G000043922

PRAISE FOR REVENGE IN BARCELONA

What begins as a romantic getaway to Barcelona for Nikki Garcia and her fiancé soon turns into a fight for her life with her enemies closing in fast to settle past scores. Nikki is no stranger to threats on her life and to using her wits to confront danger, so she is well-matched against the terrorists in this high-octane thriller. With international sites and multicultural flair, readers will be transported into a world of beauty and intrigue. From Morocco to the intimate corners of Barcelona, the suspense builds as Nikki closes in on villains and assassins devoted to their sinister mission. Deftly plotted with close calls, near escapes, and murderous plans, this ride never lets up from beginning to satisfying end.

— MICHELLE JACOBS, *US REVIEW*

Revenge in Barcelona *by Kathryn Lane is a spellbinding novel that will entice fans of thrillers and sleuth stories. Kathryn Lane begins the story in the midst of action, with the protagonist arriving at her destination. It is not long before disaster strikes and Nikki begins to sense that her life is in danger. The premise is strong and it becomes even stronger because of the background of the protagonist — a former international fraud auditor. It is hard to determine who is after her, knowing that her work often places her in the position to* make many enemies. Revenge in Barcelona *is quickly paced and the plot points are very strong. I enjoyed the fact that the key characters easily find themselves in dangerous situations. There is a lot of suspense as Nikki works hard to find out who is targeting her and why. The novel is deftly plotted and masterfully written.*

— READERS FAVORITE

I highly recommend Revenge in Barcelona. *A thrilling story with a well-researched plot - it's easily 5 Big Stars.*

— READER VIEWS

REVENGE IN BARCELONA

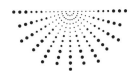

KATHRYN LANE

Copyright © 2019 by Kathryn Lane

First Edition

Copyright fuels creativity, encourages diverse voices, and promotes free speech — creating a vibrant culture. Thank you for buying an authorized copy of this book. By supporting authors, you are making it possible for writers to continue publishing their works.

All rights reserved. No part of this book may be used or reproduced in any manner, including electronic storage and retrieval systems, except by explicit written permission from the publisher. Brief passages excerpted for review purposes are excepted.

Revenge in Barcelona is a work of fiction. All the names, characters, organizations, incidents, events, and locations are the product of the author's imagination or are used fictionally. Any resemblance to real persons or events is entirely coincidental.

ISBN: 978-1-7332827-3-4

Printed and bound in the USA

Tortuga Publishing, LLC

The Woodlands, Texas 77382

Maps by Bobbye Marrs

Cover Design and Map Update by Heidi Dorey

Interior Design by Danielle H. Acee, authorsassistant.com

Editor: Sandra A. Spicher

Kathryn Lane photo by Mindy Harmon

For my husband, Bob
My son, Philip
And in loving memory of my mother, Frances Lane

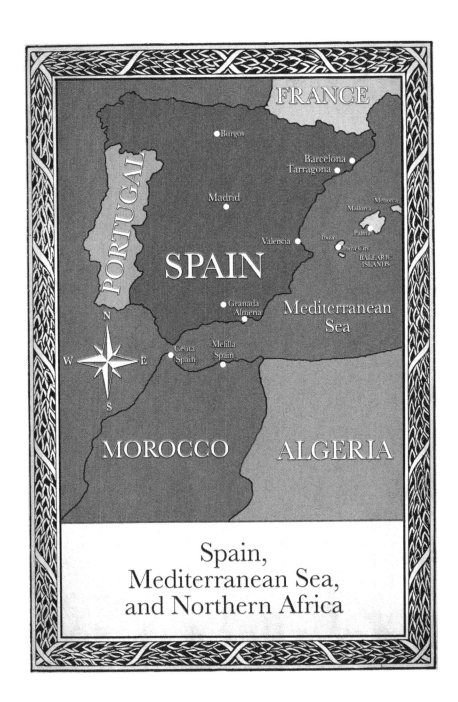

Spain,
Mediterranean Sea,
and Northern Africa

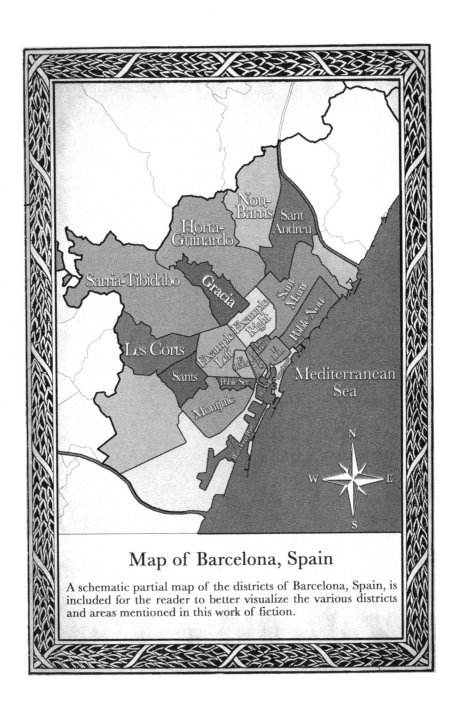

Map of Barcelona, Spain

A schematic partial map of the districts of Barcelona, Spain, is included for the reader to better visualize the various districts and areas mentioned in this work of fiction.

Basìlica of Sagrada Famìlia

A schematic map of the Basìlica of Sagrada Famìlia in Barcelona, Spain, is included for the reader to better visualize the areas mentioned in this work of fiction.

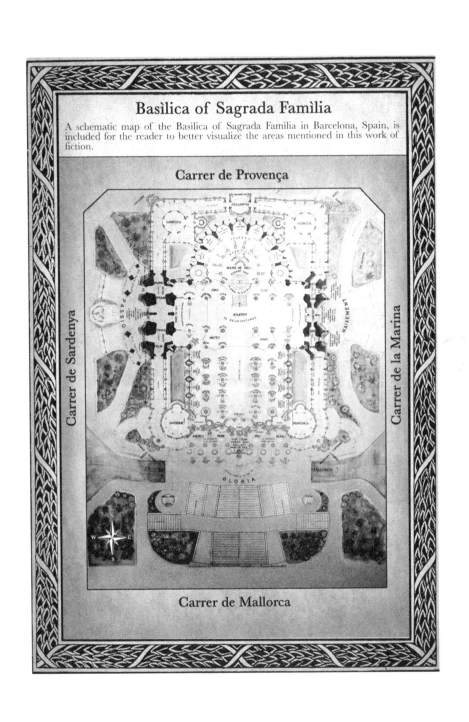

Carrer de Provença

Carrer de Sardenya

Carrer de la Marina

Carrer de Mallorca

LIST OF CHARACTERS

(This list is provided for the reader's benefit. Characters are loosely listed in order of appearance. A few minor characters are omitted.)

Nikki Garcia—Private investigator at Security Source, a firm in Miami, Florida; formerly a corporate fraud auditor
Eduardo Duarte—Nikki's fiancé, a Colombian citizen and medical doctor
Floyd Webber—Nikki's boss and owner of Security Source, a firm in Miami, Florida
Cristóbal Arenas—Colombian national
Hamilton Espinoza—Investigator at Security Source in Miami, offstage
Taiwo Adebayo—Nigerian man
Olani—Yoruba woman from Nigeria
Dayo—Olani's daughter
Kehinde (Kenny) Adebayo—Nigerian man, Olani's husband
El Saraway—A guest at the Majestic Hotel
Pedro—Concierge at Majestic Hotel
Carmen Cardoso Azar—Nikki's aunt
Luis Azar—Carmen's deceased husband and Paula's father
Paula Azar—Carmen's daughter and Nikki's cousin
Fadi Massú—Paula's fiancé
Hassan Farooqi—Florist in Barcelona

Captain—Saudi Arabian hajji, catamaran boat owner

Rafael González—Antiterrorist investigator with Grupo de Operaciones (GEO) from the Spanish National Police, Lola's husband

Lola—Yoruba woman, Rafael's wife

Selena—Romani woman, flamenco dancer, Lola's friend

Cleric in Barcelona—Imam at small Islamic center

Rosa Gebarra—Romani woman, Salena's fellow flamenco dancer, Hassan's wife

Milena Webber—Floyd's wife

Carlos Azar—Paula's uncle, her deceased father's brother

Jamila Massú—Fadi's mother

Fernando Massú—Fadi's father

Javier de la Mata—Floyd's Interpol contact

Charlotte—Floyd's assistant in Miami office, offstage

Alberto Mariscal—Detective on Rafael's antiterrorist team

Teresa—Agent, researcher, and computer expert on Rafael's team

Sonia Ussam—Owner of flower shop in Barcelona

Pepe—Rafael's driver and also an antiterrorist agent on Rafael's team

Emil El Aremi—Palestinian with Lebanese passport

GLOSSARY

STREETS IN BARCELONA

Avinguda—Avenue
Carrer—Street
Carretera—Road
Passatge—Passageway, as in narrow street
Passeig—Promenade

ARABIC WORDS OR PHRASES

As-salamu alaikum—Arabic greeting—May peace be with you (first person who greets)
Wa alaikumu as-salaam—Arabic greeting—With you as well (response)
Insha Allah—God willing
Hafiz—Person who has memorized the entire Koran
Hajji—Muslim person who has successfully completed pilgrimage to Mecca
Subḥah—String of prayer beads where units (100, 25, or 33) represent the names of God
Takiyah (not to confuse with taqiyya)—short, rounded skullcap, often worn for religious purposes

Kufi—Hand-crocheted round skullcap

Skullcap—Close-fitting cap; especially a light brimless cap for indoor wear

Thobe—Ankle-length loose robe worn by Muslim men with a shirt-like tailored top

Hijab—Traditional Islamic headscarf for women

Halal—Arabic word meaning lawful or permitted, such as *food* prescribed in the Koran

Qiṣāṣ – retaliation in kind, "like an eye for an eye"

ROMANI WORDS

Gadjo or gadji—Denotes outsiders living within Romani community, a non-Rom

Romanipen—The spirit of being Romani

Duikkerin—Fortune telling

FAMOUS BARCELONA LOCATIONS

Port Vell—Old Port, Barcelona's harbor marina area

Barri Gòtic—Gothic Quarter

Casa Batlló—Antoni Gaudí remodeled an existing building in 1904–1906, in the Modernist style, for the Batlló family for their home; now a UNESCO World Heritage Site.

Casa Milà—Gaudí designed and built the house, which was fraught with legal and financial issues, for the original owner, Pere Milá. It's popularly called La Pedrera for its façade, which resembles a quarry; now a UNESCO World Heritage Site.

Sagrada Famìlia—Famous Gaudí church, Basìlica i Temple Expiatori de la Sagrada Famìlia. The work performed by Gaudí on the Nativity façade and the Crypt of Sagrada Famìlia is a UNESCO World Heritage Site.

Parc Güell—Antoni Gaudí designed and built this whimsical park, called a "playground for the mind." The park is a UNESCO World Heritage Site and a Barcelona iconic symbol.

Templo Tibidabo—Church on Tibidabo Hill, full name: Temple Expiatori del Sagrat Cor de Jesús

WORDS OR PHRASES USED IN SPANISH OR CATALAN

Trifásico – Espresso with a drop of brandy and a bit of milk, another Catalan specialty

Gitana—Gypsy or Rom woman

Bandolero—Bandit

Tablao—Flamenco stage

Cantaor—Flamenco singer

Vale—Okay or any of its equivalents

Mi querida amiga—My dear friend

Sicario—Hitman

Hòstia—Host, or sacramental bread, a powerful swear word in Spain

Senyora – Señora in Catalan, lady, ma'am, Mrs. or Ms.

CHAPTER ONE

BARCELONA, SPAIN

<small>FRIDAY MORNING</small>

Nikki Garcia scanned the crowd gathered in the baggage claim area at Barcelona's El Prat International Airport, searching for anything unusual—a person keeping an eye on them or a familiar face hidden by disguise—as she and her fiancé, Eduardo Duarte, waited for their luggage. Satisfied she had discovered nothing out of the ordinary, she slipped her bare feet into a pair of tennis shoes she'd been clutching under her arm. One at a time, she rested each foot on the stationary outer edge of the luggage carousel to tie the laces. Twelve hours of flight time from the Yucatán Peninsula to Barcelona had made her ankles swollen and puffy. She'd walked barefoot from the plane to baggage claim to get the blood circulating in her lower extremities.

"Am I being irrational?" she asked, standing straight again. "I don't want to be mowed down like a rat." She shivered, thinking of Juana la Marihuana.

"We're safe," Eduardo said. "No one but Floyd and your aunt Carmen know we're here." He put his arm around her and kissed her forehead. "Let's just relax and enjoy ourselves."

"The Mexican job probably won't be the last time I'll work undercover," she whispered, glancing around to make sure no one was listening, "but I'm not likely to ever meet anyone as courageous as that marihuana-smoking bag lady."

"With her designer pup and that crow. They helped crack the case." Eduardo smiled, his chestnut-brown eyes beaming. "That's all behind us. We're on vacation now. And think about our wedding! Watch out, Barcelona, here we come."

"Ah, yes," Nikki said. Her expression changed from somber to bright. "Where I met my childhood sweetheart."

"When you were my mysterious Nicolasa," Eduardo whispered in her ear.

Nikki's body tightened. She tilted her head up to speak softly in Eduardo's ear. "I hate that name. That's why I changed it to Nikki when I became a US citizen."

"I saw you working before I fell asleep. Anything interesting?" Eduardo asked.

"Just researching Cristóbal Arenas." The man who had placed a price on her head. Her life in danger, her boss, Floyd Webber, had arranged for the trip to Spain to keep her safe. On the flight, she'd tried to sleep, and when that failed, she tried meditating but her mind would not relax.

"Find anything you didn't already know?" Eduardo asked.

"A little. On the I-24/7 database."

"Interpol?" Eduardo asked, his face reflecting surprise. "How can you access Interpol?"

"One of the guys who consults for us in Miami, Hamilton Esparza, set me up with an account as his admin assistant."

"Nikki, one last time. Please level with me. Are you CIA?"

"Don't start that again," she said, sighing.

"So what did you find?"

"Surprisingly little. Old mug shots from his days in prison. Arenas is suspected of international weapons trafficking. We already knew he was imprisoned in Colombia for drug charges. After being paroled, he went to Mexico where he's fallen off the map. Faded away in a puff of smoke."

"Considered a fugitive, is he?" Eduardo asked.

"Interpol has a red notice on him. He's a wanted man."

"Suspected of moving guns?" Eduardo said the words slowly. Nikki thought he was trying to burn the idea into his brain.

"Presumably there's evidence he's moved firearms into Europe and the Middle East. Military-grade Kalashnikovs from Russia through Syria into Europe."

"Smugglers are smugglers," Eduardo said. "They run guns, push drugs, and traffic in humans. Same business, just different merchandise."

"You don't suppose he's followed us here, do you?" Nikki asked. She felt tired, a weariness beyond simple jet lag.

"He won't come after us. You know he'd send someone else to do his dirty work."

"Thanks. You're so comforting," she said sarcastically as she monitored the luggage on the conveyor. She moved out of his embrace and pointed toward the carousel. "There's my suitcase."

Eduardo stepped forward and removed Nikki's luggage. His small bag was a few suitcases behind hers. Nikki followed Eduardo as he rolled both suitcases up to customs and passport control.

CHAPTER TWO

BENI ENSAR, MOROCCO, NORTH AFRICA

Atraveler carrying a well-worn duffle bag pushed open a rusty wrought iron gate as he entered the desolate yard of a shabby house on the outskirts of Beni Ensar. The traveler, Taiwo Adebayo, had arrived an hour earlier in the city of Nador, twelve miles to the south. Shortly after landing, he climbed aboard a ramshackle bus to Beni Ensar, which held the distinction of sharing its piers with the Spanish port city of Melilla, a fact of particular interest to him. The map he carried in the back pocket of his jeans showed the two Spanish enclaves in northern Africa—Ceuta and Melilla. The latter was nestled between the Rif Mountains of northern Morocco and the Mediterranean Sea. Beyond Melilla lay the city of Ceuta, opposite the Strait of Gibraltar. Across the strait, the Spanish mainland.

Tired, Taiwo stopped to look around the yard. Shriveled vegetable plants and a few herbs grew in a tiny garden, cordoned off with a flimsy wire mesh that lined up against the iron fence in the shade of a large argan tree. In the middle of the yard, a dozen or so chickens and a lone rooster rested in the shadow of an old European-style bathtub. Its underlying cast iron frame revealed itself through large chips of missing enamel. An idle electric generator on a cement slab stood behind the tub like a battle-hardened watchman. A row of Spanish lavender shrubs grew in the sunbaked ground in front of the tub. Three large spikes with purplish-pink flowers provided a bit of color in the otherwise parched, dry earth.

The rooster crowed and chickens scattered across the yard as Taiwo approached. He dusted off his clothes, stooped to dip his hands into the water collected in the bottom of the tub, and splashed his face and beard. With the back of his hands, he made a feeble attempt to dry the droplets on his face. Wiping his hands on his dirty, faded jeans, he walked toward the battered wooden door of the house, smoothing his beard before he knocked loudly.

A sliver of sunlight splashed on a woman holding a baby as the creaky door opened slightly. Her face showed surprise, and she cast her eyes downward.

"Taiwo? What brings you here?" she asked.

"Business, Olani. Strictly business. Is my brother home?"

"Kenny will come along shortly. You can sit on the bench until he arrives."

Olani pointed at a wooden bench set against the wall next to the doorway.

"I'll make you hot tea and bring it out." She started closing the door, but through the narrow crack she spoke again. "Or do you prefer water?"

"I prefer tea."

CHAPTER THREE

BARCELONA—EIXAMPLE DISTRICT

FRIDAY AFTERNOON

"Are you ready?" Eduardo asked, tapping his foot. "There's so much waiting for us out there." He parted the hotel-room curtains and gazed down at Passeig de Gràcia, a tree-lined avenue with a wide pedestrian walk doubling as a fashionable median.

"What's your hurry?" Nikki asked. Eduardo turned from the window. She unwrapped the towel she had twisted turban-style over her short, wet hair.

"Adventure. Barcelona beckons us," Eduardo said. He could hear the edge of impatience in his own voice. "If we hit the street and get a little sunshine, it'll help us get over our jet lag."

"Ah, you misled me! You said making love was the best antidote for jet lag." Nikki laughed and shot a flirty glance at Eduardo. "Or did that not work for you?" She raised an eyebrow and waited for an answer.

"Love-making works wonders." He looked across the room at her. "But the second phase of overcoming jetlag is soaking up some sunshine."

"Let me put myself together," Nikki said. She sat on a velvet-cushioned chair in front of the vanity and fastened a gold chain with its jadeite Mayan world tree pendant around her neck. She'd taken it off only to shower. Eduardo bought it for her in a market in Palenque just the previous day, replacing the one Nikki had given to ten-year-old Bibi, the child whose kidnapping case Nikki had solved in Mexico. The good-luck charm was also known as the tree of life.

She turned the hairdryer on. Using a small round brush, she dried the artificial gray tones of her short, unevenly cropped hair, a haircut and color she'd done herself, the remnants of her undercover persona from the assignment in Mexico. Eduardo knew that Nikki longed for her hair to grow back into its usual full, straight style falling below her shoulders. He wouldn't mind, either.

"What do you think about me going to light brown?" she asked. "I've heard that can give a more youthful appearance."

Eduardo knew better than to demur, even though he preferred her hair dark and long. But while it grew out, she could at least add some color. He lifted one shoulder in agreement, and Nikki dialed the concierge for an appointment at the hotel's hair salon.

"We need to call my aunt Carmen," Nikki said, placing the phone back on the desk. "Let her know we've arrived. Carmen and my cousin Paula. I haven't seen them in years."

Only half listening, Eduardo moved away from the window and picked up the remote control. He tuned in a news channel and waited for her to finish getting ready. The announcer spoke about Madrid's ongoing investigation into the pro-independence movement of Catalonia's toppled regional government. The probe concentrated on Catalonia's police force, which had created its own secret intelligence service in opposition to the Spanish state.

"Glad to know we won't be facing separatist demonstrations on the streets," Eduardo said. Over a video that must have been shot from a helicopter or drone, the announcer pointed out that crowds of over a million had brought the city to a standstill.

Nikki decided on beige slacks and a pastel green blouse. She needed to arrange things in her leather purse. Her boss, Floyd, had given it to her to conceal a Baby Glock, also a gift, when they worked a tough assignment together in Colombia. The handgun remained safely stored at home in Miami. International travel made it impossible to carry a firearm, even for a private investigator. In Spain, she would use that secret compartment for her passport and a very special lipstick case—actually a Taser.

Nikki placed her suitcase on the bed and removed the Taser from a concealed cavity. The secret chamber opened from inside the suitcase and was well hidden in one of the wheels on her luggage. When the hollow space contained the hard plastic Taser, it appeared to form part of the wheel mechanism, thus avoiding detection by routine custom inspections and x-ray machines. A flap in the suitcase lining concealed the opening to the small chamber.

Nikki cradled the little case in her palm. Its powerful defense zapper had saved both her life and Eduardo's in Mexico. She placed it next to her passport in the hidden compartment of her purse, hoping not to need it in Spain.

CHAPTER FOUR

BENI ENSAR, MOROCCO, NORTH AFRICA

FRIDAY AFTERNOON TO EVENING

As Olani finished preparing the evening meal, she became aware of a rare camaraderie between her husband Kenny and his twin, Taiwo, as they waited for her to serve dinner. They sat cross-legged on floor cushions reminiscing about their childhoods. The aroma from the kitchen permeated the living area.

All three adults ignored the simple fact that hot-headed Taiwo and quiescent Kenny had little in common despite being identical twins. They never had been close—not even as children growing up in Nigeria. Kenny, the studious one, fell back on diplomacy to resolve disputes. Taiwo used bullying tactics to solve conflicts, and when that did not work, he unleashed his wrath on those who opposed him. Different as their personalities were, they had fallen in love with the same woman. Olani had refused the hot-headed one. Instead she had chosen the quiet, unassuming Kenny.

Olani moved serenely between the brothers as she served. Her homemade garri—a mashed cassava dish—and an okra-spinach soup, both cooked with pungent spices, made the men ask for seconds.

The twin brothers had straightforward Yoruba names indicating which one came into the world to claim the honor of being firstborn. That was Taiwo. Kehinde, meaning the second-born, had left the comfort of their mother's womb twelve minutes later. Their names were hardly unique, since the Yoruba have always experienced a high incidence of twin births.

An oil lamp in the corner of the living room provided light. Olani's tall, sinuous body cast dancing shadows on the walls and floor as she placed food on the men's plates.

When she brought the main course, a communal dish of chicken with vegetables slow-cooked the Moroccan way in a clay tagine, Olani sat with them to partake of the meal. Not comfortable with Taiwo, she kept her head covered and her eyes cast downward, even while eating. The brothers, like Olani, had light skin. And for the same reason—their ancestors included either British explorers or British missionaries. Yet Taiwo's skin seemed a shade darker, possibly due to being out in the sun more than his twin brother, who had a clerical job in the Spanish city over the fence.

Kenny, with his full beard, looks so much like his brother it scares me, she thought. *Only their personalities are different.* Olani sensed Kenny's increasing anxiety as dinner progressed. She also knew his anguish was not on the grounds he'd married the woman his brother had wanted for himself. Nor was it owing to the fact that her husband had not seen his twin in five years. No, Kenny's discomfort, she knew, came from his fear of Taiwo's temper. Whenever he encountered his sibling, the normally tranquil Kenny always ended up trading punches with his twin—yelling, screaming, and kicking as he dodged Taiwo's fists.

As dinner drew to a close, Olani took the plates to the kitchen where she washed them in a small sink by the light of another oil lamp set in an open cupboard. She boiled water for tea as she cleaned up. Mint tea, made with fresh leaves she'd cut earlier from her garden and placed in a glass of water where she had kept them crisp, was the drink of choice. As soon as the boiling water hit the leaves, the entire house smelled of fresh, sweet mint. She added raw cane sugar to the tin cups and swirled the hot liquid with a spoon to dissolve the sugar. She tasted it before serving. She'd barely set the cups down in front of the men when Dayo, who had been asleep, started crying in the young couple's bedroom at the back of the house. Olani took the oil lamp from the kitchen to light her way as she went to tend to her daughter's cries. The house was small. Only a wooden screen separated their bedroom from the living area. She put the lamp on a table in the bedroom and comforted the child. With her daughter in her arms, Olani stood close to the wooden screen to watch the men in the living area and listen to their conversation.

Taiwo sipped the hot tea and took advantage of Olani's absence to change the subject.

"Brother, I need to borrow your passport so I can get into Melilla tomorrow."

"My passport?" Kenny asked. "Why?"

"To get into Spain. I have a job lined up. I'll mail the passport back when I get on the mainland."

"So you take my passport," Kenny said, glancing toward the screen that concealed Olani, "and if you get in trouble with the law, I'm the one who gets fucked over."

"I'm not going to get in trouble. I'll make sure of it."

"Look, Taiwo," Kenny said. Taiwo saw the chance of concession in his eyes. "I have a family. If you go off and do something crazy, it'd be my name, my address, and my life they'd come after. Besides, if you take my passport, tell me how I'll get into Melilla every day to work?"

"Take a week of vacation," Taiwo suggested. He made his voice sound serious and commanding. "That's all I need. One week."

"Jump the fence or take a swim in the sea to get in the way other people do," Kenny said. He should have known that Taiwo was serious.

"I need to get into Spain. And that's no joke."

Taiwo stared at his brother with hatred. "Have it your way. You always did—with mother, with father, with Olani. Especially Olani." He slammed the tin cup on the floor, spilling its contents. He stood to leave, kicking the metal cup halfway across the room.

In a conciliatory tone, Kenny explained that with a Nigerian passport, his brother could apply for a visa to Spain. Kenny even offered to help Taiwo find work in Melilla.

"I have a job. It's waiting for me in Barcelona. I can't wait for a bullshit visa." Taiwo took aggressive steps toward the door, grabbing his duffle bag.

Standing stiffly, Kenny said goodbye, holding his right hand over his heart in a gesture of sincerity. Taiwo pushed past him and thundered out of the house without looking back.

Behind the screen, Olani felt tense. She could see Kenny's pained expression over the altercation with his brother. Holding Dayo, she stepped into the living room. She wondered what had transpired in their childhood to make them so different. Kenny turned away to close the door. Still holding the baby in her arms, Olani approached her husband and hugged him. He put his arms around her and their daughter and held them tight for a couple of minutes. Olani could tell Kenny felt remorse over failing, once more, to communicate with Taiwo.

Outside, Taiwo strode to the gate. A full moon lit up the yard. Instead of leaving, he turned and glared at the house, noticing his brother had already closed the door. Angry thoughts seethed in his head as he doubled back to the electric generator. Two cats ran out from under the bathtub as he approached. They darted behind the house. The recoil starter, he noticed, was broken. He realized why they lived with oil lamps. Enraged over his brother's obstinacy, he took a pocketknife from his pants pocket and cut the rope of the recoil starter and threw it on the ground. *Now they will not be able to fix the generator so easily*, he thought as he picked the rope up and tied it loosely around his waist.

For a couple of minutes he paced around the moonlit yard. Considering his next move, Taiwo walked to the side of the house. He took the narrow space beyond the small garden for himself. The area lay between the reinforced concrete house and the wrought iron fence running along the perimeter of the property. The nearest wall adjoined the living area where they had eaten Olani's dinner. Without windows where his brother and sister-in-law could see him, it was a place he could spend the night.

Using the heel of his boot to loosen the hardened ground into a softer bed, Taiwo pushed the excess dirt into a mound. As he worked, his wrath intensified. His brother was lying on a comfortable mattress in the bedroom at the back side of the house, sleeping next to the woman who should have been his. He figured Kehinde had only married Olani to rile him. He spat on the ground. He hated his twin, hated him for having been their mother's favorite, hated him for getting it all, including a passport with a work visa to Spain stamped in it.

A mosquito buzzed about him. It landed on his nose. Taiwo slapped at it. He was too late. The insect had already bitten him. In the process of slapping himself, he accidentally poked his right eye. Seething with rage, he banged his head into the top rail on the wrought iron fence. As the firstborn, Taiwo knew he deserved more power and prestige, and resented his brother for never respecting his birthright. Another mosquito bit him.

As rancor filled his heart, Taiwo felt his chest throbbing. He thought it would burst. He doubled over in pain. He coughed. Violently. And he coughed again. That action brought the rhythm of his heart back under control. Steadying himself against a fencepost, he listened to make sure the noise from his movements had not alerted the occupants of the house. He wiped the sweat on his forehead with the sleeve of his shirt and reached for the duffle bag, throwing it on the soft dirt as a pillow.

CHAPTER FIVE

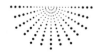

BARCELONA—EIXAMPLE DISTRICT

<small>Friday Early Evening</small>

Nikki and Eduardo stepped out of the elevator, his hand supporting her elbow. As they approached the wide doors leading to the street, white-gloved, uniformed porters, one on each side of the arched entrance, opened the glass doors for them.

"I feel like a queen," Nikki said as they walked through the grand doorway.

Soft, late afternoon sunshine bathed Nikki and Eduardo in pleasant warmth as they stepped over the threshold. A few feet away, she stopped and glanced back at the porters.

"They look so distinguished in their uniforms," Nikki said, admiring the Majestic Hotel's spectacular chamfered entryway. Holding hands, they took in every detail.

Eduardo glanced at the screen he'd brought up on his mobile phone. "Barcelona's famous nineteenth-century architects ignored traditional ninety-degree corners and built diagonal walls called chamfers at important intersections," he read. "They are called chaflanes in Spanish."

The hotel's chamfered entryway allowed for a wide sidewalk, making the entrance and the street appear more grandiose. Passeig de Gràcia, where they stood, was known as one of the most elegant avenues in the city.

As they resumed walking, Nikki noticed a tall, heavyset man with a wiry beard and wearing a khaki-colored shirt with a starched collar. He walked past them, not acknowledging them at all. Most striking was his immaculately white, crocheted skullcap. Nikki turned slightly and caught a glimpse of the white-gloved porters opening the doors for him.

Once inside the marble-floored lobby, the bulky man turned to look at the couple, glimpsing only their backs before they walked out of his sight toward Port Vell, the marina and old port. He made his way to the concierge's desk. After retrieving his wallet, he removed a hundred-euro bill and pressed it into the hand of the concierge on duty.

"Pedro, check for me if a woman by the name of Nikki Garcia is registered in the hotel."

Pedro, the senior concierge, pocketed the money with a rapid movement of his hand. He scrolled down a couple of screens on the computer, shaking his head as he searched. Using the keyboard for a more detailed query, he still shook his head.

"What about Eduardo Duarte?"

More scrolling, then a nod.

"What room?"

"I'm sorry, but I cannot—"

The man pulled another hundred-euro bill from his wallet and pushed it into the concierge's hand.

"Mr. El Saraway, I've already given you more information than I should." Scanning the lobby, Pedro pocketed the second tip. "I haven't seen your falcon recently. How is the bird?"

"Shaheen's tethered in his cage, longing for his daily three-hour hunt."

Nikki and Eduardo strolled hand in hand down the wide pedestrian median on Passeig de Gràcia.

"I thought I'd go crazy while you were undercover," Eduardo said.

"You're already crazy," she said with a laugh.

"Over you, I admit it," he said.

Nikki sighed. "I still wake up in the middle of the night worried about all those children." Some were probably back with parents who love them, she thought, but others might not be so lucky. Especially those whose parents had sold them to the traffickers in the first place. "What do you think will happen to them?"

A bus drove past with its engine revving, drowning out Nikki's voice. The fumes invaded Nikki's nostrils and she coughed.

"Father Abelardo will take care of them." Eduardo said, speaking loudly, as he leaned toward Nikki so she could hear him over the din of traffic. "Right now, we're here to decompress. Barcelona is the perfect wedding location."

He stopped and Nikki pivoted to face him. She noticed his eyes light up as he gazed at her. Pedestrians passed them in both directions on the wide median. A woman pushing a stroller while clutching a three-year-old with her other hand maneuvered around them. A newborn inside the stroller cried, his well-developed lungs finally forcing his mother to stop and tend to him.

Over Eduardo's shoulder Nikki noticed a façade adorned with luminous orange-gold colored tile that transitioned into greenish blue on the upper part of the wall, covered with an undulating roof. "What's that building?" she asked, pointing.

"Must be a Gaudí," Eduardo said, checking his mobile app again.

"The same Gaudí who designed the rooftop at Casa Milà?" Nikki asked, childhood memories of the rooftop terrace flooding her memory. As a young girl, she had been fascinated with the whimsical Darth Vader look-alikes Gaudí had created to disguise the vents and chimneys, even though she knew Darth Vader had not yet been created.

"The very same. This is Casa Batlló. Look at the roof," Eduardo said, using one hand to point and resting the other on Nikki's shoulder. "Like scales on a dragon's back. The turret with the cross at the top is supposed to represent Saint George's sword slaying the dragon."

"Looks more like a dinosaur," Nikki said.

Holding hands, they continued strolling down Passeig de Gràcia. The architecture shifted, and soon they found themselves across from stores like Louis Vuitton, Armani, Cartier, and Prada in Modernist buildings. Nikki spotted a large circular planter containing a small tree and suggested they take a seat on its modern curvilinear bench.

Pigeons hopped around on the pavers of the walkway, cooing and pecking at food morsels. Magpies screeched and flapped their wings from tree to tree or swooped down to steal crumbs claimed by other species. Nikki heard one of Barcelona's famous monk parakeets squawking until a magpie scared it away. Two sparrows, oblivious to Eduardo and Nikki, scratched the dirt surrounding the tree in the planter. She turned sideways on the bench to observe them.

"Birds are so amazing," Nikki said. One sparrow jumped on the other in an apparent attempt to mate or at least to play. Beyond the planter outside the Prada storefront, a robust, bearded man wearing a white skullcap caught Nikki's attention.

He seemed like the same man who had passed them as they left the hotel. She continued chatting with Eduardo while obliquely watching the man lingering by the storefront. It was clear that the reflection in the display window allowed him to watch the bench where she and Eduardo sat.

She nervously ran her fingers through her short hair. In her peripheral vision the tall, brawny man wearing the skullcap still lingered. Eduardo continued to read aloud from the app on his phone.

Nikki nudged Eduardo and whispered, "Don't look, but a man has been standing before a display of women's clothing for a long time."

"Probably shopping for the love of his life."

"He's wearing a skullcap."

"A skullcap?" Eduardo repeated. "Why would that bother you?"

"He entered our hotel as we left. Maybe. I'm not sure. One thing is certain. He's carrying a camera. I think he's snapped a few photos of us."

"Now that changes things," Eduardo said, looking at Nikki.

Eduardo stood to catch a glimpse but the man turned his back to the planter area and disappeared into Prada's wide doors.

"Let's follow him," Eduardo said in a commanding tone.

"No, that'd be too obvious. Besides, you're right. He has no reason to be following us. Must be a coincidence," Nikki said. "I'm still feeling panicky after those death threats in Mexico."

Eduardo leaned toward Nikki and brushed her lips with his. "I don't want you worrying about what happened in Mexico. Changing the subject, another Gaudí building is up the street a few blocks. As you can see from here, the Modernist buildings—"

"Which Gaudí?" Nikki asked.

"Our wedding venue."

Nikki's eyes widened. "Casa Milà is just steps away? What are we doing here?" Nikki jumped up and pulled Eduardo to standing, but he suggested waiting until the following day when the office would be open and they could inquire about renting the rooftop for their wedding.

"I hope we can get it on such short notice," Nikki said. "Maybe Aunt Carmen has some pull."

Pedestrian traffic picked up. Buses and taxis added to the congestion of motor vehicles at the end of the day when people headed home or rushed to meet friends. As Nikki and Eduardo walked, she kept her internal radar on high alert, and she sensed that Eduardo was also searching for the man wearing a skullcap. A small fountain provided an excuse to stop and look back to scan the street for him. But the man had vanished.

"You are so beautiful." Eduardo took Nikki into his arms and kissed her.

"This feels romantic, like the Trevi Fountain in Rome," she said.

Eduardo pulled three coins from his pocket and handed them to her. "Make a wish."

Nikki threw them, one by one, into the fountain, right hand over left shoulder. When she caught Eduardo's eye, they laughed and resumed their stroll.

Traffic continued unabated as they walked toward the marina and old port. Motorbikes, most piloted by women, traveling in both directions on Passeig de Gràcia caught Nikki's attention and she nudged Eduardo.

"Spiked heels on motorbikes?" he asked. "And they are all spiffed up, like they're going to a party."

"Maybe. Or a concert."

They continued walking on Passeig de Gràcia until it dead-ended. Eduardo consulted the map on his phone. "The Barri Gòtic, the Gothic Quarter, is where we're headed," he told Nikki.

They wandered along narrower and narrower streets that gave way to cobblestones in a pedestrian-only section. Tables set outdoors by bar owners took up a large part of the street. Nikki smiled at a portly bar patron folding a napkin and slipping it under a table leg to keep it level. People were eating tapas and drinking wine, and the aroma of rich food made her mouth water. She noticed entire families enjoying the atmosphere, from gray-haired grandmothers to babies whose prams were nestled between chairs.

Deep in the Barri Gòtic, Nikki looked up and gasped. A huge church with dramatic wooden doors almost touched the buildings on either side. She stopped to appreciate the massive structure.

"La Seu Cathedral," Eduardo read from his phone, "is the seat of the

Archdiocese in Barcelona. It's dedicated to Saint Eulàlia, a martyr during the Christian persecution under the Roman emperor Diocletian."

Deeper into the historic district, Eduardo periodically stopped to read the history of one place or another. On Carrer del Bisbe, he pointed out a covered bridge connecting two buildings facing each other on opposite sides of the narrow cobblestone street.

"The Bishop's Bridge. You'll have to make another wish. No coins this time. Just keep your eyes closed, make the wish, turn in a circle, tilt your head up toward the underside of the bridge, and open your eyes."

Nikki followed Eduardo's instructions.

"Tell me what you see."

"A skull with a dagger in its mouth."

"Oh, no," Eduardo groaned. "You were not supposed to see that."

"A superstition?" Nikki asked.

"Maybe an urban legend."

"I'm not really superstitious, so tell me what it means."

"Whoever sees the skull and dagger falls prey to an evil spell," Eduardo explained. "But there's an antidote that will overcome the curse. It's a bit farther on."

"I'm hungry. Let's eat instead. Besides, I have my tree of life," Nikki said, touching her pendant. "It works as an antidote to all evil."

CHAPTER SIX

BENI ENSAR, MOROCCO, NORTH AFRICA

Saturday Very Early Morning

Taiwo awakened when it was still dark. He could not allow Kehinde to leave for work before he spoke with him. With that intention, Taiwo had slept poorly, waking up every half hour or so to check the time on his mobile phone. Shifting position, he checked the time again, deciding to get up. After placing the phone in his duffle bag, he took a few steps from where he had slept, unzipped his fly, and relieved himself on the plants in the small garden. He returned to the area which had served as his bed, pushed aside the duffle bag he had used for a pillow, and sat directly on the mound of dirt, wishing for a cup of hot tea.

After a few minutes, he heard a creaking sound from the front door. Jumping up, Taiwo turned the corner of the house to see his brother. Taiwo felt heat rise in his chest and face from the wrath in his mind. Without acknowledging the new day, he confronted Kenny.

"I'm not going to ask politely this time. As your older brother, I have every right to your possessions. By law. Hand me your passport."

"Don't get this way, Taiwo," Kenny said, placing his arm over his chest in a reflexive effort to protect himself. "I've offered to help you get what you need. I'm willing to take a day off work and go with you to apply for a visa. But my passport—that I'm not giving you."

Taiwo's right fist connected with Kenny's jaw in an uppercut swing.

His left followed through with a powerful hook to the side of Kenny's head. The younger twin wobbled and fell to the ground.

Taking advantage of Kenny's momentary shock, Taiwo put a foot on his brother's chest and reached over to extract the passport from his shirt pocket. Kenny, still groggy from the surprise attack, grabbed his brother's arm. He pulled so hard he threw Taiwo off balance. Then he used his feet to trip his brother, dropping Taiwo to the hardened dirt with such brutal force the air was knocked from his lungs.

Kenny scrambled on top of his brother, but before he could subdue Taiwo, the angry twin ripped Kenny's shirt open, reaching for the passport. Failing to get it, Taiwo clenched his arms and legs tightly around his brother. He thrust his own body and managed to roll Kenny onto his back again. Taiwo vaulted to his feet and kicked the younger twin in the head, pinning him to the dry, sunbaked dirt with his foot. Taiwo remembered the recoil rope he had tied around his waist. Untying it before Kenny could recover from the blow to his head, he wrapped it around Kenny's neck and pulled it tight.

"Now are you going to give me what's rightfully mine?" Taiwo growled in a menacing voice. He knew Kenny was processing his threat, realizing the seriousness of his situation.

Kenny grabbed onto the rope with both hands and pulled as hard as he could, trying to force his brother to the ground again. But Taiwo overpowered him, pushing his knee into Kenny's chest.

The younger twin kicked, gaining enough momentum to turn over and stand. He dislodged the rope, letting it fall. Taiwo pelted his brother's head with hard-knuckled fists. Kenny grabbed Taiwo by the arms and threw him to the ground. Kenny looked down at his brother, breathing heavily. The lull gave Taiwo time to recover. He scrambled to his feet, grabbing the rope. Taiwo knew he had regained the upper hand. Throwing his twin face-up on the ground, Taiwo pressed a foot hard into Kenny's chest again. Before Kenny could recover, Taiwo wrapped the rope around his brother's throat.

"I'm taking your passport, even if I have to kill you."

Kenny thrashed about, his arms free of restraint, yet unable to escape his brother's grip.

Taiwo kept tightening the rope. No matter how hard Kenny struggled, Taiwo held on. The younger twin gasped for breath. The older one continued choking him.

When he felt in full control, Taiwo leveraged his legs and used his feet to turn Kenny over without letting up on the rope. With Kenny on his stomach, Taiwo put his foot on Kenny's lower back and securely grasped the rope from this position. He pulled the rope tighter and tighter until his brother stopped fighting. Soon Kenny's body went limp.

Taiwo wasted no time. He pulled on his brother's lifeless arms to drag the body behind the house, the same spot where he'd made the makeshift bed for himself.

After retrieving the passport from Kenny's shirt pocket, he searched his other pockets, taking his brother's money and phone. He laid the corpse face down at the outer edge of the soft dirt he'd loosened the night before. He spat on the ground and glowered at the passport in his hand, placing it in his shirt pocket. The other items he slipped into the back pocket of his jeans. He would find a place to bury the phone once he got far enough away from the house.

Taiwo picked up his duffle bag and walked through the gate, closing it behind him without looking back.

Taiwo watched the muted light of dawn slowly brighten, like the universe turning up a dimmer switch. He stood in the long queue of day laborers, mostly women, waiting to cross the Beni Ensar gate into Melilla. The hour difference in time zones between Morocco and the Spanish city meant he had awakened around four in the morning Moroccan time, completed his dirty work, walked to the Beni Ensar border crossing, and arrived at the gate by six a.m. on the Spanish clock. Early, yet a crowd already surrounded the crossing. He touched his shirt pocket to make sure the passport he had killed for remained there. Soon he would be on Spanish soil, unlike the desperate people pacing near the fence. He knew that some waited months, even years, to get across.

Ignoring the congestion, Taiwo had no desire to engage in casual conversation with laborers standing in line with him. Spitting to release tension, he couldn't help noticing groups of men standing by the fence. They outnumbered the crowd in the queue. He avoided staring at two such groups. One, a gang of seven would-be refugees paced like vultures holding iron hooks in their hands. Another half-dozen tottered near the fence, scraping and dragging the soles of their boots on the concrete sidewalk, breaking the silence with ear-piercing grating sounds made by cleat-like metal nails the men had hammered through the soles. They waited for an opportunity to climb over a triple-barrier wall topped off with razor wire. Their anger was palpable.

Taiwo spat on the ground again, listening to the wind, recalling Kenny's suggestion. To take actions like the men desperately waiting for a chance to get into Spain over the triple fence did not suit Taiwo's impatient disposition. Or his client's schedule. And taking a swim in the ocean appealed even less. His thoughts were interrupted by a distant whirring. It was a helicopter. He tapped the passport with his fingers once more.

The Spanish Civil Guard and police helicopter surveillance, aided by video camera monitors, mounted a thorough patrol to capture those who miraculously made it to the other side. Taiwo knew the patrol on the Spanish side broke down only when an overwhelming number of men managed to get across. In those instances, a few were allowed to remain in Melilla as political hostages. Their hope to gain access to the European mainland might never cease. *The land used to belong to the caliphate. Under Spanish rule for centuries now, the current government in Madrid makes it more and more difficult for these refugees to enter the mainland.* He spat on the ground yet again.

As the queue moved forward, the Nigerian handed his passport and attached work visa to the border official, who nodded to him in recognition.

"Buenos días."

Taiwo mumbled his greeting and looked away, avoiding direct contact with the official's eyes. He wanted to prevent being drawn into conversation, as his Spanish skills were not as good as his dead brother's.

The official returned the passport and waved him on. His eyes followed the Nigerian for a few seconds, as if the immigration officer found something a bit odd about the polite, soft-spoken man who entered Melilla every morning and left every night to return home.

"Kehinde," the official yelled after him.

A soldier standing near the gate on the Spanish side held his arm out to stop him. "The officer is calling you," the soldier said, pointing to the border gate the Nigerian had entered moments before.

Taiwo froze. He turned with trepidation to face the immigration officer.

"Is your family okay?" the official asked loudly.

"We're fine," Taiwo said as he gave the official a thumbs-up. Then he remembered his brother's habit of wearing a smile and quickly pasted one on.

For the second time in less than thirty seconds, the officer waved the Nigerian on as he took the passport from the next person in line and inspected it.

Once he stepped away from the gate and distanced himself from the soldier who had stopped him, Taiwo wiped beads of sweat from his forehead. Moving a safe distance away from other people, he returned the passport to his shirt pocket. He reached into his duffle bag to retrieve his cell phone and spoke four words into it—a code to give notice of his whereabouts. Those people who wanted him in Barcelona had told him they could arrange passage for him and provide false documents that appeared authentic. Taiwo had opted to start with his brother's Nigerian passport and current work visa. It allowed him not only a temporary convenience but also provided him a way to avenge himself on his brother for marrying the woman Taiwo wanted for himself.

After his arrival in Spain, his people could produce additional identification documents, a task made both easier and more difficult by technology. It was simple to produce false papers, but if he were caught, authorities could easily check their authenticity. Pleased he had made it to Spanish soil so easily, he walked toward the port, stopping at a corner store to purchase a Coke and two small rolls of bread topped with grilled eggplant and onions. The aroma of the onions made his mouth water, but he was anxious to buy his ticket for the next ferry to the mainland. He waited to eat until he boarded the ferry.

After the ferry departed, Taiwo relaxed. He looked out over the ocean toward Melilla and watched the steep, rugged mountains appear to shrink as they grew distant.

CHAPTER SEVEN

BARCELONA—EIXAMPLE DISTRICT

SATURDAY VERY EARLY MORNING

Eduardo awoke to the terrifying sound of Nikki's scream. He fumbled around the bedside lamp until he managed to switch on the light. Nikki was sitting on her side of the bed. He sat next to her.

"A nightmare," she said.

Eduardo took her hand. It was cold and clammy. "Tell me what happened."

"Murky images, a premonition of something bad, but I don't know what. A dim place, a sinister figure hiding behind pillars. Evil, I could feel an evil spirit, like someone out to get us."

"Not the recurring nightmare?" Eduardo sometimes heard Nikki sobbing after dreams about her son's death several years ago."

"No," Nikki said. "You and me in a meadow, which became a cave. I walked up worn staircases with large stone pillars on one side. You climbed right behind me. A figure lurched at me, then lunged at you. He had a dagger."

"A dagger?"

"He didn't have a face. Only a skull," she said. Then she described it like the one they saw at Bishop's Bridge, attached to a threatening figure that slithered off into the darkness, hiding behind large pillars in a cavern-like structure. The dream had gone from bright sunlight to a murky hell.

"It's been a while since you had a nightmare. Your mind is releasing the stress from that kidnapping case. And the Bishop's Bridge skull triggered it. Would it be relaxing if I read to you?" Eduardo asked.

She nodded.

Eduardo walked back to his side and arranged two pillows against the headboard. Leaning against the goose down, he picked up his tablet and opened an e-book he had been reading on Paleolithic cave art in Spain. But reading about caves would not calm Nikki's nerves. Instead, he opened an e-version of a guidebook on Barcelona and picked up on an explanation of La Seu Cathedral where they had been the afternoon before.

"So here we are at La Seu," he said, reading aloud.

The tourist should definitely visit the cathedral's cloister with its small chapels, gardens, fountains, medieval tombstones, and even geese whose chatter you can hear from the church building.

The thirteen white geese are said to symbolize the age of Eulàlia when she suffered her martyrdom. That may well be true, but the existence of this tradition of goose husbandry is due to a very practical feature of the geese: their deafening noise is a good barrier against unwanted intruders and thieves.

Eduardo turned to look at Nikki. She had already fallen asleep. He turned his tablet off, rearranged the pillows, and crawled back under the covers.

A long city block past the Majestic Hotel, Nikki shrieked in delight.

"It's more incredible than I remember." She hugged Eduardo, took a step away, and looked up at him. Her face glowed at the thought of being a bride. "This is so exciting. Let's climb to the roof and see the place where we met as kids. It was here you promised me a castle. Remember?"

Hand in hand, they walked across the street to the front of Casa Milà. The main entrance sat on the iconic diagonal slice of the building. As they approached the famous door, they found the building still closed and noticed a sign indicating the offices opened at ten a.m., typical Spanish time.

They strolled to Carmen's condominium on Carrer de Provença, a cross street to Passeig de Gràcia, just a block away from Casa Milà. When the elevator door opened on the fifth floor, Nikki whispered in Eduardo's ear before they stepped into the hallway. "My aunt does not need to know what I do for a living. We'd have to explain too much to her."

"I'd never give away our clandestine lives," Eduardo said, stepping out of the elevator. "Our secrets are safe."

Nikki looked at a framed photograph on the wall and studied her reflection in the glass, thinking her freshly colored and styled hair made her attractive again.

"You look very sexy," he said. "Grrrr..."

A petite woman in her early sixties, Carmen Cardoso Azar had graying hair and a smile that conveyed a tranquil, happy soul. She opened the door and gave Nikki a warm embrace, gently pulling her niece into the condo and welcoming them both. Carmen had not seen her niece for almost two decades, though they had stayed in touch by phone and email throughout the years.

After Nikki introduced Eduardo and Carmen, the three exchanged pleasantries. Then Carmen suggested moving to the outdoor terrace. Flowering plants splashed color all over the space. They were hanging from baskets, falling like canopies over the sides of ceramic planters of diverse shapes and sizes, and growing in flower boxes built into the half wall enclosing the bottom section of the balcony. The terrace took on the aroma and atmosphere of a landscaped gallery.

Eduardo whistled. "Someone must be a gardener. Up till now, I thought the balcony of my condo in Medellín had a lot of color." He stood wide-eyed, admiring the variety of blooming plants surrounding him.

"I'm a frustrated architect," Carmen said. "I came to Barcelona to study architecture. This city is a masterpiece stamped with the best Modernist and Art Nouveau designs by the patriarchs of Catalan architecture. Their buildings sit like sentinels at every street corner reminding us of the city's glorious history. What could I have contributed?"

"You added flowers," Eduardo said.

His words brought an expression of astonishment to Carmen's face, giving her the look of a mystified child despite her gray hair. "Nikki, did you tell Eduardo about my work in this city?"

"Not at all. How could I? Both times we visited, I was young and did not understand much about you, other than you'd left Mexico for Spain."

Carmen gazed at Eduardo. "In my working days, I designed and supervised the plantings along the main boulevards and the parks of the inner city."

"Do I hear a hint of disillusion?" Nikki asked.

"Not at all. Barcelona stole my heart. I dreamed of staying here instead of returning to Mexico. Then I fell in love with a fellow student and became a wife, mother, and landscape architect when I completed my degree."

"Casa Milà is down the street," Eduardo said, a comment that brought a long explanation about Carmen's late husband, Luis, who had decided they should live near La Pedrera, the name given to Casa Milà by the locals, due to its resemblance to a stone quarry.

"It's the chimneys I have such fond memories of," Nikki said. "Do you remember when I visited here as a child? My father stood me up on the table so I could see those magical structures."

Carmen nodded. "We took you and Paula to admire the whimsical vents and chimneys up close. Paula was just a toddler."

"Casa Milà is an experience I've never forgotten. See that cluster of white Darth Vaders and the Greek cross?" Nikki pointed.

"How could I ever forget?" Eduardo asked. "Though what you call white Darth Vaders look more like stormtroopers to me."

"It's definitely out of this world," Nikki said, smiling at Eduardo. "Tía Carmen took us to visit, and a mischievous boy got me in trouble with my mother."

Nikki shared their chance encounter as kids at Casa Milà with Carmen.

"On our very first meeting, he convinced me to explore the crawlspace. My mother was livid, thinking he was endangering me."

"It was obvious I was smitten by you, and maybe she thought I would steal a kiss as we hid in the crawlspace," Eduardo said, smiling at the memory. "If she'd only known I was too shy."

"So you admit you did think of kissing me," Nikki joked.

They all laughed.

Eduardo turned to face Carmen. He told her how he had returned to Casa Milà for the next two days hoping to see this exquisite girl again before returning to Colombia. His family left Spain and the adventure on the terrace had become a fantasy. But over time, he forgot it.

"That's very romantic," Carmen said.

"Twenty-five years later a remarkable woman arrived in Medellín. I fell in love with Nikki at first sight, which made no sense. You see, I didn't make the connection with the impish ten-year-old who had stolen my heart."

"Destiny," Carmen said, "works in strange ways. When is the wedding?"

"We thought we'd visit Casa Milà later to see if we can arrange it as our venue," Nikki said. "We'll set the date once we see what's available. We may have to make another trip to Barcelona if they can't accommodate us this time."

"A rooftop ceremony will cement your childhood memories forever," Carmen said. She added that Casa Milà scheduled rooftop concerts on summer evenings and suggested they see one. "Speaking of weddings, Paula is also getting married this month."

Carmen's face changed from a joyful expression to one of concern.

"Reservations about the marriage?" Nikki was surprised.

Carmen hesitated. "He's a well-educated young man, born and raised in Spain, but I worry. His parents are very nice, especially his mother. They are Muslim, and I know mixed marriages can create enormous challenges."

"All marriages have their challenges. If he's a good man, that's what counts," Nikki said.

"He seems to be. He's agreed to marry Paula in a Catholic service at Sagrada Família."

"Sagrada Família? Really? My cousin is going to marry in the most famous church in Barcelona?"

"In a crypt church built in the basement under the high altar of the basilica," Carmen said. "As longtime parishioners, we are privileged to hold the wedding there. Paula and Fadi will also have a Muslim service."

"A month of weddings—I love it," Eduardo said. He put an arm around Nikki and they both turned to face Carmen. "If we cannot arrange our wedding at Casa Milà, then this balcony, Tía Carmen, is our next choice."

Carmen gave him a warm hug. He glanced at Nikki, and she saw his eyes brimming over with love. He reached out to bring her in for the hug too.

"If you have trouble renting the rooftop," Carmen said, "Fadi knows people who might help you get it for an evening."

"Wonderful," Nikki said.

"I'll see if Paula and Fadi can join us here for dinner tonight. I'll make paella, Fadi's favorite dish."

Carmen led them into the kitchen, where they sat at tall stools around a bistro table while she made cappuccino.

From the black leather seat, a modern design in shiny chrome, Nikki looked through a doorway leading off the kitchen into a room with built-in bookcases and a desk piled high with books. A floor lamp was positioned next to a recliner.

"You must still be an avid reader?" Nikki asked.

"For sure. I use the recliner in the office, except when Paula is here. Then she takes the desk for her computer."

Carmen moved around the kitchen with the efficiency of a barista as she ground coffee and arranged pastissets, small Spanish cookies filled with caramelized fruit paste, on an elegant porcelain plate with gold trim around the edges.

"You haven't seen Paula since the second time you visited. She was about four years old then," Carmen said as she removed cups, saucers, and napkins from a cupboard and spoons from a cabinet drawer.

"Paula is younger than I am," Nikki told Eduardo as she watched Carmen's efficient movements in the kitchen. "She was like a little sister to me during that trip. Tell us about her. Is she still working at the university?"

A pint-sized milk carton from the refrigerator poured into a small glass container became pure froth seconds later under a nozzle of the espresso machine.

"She works with the United Nations at the Institute for Globalization, Culture and Mobility. It seems to suit her perfectly," Carmen said as she poured espresso into each cup and topped it with frothy milk. She sprinkled a little cinnamon on the froth and arranged the coffee, sugar bowl, and the plate of pastissets on a silver tray. She led them back to the balcony, balancing the tray through the open sliding doors and placing it on the table. "Primarily research, but she reaches out to migrant groups in the community as part of her work."

"Does Paula work to integrate these migrants into Spanish society?" Nikki asked.

"Exactly. Though I worry her idealism will collapse under the realities of cultural diversity," Carmen said. She placed a napkin, a cup of coffee, and a spoon around the table for each of them.

"Love this cappuccino," Eduardo said after a second sip. He nibbled on a cookie and added, "the cookies too."

Carmen beamed at the compliment.

Eduardo continued. "Paula's work sounds interesting and certainly worthwhile."

"Many of the migrants she works with are young men in ghettos. It's satisfying to bring hope to them, she claims."

"That's what counts," Nikki said.

"It's consuming her life. She's even given up her dancing to work longer hours. She's studied flamenco since she was six years old, and she's pretty good."

Nikki murmured sympathetically.

"But I need to call Fadi to arrange a celebration for your visit," Carmen said, returning to the kitchen. When she rejoined her guests on the balcony, she beamed and announced that Fadi and Paula would join them that evening for her world-famous paella.

CHAPTER EIGHT

ALMERÍA, ANDALUCÍA, SPAIN

Saturday Midday

"This land belongs to the caliphate," Taiwo whispered to himself when he got his first glimpse of the Almería port and its surroundings as the ferry approached. "We will regain this land in the name of Allah."

Taiwo, not usually appreciative of nature, was impressed by the Andalusian town nestled on a cove overlooking the Mediterranean. Before undertaking his trip to Spain, he'd studied a bit of Spanish history, especially places he would pass through. He'd learned that this area had formed part of the Caliphate of Córdoba in the tenth century. The nearby Moorish castle, Alcazaba de Almería, was second in grandeur and importance only to the Alhambra in Granada. Due to the Alcazaba's strategic location, it saw countless sieges during the Christian–Muslim wars until it fell into Christian hands in 1489 under Ferdinand and Isabella.

The land of Andalusia, he had read, was as harsh and rugged as the history it had witnessed over three millennia. Going back to its origins, the native Iberians were conquered by many peoples—Greeks, Romans, Visigoths, Byzantines, and Moorish Muslims to name a few—all of whom left an imprint of their customs and traditions imbedded in the local culture. Later the Muslim conquerors fought against the Iberian

Christians for almost eight millennia, the longest war in history. Eventually the Christians, he knew, had reclaimed the territory. The Reconquista, as the war was named, finally concluded in 1492 in Granada. The Christian victory coincided with Spain's expansion into the New World.

As a harbor pilot escorted the ferry into port, Taiwo pulled both his cell phone and the stolen passport from his pocket.

"The ferry is almost in port." He listened to instructions before hanging up. As he moved to the front of the ferry he picked up his duffle bag and looked over the seaport with disgust at the pleasure boats in the harbor. *Those boats are owned by infidels.*

Once he cleared the checkpoint, he headed for the café on the waterfront where he had been instructed to wait. Hungry again, he ordered a red fish stew and a double espresso. Heavy on garlic and cumin, the stew contained more potato than fish. He dunked the crusty bread that came with his meal into the stew to soften it. He finished eating, wiped his mouth, pushed his bowl away, and replaced it with his coffee cup. As he stirred the heavy espresso, a thin man of about thirty years of age with curly, shoulder-length black hair entered the café. The young man scanned the tables and then strode toward Taiwo.

Taiwo held his espresso cup with both hands and passed it under his nose as if to overcome his garlicky breath with the aroma of coffee. He continued watching the young man. He half smiled as he took a sip.

"As-salamu alaikum," the man said, his right hand over his heart as he approached the table.

"Wa alaikumu as-salaam," Taiwo responded spreading his hand over his heart. Still contemplating the man, Taiwo gestured with his head for the young man to join him at the table.

The man's sullen eyes beneath bushy, black eyebrows accented his thin face. Those eyes bored into Taiwo's in a piercing manner.

"I'm Hassan. I'm to take you to the next location. Insha Allah—God willing, I'll help you with the assignment."

Together they walked to the train station. Hassan purchased one-way tickets to Valencia, where they would spend the night at a mosque near the center of town. Further instructions would be given once they reported in at the mosque.

On the train, after a few formalities, Taiwo tried to converse with his companion, but soon discovered Hassan was not interested in talking. After that, Taiwo pretty much ignored Hassan. *If he doesn't want to talk, that's fine with me,* he thought. *It's just a job.* Besides, Taiwo would keep his information secret, like his stolen passport. He turned to view the landscape as the train clacked away.

Despite the strong espresso he had consumed, Taiwo felt sleepy. Usually a good sleeper, he'd been on vigil to confront Kenny and obtain his passport the night before. Now he felt the effects of sleep deficit. The landscape reminded him of the West African desert. Even the dry, hot climate seemed reminiscent of his homeland. The passing olive groves and the occasional highly irrigated vegetable farms and greenhouses that dotted the hills soon hypnotized him. After what seemed like an interminable period, he checked the time on his phone. Realizing they still had four more hours of train ride, he propped his duffle bag against the window and the back of the seat and leaned his head against it. Closing his eyes, he thought how good it would be to dream about Olani's face when she found Kehinde. *My brother never considered I'd get even with him for marrying her.*

CHAPTER NINE

BARCELONA—CARRER DE PROVENÇA

Saturday Evening

A fresh flower arrangement of crimson stargazer lilies and white hydrangeas set a festive tone at the dining room table. Yet no one sat at the table. Nikki, Eduardo, and Fadi were outside on the balcony, where Carmen labored over the portable grill. She stood half hidden from sight behind two clay pots hanging from the rafters.

"There's nothing worse than overcooked, soggy rice," Carmen declared, lowering the heat on the portable barbecue and emerging from behind the greenery.

"You've never served soggy paella," Fadi countered.

Carmen smiled and nodded. "But it could be tonight."

Paula had called to say she would be late. Fadi, Nikki, and Eduardo indulged their palates with big, fat olives Carmen had filled with roasted Marcona almonds, plus fresh boquerones—white anchovies—she had prepared in a traditional Spanish pickled style with vinegar and spices before patting them dry to place on toast tips. As soon as Carmen brought a dish of steamed clams from the kitchen, they helped themselves to the buttery shellfish.

"Clams are my favorite tapa," Carmen said. She discarded an empty shell in a bowl she'd placed for that purpose.

"Sorry I'm late," Paula said as she swept onto the balcony. "I had to finish a report. Plus, I had to pick up the baklava I keep in my freezer for spontaneous occasions like this."

"Stop apologizing and greet your relatives," Carmen said.

Introductions, hugs, and cheek kisses made the rounds. For a while, Nikki and Paula stood by the table on the balcony and engaged in conversation. First, they exchanged small talk on the number of years since they had seen each other. Shortly the conversation became more intimate, discussing the upcoming weddings.

"Looks like you've had prenuptial tests," Eduardo said, pointing to a self-adhesive elastic wrap around Fadi's elbow.

"No. It's a genetic test I had done to placate my dad. He has Parkinson's and wants to make certain I did not inherit the genes from him. Not that I would necessarily get Parkinson's even if I did inherit the markers."

Eduardo expressed sympathy for the father's health condition, and the conversation turned to soccer—specifically the Barcelona team. Soon the two men were talking as if they had been lifelong friends.

Carmen interrupted by asking her guests to take a seat at the table in the dining room. She moved indoors holding the hot paella pan with heavy kitchen gloves. Paula took a large spoon to serve the succulent rice and seafood delicacy on each dinner plate as she and her mother walked around the table. Once they finished serving, Carmen returned the paella pan to the outdoor grill. Mother and daughter joined their guests at the table.

"Tía Carmen, your table setting looks very elegant. I assume you arranged the centerpiece?" Eduardo asked.

"You know I need to be surrounded by flowers," she said. She looked happy.

"Besides growing flowers, my future mother-in-law is a great cook. I think I've told you she prepares the best paella in the world," Fadi said, looking across the table at Carmen. The contrast of Fadi's jet-black hair against his pale ivory skin, combined with almost perfectly symmetrical facial features, gave him the appearance of a movie star.

Carmen smiled and nodded ever so slightly to acknowledge the compliment.

"You are a lucky man," Eduardo said.

Fadi nodded in agreement as he took Paula's hand and kissed it. With his other hand, he lifted his wine glass for a toast.

As he did so, Nikki's eyes flickered in confusion.

"I saw that." Fadi laughed as he held the wine glass up high. "I'm a Spanish Muslim, which explains why I drink wine. My ancestors enjoyed wine with their meals, so I'm honoring a family tradition. To a fine wine!"

"To a fine wine," Eduardo echoed.

Fadi took another sip, lingering a few seconds as if to appreciate the flavor before placing the glass on the table. "This tinto is truly exquisite. Wines from the Rioja region are known for their structure and tannins, yet the connoisseur will detect a fruity, cherry characteristic in this red."

"If Fadi can discuss Spanish wine, I want to explain another purely Spanish tradition—paella," Carmen said, "even though each region has its own version. Valencia claims theirs is best since they invented it."

"Ah, but the Spanish would not have invented paella," Paula said, "if the Arabs had not brought rice to Spain. Rice is one of the many gifts brought here by the Arabs." Changing her gaze from the guests to her plate, she took a forkful of shrimp-laden paella to her mouth and turned apprehensively to face her mother.

For a few seconds everyone was quiet as each indulged in the saffron-infused rice with shrimp, mussels, chunks of lobster, and Spanish sausage.

"Nikki, do you like flamenco?" Fadi asked, breaking the silence.

"Yes, but I've never seen much of it," Nikki responded, as she turned to Carmen. "Mmm, this is the most delicious paella I've ever eaten."

"We thought a good flamenco show would be the perfect way for the three of us to welcome you and Eduardo to Spain," Carmen said. "We will go after dinner tonight."

"I love the idea," Nikki said. She touched Eduardo's hand under the table and squeezed it to let him know how happy she felt.

As the five people around the table continued to eat and sip and laugh, Fadi pulled an envelope from his pocket and passed it to Nikki.

"Tickets for you and Eduardo to attend a jazz concert on Monday night at the Casa Milà rooftop."

"How did you get them?" Eduardo asked. "The event was sold out."

"Connections. Fadi is like a magician," Carmen said. "Our plan is for the two of you to fall so madly in love with Spain, you won't want to return home."

"I'm already in love with Spanish food," Eduardo said.

"For dessert, you will sample Paula's baklava," Carmen said. "She's mastered the technique of layering phyllo dough."

"Her pastry is exquisite," Fadi added, smiling at his fiancée. "And after dessert, the most sought-after show in town: Tablao Flamenco Cordobés.

The dancers are quite good, though Tablao is best known for their world class cantaores—singers of cante jondo."

"But Tablao's singers have been outdone lately by a flamenco dancer who is all the rage. A Gypsy named Selena," Carmen said. "And sitting with us here is a wonderful flamenco dancer—"

"Mama," Paula said, "don't start—"

"Let us give them a taste of flamenco," Fadi said, interrupting his fiancée. He grabbed Paula's hand and pulled her to standing.

She shook her head. "I'm out of practice. Let's leave it to the pros."

"Paula took dance lessons until six months ago," Carmen said. She looked down at her plate. "Unfortunately, she's lost interest in dancing."

"I don't have time anymore," Paula responded swiftly. "The coffee should be ready." She walked to the kitchen.

"I feel like such a foreigner in this country," Nikki said. "The culture is so different despite the many ways Spain is linked with Latin America. I've never given much thought to flamenco."

"The history behind it is compelling," Paula said as she poured coffee into demitasse cups already set on the table.

"True," Fadi said, waiting for Paula to finish filling his cup. He took a sip. "It's the melding of Arab song and string instruments, Jewish synagogue chants, and ancient north Indian classical music. And Gypsy women dance with such passion. It's become the fiery, passionate Gypsy sound of Spain."

"We should say Rom or Roma instead of Gypsy," Paula said, smiling as she corrected her fiancé.

"As I was saying," Fadi said with a wide grin, "impassioned Rom women dancing does not sound right. The word Gypsy is beautiful. It sounds spirited and energetic. Gypsy women dance in provocative blouses and long skirts. It's all wrapped up in the Andalusian folk tradition of song and dance where flamenco and cante jondo originated."

"I've read of the golden age of Spain when Christians, Muslims, and Jews were at peace and influenced each other in positive ways," Eduardo said. "Would you say music brought people together?"

"Music no doubt is partly responsible, but a thriving business environment remains the common denominator," Fadi said.

"How is that?" Nikki asked.

"Spain offered commodities in much demand at the time—silver, gold, spices," Fadi said as he reached for one more piece of baklava. "Trade with other countries thrived. Christians and Muslims needed money to expand their businesses, yet both religions condemned usurious practices, like charging interest. As demand grew for financing loans, the Jewish community resolved the issue by becoming bankers."

"So everyone was happy, and business flourished," Eduardo said.

"And everyone got along," Paula said, "and the Muslims were not marginalized as they are today."

"We live in different times, Paula," Carmen said. "We cannot compare what happened centuries ago to our world today. The cultures came together and pieces of each one contributed to the rich tapestry of Spanish heritage."

"But those golden years of cultural understanding," Paula said, "as you called them, Eduardo, happened before the Christian reconquest of Spain. The longest war in history."

"And by 1492, when Christopher Columbus went to the Americas, Christian Spain reigned supreme," Nikki said.

"After the reconquest, we all know how the Moors, the Muslims, either converted to Christianity or were expelled from Spain. Sometimes both," Paula said. "Of course, a number of them converted to Christianity and remained here, like my father's family."

"And the Jews met the same fate. They converted, and some were still driven out of the country," Carmen added. "My understanding, Paula, is that your father's family was already Christian Lebanese before they migrated to Spain."

Paula visibly stiffened.

"We're digressing," Fadi said, attempting to take the conversation to more neutral ground. "About flamenco, we don't know when it originated, but its earliest roots can be traced back to music and dance traditions from northern India."

"Northern India? Amazing," Nikki said. "I had no clue."

"Gypsies," Fadi said, glancing at his fiancée, "or as Paula prefers, the Roma people, first moved westward about two thousand years ago, bringing their folklife with them. Their musical traditions melded with ours even when the Roma themselves did not integrate into our society."

"All I know is the vibrancy of the dance. Stomping of feet, clapping of hands, the deep, sonorous voice of the cantaor, and guitar music are a feast for the eye and ear," Carmen said. "The very spirit of Spain."

"Centuries of dance forms converged in Andalucía, and over time flamenco emerged. The intensity of the cante jondo lyrics are deep-rooted," Fadi said, looking at Paula. He winked at his fiancée.

"The dance itself probably rose as an expression of defiance at the time Spain banished Moors, Roma, and Jews," Paula said. "So, to respond to Eduardo's question, flamenco music served to unite the outcasts of society in the new Christian Spain."

"We don't know that flamenco united the outcasts," Carmen said, moving her dessert plate toward the center of the table in an absent-minded gesture.

"What else should Eduardo and I see while we're here?" Nikki asked, wanting to change the subject.

"You mean in Barcelona or in the whole of Spain?" Carmen asked.

"The whole country," Nikki said as she looked around the table, anticipating another long discussion. Her gaze fell upon her cousin, as if waiting for her to speak first.

"Sights not to be missed are the Alhambra, the Moorish castle in the city of Granada, and the city of Toledo," Paula said.

"This country offers so much to the tourist," Fadi said. "In antiquity, so many different tribes conquered Spain, each one left us a legacy, a delicious morsel of their own culture making each region different. But if I were visiting Spain for the first time, I'd start with the prehistory, our earliest ancestors. Yes, the Paleolithic cave art."

"Cave art?" Eduardo repeated.

"That's my choice, but there is so much to choose from," Fadi said.

"I'd love to see Paleolithic art," Eduardo said. He reacted with so much enthusiasm, his body moved forward toward the table in an assertive gesture. "I've been reading a book on it."

"You should start at the Museum of Humanity in Burgos," Fadi said. "Next you should visit Atapuerca where some of the earliest human remains have been found. By that point, you'd logically conclude you should visit a few caves."

"I suggested the idea, but Nikki does not like caves," Eduardo said.

Nikki nudged him under the table.

"Some, like Altamira, are replicas, not actual caves. So you don't get your feet dirty."

"It's not fear of getting her feet dirty," Eduardo said.

"Replica caves? That sounds like fun," Nikki said, pinching Eduardo's thigh under the table. "Are the caves well-lit?"

"Good lighting? Inside the caves? Fadi asked. "I think so. You can see the art very well. You're allowed to bring your own flashlight to most of them."

"Our Paleolithic art goes back forty thousand years. Maybe even more. Recent studies take our art back to the Neanderthals," Carmen said. "It's truly a national treasure, as it is in France too."

Fadi checked the time on his smart watch. "It's time for us to head over to Tablao and watch Selena take command of center stage."

"I thought you said it was all about the cante jondo." Nikki said.

Fadi smiled and held his hands up in a mock "you win" stance.

CHAPTER TEN

BENI ENSAR, MOROCCO, NORTH AFRICA

SUNDAY EARLY MORNING

Awakened by her baby daughter at six in the morning, Olani discovered Kenny was not next to her in bed. When she had retired the night before, he had not yet returned home.

She'd worried yesterday evening when Kenny did not get back. Yet she decided to get some sleep, deducing he'd gone to a café with Taiwo. The thought of Taiwo gave reason for her concern. She had considered going out to look for Kenny, but it was getting dark by the time she had started to worry. She had been busy in the kitchen, preparing and cooking lamb with vegetables for the week, taking care of the baby, and cleaning the house. Jobs that had kept her indoors. She had only stepped outside her house once yesterday morning, to throw kernels of corn to her chickens from the front door. Busy with cooking and household chores, she even forgot to collect any eggs they may have laid.

With the aroma of cooked food still permeating the small house, she surmised her husband had returned home late and, not wanting to awaken her, had slept on cushions in the front room. She got up and walked into the kitchen only to discover it in the same condition as she had left it the night before. Kenny had not slept in the living area either. That's when her worry slid into panic. Checking her cell phone to see if he had called, she found he had not. She dialed his number, but no one answered. Kenny had left for work yesterday at his usual early time, an hour before sunrise. Whatever the problem, she knew it involved Taiwo.

In desperation, Olani took the baby in her arms, whispering soothing words in Spanish, a language she wanted her daughter to speak. Kenny wanted to move the family to Spain, so they spoke Spanish at home, unless they had visitors from Nigeria. She changed the child's diaper and decided against wrapping her in a light blanket, since it was very warm, even this early in the morning.

Hurrying from the house, Olani hastened through the yard to awaken a neighbor down the street who could help her. Near the iron gate, she noticed the cats watching three large, semi-bald black buzzards. She had encountered her cats behaving this way almost a year ago when a stray dog had wandered in through the open gate and died inside their yard. The dead dog had attracted the same type of buzzards.

Another dead dog, Olani thought. *As if I didn't already have enough to worry about. In this heat, I'd better get rid of the dead animal first.*

As she rounded the corner of her house, Olani let out a muffled scream. She fell against the wall, almost losing her grip on the baby, who started crying. Slowly, she slid down the plastered concrete wall to the ground and placed her daughter on a mound of soft soil. Dayo whimpered but stopped crying.

Olani's hands trembled as she turned the corpse over. A rope, which looked like the cord from the starter coil, formed a loose-fitting noose around her husband's neck. The cord had left visible dark bruises and rope burns on his skin where it had been pulled tight to strangle him. His face was purplish-blue, and the flesh surrounding his lips was black. Tears flooded her eyes as she looked at her husband's stiff body. She knew who had committed this vile act.

With trembling hands she closed her husband's eyes and his lower jaw, reciting the traditional words "when the soul leaves the body, the vision follows it" as she knelt by his side. She kissed his forehead, turned him to face Mecca and made a simple du'aa' for his eternal rest, a supplication for Allah to forgive her beloved Kenny. She used a du'aa' with a rhyming scheme she had learned long ago and was surprised she could recite it despite her unbearable stress.

After picking up her daughter, Olani returned inside the house and put the baby on the mattress in the bedroom. She sobbed violently for several minutes. But things needed to be done, so she dried her eyes and picked up her mobile phone. She called her mother, which started her tears again and brought an occasional outburst of sobs. Olani explained what had happened and what she planned to do. Her mother promised to fly in later that day, though she asked Olani not to delay the funeral. They both knew that Kenny had to be buried as soon as possible. Only her mother would make the trip. Kenny's parents were both deceased. Olani called Kenny's sister to notify her, but she knew his sister would not be able to make it to the funeral since she lived in Washington, DC. Her own half-sisters would be too busy with their own families to travel.

Olani opened a long, narrow wicker basket, used as a makeshift headboard for the bed. From it she removed a thin, white blanket. Talking softly to her daughter for a few seconds, Olani left the baby in the room and walked back outside.

Through tears, she gazed at her husband's corpse. She noticed his shirt was torn. On instinct, she reached down into Kenny's pockets to check for his passport. It was missing. She checked for other personal belongings, but his pockets were empty.

After a few seconds of silence, with minimal movement but great effort, she covered her husband's body with the blanket. She moved slightly away to avoid negative ideas so near Kenny's body.

You murdered your own brother to steal his passport. I will report this atrocity to the authorities. And you will pay, Taiwo, for your heinous crime. Even if it's the last thing I do on this earth. You barbaric dog, you will pay.

After Kehinde's close male friends removed his outer garments, they performed the ritual ghusl, bathing the corpse to cleanse it. The men then wrapped him in a simple shroud. Since Kenny had suffered trauma in his dying moments, and the body had not been found until twenty-four hours later, the janazah, or funeral, was rushed even more than usual to get the deceased to al-Dafin, his final resting place. The grave was aligned so it would be perpendicular to Qibla, or Mecca. The body was interred without a coffin, facing Mecca, as required by sharia.

After the burial, Olani asked one of Kenny's friends to report her husband's murder to the police in Port Nador. Although she had called and reported the murder at Beni Ensar, the police, knowing the Adebayo family was Nigerian, had only sent an examiner to verify the death and issue a death certificate. Kenny's friend said he would drive the twelve kilometers to Port Nador to report it at the police station. He also said he would drive an officer back to discuss the details with Olani.

Female friends spent time with Olani after the janazah, which had taken place less than three hours after she'd found his corpse. When her mother arrived from Nigeria in the afternoon, the women returned to their own homes.

A couple of hours after her mother's arrival, Kenny's friend knocked on the front door. A police officer accompanied him. Olani covered her head, opened the door, and joined them in the yard. Beyond the iron fence, she could see the police jeep they had driven.

"Let me show you where I found my husband's body. Before I tell you anything else, you need to know this was premeditated murder. My brother-in-law wanted my husband's passport. He had an urgent reason to go to Spain. So urgent, he killed his own brother."

The three of them walked to the area where Taiwo had hidden his victim. Evidence showed on the ground where digging had taken place. Still visible along the ridges of soft upturned soil, Taiwo's boot tracks had made discernable impressions.

"There is no evidence of a murder here," the police officer said.

"I'll show you the starter coil from the electric motor he used to strangle my husband. It's on the bench by the front door."

"May I also see the death certificate? And I'll take his mobile phone."

"The murdering devil," Olani said, "took all his personal belongings, money, phone, everything. The death certificate I'll show you. It's inside the house."

Despite trying to contain her emotions, tears welled up in Olani's eyes. She could not stop thinking about her little Dayo growing up without her father.

As if reading her mind, Kenny's friend told her she was a strong woman and he knew she would do a fine job raising Dayo.

"You need to know," Olani said to the officer, "that Taiwo Adebayo is a terrorist. You need to report him to the Spanish authorities. In Barcelona. That's where he has a job to carry out in the name of jihad."

"Did he say that?"

"In different words. His urgency for the passport speaks of his desperation. He definitely stated his assignment would take him to Barcelona."

"Can you be more specific?" the officer asked. "Did he mention accomplices? What job they intended to carry out?"

"That's all I know. He needed to get to Barcelona for an assignment. If it had been legal work, he would not use a stolen passport."

Olani saw the officer's eyes glaze over when she was unable to provide the detailed information he requested.

"The office will check the Interpol database and see if he's on the watch list. If he is, that will make it easier to put out an alert," the officer said.

"Kenny was a good man." Olani's voice broke as she spoke. "The good man is dead and the evil one is alive." She started crying again.

"I'm sorry," the officer said. "Can you show me the death certificate and I'll get out of here, so you can return to your child."

"Yes, of course. Follow me." She led the men into the house where the officer verified the death certificate and took a picture of it with his phone. After the men departed, she went to the kitchen, where her mother was busy entertaining Dayo.

Despite the late hour, neither Olani nor her mother had eaten. Dayo was asleep and Olani had spent the last two hours crying. She had also talked to her mother about what her life would be now without Kenny.

"Never mind the three-day waiting period. Who is to know if you do not observe the widow's three-day waiting period?" Olani's mother asked rhetorically.

"Are you sure?" Olani asked. She had always considered her mother to be a very sensible woman and was pleased to have her mother's blessing.

"Pack a suitcase and leave for Spain as soon as possible—you must do what you must do. The Spanish authorities must punish him. I've come to take care of my granddaughter. Go without worries."

Though his murder was reported in Beni Ensar and in the city of Nador, Olani knew she'd need to report his death to the Spanish authorities to make certain Taiwo suffered the consequences for murdering his brother. Normally the Spanish government would not be interested in the death of one more Muslim man in the Melilla area, but she knew they would listen when she told them of the terrorist carrying her husband's passport. As the widow, she should wait until the end of the third day following Kenny's death before leaving the house. But with her mother supporting her decision to travel to Spain and stay with relatives who could help her, she took out her suitcase and packed. Knowing her mother would take care of Dayo, Olani could act before it was too late and Taiwo got away without punishment. She dialed a number in L'Hospitalet de Llobregat in Spain. Then she called a taxi and set an appointment for pickup at four a.m. to be driven to Melilla, in time for the first flight to Barcelona the following morning.

Olani knew her mother had always detested Taiwo. The woman had been so pleased when Olani and Kenny married. After all, Taiwo's constant harassment would have to stop after Olani married another man. Especially since that man was Taiwo's twin brother. Except that now, four years after Olani's marriage to Kenny, Taiwo's aggressiveness had taken a sinister turn. And there was a corpse to prove it.

CHAPTER ELEVEN

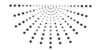

MEDITERRANEAN SEA

The Mediterranean is almost completely enclosed by land—the European continent and Anatolia to the north, Africa on the south, the Levant to the east, and the mountainous Spanish and Moroccan coasts separated by the relatively narrow Strait of Gibraltar to the west. Bobbing in the rough waves of the Mediterranean, a forty-foot catamaran was en route from Valencia to the third largest Balearic Island, Ibiza. This archipelago is an autonomous community and forms a Spanish province, with Palma de Mallorca as its capital. The islands' history followed the ups and downs of the Christian–Muslim power struggle on the mainland. Over the millennia, the islands saw conflict involving many different armies, including attacks from the Turks to the east and the Barbary pirates from North Africa.

Taiwo clung to the steel handrail attached to the interior of the small center cockpit, feeling as if his very life depended on how tight he held it. The captain steered the boat head-on into monstrous, unruly waves. Taiwo gritted his teeth as he tried to stand and look out over the ocean. All he could see were waves, huge waves—rising, falling, and then the sudden swells breaking against the hull of the boat. With each upsurge of the vessel, he felt the heaving of his stomach, which had already spilled the remnants of his last meal. Not accustomed to rough seas, Taiwo had thrown up all over the floor. And he still felt sick. If not for the endless nauseating bouncing of the boat, he would have lain down. He could not understand how Hassan and the captain kept the contents of their stomachs in the rough sea. The city of Valencia had not been visible for over three hours, but the island they were heading to was nowhere on the horizon either.

The violent winds ceased as suddenly as they had arisen. The sea grew calm. The sun was low in the sky. Taiwo watched the captain turn off two of the four outboard Yamaha engines and reduce the speed of the boat to a mere crawl. Though the captain had remained silent throughout most of the trip, he spoke as they approached land.

"I'm from central Saudi Arabia. One day, I felt called to exchange my seminomadic life in the desert to the life on a seaworthy motorboat," he said as he looked out over the horizon with expressionless eyes, almost as if he were talking to himself.

"One lonely life to another. You must have had trouble with women," Taiwo said.

"No, no trouble."

"A man your age," Taiwo said, "does not leave his home to come so far away without some form of shit with someone."

"I'm a hajji. I came to where I was needed," he said, standing a little taller and puffing his chest out like a frigatebird. "How about the two of you?" As the short man stood on the platform by the controls, Taiwo felt the captain's stare. He appeared to take pride in having fulfilled his duty to make the sacred pilgrimage to Mecca.

"Not yet. But I will someday," Taiwo said. Irritated by the captain's bragging on attaining hajji status, the Nigerian could not conceal his feelings. Although Taiwo had recovered from his seasickness, he still felt pale and shaky. He noticed the normally quiet Hassan ignored the hajji's comment and fixed his gaze on the horizon.

The captain went silent again, as if he should not waste too many words on them.

"You must feel we are mere foot soldiers. Let me tell you, hajji man, we all find our way to serve Allah. You're not the only one who has devoted his life to Allah," Taiwo said. He felt ill-humored after the rough seas. It made him feel better to spit out the venom building in the pit of his stomach by confronting the captain.

Uttering an unintelligible growl, the captain turned back to the control panel.

Straight ahead, Taiwo saw white bluffs loom over the horizon. As the boat approached a cove, the bluffs became stratified rock, chiseled by the wind and sea into horizontal planks.

The captain moved and Taiwo saw him scanning the cliffs. He seemed to be making certain no people were perched on the outcroppings waiting to watch the sunset—or keeping an eye on the comings and goings of small vessels in the sea.

A lone figure walked along a distant ridge. Out of nowhere, a small speck that Taiwo realized was a bird flew to the man's uplifted hand. *A falconer is out hunting with his raptor,* Taiwo thought. *I'm a hunter too, just different prey.*

The boatman either did not see the falconer or he did not perceive the man to be a threat, for he proceeded to steer right up to the rock ledges. He signaled for his two passengers to scramble out onto one of the protruding flat rocks. He passed two boxes containing food, water, cooking equipment, and light blankets to them. He informed Taiwo and Hassan he would tie the boat further down the coastline.

"When I return, we will climb up to that cave to eat and sleep there," the captain said, pointing to an opening visible on the upper part of the rocky cliff. "While you wait for me, gather dry driftwood along the bluffs so I can cook tonight."

Taiwo spat on the ground as he watched the captain turn the boat around in the cove. Looking back to where he'd seen the falconer, he saw that the cliff was deserted.

Awakening in the predawn hours, Taiwo saw the captain moving about, lighting his way to the mouth of the cave with a flashlight. When the captain gave no indication that he knew he was being watched, Taiwo got up after the Saudi left the cave. Taiwo relieved himself near the mouth of the cave and kept an eye on the captain walking down the cliff. He assumed the hajji would collect more pieces of driftwood. The wood he and Hassan had gathered the night before while the hajji moored his boat had been consumed during the preparation of dinner.

Taiwo laid down again but was still awake when he heard the captain piling driftwood inside the opening of the cave by the circle of rocks where he had made the campfire the night before. He pretended to sleep as he saw the hajji take his prayer rug and perform his morning salat. After his prayers, the man again stretched the rug between the two metal stakes he had used the previous evening to prevent the fire from being seen from the bluffs below. Taiwo watched the captain light the sun-dried tree branches and other debris.

When Hassan awoke, Taiwo decided it was time to get up. After their daybreak prayers, the two men joined the captain at the campfire. He handed them cups of strong coffee and the results of his campfire cooking. Each man indulged in freshly made hunayua, a typical Saudi breakfast made with ground dates, butter, and semolina and seasoned with cardamom seeds. The captain had simmered it until the liquid evaporated, leaving the consistency of dry porridge. The robust aroma and flavor of the coffee enhanced the taste of the hunayua.

After they ate, the captain announced it was time to pack up camp. He gathered the few pots and utensils he had used for cooking dinner the night before and breakfast this morning. Using a dirty, char-covered cloth, he wiped the excess soot from the pans before banging them into a backpack. In between the butter and flour tins and his cooking pots, he slipped sacks made from coarse cloth containing dates and other leftover ingredients. The arrangement kept the metal pots from rattling. The captain crouched down at the opening of the cave to kill the campfire embers with water from a flask he carried on his belt. Then he scraped dirt from the cave floor with his hands and poured it over the ashes. Finally he untied his prayer rug, removed the two stakes from the ground, and rolled them up inside the rug. This he tied securely to the outside of his backpack.

Taiwo gathered up his own stuff. The two men followed the captain down the cliff to the place he had moored the boat.

A man in a skiff met them in the cove near the catamaran. The captain kissed the newcomer on both sides of his face. Taiwo and Hassan gave the usual greeting in Arabic with their hands over their hearts, to which they received the expected response. The smaller boat had wooden boxes in various sizes and shapes—some long, some rectangular, and a few square ones. The captain organized Taiwo, Hassan, and the newcomer as they moved the cargo from the skiff to his catamaran. Overseeing the transfer of boxes, the hajji took great care to fit part of the load in his small sleeping quarters below deck. The rest of the cargo was placed in the forward holds meant to store and refrigerate fresh fish. On top of these boxes, the captain laid ice the newcomer had brought with him. Over the ice went fresh fish that the newcomer had also brought.

"Insha Allah, God willing you will have a successful mission," the captain said, nodding at Hassan and Taiwo as he started the engines.

The captain departed. Taiwo and Hassan joined the newcomer on his skiff. Without the load to steady it, the vessel wobbled as the men jumped aboard. The skiff hugged the coast until they came to the town of San Antonio, where the newcomer moored it at a small wharf. The three of them walked to the bus station and boarded a bus to Vila.

CHAPTER TWELVE

L'HOSPITALET DE LLOBREGAT, SPAIN

Monday Early Morning

Rafael González, an agent with the tactical unit of the Spanish National Police Corps, Grupo Especial de Operaciones—better known by its acronym, GEO—sat with his wife Lola in the breakfast nook of their condo in L'Hospitalet de Llobregat. A municipality to the immediate southwest of Barcelona, L'Hospitalet was Rafael's hometown. Often considered a depressed suburb, it was Catalonia's second most populous city. Yet Rafael and his wife found the more tranquil lifestyle in L'Hospitalet more to their liking than the hustle and bustle of Barcelona. Lola also appreciated the town's diverse population. Their condo was situated high on a hill away from the busier area along the coastline. Its location about forty minutes from Barcelona gave Rafael easy access by metro to his office.

After learning of Kenny's murder the night before, neither Rafael nor Lola had slept well. Now they sat in their kitchen reminiscing about how they met. Rafael had served as an antiterrorist agent on the border patrol detail in Melilla, North Africa's Spanish enclave. Lola, a Christian Yoruba woman, had made his pursuit of her into a ritual. And he liked to savor those memories.

Rafael recalled watching her graceful figure cross the gate into the Spanish city every morning. For months he had waited every evening to watch her return to Beni Ensar. Finally finding the courage to introduce himself, he discovered the svelte woman with the creamy brown skin had a tenacious resolve to protect her independence.

"I remember the day I asked if you were single or married," Rafael said.

"And you looked scared to hear the answer," Lola said. "I was not going to mess around and ruin my life. No matter how handsome and nice you were, Rafa." Now they were the proud parents of twins.

Rafael knew that her search for better work had prompted her to leave her native Nigeria for Beni Ensar. Being one of the few lucky women who had found regular employment as a cook for a Spanish family in Melilla, she was not about to jeopardize her position. He had understood.

"When I proposed, you still insisted we get to know each other before making promises," Rafael recalled.

They continued to reminisce. When Lola's cousin Olani, living in Nigeria, had married Kenny, Lola suggested they look for work in Melilla. It was the same year Lola had given birth to twins. Having her cousin move to neighboring Beni Ensar had meant a lot to her. Then Rafael received a big promotion as an antiterrorist operative with the GEO office in Barcelona, which brought them to L'Hospitalet two years ago.

"Kenny was a good man," Rafael said.

The mention of Kenny's name brought tears to Lola's eyes.

"Yes, he was," Lola said, wiping her tears. "So hard to believe he's gone."

Rafael had taken an immediate liking to his wife's relatives. He had helped Kenny get a Spanish work visa and a visitor visa for Olani so she could visit Lola and help with the twins. That was before Dayo was born.

"I regret not using my influence to speed up the process on their immigration," he said sadly "Kenny would still be alive."

"You can't say that," Lola said. "You both did the right thing. Kenny wanted the normal process, not to use his wife's relatives to intervene."

Rafael reached across the table and patted his wife's hand. "Yet we are the sponsors of their petitions."

Lola sighed. "We cannot live the rest of our lives regretting Kenny's wishes to let the legal process run its course."

Rafael knew his wife would be happier with Olani around. After she arrived, he'd do what he could to speed up her immigration. She could even live in L'Hospitalet. It'd be good for both of them, he thought. Despite the tragic circumstances, he knew Lola looked forward to welcoming Olani into their home. They had not seen her since leaving Melilla two years earlier.

His wife rose to start coffee. Her movements in the kitchen brought him back to the present.

As a GEO agent, Rafael had encountered many horrific events in his work, but this one hit too close. He still could not absorb Kenny's senseless death at the hand of his own brother. His mind drifted to the future, specifically how he and Lola could help her cousin. They would not know what or how much they could do until Olani was here.

Rafael took the covered mug of coffee his wife handed him. He kissed her and left the condominium.

As he drove his Renault Clio to the Barcelona airport, Rafael wondered about Olani's emotional state. Would the widow have used her time while traveling to sort through the details of the tragedy? And would she have a plan for her future? He admired the woman who had boarded a plane in Melilla to fly to Barcelona by herself so soon after her husband's murder.

When he found her at the luggage retrieval area, Olani dissolved into a flood of tears in his arms. On the return drive to the condo, she did not stop crying. Rafael drove in silence, not knowing how to comfort her.

Upon seeing her cousin, Olani fell into Lola's arms, convulsing with sobs. Lola embraced her cousin. After some time, Olani managed to compose herself.

Darkness hung in the room like a brooding storm. Rafael sat at the round table in the breakfast nook with Olani, thinking about the questions he wanted to ask. Lola placed coffee cups and a plate of chocolate-filled croissants she had made a day earlier on the table. Rafael seized the opportunity to inquire about Kenny's murder.

"Taiwo is up to no good. That man killed his brother to steal his passport," Olani said. "He's involved in a terrorist plot that will take place in Barcelona. I overheard him say he had a job in Barcelona—the reason he wanted Kenny's passport. He wanted it so desperately he killed his own brother."

"You know that as an officer in the Catalonia National Police Corps, I'll be able to report the murder and his motive. That should suffice for placing him on a watch list."

"Rafa," Lola said in an endearing tone of voice as she shook her head.

"Watch lists never work. Can't you track his movement within the country?"

"If he uses Kenny's passport, we can track him. By any chance, do you have Kenny's passport number?" Rafael asked.

"I do," Olani said. She rummaged through her purse, handing the results of her search to Rafael. "Kenny's passport number, a photo of my husband, and an old photo of Taiwo. Taiwo looks so much like Kenny. Even the beards are similar. Can you make copies for me?"

Rafael nodded. "This helps a lot. At the agency, we have a few other methods I can use, but I can't really inform you about his movements."

"Unless Olani is in danger," Lola said.

"Under those circumstances, yes. I will do everything I can to track him," Rafael said.

"A Moroccan police officer came to my house the day we buried Kenny. He took all the details and I asked him to inform Spanish security forces of a possible terrorist. I gave him all the information on the passport."

"He should have entered the stolen passport into the international criminal database," Rafael said. "I'll be able to check if he input it on Interpol. If he did, that will flag the passport and anyone using it will be apprehended."

"I hope he followed up," Olani said.

"I'll check if Taiwo is wanted in other countries. Unfortunately, killing his brother in Morocco does not make him a wanted criminal in Spain until Morocco asks for extradition."

Rafael got up to leave for work when the doorbell chimed.

A stunning woman, their neighbor Selena, leaned against the door frame. She wore a blue low-cut blouse with flared sleeves and a skin-tight, calf-length skirt. High heels made her appear even taller than she might have been. Her long, curly black hair was loosely gathered in the back with several strands falling over her face giving her a savage, wild appearance.

"May I come in?" she asked in a husky voice.

Rafael bowed slightly as he made a sweeping motion with his arm into the middle of the room.

Lola stood and hugged Selena. She introduced Olani, who got up to greet the visitor.

Rafael smiled for the first time all morning and shook his head as he glanced at the three women. They shared similar qualities—tall, lithe bodies, high cheekbones, large black eyes, long, curly dark hair, and creamy brown skin.

"I can't believe it," he said.

"What's that?" Lola asked.

"You three could be sisters," Rafael said, shaking his head. His smile grew.

Lola and the visitor laughed.

Rafael grabbed a lightweight jacket as he headed down the hall to call the four-year-old twins to drop them off at their kindergarten and day care. Quiet until now, the twins burst into the room like firecrackers. They hugged their mother. She instructed them to say goodbye to the two visitors.

"I'll see you in the afternoon. Call me at the office if you need anything," Rafael said, ushering the twins out the door in front of him.

After Rafael and the children left, Olani found herself crying again in her cousin Lola's arms. Then she straightened up.

"Is Rafa okay with my desire to get justice?"

"Absolutely. If he were not in agreement, he would tell you. As a detective, he does have rules to follow, but I'll make sure I get as much info from Rafa as I can," Lola said. "You should—"

"You've lost your husband in a tragic accident," Selena said, interrupting. "I'm sorry you are suffering. Maybe I can help."

"I've lost him. And it's tragic, but it was no accident. Premeditated murder." Olani felt tears slide down her cheek. With the back of her hand, she wiped them. "How did you know?"

"I'm Roma," Selena said. "What many call Gypsy. We have a knack for recognizing the torments afflicting other people. I'm attuned to your suffering. I lost my own husband seven months ago. When you feel ready, I might be able to help."

"I need help right now," Olani said, sniffling again. Any avenue that could help her stop Taiwo would be welcome. "Can you tell fortunes?"

"Duikkerin?" Selena raised an eyebrow. "Fortune telling is in my blood. Even though some say I'm not a Romanipen." A strand of curly hair fell across her eyes, and she flicked it away.

"Not a Romanipen?" Olani looked confused.

"Not a real Rom. My fellow Romani think I've slipped away from our traditional way of life."

"It doesn't deter from her duikkerin capabilities," Lola was quick to explain. "But the Rom don't like the police and they normally don't befriend police either. They have their own way of regulating their communities and enforcing their laws. Yet Selena is our friend despite Rafa being a detective."

"Let me see your palm," Selena said. The fortune teller studied Olani's right hand, turning it over, looking at each finger and her wrist. Then she took Olani's left hand and examined it in the same close manner. After her evaluation, she patted Olani's forearm. "This is interesting. Very interesting."

"What do you see?" Olani asked.

"You're determined to find the man who killed your husband."

"That's true. If I don't, the police in Morocco will probably do nothing. And Rafa said if Morocco does not ask for Taiwo's extradition for killing his brother, he can hide out in Spain with impunity."

"You will find justice, but only after more challenges and afflictions."

Olani took a deep breath. "As long as I get justice, I'll be satisfied."

"I see that you have a child. A girl. You need to take care of yourself to be there for her as she grows up. Eventually you will remarry. Several years from now. He will be a good man. Like the one you lost."

The women sat, talking and sipping coffee for hours. When Selena asked to hear more details surrounding Kenny's death, Olani cried again. Selena and Lola cried with her.

Midday gave way to early afternoon and the women offered Olani encouragement in overcoming her present suffering and suggestions for bringing justice to honor Kenny's memory. At two in the afternoon, Lola fixed a light lunch of leftovers she pulled from her refrigerator—Spanish tortilla, Manchego cheese, chorizo, and homemade bread rolls. Finished with the early afternoon meal, Lola brewed fresh espresso and served it with Scarlett Royal grapes for dessert.

Selena looked pensive as she bit into a grape, cutting it in half with her teeth. "The closer you are to that malicious man, the easier it will be to find him. You said he's planning something in Barcelona. My work keeps me in the city at least five days a week, so I keep an apartment there. Come stay with me. We can locate that worthless bastard easier in the city through informal channels."

"I like the idea," Olani said with a forcefulness that surprised her. She stopped to think and turned toward Lola. "But what will Rafa say?"

"He'll worry," Lola said. "And he may not agree with your decision, but he will respect it."

"Police officers have legal constraints that can waste time–time that criminals, even the ones on watch lists, can use to commit further atrocities," Selena said.

"It won't hurt to get information on Taiwo's whereabouts through informal channels. Just be careful. Both of you," Lola said, getting up to give Olani a reassuring hug. "And Rafa and I want you to know you and Dayo have a home with us."

CHAPTER THIRTEEN

VILA D'EIVISSA, IBIZA

Vila d'Eivissa, known on the island simply as Vila, is built on a hill jutting up out of the sea. The hill is crowned with the cathedral, Santa María d'Eivissa. Whitewashed houses of the old town sparkle in the sunlight, rising from sea level to the cathedral, like parishioners kneeling as they make their way up the hill to approach the seat of power.

Ibiza was surrounded by a calm sea on the morning Taiwo, Hassan, and the newcomer entered Vila through the main gate of Portal de Ses Taules. They stepped right into the main square as they got off the bus.

Taiwo did not stop to contemplate their surroundings. He followed the newcomer who led him and Hassan up the winding, cobblestone street to an open space near high ramparts. The newcomer stopped and leaned against the historic cannon on display. He pulled his mobile phone out and made a quick call.

As they paused, Taiwo wondered how Olani had reacted to Kenny's death. Spanish authorities in Melilla might investigate, but he'd killed before. Many times. He was a professional and had never been caught.

The newcomer spoke. "Our supplier said to bring you up. He has a request to make of you."

"Supplier?" Taiwo asked.

"Supplier of services, guns, whatever customers need."

The men continued walking up the labyrinth of narrow streets until they arrived at a small open plaza. The newcomer made another phone call. After he hung up, the newcomer took the men to a table at a small outdoor café on the edge of the plaza with a view of the harbor.

Instead of looking toward the harbor, Taiwo sat facing the cobblestone street. He stared at a staircase built between two white buildings. The passageway obviously connected to the next parallel street up the hillside. A tall, robust man walking down the steps was the object of Taiwo's attention. The man wore a traditional Muslim skullcap but otherwise was immaculately dressed in Western attire. Distinctive in appearance, he reflected restrained grace and strength of character. Yet the most interesting aspect of the personage was not his serene and commanding presence. Instead, it was a thick, one-sided leather vest worn over his left shoulder. A hooded falcon tethered to a vest, in the right country, would thrust him into a position of stature. Taiwo felt a sudden impulse to stand up and bow, as if he were in the presence of a member of the royal family of Saudi Arabia.

Taiwo wondered if this was the same man he had seen standing atop the cliff when the captain had landed at the cove the day before. More than one falconer could live on Ibiza, but the robust figure seemed similar to the one he had seen at a distance.

A younger man walked down the stairway at a fast pace and passed the falconer. The younger one continued toward the newcomer's table. The distinguished gentleman turned to the right when he hit the street level and disappeared into a shop opposite the café where they sat.

Taiwo knew instinctively that the dark-skinned young man who had just joined them could not be the supplier. He must be an intermediary. The supplier would want to remain anonymous. Upon hearing the young man speak Arabic, Taiwo tried to pinpoint the accent. Although he spoke five languages, he was not fluent enough in Arabic to discern the origin of the accent.

The intermediary ordered a round of espresso and an assortment of breakfast pastries. It did not take long for him to come to the point. He told Taiwo and Hassan that he had arranged a taxi to the airport where a pilot would fly them to Reus Airport outside Tarragona in a private plane. Once they landed, either the imam or a person in his confidence would meet them, take them to a mosque, and convey the next steps for the assignment in Barcelona.

"You will receive documents and equipment you may need," he said, looking at Taiwo before turning to Hassan. "I understand you already know the imam."

"I do. In fact, my car is at the mosque."

Next, the intermediary asked Hassan and the newcomer to let him speak privately with Taiwo.

"I've been told your previous work involved killing for a fee," he said in a quiet voice after the other two men walked away.

"I've done that," Taiwo said, without blinking.

The intermediary pulled a folded sheet of paper from his shirt pocket. He opened it and spread it out on the table in front of the Nigerian.

"Let's discuss the reason I arranged for you to come to Ibiza. See this." He ironed out the creases with his index finger.

Taiwo leaned in for a closer look at the pictures printed on it.

"After your visit with the imam in Tarragona this afternoon, you will travel to Barcelona for the main assignment. This is a side job and you must make it appear accidental. Carry it out when you find the appropriate moment."

The man handed the sheet of paper to Taiwo.

"For me?"

"Yours to keep for now. Memorize the faces and then throw it away. We don't need any problems. Understand? You are to take care of this assignment only when you won't be discovered. Once you complete the job, you will be paid for your trouble."

"How will I notify you when I have carried out your instructions?"

The intermediary placed an envelope on the table. "Here's your advance."

Taiwo picked it up.

The man pointed to handwritten numbers on the corner of the envelope. "Report in to keep me updated. Use this number. I will get the message. After you have completed both jobs, you will get information on where to collect the rest of your money. Keep yourself alive. We may need you for future assignments."

———

When the Cessna Citation prepared for its final approach to land, Taiwo regretted the briefness of the flight. It had been only forty minutes, hardly giving him time to enjoy the luxury of the jet. One final time before landing, he stretched his legs in the elegant, roomy cabin. He looked out the window. Below them was a beach with small clusters of white buildings, the front row invading the golden sand. The buildings looked like oversized children running toward the Mediterranean Sea, vying to be first to touch a toe in the tepid water. In the distance, a bluish maroon mountain range seemed poised to protect the beaches from marauding invaders, yet the mountains had already failed to keep the hordes of tourists away.

"The Costa Dorada," Hassan said. "And the city is Tarragona, where we pick up my car. We land in Reus, a short distance away, and come back to Tarragona."

Taiwo looked out the window again and saw farmland and a few small buildings scattered along two highways below. The plane descended and the tires hit the ground with a punishing thud.

Taiwo and Hassan climbed out of the jet, met by a youth of high school age. The young man led them through an entrance used exclusively for passengers arriving by private planes. Taiwo offered his passport to a lone immigration officer, who held his hand up signaling he did not need to review it. The man nodded at their young escort as they passed.

The young guide drove, speaking to them in broken Spanish, pointing out the few landmarks. After less than half an hour, their guide parked the car in a spot marked as reserved for the imam. All three men stepped out and walked toward the mosque. They removed their shoes and continued inside. Arriving in time for the late afternoon prayer, they joined the congregants already filling the mosque.

After the prayer ended, the crowd, mostly consisting of men, departed. Their guide took them to meet the man dressed in a white robe who had led the prayers. Each one performed the usual greeting.

"I'm a member of the congregation, not the imam," the man said as he removed a key chain from an inside pocket of his thobe, an ankle-length robe. From another pocket he retrieved a wad of euros, peeled off several bills, and handed the money to the young man. "Go fill the tank of Hassan's Honda while I speak to our visitors."

The three men sat down on a carpet covering a section of floor in the prayer room. The prayer leader gave specific instructions to each man on the assignment in Barcelona. He spent more time explaining Taiwo's responsibilities and discussing the electronics he planned to use, specifically the circuitry and programming to make sure the project worked correctly. The man had worked with Hassan before, but not with Taiwo. When he completed his inquiry, he turned to Hassan.

"Fetch us water. Go to the rear of the imam's living quarters. Step outside to the small courtyard. On the south wall, a stone container mounted on a metal rack contains a clay pot of filtered rainwater. You will find cups hanging on the outside of the rack. Take one for yourself. Drink it. When you finish, bring two for us."

Left alone with Taiwo, the prayer leader escorted him to a large bathroom. Once inside, the religious man moved next to a cabinet built into the wall. He took out his key chain and unlocked the small door. First pushing aside cleaning supplies and rolls of bath tissue, he reached to the back of the space, withdrawing a shoebox. He placed it on the counter in front of the Nigerian.

"Our man in Ibiza asked me to give you this. Open it."

The Nigerian lifted the lid.

The box contained a Russian Nagant M1895 seven-shot revolver outfitted with a Bramit device. Taiwo could feel the prayer leader watching him as he examined two packages of sabot .22 bullets designed for use with the silencer.

The leader returned to the cabinet and retrieved a 10-megapixel Canon PowerShot.

"Stand against the wall. Right there. Look up. Now look straight into the camera," he instructed as the shutter sounded repeatedly.

As they walked back to the prayer room, Taiwo noticed the mihrab, the niche indicating the direction of Mecca, for the first time. He held the shoebox firmly against his torso to prevent its contents from falling out. *An old gun*, Taiwo thought. *The supplier could have arranged for a newer model. Arriving by private plane and walking through a private immigration entrance, I could even have carried the revolver with me from Ibiza.*

Both men returned to the same spot of carpet where they had sat before. The prayer leader placed the camera on the floor next to him. Almost immediately, the young guide came in and handed the Honda Beat's key to the robed man who in turn gave the camera to him and asked him to print the appropriate photos and produce the corresponding documents.

Hassan appeared holding their cups of water. The prayer leader gestured for Hassan to sit with them as he finished speaking with Taiwo. Shortly the young guide returned with a packet for the prayer leader to review. Looking satisfied with what he saw, the leader presented a driver's license, passport, and national identity card to Taiwo, documents intended to facilitate Taiwo's mobility within Spain.

Taiwo took the packet and shoved it into the shoebox, closing the lid again.

"May Allah be with you always," the prayer leader said. Then he added the last words Taiwo heard before he climbed into the Honda Beat. "Be wise before you use the weapon."

Hassan drove Taiwo the sixty-two miles from Tarragona to Barcelona in his small yellow Honda. The kilometers shown on its odometer had increased exponentially during the time it had been parked at the Tarragona mosque.

"I liked that small city. A good following at the mosque," Taiwo said, interrupting Hassan's silence. "Good atmosphere."

"Many people are committed to establishing sharia in Catalonia," Hassan said before focusing exclusively on his driving.

After a drive of an hour and a half, Hassan arrived at a small mosque in Barcelona. He introduced the Nigerian to its cleric, a sympathizer of the Tarragona imam's cause. After Hassan left, the cleric showed his guest around.

"My friend in Tarragona has a full mosque. Here in Barcelona, I have a small Islamic center, not a mosque with minarets or rich furnishings."

Taiwo had already taken notice of the bare-bones structure when he had arrived. It lacked a qubba, the dome representing the vault of heaven. It lacked an ablution fountain for cleansing before entering for prayers. The customary sahn, a courtyard where people could meet without disturbing those inside, was also missing. It did house the religious essentials: a mihrab indicating the direction of Mecca and a minbar, the raised platform used by the imam to deliver the sermon at Friday prayer gatherings.

As they strolled slowly through the prayer room, the host pointed out his personal quarters before taking Taiwo to a compact room with adjoining bathroom that the imam's wife had prepared for the Nigerian's stay.

Taiwo explained he would stay two or three weeks before returning to his native Nigeria. After a few minutes of small talk, the imam returned to his quarters. Taiwo closed the door to his room and unpacked his belongings from the duffle bag. Since it was dark when he arrived, Taiwo had not seen the layout of the neighborhood. A bit of research on his phone made him realize the small mosque was located at the rear of a building fronting on Carrer de San Gil. It had its own private entrance off a small alley. He found the building also housed offices for a realtor, a dentist, two doctors, an attorney partnership, and an interior design boutique. He closed the map app on his phone knowing he would spend time tomorrow learning how to get around the city.

Removing the shoebox from his bag, he placed it on the bed and sat down to examine the revolver and silencer again.

Be wise before you use the weapon, words Taiwo kept hearing in his mind, even after crawling into bed.

CHAPTER FOURTEEN

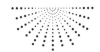

BARCELONA—EIXAMPLE DISTRICT

Monday Evening

Nikki tingled with excitement, standing with Eduardo in a queue at Casa Milà. Bright streetlights provided good illumination for people lined up outside the nine-story curvilinear building waiting to ascend to the rooftop for the jazz concert.

The ticket collector, a young woman, asked if they had visited Casa Milà before.

"As children, we met here," Nikki chirped excitedly.

"Do you want to walk up or take the elevator?" the woman questioned in a robotic sounding voice.

"The stairs," Nikki responded.

The ticket taker used her head to signal the direction toward the stairwell.

"The most interesting way," the young woman said, showing a bit of enthusiasm for the first time. "Gaudí turned them into pleasing spaces."

At the fifth-floor landing, Nikki stopped to catch her breath after running up four flights. She lingered, looking down the stairwell, waiting for Eduardo to catch up with her.

Eduardo joined her on the landing.

Nikki laughed. "You're breathing pretty hard, old man."

"Who else is out of breath?" Eduardo glanced at Nikki before observing the stairwell. He shook his head in amazement at the walls. "What a genius."

True to the concept used throughout the entire building, the stairwell's walls were curvilinear. The doorways connecting to each floor echoed the sinuous design. Two high-gloss colors covered the unique space. Frog green painted in an undulating pattern covered the upper part of the wall and the ceiling while a toad brown blanketed the lower portion of the wall along the well-worn stairs.

"Lead on, my loved one," Eduardo said.

Nikki ran up the stairs of the remaining floors and pushed open a heavy door where the stairwell ended. As she stepped outside onto the flat, well-illuminated terrace, cool evening air enveloped her in a silky embrace. She gasped at the sight before her.

She felt Eduardo behind her snuggling up close, placing his hands on her shoulders, and giving her a loving squeeze. She turned toward him slightly. They looked at each other, then stared in awe at the artistic terrace, site of their childhood memories. Joy overtook them both as they marveled at the legacy Gaudí left on this unique rooftop overlooking Barcelona.

"They've come to life," Nikki whispered as she observed the structures in the tenuous light.

"Our private chimney," Eduardo said, pointing to the white-tiled stack. "They've made the pyramid space under the Greek cross into a room. The opening where we crawled in has been expanded to a full doorway."

"With its own private door, our romantic hideaway is transformed into our petite castle," she said.

"Am I dreaming?" Eduardo brought Nikki closer to him. She leaned her body against his.

"We both are," she said. Her eyes glistened as if the dew in the air had drifted into them, reflecting back like diamond dust.

Eduardo hugged her as he kissed her ear. Then he took a step away from Nikki and turned toward the chattering concertgoers emerging from the elevator twenty feet behind them.

Nikki laughed. "Romantic hideaway, indeed. If not for all the people standing around waiting for the concert."

"When Fadi gave us the concert tickets, I thought we might be disappointed," Eduardo said, contemplating the fairytale scene where he and Nikki had met. "But it's even more wondrous than I remember."

Nikki tugged Eduardo's arm. "Those Darth Vader stacks are my favorites. I wonder if George Lucas got the idea for Anakin Skywalker's Darth Vader mask here. Of course, Darth Vader is dressed in black instead of beige like these sculptured stacks."

"Probably a coincidence," Eduardo said. "They still look like stormtroopers to me."

Nikki led Eduardo across the expanse of tile-covered concrete steps and walkways toward the Greek cross. She stopped and turned back to gaze at the stacks, deciding they did look more like stormtroopers. Taking her smart phone, she snapped a selfie of the two of them with the stormtroopers in the background.

Eduardo was looking toward their romantic hideaway. When she looked over, she saw what had caught his attention—a unisex restroom sign.

"Nikki, look what they've done to our romantic hideaway," he said, his voice full of disappointment.

"Shatters any amorous ideas we were harboring." She stepped toward their meeting spot at the base of the chimney stack. Leaning against the tiled wall next to the door that had not existed when they were children, she took off her shoes and propped them against the wall.

"Taking off our shoes, like when we were kids? That's when I fell in love with you," Eduardo said, reaching out to touch Nikki's face gently with the back of his hand.

"This is paradise. You know Eduardo, this is where you promised me a castle."

"I meant the chimney was our castle," Eduardo said. "If only Gaudí had left written instructions to prohibit building bathrooms in the cavity of our palace."

"From castle to bathroom. That's pretty crappy," she said. Eduardo groaned at her pun. He glanced toward the makeshift stage where the musicians were beginning to gather. "We could find a place to sit for the concert."

"I'd rather listen from here. It's a better view—I can see all the sculptured elements. Isn't that why we came?"

As Eduardo walked away, she thought he had gone on a chair-finding expedition until she noticed him standing by the makeshift stage.

People streamed in, most arriving by elevator, a few drifting out of the stairwell. The crowd ranged from teenagers flaunting body piercing, tattoos, and orange or purple hair to gray-haired men and women wearing drab, outdated clothes. A group of three fashion-conscious women dressed in outfits too elegant for the occasion seemed a bit out of place as they emerged from the elevator. A man rushed to meet them and escorted them rather ceremoniously to reserved seats.

One lone man, his white beard accenting his bohemian-style clothes, fidgeted with his handlebar mustache as he contemplated his surroundings. Moving as if he had recognized someone, he headed toward Nikki, his path taking him right past her. He turned slightly and wished her a good evening as he opened the restroom door. The old man's unusual attire captured her imagination and she wondered if he was an artist she should recognize. Yet as soon as he was out of sight, she turned her awareness back to the roofscape.

Nikki scanned the crowd. She had lost Eduardo in the multitude. The cool night air refreshed her as she refocused and searched for him. Locating him as he stepped up on the stage, she noticed he started talking to a lanky man setting up musical instruments. She watched her fiancé reach into his pocket, retrieve his wallet, open it and hand something to the man.

Eduardo turned and elbowed his way back to her.

"What were you doing?" she asked. Glancing at the crowd again, she noticed the number of people gathering for the concert continued to increase. All seats seemed occupied and standing room space near the stage was crowded to the point that a few spectators were edging into the area around the stormtrooper cluster closest to the stage.

"Asking the musicians how much they charged for a private event up here. They said they'd get back to me."

"I'm not sure jazz is my choice for our reception," Nikki said. "Where would you set a band up?"

"How about the area by the second group of stormtroopers? It allows a smoother floor for dancing." Eduardo escorted Nikki around the only open space left on the terrace. Using both arms like ground crew directing a plane to a terminal gate, he pointed out where he would place every component of the event from wedding party to dance floor to guest tables. "This way, people can dance," he said.

Nikki glanced at the concrete floor and noticed it was smooth, without embedded tile.

As he spoke of the plans, Eduardo's voice became ever more animated. "The bridal table should face the band with a few tables for guests completing the circle at the outer edge of the dance floor."

The band started playing. Eduardo took his fiancée into his arms.

"That's Mendelssohn's 'Wedding March,'" she said, surprised.

Eduardo twirled her around as he hummed the march. The band played a shortened version, and when it concluded, Nikki and Eduardo collapsed into each other's arms, laughing. Eduardo found her lips and kissed her passionately.

"That was beautiful," Nikki said, catching her breath. "I guess a good jazz ensemble *can* play at a wedding. You arranged that, didn't you?"

"Of course," Eduardo said, kissing her again.

Nikki pulled slightly away and admired the space around her. "Such a gorgeous setting. Our personal story makes this a perfect venue for us. I feel like a princess." She lifted her arms in a dancelike stance as she pirouetted around Eduardo.

"You *are* my princess. My Star Wars princess," Eduardo said. "We'll return tomorrow to leave a deposit."

"And what about our castle?"

"The entire rooftop is our castle," Eduardo said. "The reason we're getting married here."

They sat, barefoot, on a tiled step to listen to the concert. Nikki leaned her head onto Eduardo's shoulder. As the concert ended, he retrieved their shoes and set them on the step below where Nikki sat.

"My Cinderella, it's time to put your glass slippers on."

The next morning, Eduardo and Nikki enjoyed an early breakfast buffet and cappuccino at the Majestic while they planned their wedding. They refilled their cappuccinos at least three times while they discussed their ideas. Then they set off for Casa Milà, hitting the street slightly past nine-thirty. They enjoyed walking in the bright sunlight on their way to their wedding venue. With a Casa Milà wedding coordinator they discussed catering, table arrangement, and space for the musicians. "Fadi Massú and I attended the university together. He's a great guy," the coordinator said. "When he called to ask that I help you, I told you you were so lucky. We had a cancellation for Saturday night. We had been completely booked."

"It works great for us. Fadi and my cousin are getting married the following Saturday," Nikki said. "At Sagrada Família."

"Fadi mentioned it," the planner said, then changed the subject. "What about flowers?"

"My aunt is doing them."

"I forgot. Fadi told me. Said his future mother-in-law is quite the expert. How about monograms or a special phrase on the cocktail napkins?"

"Special phrase?"

"We can print something meaningful to both of you, a romantic saying, the place of your first kiss, or anything you'd like to share."

"Ah, yes," Nikki said. "Like meeting on this rooftop as kids."

Later, sipping espresso at a small outdoor café in Parc Güell, Nikki chatted about their upcoming reception. Although other people were sitting at nearby tables, she was so engrossed in conversation with Eduardo, she felt she owned the world. "When we used the tickets Fadi gave us, it solidified my desire to marry on the rooftop."

Eduardo took her hand in his to admire the engagement ring he'd given her in Colombia. "You know we have to choose wedding bands."

"Tomorrow we can shop for them. Changing the subject," Nikki said, "We never discussed Carmen's dinner party. "Did you enjoy it?" She searched Eduardo's eyes. "More specifically, what did you think of Paula?"

"She's sure defensive of Arabs and Muslims."

"Her father was Lebanese. Paula was very close to him." Nikki took the last sip of espresso and put the cup down.

"I meant the tension between Paula and Carmen."

"You noticed?" Nikki asked. "Though Carmen seems to genuinely like Fadi."

"Fadi is great," Eduardo said. "It's the tension between mother and daughter that caught my attention."

"And Fadi is caught in the middle."

"Or Paula is influenced by the immigrants she's working with," Eduardo said.

"That's what Carmen is concerned about. But maybe Paula is simply nervous about her wedding."

"Wedding jitters? I hope you don't get feisty like that with me," Eduardo said as he took the last sip of his coffee and opened the brochure the ticket office had given him showing a map of the buildings, pathways, and other points of interest in the Gaudí-designed park.

"The dancer at Tablao Flamenco afterward was beyond phenomenal," Nikki said. "And she was striking. I loved the dance where she used a fan."

"Beautiful, indeed," Eduardo said, sliding the brochure toward Nikki.

"Sultry and exotic. Now help me decide which route to take within the park."

They opted for the route recommended in the pamphlet. Encountering an outdoor staircase with a whimsical dragon, Nikki laughed with delight. "Look how perfect he is. Every city should count a genius among its architects. One who thinks creatively in such fun and frivolous ways."

"Stand next to the dragon so I can snap your picture." Eduardo no sooner asked Nikki to stand by the dragon than she moved through various poses, making faces, leaning on the dragon, kissing the dragon's snout, and backing away with her arms stretched out looking terrified. As Eduardo moved in to take a close-up, Nikki held her hand out to block the camera.

"That's enough, paparazzo—I need to visit the ladies' room. I'll meet you right here."

Nikki entered the restroom. A paper taped to the first cubicle door stated OUT OF SERVICE in childlike block letters. She chose the second stall instead. When she stepped out and started toward the wash basin, the door to the first stall swung open. Nikki turned and was shocked to see a man with a stocking over his face. Almost simultaneously, two women walked in from the park. The man dashed for the exit. The women screamed. As he rushed past them, he pushed one out of his path, nearly knocking her over.

Nikki took a couple of seconds to react before sprinting after him, yelling for Eduardo's help. She pointed to the runner. "Grab him."

Holding the camera hanging around his neck with one hand, Eduardo raced after the escaping man. But the young, athletic guy ran through the gates into the street and jumped in a waiting taxi. Nikki and Eduardo tried to glimpse the license plates or cab number, but the taxi disappeared around a corner. Still, they ran to the intersection, hoping to find it caught in traffic. When they reached the corner, only three cars occupied the street. The taxi was long gone.

Eduardo put his arm around Nikki's shoulder. She turned to face him.

"After my experience in Tayrona, I don't like isolated bathrooms."

"But this one is hardly secluded," he said. "Did he hurt you?"

"Just a nasty surprise."

"What exactly happened?"

Nikki was visibly upset as she explained about the handwritten notice and the man who had scared her and run away when two women entered.

Eduardo took Nikki into his arms.

"It was so reminiscent of what happened in Colombia," she said, "that's what scared me. I turned and saw a guy standing there."

"Most of the bathrooms here are unisex. Do you think he went in thinking it was unisex?" Eduardo asked, still holding Nikki in his arms.

"Didn't you see he had a stocking over his face?"

"No, I did not," Eduardo said. "That means he was waiting to assault someone."

"His intentions could not have been good. When two women came in as he stepped out of the cubicle, he split."

"Nikki, do you think he was there waiting for you?" Eduardo asked. His voice reflected concern.

"Either me specifically, or some other unlucky woman. He planned to hurt someone."

"Who'd even know we're here? Who in Barcelona would want to hurt you?" Eduardo asked. "This is a threat."

"I'm a little spooked is all," she said. Nikki remembered when she had been at risk in Colombia and later in Mexico. But those situations had been work-related, and here she was on vacation. "Maybe he's just a voyeur."

"With unisex bathrooms all over this city, wouldn't it be easier to be a voyeur in one that's unisex?" Eduardo asked. He studied the sign over the door clearly indicating a ladies' room.

"Maybe he was trying to steal a handbag."

"Could be, but coincidences don't happen. That's the second incident since we arrived," Eduardo said.

"Second incident?" Nikki asked.

"Skullcap," Eduardo said. "The one who may have taken photos of us."

Nikki nodded.

Before leaving the area, they searched the bathroom but found nothing out of the ordinary and decided to forget about it and see the park.

Nikki stepped out of her shoes as soon as they left the restroom. "After chasing that guy, my feet deserve a barefoot walk through the park."

"Barefoot? Here? Surely your joking, my princess."

"Can't I roam barefoot in Barcelona?" Nikki asked. She smiled seductively at Eduardo and added. "One less item of clothing to take off."

CHAPTER FIFTEEN

BARCELONA—EL RAVAL DISTRICT

The landlord of the small mosque, Taiwo learned in conversation over breakfast with the imam, was a Barcelona-born Muslim who belonged to the congregation of the much larger Islamic Center four blocks away.

"My landlord turns a deaf ear to complaints about activities at our place of worship," the imam said, laughing. "He's told me the Catalonia antiterrorist police suspect my alleyway mosque to be radicalized. They keep me on their radar. But they have no proof of wrongdoing, so all they can do is watch."

The imam's wife approached with second servings of khatchauri. The savory pastry filled with cheese was her husband's favorite breakfast item. She returned once more to refill their teacups.

Taiwo mentioned to the imam that before going to sleep the night before, he had researched the area on his mobile phone. He needed to familiarize himself with the part of town he was in and verify the location of several Barcelona landmarks. He pulled out handwritten notes about buildings and other landmarks that might help him navigate the city.

Taiwo had checked the metro lines and discovered, by studying the online maps, that he was within walking distance of the Ramblas and the historic Gothic Quarter, described online as vibrant areas of the city.

"Is it true Barri Gòtic still stands today because the Moors captured it in the eighth century without resistance?" Taiwo asked.

"I don't know. Maybe a few restored remnants of ancient city walls come from that era. Mostly it contains museums and famous landmarks," the cleric said. "Not too far away, El Born contains what the nonbelievers consider priceless treasures, such as the Picasso Museum."

"Tell me more about this neighborhood," Taiwo said.

"El Raval," the cleric said, "is known for its many bars, both high-end and low-end. And prostitution. It has a mixed reputation. Slowly, it's changing. Over the last few years, former cabarets have been remodeled into cultural and educational spaces. Bringing tourists in. Our own people visit the Museum of Contemporary Art."

Taiwo gulped the last of the mint tea the imam's wife had prepared.

"Breakfast was good. Shukran jazilan," Taiwo said as he stood. "Thank you." He took a baseball cap he had laid on the table and put it on his head.

"Ahlan wa sahlan," the cleric responded. "You are welcome."

"Before I leave, may I borrow your computer and printer?" the Nigerian asked.

The imam took him to the computer. After bringing a map up, Taiwo printed it, folded it, and tucked it into his shirt pocket, which already held a ballpoint pen.

Taiwo felt good as he left the mosque. The research he had done plus the information the imam had given him had helped him plan his schedule. He would visit the sites where his job would take him, try to locate his target and her companion, and learn the metro lines.

By late afternoon that day Taiwo had caught the metro back to Universitat station. From there to his borrowed quarters was a relatively short walk. In less than a full day, he had managed to navigate within the city to all the places he would need to be. Plus, he had identified the woman he was supposed to eliminate. He'd followed her and her companion to that park and had seen them up close. His planning for both jobs was progressing and he was feeling confident his execution would be faultless.

Tomorrow, his work would take him across the street from the iconic Catholic church, the Basilica of the Sagrada Família, one of the most popular tourist attractions in Spain. It brought in over four and a half million visitors a year. Also known as the only church under continuous construction for more than a hundred years, it was not nearly as big as the Hassan II Mosque Taiwo had visited in Casablanca nor as beautiful as the Blue Mosque in Istanbul, but Sagrada Família packed in the tourists.

That is the difference, he thought with disdain, *mosques attract worshippers, Sagrada Família attracts tourists.*

Tomorrow he would start the new job. Right now he was hungry. As he walked in El Raval, he saw many halal restaurants. He stopped at Habibi, a small one advertising Moroccan food, and ordered lamb and rice to go. When he pulled a roll of money from his pocket to pay for the purchase, a nylon stocking fell to the floor.

A busboy clearing tables eyed the stocking with suspicion as Taiwo left it where it had fallen. The boy took a soiled napkin and picked it up, throwing it in the trash.

Taiwo arrived early the following morning for his temporary job. The assignment provided a cover for him. It consisted of selling selfie sticks and Sagrada Família souvenirs to the infidels on the west side of the famous basilica. The vendors were allowed to set up on the sidewalk in the park on Sardenya, across from the basilica. It was the only street surrounding the church that was open to vehicular traffic.

The large Passion portico, a huge structure supported by six mammoth-sized columns, rose above an entrance that remained temporarily closed. This west entrance as well as the east side Nativity portico built to greet the sun every morning in celebration of the birth of Christ would form grand entrances after the completion of the third one, the Glory façade on the south side. Construction had only recently begun on the south entrance. From the time of Gaudí's earliest drawings, the Glory façade had always been intended to be the grandest of the three.

Most tourists who walk on Sardenya or snap pictures of the basilica's west side never notice a discreet entrance leading to the parishioner church, tucked away in the underground crypt. The Passion portico juts out from the basilica toward the street further minimizing the parishioner doorway made of carved stone. Set apart from the street with a good-sized courtyard enclosed by a decorative wrought iron fence, the parishioner church entrance is totally inconspicuous. For keen observers, two guards stationed inside the narrow gate of the wrought iron fence provide a clue for entry to the parishioner church, also called the crypt church.

The cleric from Tarragona had prearranged Taiwo's cover with a young Pakistani who already held a permit to sell his goods in the west park. Street vendors, allowed exclusively on that side of Sagrada Família, consisted mostly of Muslim immigrants from various countries who set up portable tables every morning on the wide sidewalk to display their wares. The goods offered were similar from one vendor to the next, and tourists tended to purchase from the person who struck their fancy.

A slow morning for sales, a few vendors talked among themselves. One was eating his breakfast as he carried on a loud conversation in Arabic with two other sellers, each holding tea mugs refilled periodically from thermoses. Still other vendors wearing expressions of tedium watched silently as tourists overflowed from the basilica to a small courtyard under the Passion portico. This tight courtyard, fenced in by tall iron stakes, allowed visitors to get a close glimpse of the giant, austere apostles sculptured in raw marble. The fence around this smaller courtyard also eliminated tourist access from the street to the west entrance into the basilica.

The hordes of tourists seemed more engaged in viewing Gaudí's representation of nature inside the basilica's well-illuminated interior than in spilling over to buy goods from the park's vendors.

Taiwo found his idle time useful. He pulled the map he had printed at the mosque the day before and took the pen from his pocket. After adjusting his baseball cap low over his face, he walked the perimeter of the church. Covering the entire city block surrounding the basilica, he stopped periodically to make notes. He also mentally compared written notations he had recorded the day before. From time to time he stopped to search for video surveillance cameras or closed-circuit television. He covered his mouth and nose with his hand whenever he looked up, leaving only his eyes uncovered. He moved to areas he considered lacking surveillance whenever he needed to mark his map with an X to reflect the locations of cameras. For almost three hours, he worked the perimeter and grounds of the basilica. He examined the side streets for cameras. He noticed tourists were funneled through the east entrance, dedicated to handling crowds. As he walked the east side he noticed how security managed throngs of people more efficiently by permanently banning vehicular traffic, leaving the street between the church and the park for tourists and whatever security forces, whether uniformed or plainclothes, monitored the area. The park on the east side, Gaudí Park, took up a complete city block, as did the stone façade and sandstone towers of the basilica. The complex dwarfed the apartment and office buildings in the area. Gaudí Park contained a lake and large shade trees. By contrast, the park on the west side, Park of the Sagrada Família, where vendors set up their tables, was half the size and not as well groomed as its counterpart on the east.

Taiwo walked through the east park, noticing its lush grounds and variety of trees. Stopping to observe the Nativity portico, he watched as visitors waited in a line that crawled up the stairs to the entrance. It reminded him of a snake brumating in cold weather, its energy diminished by its sluggish metabolism.

Like a lion stalking its prey, he circled round the basilica for the third time. Taiwo searched one last time for security cameras on the exterior walls. He surveyed all side streets and buildings, making mental images of possible escape routes. Continuing his final walk around the area, he noted the number of police and uniformed security personnel, their locations, and their vehicles. Police vans, parked in the ample space provided by street corners where vehicular traffic and parking were prohibited, appeared to be equipped with cameras, antennas, and surveillance instruments. In his final analysis, he compared today's written notes to his previous notes. He tucked his map and his written information back into his pocket.

Taiwo cut the corner back to Sardenya, the street where his Pakistani companion manned the table of trinkets. As he approached the small parishioner entrance, he almost bumped into three people. Taiwo could not conceal his surprise. It was Hassan. In the company of two Western women. Taiwo's surprise was not upon seeing his mission comrade. No, his shock came from seeing Hassan with the woman he'd been instructed in Ibiza to eliminate.

CHAPTER SIXTEEN

BARCELONA—EIXAMPLE DISTRICT

Wednesday Night of First Week

"Tonight," Selena informed Olani as they walked up the metro station steps, "I need to make a few inquiries about the underground movement. A fellow dancer can provide answers. Her name is Rosa. She's married to a Muslim. An angry radical guy."

"And she's not Muslim?"

"No, she's Roma. Like me. We met at the Catholic orphanage as kids."

"A Muslim man lets his wife dance publicly?" Olani asked, astonished.

"He works at a flower shop and doesn't earn much. Allows his Gypsy wife to dance for the money. Pure hypocrisy. We'll take her to a café after the show."

As she listened to Selena, Olani figured this man must be using Selena's friend. Lots of radicalized men use women. Unlike her Kenny, who was a good man, this man sounded bad. She could not imagine being married to a radical. Olani slowed the pace, shook her head, and voiced her thought out loud. "Rosa's husband would be like having Taiwo for a husband."

"Don't even think about that. Enjoy your outing tonight. You're doing things you've never done before."

"Never been a widow before, either," Olani said. "As a widow, I should be at home, taking care of my daughter. But it's my duty to seek revenge for Kenny's murder. No one else will bring justice. Though I could not do it without you and Rafa helping me."

The two women entered the employee entrance at Tablao Flamenco. In the dressing room, Olani sat in a chair watching the two female performers, Selena and Rosa, use a ballet bar to work through their warm-up routines in preparation for the show. Olani continued watching the women intently as they dressed for their performance.

Selena slipped into a body-hugging dress with ruffles accenting the sleeves, bodice, and a skirt slit from the hemline to midthigh. She gazed at her fellow dancer. "We're going to a café after the performance. Rosa, I'd love for you to join us."

"That'd be nice," Rosa said, applying eyeliner to enhance her large eyes. She added blue eyeshadow on the upper eyelids and completed her look with a sparkly, golden bronze color from the crease in the eyelid to her eyebrows.

"You can stand offstage to watch our performance," Selena told Olani as the three women left the dressing room. She showed Olani to her place and the women walked on stage.

The curtain rose and the music started. Dancers, both men and women, clapped their hands and stomped their feet in frenzied rhythm to the guitars and percussion instruments. Olani felt nervous and guilty, overwhelmed by the performance. She had to refrain from running to the dressing room. She wondered what Kenny would think and, strangely, felt his presence. She knew that was impossible, yet feeling him close calmed her, as if he were sending a message of approval.

Shortly, her psyche assimilated the intensity of the music and the dancing. She remembered the African music and dance she had participated in as a child. Her head began to sway to the beat set by the percussion instruments and her skin tingled with excitement. She tried to remain focused, suddenly afraid that in her fascination for the spectacle, she might step out from her hiding place and accidentally join the performers on stage.

Almost midnight, it was an early night for the flamenco performers owing to a sparse crowd at Tablao Flamenco. Still, the enthusiastic audience applauded, their voices erupting in several rounds of bravos. Olani returned to the dressing room after Selena took her final bows.

The three women left the Tablao. Rosa, dressed in street clothes, also wore a hijab. She lit a cigarette.

"Dancing flamenco always leaves me with so much energy," Selena said. "Let's have something at the Bosc de les Fades Café. It's inside the Wax Museum building on Passatge de la Banca. The place brings my adrenaline down. Soothes me."

"The dancing looks exhausting," Olani said.

"On the contrary, it excites me. I never indulge in drugs to relax as some of my fellow performers do," Selena said. "I rarely drink alcohol. Except for trifásico. I enjoy one after a night of performance."

"What's trifásico?" Olani asked.

"Coffee. An espresso with a drop of brandy and a little milk—that does the trick."

"Coffee calms you?" Olani sounded surprised.

"I've been drinking espresso since I was a kid. It's like a security blanket," Selena said.

The three women continued down La Rambla. After a block, Rosa put a second cigarette to her lips and used the first one to light it. They stopped again a few steps later as Rosa had a severe coughing episode. Once she recovered, the women resumed their walk toward the café.

"If you're not Muslim, why do you wear a hijab?" Olani asked, looking at Rosa with curiosity. Under the bright streetlights, Olani noticed Rosa looked more relaxed after her smoke, despite the coughing attack.

"Too many idle Muslim men come to the Ramblas at night. They have nothing better to do than hang out. One of them could be a friend of my husband," Rosa said.

"But if you're not Muslim—"

"My husband is Egyptian. He asked me before we got married to wear a hijab if I ventured out in neighborhoods where his friends might recognize me."

"Yet you continue to dance," Olani said.

"We need the money. He told me belly dancers in his country are allowed to dance. So I guess he takes it in that spirit. I don't talk about my work to people we know as a couple," Rosa said as she lit a third cigarette. "And I only smoke away from the house. It's *my* way of relaxing after a strenuous performance."

"I liked the show," Olani said in a rather timid voice as she was experiencing pangs of guilt again. "But what happened to the castanets?"

"They are only used when we dance zambra or siguiriyas," Rosa said.

"Zambra?" Olani asked. "What is that? I thought you danced flamenco."

"That's right, we do," Selena said. "Zambra and siguiriyas are forms of flamenco which use castanets, but most flamenco does not call for them. Only the palmas, or hand clapping and finger snapping. Confusing, I know."

"In any case, it was mesmerizing," Olani said.

"Here we are," Selena announced as they approached the entrance to the café.

Before entering, Rosa threw half a cigarette into the gutter. She removed the hijab and tucked it into her handbag as soon as they stepped inside.

Escorted to a table, they passed through a room with deep forest foliage where two young women, scantily clad as forest nymphs, were half hidden in the dense vegetation. Olani thought the entire setting was artistic and was surprised she did not feel uncomfortable. Soft music played in the background, enhancing further the feel of an enchanted forest. Walking into the next room, dark and jungle-like, they were seated at a round table made from a large tree trunk.

A cocky yet appealing server in a highly starched white apron over dark shirt and pants took their order. His jet-black hair pulled back into a ponytail at his neckline accented his black eyes.

"Rosa, I need to ask you for a favor," Selena said after the server left.

"Anything for you, querida," Rosa said as she watched the server walk away.

"A bit of noise is going around about an attack being imminent in Barcelona. Your husband knows people in the radical Muslim community. By any chance have you heard anything?"

Rosa's expression changed instantly from relaxed to stressed. She looked at Selena. Then she glanced at Olani. "He does not tell me things like that."

"No, but you overhear conversations. You check his cell phone, his email, his computer," Selena said.

"All I can say is he's left town recently. For a night or two each time. That usually means he's working a job somewhere. I don't have access to his phone when he's gone. His email account, I only see when he's logged in and leaves the room to use the bathroom. He'd be furious with me if he knew I check his email. Besides, a lot is in Arabic, so I can't read it."

"I need to find a Nigerian fellow who owes me something," Selena said, as she took a photocopied picture from her purse and handed it to her friend. "His name is Taiwo and this is what he looks like."

Rosa stared at the photo. She glanced at Selena with startled eyes.

"Have you seen him?" Selena asked. "He might be using the name Kenny."

"You're asking dangerous questions, my friend. Be careful who you ask. Hassan has not brought him around, but—"

A clap of thunder invaded the room.

Rosa stopped in midsentence to let the thunderous sound roll.

Olani, shocked by the noise, ducked until she realized they were not in danger.

Both Selena and Rosa seemed accustomed to the sound effects, intended to surprise and delight tourists and make them feel the atmosphere of an enchanted forest. The thunder reverberated through the café, making conversation impossible for a moment.

"As I was saying, my husband hangs out with people who seem aware of happenings, both good and bad. I overhear him mention a lot of places, but he speaks Arabic in most phone conversations. I've overheard 'Sagrada Família' when he's been on the phone, but I don't want anyone getting killed over your question or the photo," Rosa said, handing the picture back to Selena.

Selena put it back in her purse.

Olani looked away. A shiver of fear ran down her spine. From Rosa's reaction, her husband had to be a terrorist.

"You live in fear of him," Selena said.

"I know my limits. My little girl comes first. I know what I can do, what I can ask, and what I must stay away from," Rosa said with a resigned smile.

"If you ever need to leave him," Selena said, "I can help."

"What did this guy do to you?" Rosa asked.

"Oh, it's a score left over from my husband," Selena answered, looking across the room, studying other patrons. Their server walked up with their drinks.

He placed a small dish of peanuts on the tree-trunk tabletop before setting down Selena's trifásico and Olani's nonalcoholic horchata, a silky sweet drink of rice water, vanilla bean, and sugar with cinnamon dusted on the frothy top. Next he moved around the small table to set down Rosa's leche de pantera, a mixture of sweet condensed milk, rum, and brandy. Topped with a sprinkle of cinnamon, it looked as innocent as

Olani's horchata yet contained a powerful punch. As Rosa tasted her cocktail, she called the server back, and handed him the glass.

"I requested double rum and brandy." She flashed a seductive smile at him. "Please ask your bartender to make me un doble. ¿Vale?" After he left, Rosa turned to Selena and said, "Joder, chica, ese majo merece otra mirada—¿vale? Shit, girl, that handsome guy deserves another look —okay?"

"You won't get in trouble with your husband with alcohol on your breath?"

"He's not coming home tonight."

"You don't need to pick the waiter up," Selena warned.

"I'm only looking. A married girl can still do that, can't she?"

"Have you forgotten you are Rom?" Selena asked.

Olani was not sure what that remark meant.

CHAPTER SEVENTEEN

BARCELONA—EIXAMPLE DISTRICT

THURSDAY MIDMORNING

As Nikki and Eduardo sat at a table, their plates piled high with the Majestic's breakfast buffet, they reviewed a list of guests for their wedding. Twenty people were flying in on various airlines at differing hours and they had committed themselves to meeting all of them at the airport and driving them to the hotel. Nikki placed her tablet on the table and picked up her cup of cappuccino, her second one.

She had spent time the day before organizing wedding details. Without the need to mail save the date requests or invitations, attend dress fittings or coordinate bridesmaids' attire, or myriad other tasks such as selecting a photographer, it had been easy. She'd spent most of her time preparing a schedule for picking up guests at the airport. One of the big items, their wedding bands, they had purchased at a jewelry shop on Passeig de Gràcia the day before, but today she and Eduardo would visit gift shops to select wedding favors. If only she knew the name of the florist shop her cousin had picked for her wedding, they could visit it. But Nikki dismissed the idea as intruding on something that was not her business. It did not take away from the fact Nikki was very curious why Paula had chosen anyone other than her mother to do the flowers.

She handed Eduardo a printout of the airline schedules and suggested renting a second car in case delayed flights made them scramble to accommodate everyone. Floyd and his wife could keep the extra car.

"More amazing is the way it's come together—caterer, venue, and flowers. Even the jazz band. So easy. No real effort." Nikki used a spoon to scrape the last bit of coffee-tinted foam from the bottom of her cappuccino cup.

"When you pay big bucks, it's a breeze to organize a party," Eduardo said with a laugh. Then turning serious, he added, "I'm so glad Floyd can walk you down the aisle."

"It's more like down the steps and past the stormtroopers to where you and the judge will be standing."

"That reminds me," he said. "We need to thank Carmen for getting the judge and the legal aspects approved in two days."

"And Fadi for arranging the rooftop. Without them, we would have waited months." Sipping her coffee, Nikki looked across the room and noticed skullcap also eating breakfast. Sitting by himself, he read a newspaper. She nudged Eduardo.

"He's obviously a guest here," he said. "Getting back to our planning, I'm glad we don't need to order flowers. Carmen will turn the place into the castle I promised you."

Nikki smiled. Then with a more somber expression, she added, "It's sad that Paula won't let her mother do her wedding flowers. It must hurt Carmen's feelings. The shop doing her arrangements is Muslim-owned. Must be one of Fadi's connections," Nikki said. "When I met Paula at the church yesterday to decide on the placement of the flowerpots, she brought the florist with her. Hassan. Quiet man. Strangely quiet."

"Are Floyd and Milena vacationing after our wedding?" Eduardo asked.

"He mentioned catching up with an old friend at Interpol. He relishes his direct cooperation with that agency. Since he's coming for our wedding, he's taking advantage to find out more about Cristóbal Arenas and the possibility he may have a vendetta against me. Plus Floyd cannot pass up an opportunity to network and make inquiries beyond what can be done from sitting in our Miami office. And Carmen invited them so they're staying for Paula's wedding."

Stepping to the music of Mendelssohn's "Wedding March" two days later, Nikki's heart swelled as she turned the corner past the stormtroopers. Overcome with emotion upon seeing Eduardo waiting for her under a trellis covered in red carnations, she could hardly place one foot in front of the other. She leaned on Floyd's arm to steady her.

The guests broke into applause as Floyd delivered Nikki to Eduardo under the trellis. Her dress was ivory lace with flamenco-style sleeves, snug to the elbow where elegant ruffles fell midway to her forearm. The tight bodice, with an organza underlining, accentuated her slim figure. Scarcely above the knees, the dress cascaded into more flamenco ruffles with the fabric trailing to the floor in an undulating fashion to form the bridal train. Instead of a traditional veil, she wore an off-white hat adorned with three red carnations and crystal earrings borrowed from Carmen that sparkled as they dangled from her ears. Her bouquet, also red carnations, was accented with white baby's breath.

When the wedding march stopped, the judge proceeded with the ceremony. Repeating after the judge, they pronounced their vows, which they had each written.

"I pledge myself, my love and devotion, to you, Nikki, to live each day as beautifully and fully as God intends for us." Eduardo turned to Fadi, who was bearing the rings, and placed the ring on Nikki's finger, saying: "Take this ring as a symbol of our love and a reminder of the blessings of finding each other again."

Nikki's vows were similar, adding "as we join our lives, we will live together in honor, love, and commitment" as she slipped his ring on.

The judge declared them husband and wife. Nikki inched closer for Eduardo to kiss her. The guests broke into applause again and they cheered in various ways and languages. A man Nikki did not recognize walked toward the trellis and faced them. Before she had time to determine if he should be there, he broke into "Ave María," an old favorite of Nikki's, especially when sung by such a beautiful tenor voice. Tears brought on by happiness filled her eyes. She mouthed a thank you to Eduardo for surprising her with this traditional wedding solo.

The hugs and congratulations took very little time after the ceremony.

Last in line to congratulate them, Fadi introduced his parents, Jamila and Fernando, to the newlyweds.

"Carmen turned the space into an elegant setting," Jamila said, complementing Nikki for letting her aunt manage the decorations. "I wish Paula had allowed her mother to do the flowers for their wedding."

Pleased to know her aunt's creativity had been appreciated, Nikki continued speaking with Jamila Massú as she studied the placement of a circular row of planters containing white calla lilies and pink tulips with a second, higher tier of planters of four-foot bamboo behind the white and pink flowers, turning the space into a garden. The backdrop of Gaudí's playful chimney designs added pizzazz. Carmen had indeed taken all the elements available to her and turned a large expanse of the roof into an elegant and intimate setting. The guest tables, trellis, and dance floor were enclosed within the perimeter, leaving an opening in the circle where Floyd had escorted Nikki past the stormtroopers to the waiting bridegroom.

Servers offered champagne to the guests and handed out the cocktail napkins Nikki had ordered. Floyd glanced at the one in his hand and smiled. Milena looked at hers. Below the selfie Nikki had taken a few days earlier of herself and Eduardo by the stormtroopers was a caption:

> *We first met on this rooftop as kids and we thank you for*
> *celebrating our wedding among the stormtroopers!*

Fadi, designated photographer for the evening, had posed Nikki and Eduardo for several dozen pictures. For the last formal picture, he positioned the newlyweds with Paula and Carmen. Milena waited until the photo shoot was complete before approaching Carmen.

"Your flower arrangements are so gorgeous. I love the amaryllis and rosebud centerpieces on the tables. I can hardly wait to see what you do for Paula's wedding."

"Mama is not doing them," Paula said. "I've asked a friend who works at a flower shop."

Seeing Carmen's expression, Nikki quickly stepped to the rescue. "As mother of the bride, my aunt is so busy that Paula thought it best to order her arrangements."

Eduardo saved Carmen from further embarrassment by escorting her to the wedding table. On his way, he turned to the musicians and signaled for them to start playing. Nikki asked Fadi, Paula, Milena, and Floyd to follow her so they could be seated.

Other guests took the hint and sat.

Enya's "Dreams are More Precious" started, and Floyd took Nikki's hand for the first dance. They pranced and pirouetted their way to Eduardo, where Floyd delivered her to the bridegroom.

"Thanks for saving Carmen," Nikki said as she slipped into Eduardo's arms. "I don't understand Paula's behavior."

"Don't let it upset you," Eduardo said. "This is our special day." He guided her around the dance floor like a professional.

Dinner was served and the newlyweds joined their guests. Fadi took a few minutes to snap spontaneous photos of the guests before returning to sit at the main table with the newlyweds.

Nikki looked up and heard Paula continuing to discuss her wedding plans with Milena. "Our food selection is Lebanese. I think it's the best food in the world. Have you tried it?"

"Delicious gastronomy," Milena said. "So are Spanish dishes."

"I agree both styles of cooking are good," Carmen said, trying to participate in the conversation.

"But food from the Middle East contains so many wonderful spices. I consider it superb. It's the reason I chose it for my reception."

"I look forward to it," Milena said.

"Well, I'm speaking of my Muslim wedding reception. Maybe you can stay and attend that one too. It's a week after my Christian ceremony."

Nikki sighed as she listened. She couldn't believe Paula's hurtful words. Besides being rude to Milena, why was she purposely insulting her mother? Paula had moved back in with Carmen, intending to remain there for the week before her own wedding. Had mother and daughter quarreled? Eduardo was engaged in conversation with Fadi. While it was man talk, Nikki was relieved when Fadi included Carmen in their discussion of sports teams.

Early the next morning, Floyd drove the newlyweds to Barcelona Sants, the city's main train and mass transit station in the Sants-Montjuïc district. He parked the car at the passenger drop off and they all stepped out. He popped the trunk and Eduardo removed their luggage.

"Being a man," Floyd said, clearing his throat, "I'm not much of a fan of weddings. But I have to say, I've never been to a nicer one than yours. Have a wonderful trip. We'll see you for Paula's wedding."

He embraced Nikki and then hugged Eduardo. Floyd felt his eyes get watery with emotion, as if Nikki were his own daughter. He stood by the car at the curb and watched Nikki turn and wave at him before she and Eduardo entered the station.

CHAPTER EIGHTEEN

TRAIN TO BURGOS, SPAIN

E duardo pulled the tickets from his jacket pocket as a conductor sporting a hat knocked on the frame of the open door of their first-class cabin. After the conductor left, an officious server wearing the same conductor-type hat, and dressed in a white jacket over a black shirt with a stand-up starched collar and black pants, came through to take drink and snack orders. When he returned with a cart, he delivered fresh grapes, Serrano ham, Manchego cheese, Spanish olives, crackers, and two slices of Spanish tortilla. He also poured coffee and left two small glasses of freshly squeezed grapefruit juice.

As the train sped down the tracks, the newlyweds picked up their glasses of juice and toasted as if they were drinking wine.

"Salud," Nikki said. She clinked her glass against Eduardo's. "Cheers."

Nikki sipped her juice and put the glass down and sliced the Manchego. First, she placed a bit of ham and a piece of cheese over each cracker, then topped each one with an olive. She sampled the tortilla. Not exactly finger food. She had to wipe her fingers on the napkin and discovered a fork wrapped inside. She continued to savor the tortilla without getting her hands soiled. When they finished snacking, Nikki took out her tablet to check their wedding photos. Before leaving the reception, Fadi had uploaded the pictures from his camera to her tablet.

Nikki browsed through the file, discovering three images she had not expected.

"Looks like Fadi included photos of Paula with his father," she said, passing the tablet to Eduardo.

"Nice Ferrari," he said as he peered at the screen. "If I had one, I would not paint it gray, though."

"Yours would be red hot," Nikki said.

"Red hot is right," he said. "Who is the other guy?"

"Paula's florist. He's the one I told you seemed creepy."

"Start over at the beginning," Eduardo said. "I want to see all the photos."

She scrolled slowly, stopping to contemplate the photos she or Eduardo liked best.

"We should enlarge that one," Eduardo said, pointing. He sipped the rest of his grapefruit juice as he admired the picture. "I want it framed for my desk. I really loved the way you looked in your flamenco wedding dress."

"I loved how romantic our wedding was," Nikki said. "I only wish Robbie could have been with us. You would have loved my son."

Eduardo touched Nikki's arm. "I know I would have loved him. It's so unfair to lose a child."

They returned to the photos, spending the next half hour selecting the ones they liked, discussing which ones to enlarge and frame once they returned to Miami. When they finished sorting and choosing, Nikki copied their favorites into a separate file. She closed the picture app, opened her Kindle, and selected a novel to read. She removed her jacket, reclined the seat, and settled in. Eduardo, next to her, also reclined his seat and fell asleep.

When Eduardo awakened, he noticed Nikki was snoozing and her tablet was on her lap. He picked it up, closed the cover, and placed it in the rack mounted on the wall in front of their seats.

Feeling thirsty, Eduardo opened the door, stepped into the hall, and closed the door behind him. He walked to the rear of their coach to get a glass of water from the bar located in the adjacent car which served as the dining room. As he walked down the narrow hall which curved into an open seating space immediately before the electronic doors connecting to the dining car, he decided mimosas would be appropriate since the noon hour was approaching. He would get one for Nikki too. And a bottle of water. Eduardo turned to head back to their cabin and retrieve his wallet.

A man with a full, black beard stood at the door to their cabin. The man reacted by avoiding Eduardo's inquisitive glare. He walked three cabins beyond and knocked on the door. When there was no answer, the man marched on ahead into the next coach.

Alarmed at first, Eduardo thought about asking what he was doing. He reconsidered when he realized the man wore the same white jacket and starched-collar uniform, complete with the hat, as their server.

Nikki stopped Eduardo under the Arco de Santa María, the archway forming the city gate that had protected Burgos since the fourteenth century. "Any superstitions I should know of before I look up?"

"No skulls and daggers here," Eduardo said.

They enjoyed the stroll over the Arlanzón River as they walked toward the museum Fadi had recommended. When they turned the corner, Nikki groaned at the huge crowd of tourists and school kids standing in line on the sidewalk, occupying the stairs, and congregating on the landing all the way to the museum doors.

Nikki stood in the queue while Eduardo went to the ticket office to purchase their entry. A school bus stopped at the curb. Three museum guards wearing orange vests over their uniforms rushed down the steps to direct traffic while a group of twelve-year-old students exited the bus and squeezed onto the already crowded sidewalk. The kids spread all around Nikki, a few of them invading her space. Two boys right next to her started shoving and fighting, hardly being disciplined by the three accompanying teachers. Once the bus left, Nikki noticed how fast traffic drove on the street, only a few feet away from the curb and the congested sidewalk.

Taiwo wore his cap low to shield his face. He carried a walking stick, a very sturdy one like he'd used as a kid in Nigeria. Following his target from the moment she and her companion had left their hotel, he saw his opportunity from where he stood at the intersection a block away. He moved in while the school bus activity shielded his movement and he could blend in like another tourist. Acting quickly to take advantage of a perfect setup, he positioned himself by moving into the back row of rowdy kids. He looked down to avoid catching anyone's attention. Standing close to his target, he waited until the bus had driven away and the guards had returned to their posts near the museum doors. Timing was essential. The traffic light a block away turned green and oncoming traffic sped toward them.

Then Taiwo did it. Pushing the two fighting boys, making them collapse against his target while simultaneously using the stick against her upper calves, he tripped her backward as the boys fell into her. A delivery truck swerved and applied its brakes, hitting a car in the next lane. Screeching tires, screaming kids, and yelling teachers created the chaos he needed to divert attention toward the accident and away from himself as he crossed the street behind two trucks whose drivers had scrambled into the scene trying to help.

Not running, Taiwo merely walked fast to the small park. His adrenaline pumping, he did not look back until he positioned himself on the far side of the park. He turned to face the museum and observe the damage he had caused. He was unhappy with the unfolding scene. He had failed.

His target was standing. A man was helping her, probably one of the teachers. Her companion was running toward her, and when he reached her, he eased her toward the museum. The woman had not fallen into oncoming traffic as Taiwo had intended. He wasn't sure what had gone wrong. Since his teenage years, he'd used this technique to throw someone into oncoming traffic. And it had worked. Several times. But this time, he had failed. Angry, he spat on the ground. The sound of sirens filled the air. He disappeared into the alley between two buildings.

Aching from the nasty fall she had taken a couple of hours earlier, Nikki ignored the pain as much as possible and leaned forward in a chair to get more comfortable. Eduardo reached out to touch her.

"Are you sure you want to stay?"

Glancing at him, she nodded. "My legs hurt the most. When I cleaned up in the bathroom, I noticed bruises already showing on each calf. The kids fell into me from my right side. The teacher caught me as I lost my balance and we both crashed to the sidewalk. So I don't understand why my shins and calves hurt." She leaned over and rubbed the sore areas of her lower legs through her pants.

"Probably from the fall. We can return to the hotel—"

"I'm fine. Very lucky, in fact. If that teacher hadn't intervened, I might have fallen under the delivery truck. Let's stay and enjoy the museum."

Nikki turned her attention toward the three large monitors suspended from crossbeams in the ceiling, showing monochromatic photos of Paleolithic art. After a couple of minutes, she sensed Eduardo had noticed her hypnotic attraction to the images projected on the screens.

"Not bad for art painted thirty thousand years ago," he said.

Nikki glanced sideways at him.

"Unbelievable," she said, turning her focus back to the screens.

She became aware of the ethereal silence surrounding them. They sat at the end of an open floor plan on the second level of the museum facing oversized screens. Although several exhibits covered the rest of the floor, the monitors in front of them provided the only movement in the huge chamber, minimal fluttering as a sepia-colored bison image dissolved into a herd of ochre-hued deer on one monitor while another screen showed a maroon-tinted elk morphing into flowing charcoal lines of mammoths. Rust red pixels forming human hands disintegrated and reappeared as gray and black images of horses on the third monitor.

Nikki detected movement along the wall to the right of where they sat. With a sidelong glance, she saw it was the elevator doors opening. She barely caught a glimpse of a man with a cap, dark glasses, and a beard peering in their direction. When she turned to get a better look at him, the elevator door had closed and he had disappeared.

The hall filled with chatter and giggling. A group of kids, the twelve-year-olds who had been roughhousing outside when she fell, climbed the stairs from the first floor. They marched past the monitors to an exhibit containing a boat-like structure where they could climb, tackle one another, and shout. Each shouted to be heard over the jabber of the others. The teachers who escorted them made no effort to keep the noise level down.

"These kids are about the same age as Robbie was when he died," she said. She glanced at the group. "It still hurts so much."

Nikki saw one of the boys who had fallen into her looking at her from his perch on the boat-like structure. He waved. She waved back, knowing it had all been an accident. Plus the teacher who had kept her from falling into the street had made both boys apologize to her.

"I could overcome my fear of caves for the pleasure of viewing this art in the environment where it was painted," Nikki said.

"You think you can handle the dark caves?"

"As long as these raucous kids don't follow us," she said, "and ruin the meditative atmosphere where the artists worked."

"That could be our real honeymoon. After Paula's wedding," Eduardo said. "I'll book the trip tomorrow."

CHAPTER NINETEEN

BURGOS, SPAIN

The loudspeaker at Burgos Castle announced closing time was in five minutes.

Nikki sighed. "What a shame we have to leave. So quiet after all the confusion at the museum."

"We can return tomorrow," Eduardo said. "After we plan our cave trip."

Nikki reached for Eduardo's hand as they passed through the gate leading to the park outside the castle walls. People were getting into taxis to take back into Burgos.

"Hurry, let's grab a cab before they are all taken," Eduardo said.

"On such a gorgeous night? With a full moon barely over the horizon," Nikki said. "It's so romantic. And isn't this our honeymoon? Let's walk back to town."

"Are you sure? I thought your legs were hurting?"

"A little exercise will help," Nikki said.

They walked in the moonlight, following a dirt trail leading from the hill of San Miguel toward the township of Burgos.

"Fadi is right. Spain has so much history, so many sites to see," she said. "I had no idea an old castle in absolute ruins would be so interesting to visit."

"Archaeological sites are always in ruins," Eduardo said.

Nikki stopped. She turned to admire the remnants of the palace fortress. Four large floodlight panels like those used at football fields illuminated the crumbling castle, giving it a look of both fantasy and horror, a sense of the mysterious where anything could happen.

"Look at the outline of the castle against the black background of the surrounding park. It's magnificent. And scary," she said, "especially under this full moon."

"Earlier you called it romantic," Eduardo said.

"Tell me," she said as she gazed up into the night sky, "have you ever seen such an exquisite rabbit in the moon? His ears curve along the top of the moon. His body then flows from his head through the trunk all the way to his feet."

"Ancient civilizations always saw a rabbit in the moon, Nikki, but most people now see a man. Hold it," Eduardo said, suddenly changing to a whisper. He put his hand on her shoulder. "Did you see something move behind those bushes?"

"Probably a wild animal or a dog from the town."

"Could have been your rabbit. Might have jumped from the moon to the bushes," he said.

They laughed. Eduardo led her to a rock outcropping that overlooked the town lights below. She leaned against a waist-high stone and raved about the sights they had seen in historic Burgos that afternoon.

"There are places where I could move to in a flash. This town is one of them," she said. She sounded joyful.

"So, Señora Duarte, you'd like to move here?" Eduardo asked. He relaxed against her body. "Maybe you can convince me to move here with you."

"It will be a pleasure to persuade you, Señor Duarte," she said, nibbling on his ear.

Eduardo pecked lightly at Nikki's neck, then ran his tongue along her collarbone up to her chin. He resumed nibbling the silky skin of her face, seeking her mouth. As he kissed her on the lips, she responded with passion. He stopped to pick Nikki up and eased her onto the flat surface of the boulder. She grabbed a handful of his hair as he positioned her on the smooth area of the rock. She laughed. With outstretched legs, she encircled his body and pulled him in close to her. Their bodies intertwined in an impassioned embrace as he slipped his hands under Nikki's loose-fitting blouse and caressed her breasts.

In daylight, a lone figure would have been seen following Nikki and Eduardo. But it was dark. Taiwo had hidden behind a tree about twenty paces away. He leaned on his walking stick as he watched them. Thinking he might be able to throw them from the outcropping or otherwise cause an "accidental" death before they realized what was happening, he moved from his hiding place closer to them. But he stepped on a dry branch. It snapped.

Eduardo pulled away when he heard the cracking sound. Startled, Nikki sat upright, pulled her blouse down, and straightened her hair.

A young couple walking the trail, probably pilgrims hiking the Camino de Santiago who were overnighting in a Burgos hostel, strolled up from the town on their way to the palace fortress.

"Is the Burgos Castle straight ahead?" the young man asked the older couple. "Have you seen it?"

"We loved it," Nikki said, "but we left when it closed."

"Ah, we thought it'd be incredible to visit by moonlight. We were expecting it would be open till ten tonight," the young woman said. "I guess we should return to town."

The foursome continued talking until Eduardo invited the pilgrims to join them for dinner in Burgos.

As the two couples set off to find a place to eat, Taiwo picked up the branch he'd stepped on. He waited a few seconds before throwing the broken twig against the ground with force. Twice he had failed. In the same day. But the opportunity would present itself again. *Soon*, he thought. He spat. Then he turned, carrying his walking stick, toward town and his hotel room.

CHAPTER TWENTY

BARCELONA—EIXAMPLE DISTRICT

Two Days Later—Tuesday Morning

Olani and Selena reached the southwest corner of the park opposite the basilica, crossed the street, and headed toward the Passion portico. Both women wore long, colorful skirts with the loose, long-sleeved blouses typically used by much older Roma women. They carried fans despite the weather not being warm enough to warrant them.

Olani listened as Selena reminded her of the code they had practiced with the fans. They would communicate this way since they would beg in different places near the basilica.

"I was thinking that your friend Rosa thinks an attack is planned around Sagrada Família," Olani said, "why can't we just call Rafa—"

"No way!" Selena answered.

"Can't we tell him what we know? Let him report the possible bombing to authorities here?" Olani turned away from Selena to hide her fear.

"Give Rafa that information and you'll get several people killed. Like Rosa. Her husband would kill her. Then he'd come after you. And me too."

"I want justice for Kenny. For Dayo. Why must it all be so convoluted?"

"It's the way the police work. They play by the rules, getting subpoenas. Taiwo would be long gone by the time the legal approvals came through. Rafa may be your cousin's husband, but he has to follow standard procedures."

"The laws are made to benefit the criminals," Olani said.

"What will you do if you find Taiwo?" Selena asked.

"Turn him over to the police."

"Remember, only if you can link him to an obvious attack," Selena said. "Do not get involved unless he commits a crime *and* you can turn him over with minimum attention to yourself. Anonymous is better."

"Understood. The police number is on my phone."

Olani changed the subject to a phone call she had received from her cousin Lola the night before while Selena had been practicing her dance. Lola reported on Rafael's progress toward finding Taiwo. Which was no progress at all, since the Moroccan police had not issued an international extradition request.

Selena wanted to know if Olani was prepared to take matters into her own hands if the authorities did not catch him.

"I lie awake at night wondering about that," Olani said.

"And?"

"I will kill him myself if I must. Qiṣāṣ—retaliation in kind. But the ideal would be to catch Taiwo with a bomb," Olani said. "I'd scream for the police to arrest him."

"It doesn't work like that. If you see him, do not let him see you. Do not forget he killed his brother in cold blood. He has no reason to spare you if you get in his way."

Olani considered Selena's words. Taiwo would not even recognize her if he saw her. Not now that she used makeup and resembled the American singer Beyoncé. Plus she was not wearing a hijab. *Selena has made me look so different.*

They approached the Passion portico. Selena gave Olani instructions to signal her by using the fan if she saw Taiwo. "Did you bring the cell phone I gave you? And the knife?" Selena asked.

"Yes, and sunglasses, too."

Selena pointed to a spot near the parishioner entrance. "That's a good place for you to appeal for donations. I'll be across the street in the park. Remember what I've taught you about approaching tourists. How to ask for money. If I get near, use the cards I gave you."

"Solicit people for fortune telling?"

"Yes, they love to hear about their future, especially women. Hold those cards the way we practiced. Talk to them about romance. Weddings. Children. That way you can keep them distracted. I'll come along and pick their pockets."

"Are you really going to do that?"

"Pick their pockets?" Selena asked. "Keep in mind, gadji, you need money to survive on. Consider it your pay for turning over a terrorist."

Olani figured she could beg for money, but she was still a gadji. She'd figured out the endearment meant something like "bumpkin." She was definitely that when it came to fortune telling. She was pleased every time she heard the clink of coins falling into the small steel pan she held, but pretending to tell women's fortunes? That was beyond her abilities.

Three hours later, Selena walked to the parishioner entrance to rejoin Olani.

"Hey, Morocco, it's time for lunch."

Olani felt a flush of acceptance into Selena's life. She could not contain her exuberance. "Would you believe people gave me money?" Her voice rose in excitement.

"Of course. You're a beggar. People will feel sorry for you and they *should* give you money. They have more than you do. How much did you earn?" Selena asked.

"Twenty-two euros. Just for standing there. And you?"

"One hundred and forty-five," Selena said. "And some change."

Olani's eyes grew bigger.

"But I gave the pizzo forty-five to cover both of us." Selena explained that the pizzo collected money for space to panhandle. She handed Olani a small silk bag containing coins and bills.

Weighing the pouch in her hand, Olani exclaimed, "So much!"

Although the café they entered had no outdoor seating, its large windows were open. After freshening up in the bathroom, they found chairs at a bistro type table. Olani confirmed to Selena that Taiwo had not arrived on the scene.

Olani picked up a menu. "Maybe he's gone back to Morocco or Nigeria."

"Not likely. We may have to wait several days before he shows up. Maybe he's doing other jobs in preparation for the big one."

"You think we'll find him?" Olani asked, sounding discouraged.

"Yes."

Olani asked her friend how she learned to beg if she was a flamenco dancer, not a beggar.

"As a child, I was taught to beg. My mother and I had to survive after my father was killed."

Olani gaped in amazement.

"Later my mother met the man who would end her life. A talented and charming musician. She married him. He strummed guitar and sang while we danced. Mother would get very close to the patrons, distracting them while I combed through pockets and purses."

"She had you do that?" Olani asked.

"My stepfather was a bad man. He had me pickpocketing tourists by age ten. He strangled my mother right in front of me. I ran away and never saw him again."

"That's terrible. I'm so sorry. How did you make it?"

"A Catholic charity picked me up off the street." Selena sighed. "The charity saved me. That's where I met Rosa. I graduated from high school. My Rom blood and my mother's training helped me excel at dancing, especially flamenco," Selena said. Her face took on a sultry expression and she arched her arms above her head in a typical flamenco posture.

Olani smiled. Despite the dowdy clothes her friend was wearing today, Selena looked the part of a seductive dancer.

Selena continued talking about her background. After high school, she had run away to Sevilla. By day, she had studied at a dance school. By night, she had begged for money, including picking a few pockets when she failed to get enough from begging. The school had never found out about her panhandling, and later hired her to teach. For the past ten years, she had worked at flamenco dinner clubs in Barcelona. And supplemented her income with private dance lessons she taught at her apartment in Barcelona.

"It's never occurred to me to dance for a living," Olani said.

"Your religion would never allow it," Selena said, "whereas, for the Roma, it's honest work."

CHAPTER TWENTY-ONE

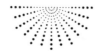

BARCELONA—EIXAMPLE DISTRICT

FRIDAY EVENING

Back in Barcelona after their five-day honeymoon, Nikki sat by an open window inside a small café on Carrer de Sardenya waiting for Carmen and Eduardo. The window was propped open by four tattered, dirty books: *Catalonia*, *Barcelona*, and two volumes of *Great Small Hotels*. Nikki admired the care someone had taken in placing the books exactly where they would hold the window open.

Carmen had recommended the boutique restaurant. She knew the owners, the food was good, and dinner was served much earlier than in most restaurants in Barcelona. Besides, it was close to Sagrada Família and within walking distance of her condominium. Nikki and Carmen had attended the rehearsal for Paula's wedding an hour earlier at the Sagrada Família parishioners' church. Eduardo had stayed in the hotel studying for his comprehensive medical licensing exam. He would be taking it when they returned to Miami so that he could practice medicine in the United States.

Since Paula did not want a rehearsal dinner, she had left with Fadi and his family as soon as the walk-through at the church was completed. Nikki, sensing the rejection that her aunt must have felt when Paula departed, invited Carmen to dinner so that she would not be alone after the rehearsal. Eduardo planned to walk from the hotel to meet them.

Despite Carmen's many friends in the city, Nikki surmised that she regularly dined alone, considering Paula's long hours at work and her apparent lack of interest in spending time with her mother. Nikki welcomed her aunt's company. Carmen reminded her of her late mother.

Glancing toward the door, Nikki saw Eduardo walk in. Her body straightened, and she felt the familiar tingle of excitement upon seeing him. He leaned in to give her a kiss before sitting down.

"Where is Tía Carmen?" he asked.

"In the bathroom—she'll be back soon."

"How did the dress rehearsal go?"

"Fine." Nikki responded with a shrug of her shoulders.

Carmen approached, and Eduardo stood to pull out a chair for Carmen to sit.

"Did you and Nikki enjoy your honeymoon?" Carmen asked upon seeing Eduardo for the first time since the Casa Milà rooftop wedding reception.

"Short but great!" Eduardo said. His voice sounded full of joy. "But we've already booked a longer one. A tour through caves in northern Spain and the Dordogne in southern France."

"You've overcome your fear of caves?" Carmen asked, looking at her niece.

"It's the Paleolithic art Nikki wants to see," Eduardo said, answering for her. "You should have seen how entranced she was at the museum in Burgos."

"I'll talk to Floyd about extending my vacation," Nikki said.

Carmen cleared her throat. She thanked Nikki for letting her arrange the flowers for their wedding. Obviously hurt by Paula's choosing a florist instead of her, Carmen seemed resigned to the fact. She reached across the table and squeezed Nikki's hand. "Thanks for being here. It means so much to me."

"And to us," Nikki said, squeezing back.

"I hope my daughter is happy about her marriage," Carmen said. "Tonight she told me she just wants to get it over with. It made me sad to hear that, like she's having second thoughts."

"Paula may not be interested in the fuss over being a bride," Eduardo said.

"That's true," Nikki added, "but last week before our own wedding, she invited me to Sagrada Família to take measurements and she seemed very happy."

"Measurements?" Carmen asked. Her brow furrowed in a perplexed expression.

"For placement of the flower vases around the altar and up the central aisle."

Shouting outside caught their attention. "A parade?" Nikki asked.

"Or soccer hooligans," Eduardo suggested.

Men wearing black T-shirts and holding red and yellow striped flags with a blue triangle and white star marched along the sidewalk toward the café. "Isn't the Catalan flag just yellow and red?" Nikki asked Carmen.

"Those are the Catalunya separatists," Carmen explained. "They carry the flag we call L'Estelada Blava, the Blue Star."

A shouting demonstrator knocked the books off the windowsill, and they crashed to the floor. Nikki jumped and the window slammed shut.

A server moved in with haste to pick up the fallen books and prop the window open again, apologizing for his rude countrymen.

Nikki watched her aunt pacing back and forth on the balcony. She had arrived early that morning at Carmen's place to help with any final details. But she could only witness her aunt's anxiety and wonder why Paula was taking so much time getting ready.

Paula had moved in with her mother the final week leading up to her wedding, vacating her apartment. She would move in with Fadi once the priest married them at the Sagrada Família ceremony.

"I've never understood my daughter," Carmen said. She stopped pacing and glanced at Nikki sitting at the table on the balcony. "At least not the way my husband did when he was alive. Paula and her father enjoyed a special bond. At times like this, I really miss Luis."

"Paula is so lucky to have you, Aunt Carmen," Nikki said. "After she has children of her own, she may appreciate you more."

"Luis could persuade Paula to be sensible. He understood how difficult it was for her to express herself. She responded to him. But not with me."

"Weddings are emotional times. She will get over it," Nikki said. "Give her time."

"On the contrary, Paula's been very rational this past week," Carmen said. "She's paid every utility bill. She's returned borrowed items to her friends. She's even paid off her car loan."

"Paula is probably a little nervous," Nikki said.

Nikki watched her aunt's exasperation. Carmen must have been wondering what Paula was thinking, not even getting dressed as the hour of the wedding fast approached.

The doorman called on the intercom and Carmen stepped into the living room to answer it. After giving her consent for Eduardo, Floyd, and his wife Milena to come up to her condo, she moved toward the door to greet them.

As her guests stepped out of the elevator, Carmen cheek-kissed them and ushered them into her living room. Turning to Milena, she said, "I'm so glad you and Floyd could stay for Paula's wedding. Assuming we actually have a wedding today."

"She's not backing out, is she?" Nikki asked, thinking about Paula's lack of enthusiasm for her nuptials.

"She's having trouble getting dressed," Carmen replied.

Nikki offered to see if she could help her cousin, heading down the hall to Paula's bedroom and knocking. When she received no answer, Nikki knocked again.

Still not getting a response, Nikki cracked open the door. The beaded white lace wedding dress lay pooled in a heap on the floor. Beyond it, Paula was also on the floor.

Closing the door behind her, Nikki realized that Paula was praying. In the Muslim way, kneeling on a prayer rug and bowing to the east. She wore only her underwear and wedding veil. Neither woman spoke until the prayer was finished.

"I did not know," Nikki said, stuttering.

"Of the family, only Fadi knows."

"If you have converted to Islam," Nikki asked, "why are you getting married in the Catholic church?"

"For mother. She would be devastated if I didn't. And in memory of my father. He would want me to marry in the Christian tradition."

"You should not do this if you don't want to."

"I want to," Paula said. "I'm just nervous."

"Okay," Nikki said as she continued to digest the news. She picked up the gown from the floor. "But you won't have a Christian ceremony if you don't hurry and get dressed."

CHAPTER TWENTY-TWO

BARCELONA—SAGRADA FAMÍLIA

Arriving three minutes before the wedding was scheduled to commence, the bride and her party, including Floyd and Milena, cleared the minimal security check at the entrance to the parish church courtyard. Most of the guests were already inside, with only three tourists milling around the small courtyard. Paula's uncle Carlos Azar, her late father's brother, waited in the courtyard next to Jamila Massú. Carlos was dressed in a midnight blue tuxedo accented by a cummerbund with a paisley design in red and midnight blue. He might have just popped out of the pages of Vogue. He looked like the perfect escort for a bride. Paula approached them, kissing Jamila and then turning to her uncle, kissing him on both sides of his face and latching her hand through his arm. Jamila turned to Eduardo, spoke briefly with him, and stepped closer to Paula and fussed with her veil.

Together Paula and her uncle led the family toward the carved stone arch of the crypt church.

"I hope security is not this lax throughout Sagrada Família," Floyd whispered to Nikki. "They must have cameras somewhere, but I can't see any."

Eduardo and Nikki searched the walls of the basilica for outdoor cameras but saw none. "Maybe inside those windows. Surely, they record videos of outdoor activity," Eduardo said. "Perhaps cameras are hidden among the figures and vegetation on the façades."

"Let's hope so," Nikki said.

"I did see closed-circuit television out on the streets," Floyd said.

The wedding party disappeared through the passageway with stairs leading into the crypt church. From the dimly lit arched stairwell, they proceeded to the landing, which ended across the hall from a large archway where the altar was visible. A barricade obstructed the floor under the archway to prevent parishioners from entering the sanctuary. The wedding party followed the bride and her uncle, who turned left into the hallway. They walked the circular hall to the apex at the rear of the church, the intended entrance for worshippers.

As they stopped in front of the main arch, a waiting priest approached them and pulled Carmen, Carlos, and Paula aside to coordinate last-minute details. Paula wiped tiny beads of perspiration from her forehead.

Milena glanced toward the altar. "The flowers are nice," she whispered to Nikki. "But not nearly as lovely as the ones for your wedding."

Nikki gazed down the aisle and saw the display of red roses and white lilies with palm fronds set in pots on metal stands lining the center aisle. A profusion of white and red flowers was arranged on the altar against the greenery of the palm leaves.

"Beautiful, yes, but not as splendid as my aunt could have done."

"I've never seen palms used for weddings before," Milena said.

"Most likely an Arabic tradition," Nikki said. "Like the roses."

An usher led them down the aisle. He seated Floyd and Milena first, in a row midway to the altar. Nikki and Eduardo were seated in the second pew, where Paula's other Spanish relatives congregated. Carmen and Mrs. Massú were seated on the front row. Fadi stood by the altar. He kept looking around. No sooner were the two mothers seated than the organ music started.

Nikki held her breath as her cousin proceeded slowly down the aisle. Paula had asked her father's brother to walk her to the altar. Nikki hardly knew her cousin, yet she felt emotional as she watched her walking to "The Arrival of the Queen of Sheba," a composition by Handel. She thought it an unusual selection the couple made for their Catholic ceremony. Experiencing mixed feelings, Nikki couldn't help but think how Carmen's sentiments might play out once she discovered her daughter had married at Sagrada Família as a conciliatory attempt to keep peace with her mother. *Would Carmen be understanding of her daughter's conversion to Islam?* Nikki wondered. *I think Carmen will accept it just fine if she knows it was Paula's true desire to convert. That she was not pressured into it.*

"Do you see Fadi's father?" Eduardo asked as he leaned toward Nikki and whispered in her ear.

The question made Nikki glance at the guests near them. Not seeing Mr. Massú, she turned to look back at the altar where Fadi waited for his bride. His mother had moved close behind him between the altar and the first pew. Mrs. Massú frowned and seemed to be searching for someone, most likely her husband, among the people gathered.

"Oh my god," Nikki said. "He's not here."

"They've started the service without him. Mrs. Massú told me her husband was running late. She asked me to make sure he found the entrance to the crypt," Eduardo said.

"They should have waited for him. Didn't Paula know?" Nikki rolled her eyes in exasperation.

"I'll go look for him," Eduardo said.

"No, let me go," Nikki whispered as she placed her hand on his arm and held him back. "After I find Mr. Massú, I'll ask one of the ushers to direct him to the altar. Then I'll visit the restroom. Too much coffee this morning."

Nikki left the pew before Eduardo could react. She hoped guests would be watching the bride and not notice her. She slipped into the hallway and toward the stairs with determined steps. How could a man be late for his own son's wedding? What could possibly be so important he couldn't arrive on time? Since she had only met Mr. Massú briefly at her own wedding reception, Nikki hoped she would recognize him. She put on her sunglasses upon emerging from the crypt into bright sunlight. Searching the immediate courtyard, she only saw a lone beggar, a girl about fifteen, leaning against a pillar buttressed against the main church.

Una gitana. Poor girl. Nikki opened her purse and walked a few steps out of her way to hand over five euros.

"Que Dios la bendiga," the teenager said in a soft voice as she glanced at Nikki. "May God bless you."

What a shame the girl must beg. Nikki hurried on toward the two apathetic security guards who had checked her handbag earlier.

She told the men she had to look for a lost guest and would return shortly. One of them nodded. On the street, Nikki looked up and down for Mr. Massú, to no avail. She crossed into the park and was immediately the object of hard-sell tactics from a tall, lanky man. She thanked him and rushed past, then doubled back toward the café where she, Carmen, and Eduardo had eaten dinner the night before. She scanned the parked cars along Carrer de Sardenya for a gray Ferrari, the one she had seen among her wedding photos. She proceeded the full block but did not see the sports car. Deciding to give Massú a few more minutes, she went into the café to use the restroom.

Inside the parish church, Eduardo grew increasingly uneasy as mass started and Nikki had not returned. From where he stood in the pews near the altar, he could see through the archway to the marble stairs leading to the parish courtyard on the street level. Anxious to see Nikki return soon with Mr. Massú in tow, he glanced toward the stairway every ten or fifteen seconds.

Blood drained from Eduardo's head and his stomach tightened when he saw a bearded man leaning against the wall at the midpoint of the stairs. He knew that face. Yes, that face had been on the train to Burgos. On the train, the man had worn a conductor's hat. Here he wore a baseball cap, but it was the same face.

Turning to avoid being recognized by the man on the stairs, Eduardo eased out of his pew, hoping to escape the bearded man's attention. He quickened his pace when he was out of the line of sight from the stairwell. Still out of view, he crossed to the far side of the circular hallway and followed it to the staircase.

At the bottom of the steps, Eduardo looked up and glowered at the bearded one standing more than halfway up the staircase. They stared at each other for a split second.

The man turned and started running up the final few steps toward the street level. Eduardo followed, taking two stairs at a time. Emerging from the basilica, he saw the suspicious character running through the exit to the street. Beyond the exit, the man stopped momentarily to check if he was still being followed. He took his cell phone out of a pocket and started running again, holding the phone in his hand. The security guards posted at the gate chatted as Eduardo sprinted past them. The bearded man had put more distance between them. Eduardo kept running, and the guy stopped to look back. Then he pointed his phone at Eduardo.

Nikki stood in front of the café scanning the street, not knowing where else to search for Mr. Massú. With no way to contact Fadi's father by phone, she turned back toward the church. She did not want to miss too much of the wedding ceremony.

An explosion came from the direction of the basilica. Nikki's heart skipped. She stared down the street in disbelief. People emerged from cars and buildings, responding to the blast. They spread like ants abandoning an anthill.

An eerie, surreal silence spread over the street. When she heard noise again, it was her own heartbeat. People on the sidewalk rushed for cover into buildings or crouched between cars. Paralyzed for a split second, Nikki's stomach plunged as the image of Eduardo as she'd last seen him flashed through her psyche. She raced toward the church. She thought of Carmen, Paula, and Fadi. Floyd and Milena, too. She had to get to them.

On the side street next to the park, Eduardo tackled the bearded man and brought him to the ground moments after the blast. As the man fell, his mobile phone tumbled out of his hand and bounced onto the asphalt out of reach. The man stretched, trying to grasp it, but it was too far out of range.

A car sped toward Eduardo. He jumped onto the sidewalk out of its way. The bearded man leaped up from the asphalt and scrambled. The oncoming car veered to avoid hitting him.

Eduardo, still running, grabbed hold of a tree in the park to help him stop. He lunged behind the tree for protection. As soon as the car had sped by, three police vehicles traveling in caravan style followed.

The bearded man ran in the opposite direction, away from the basilica, his phone left abandoned on the street.

At the intersection the car, which he now saw was a light blue Mazda 3, veered to the right, skidded, and smashed into a group of three policemen, striking two of them and knocking them to the ground like bowling pins. Police on the sidelines fired at the driver. Without stopping, the car swerved and picked up speed as it disappeared down Carrer de Sardenya.

Sirens sounded and lights flashed as two police vehicles parked near the basilica started their engines to chase the Mazda.

Leaving the security of the tree, Eduardo moved toward the street. He looked in both directions for the bearded man. There was no trace of him. Turning back to the basilica intending to report the man to the police, he noticed the officers had dispersed, taking positions around the basilica with their weapons drawn. People poured forth from the church, scattering into the street.

Eduardo stepped into the street to recover the abandoned phone before its owner could return. He picked it up using a handkerchief and held his breath. Surprised to find it intact, he turned it off. Consciously trying to avoid leaving his fingerprints, he wrapped it securely in the handkerchief and slipped it into his pocket. He took out his own phone and dialed Nikki.

"Where are you?" Eduardo was relieved to hear Nikki's voice, though she sounded anxious.

Sirens' piercing dissonance fell heavily on Eduardo's ears, almost making him dizzy. "By the park. Where are you?" Eduardo yelled into his phone so Nikki could hear him over the din.

"In the courtyard. With Floyd. It's a mess."

Firetrucks and ambulances crammed the streets, edging into whatever space they could find. Eduardo ran toward the parish courtyard, passing between two parked ambulances. The drivers and first aid personnel were opening the rear doors and removing stretchers and trauma kits.

By now, police were setting up barricades at the intersection closest to the parish entrance when another speeding car, a small yellow Honda Beat, smashed through one side of the barricade. The car jumped the curb onto the sidewalk and charged ahead on the park's concrete path, aiming for victims who had escaped the church. People dispersed at the sight of the oncoming car. Police shot at it. The flattening of the two rear tires slowed the Honda before it hit anyone. Then it halted.

A man jumped from the passenger side. He used the Honda for cover as he opened fire, with what sounded to Eduardo like a semiautomatic, on people running in every direction. In the chaos, people who had poured out of the basilica to find safety outside were running again, desperate to find shelter.

Eduardo joined emergency personnel who ducked behind an ambulance for cover from the shootout between police and the terrorists. He heard bullets zing overhead.

Eduardo's stomach tightened. Fear gripped him. His palms were sweaty. He felt paralyzed for a few seconds. Two rounds hit the ambulance. Eduardo crouched closer to the tire, clinging to it as if it were a shield. He held his breath as more bullets pounded the ambulance. He knew that if the rounds penetrated both walls of the van, he and the others could be wounded or even killed. The heavy vehicle might not protect them from the terrorists in the park or even from a ricocheting police bullet. He swallowed hard.

As soon as the gunfire subsided, Eduardo peered around the tire toward the park. On either side of the Honda, a cluster of police stood, probably over the lifeless bodies of the terrorists. People littered the ground. He could not tell if they were dead or injured or protecting themselves. Then a few moved, some crawling to safety behind a tree or sculpture, and in a manner of seconds, others stood and sprinted toward the side streets. One man ran with a child in his arms.

Eduardo raced to the courtyard entrance. The very security guards who had been so derelict in their duties earlier now prevented him from entering. Floyd appeared.

"This man is a medical doctor. We need him to evaluate the injured. He can triage who needs to be taken to the hospital immediately." Floyd spoke in English. Eduardo wondered if the guard would understand.

"No authority," one of the guards said.

"Call the officer in charge," Floyd shouted.

As both men waited with the guards, emergency personnel rushed past them carrying trauma kits and stretchers. Plainclothes security personnel placed orange traffic cones on the sidewalk and strung yellow crime scene tape around the gate and iron fence, cordoning off the patio and entrance to the parishioner church. Floyd yelled at the guard one more time to call the person responsible for security.

"He gave me this badge!" Floyd said, beating the laminated card clipped to his shirt. "Authority!" The guard muttered into a cell phone. Across the courtyard, Eduardo saw an officer with a cell phone wave at Floyd. The officer jogged over.

"Eduardo Duarte is related to the bride," Floyd said as he placed his hand on Eduardo's shoulder, "More importantly, he's a medical doctor. He can help us. Authorize him to come in."

The officer requested Eduardo's identification. He looked over the passport and medical ID and took photos of them with his mobile phone before returning them. Handing Eduardo a badge identical to the one he'd given Floyd, he permitted the Colombian doctor to enter.

"Extra hands are useful today," the officer said. "Thanks."

As soon as Eduardo was in the courtyard, he grabbed Floyd's arm to keep him from walking away.

"Without going into the full story now, I may have the cell phone for the guy who caused this."

"A cell phone?" Floyd asked.

"The detonator."

"The device that triggered the bomb?" Floyd asked, dumbfounded.

"To turn over to the police."

"Nope, we'll give it to Interpol." Floyd said. "You have it on you? Where did you find it?"

"I chased him, and he dropped it."

"You *chased* him? Chased who?" Floyd asked, shaking his head and sounding confused.

"I left the church service when I saw the guy," Eduardo said.

"You left the church? Where was the guy?"

"On the stairs. I saw him through the side archway. I hustled after him. All the way to the street. He stopped and turned to look back. As he stood there, he did something with his phone. I'm not certain, but I think he used it like a remote control."

Floyd shook his head. "How did you know he was a terrorist?

"I didn't. Not at the time. What scared me is he's after Nikki."

"Shit, man, how could anyone be after Nikki?" Floyd asked.

"He pointed his cell at Sagrada Família instants before the detonation. At first, I thought he wanted to check to see if I was still on his tail. But in retrospect, I figure he stopped to cause the explosion."

"I'm confused, Eduardo. Tell me why you think he's after Nikki."

"He was on the train. Wearing a uniform, so I dismissed him as an attendant." Eduardo unconsciously wiped his sweaty hands, one at a time, down the sleeves of his jacket.

"What did the guy look like?" Floyd asked.

"Light-skinned African. With a bushy beard. Could even be Middle Eastern. No, I'll take that back. He's definitely African, I'd say."

"And you're sure it's the same person? Beyond any doubt?" Floyd asked.

"I'm pretty sure."

Floyd informed Eduardo he would call his contact at Interpol, and advised against Eduardo walking around with a detonator in his pocket since there could be more bombs.

"I've turned it off."

"Shit, man," Floyd said. His voice went up an octave. "Don't touch any buttons on it. You could blow this place."

"It's off, Floyd. Why don't we turn the phone over to the head police officer?"

"If I personally give it to Interpol, I might retain a bit more control on the results of forensic findings," Floyd said. "If someone is after Nikki, we need to know who and why."

"I need to warn her about the bearded man," Eduardo said.

"Stay here until I call Interpol," Floyd said. "The place is crawling with police, so your fellow is probably long gone."

"In this confusion," Eduardo said, "he could be waiting. He's dangerous." He looked down the street and saw the police were evacuating nearby stores. They were probably running searches through apartment buildings, and he thought Nikki would be safe.

Eduardo took a deep breath. He looked at the people in the courtyard, some with obvious injuries, all of them looking frightened. Catalan police, wearing vests printed with the words Mossos d'Esquadra, were lining the uninjured against a stone wall of the basilica. Then he noticed Milena, Floyd's wife, sitting on one of the three metal benches permanently installed near the basilica's stone wall. Her arms were raised with her hands resting on her head. Another mosso d'esquadra was walking among the people in the patio area asking them to raise their arms up.

Floyd dialed Javier de la Mata, his Interpol contact, on his mobile phone. Eduardo stood close to Floyd, making sure no one would overhear the call.

"Look, Javier, I'm at Sagrada Família."

"My god, get away from there. It's under attack," his contact said over the phone in a voice loud enough even Eduardo standing two feet away could overhear.

"I know. We were attending a wedding and we're lucky to be alive. In fact, the reason I'm calling is that I need advice who to give a phone to."

Floyd listened and then spoke again. "The phone may belong to one of the terrorists. A light-skinned African with a heavy beard. You might want to get that intel to the appropriate channels."

After talking a bit longer on the phone with his Interpol contact,

Floyd hung up. He took a few steps away and approached one of the paramedics to ask for an empty plastic bag. Then he rejoined Eduardo and opened the bag.

"Drop the phone in here. Javier is going to pick it up. Then later, we have an appointment to talk with him. We'll meet at a coffee shop," Floyd said, handing the plastic bag to Eduardo. "I'll try to get a safehouse for you and Nikki."

"How long will it take him to get here?"

"He said about twenty to thirty minutes," Floyd said. "And put the phone in your pocket until he arrives. In the meantime, be vigilant about Nikki. I don't want to over-react until we know more. Ask Nikki to keep an eye on my wife. That should keep her here."

"I'll warn her though," Eduardo said as he placed the bag into the pocket of his pants.

Floyd winced. "Careful not to trigger that damned detonator."

"Relax, it's turned off. It should not be a danger," Eduardo said. "Though, I admit I'm not comfortable with it in my pocket."

"I'm going below to check on the situation inside the church," Floyd said. "You stay up here. I'll come back when Javier arrives."

———

Eduardo assessed the scene. Forty or so people stood in the courtyard like zombies. These people would not have been near the altar. A few of them may have been hurt in the panic as they rushed out of the church, into the hallway, and up the stairs to the open space outside. Most of the emergency personnel had gone inside the parish church, but one EMT knelt as he administered first aid to an elderly gentleman stretched out on the ground.

Eduardo spotted the one person he needed. Nikki knelt next to a metal bench examining an older woman. He went straight to her. As he gently touched her shoulder, Nikki stood.

She embraced him.

"I'd like to cry, but that won't help matters," she said as she clutched Eduardo.

"No harm in crying," Eduardo said.

Nikki gestured to the seated woman. "She said bombs went off at the altar. If that's true, I fear for Tía Carmen's life." Nikki's voice faltered, and she started crying. "And Paula and Fadi. They could all be injured or dead. I can't believe this. Why?"

"Don't give up hope. We'll pray they survive."

"This is unfathomable," Nikki said. "How can people be so evil?"

Eduardo saw a man collapse. He yelled for the EMT to assist him. Acting quickly, Eduardo found a palpable radial pulse.

"Apply high flow oxygen," Eduardo snapped.

"Get gloves out of my bag," the medic said.

Eduardo slipped the gloves on and opened the man's tuxedo jacket. Blood covered the cummerbund, which acted as a pressure dressing, slowing abdominal bleeding. He tore the man's shirt off, popping all the buttons. Next, he ordered the EMT to bandage the man's abdomen and apply pressure to the puncture to stop the bleeding as Eduardo performed a head-to-toe exam. When he found a wound on the front left thigh hemorrhaging bright red blood, he applied hard, direct pressure. When he could not get the bleeding to stop, he asked for scissors and a tourniquet. The EMT handed them to Eduardo. First cutting the pant leg to see the injury, he placed the tourniquet on the limb and watched the blood flow stop. Then the EMT handed him a cloth, which the doctor wrapped around the man's leg. Once the bleeding had subsided, Eduardo removed the tourniquet.

"Get him to the hospital," Eduardo ordered.

As more medics brought a gurney, Eduardo continued to apply pressure and talked to the man in a reassuring voice. The medics placed the man on the stretcher, secured him, and rolled him toward a waiting ambulance.

Nikki had watched Eduardo tend to the patient. Now he stood up and took her into his arms.

"Sorry about the blood," he said.

Nikki put her arms around his shoulders and squeezed her body tightly into his as if seeking protection.

"Please listen to me," Eduardo whispered in Nikki's ear. "I need to warn you about an African with a heavy beard. He may have set off this bomb. I ran after him. I've got his phone. It may have triggered the explosion."

"You ran after a terrorist? You have the phone he used to detonate the explosives?"

Nikki pulled away from Eduardo with tears filling her eyes.

Eduardo assured her there no reason to worry about the phone. He'd turned it off. Besides, Floyd had arranged to turn it over to the man from Interpol.

"Is the terrorist in custody?"

"He ran away. The police were busy with two shooters by the time I realized he was the one who may have set the bomb off. By then he'd disappeared."

"Have you reported him?"

"Floyd has called it in to Interpol. But I'm asking you to be alert for an African with a beard. He may have been on the train to Burgos with us."

Nikki collapsed into his arms.

Gently grabbing her chin, Eduardo turned her face toward his. He gazed directly into Nikki's eyes. "I'm asking you to be cautious, that's all. If you see a man with a heavy black beard, be prepared to scream or hide. He's dangerous."

Nikki sighed audibly. "Why is this happening?"

"I wish I knew," Eduardo said.

For a few seconds, Nikki remained in Eduardo's arms. Then she pulled away again. Scanning the courtyard, she said, "These people need you more than I do."

Eduardo knew it was true. "And Floyd asked me to see if you'd look after Milena," he said, directing his gaze to where she sat. "You could probably also help out the medics."

Eduardo analyzed the situation as if it were an emergency room. In triage mode, he put patients into groups based on the severity of their injuries or emotional state. The EMT who had helped him a few minutes earlier continued to work with him after securing the cervical brace on a woman. The young man relayed messages to ambulance leads about five more people the Colombian doctor had stated needed immediate transport to a hospital.

Floyd returned and asked Eduardo to take a break. "Javier is here. Let me introduce you so you can give him the African's cell phone."

Eduardo and Floyd walked past the guards, out to the street and located Javier standing near the street corner beyond the barricade.

After returning to the courtyard, Eduardo approached Nikki. She glanced at him as she opened a package of gauze to hand to the EMT tending to a middle-aged woman.

"Can you check on Carmen and Paula?" she asked, looking at her husband through teary eyes.

"Of course, Nikki, but you must stay in the courtyard. Floyd wants to make sure you are around in case Milena needs anything," Eduardo said. "I'll go downstairs and try to find Carmen."

"And Paula and Fadi," Nikki said.

Eduardo choked up, but he turned to the EMT to gain control of his emotions. "After cleaning this woman's wound, please take care of the one in the blue dress sitting on that bench. She has blood down the front of her dress. I'll be back."

The EMT nodded.

Two officers exited the arched stairwell passing Eduardo on his way in. He deduced they had performed a preliminary walk-through and search in the crypt church. Both men talked on their cell phones, possibly reporting early information or requesting backup.

Nikki saw a man in a black tuxedo running toward the stone-carved doorway. In his haste, the man bumped into a police officer. Nikki rushed toward him.

"Mr. Massú," Nikki shouted as she moved out of the way to let a stretcher get past, "Mr. Massú, my husband is down there checking on Fadi and your wife."

Massú turned to face Nikki.

"Is this a terrorist attack?" he asked. His face was contorted into an expression of horror. Without waiting for an answer, he rushed into the stairwell.

Floyd came up assisting a man with a blood-stained jacket. Nikki indicated she would take the injured gentleman to an EMT for triage.

"Where's Eduardo?" Floyd asked.

"Downstairs. I asked him to check on Carmen. You may not have noticed, but that was Fadi's father who just went down," Nikki said.

"I'll talk to him," Floyd said.

In the crypt church, the police had stopped Eduardo near the back row of pews. The odor of burned flesh overwhelmed him as he evaluated the scene. He turned as Massú arrived.

When the officer prevented Massú from advancing toward the altar, the man became agitated.

"It's my wife. My son. They are up there. They need me. Coño, hijo de puta, let me through." Massú tried to push past the officer. "I will kill the bastards who did this."

"It's dangerous to get closer. We *must* wait here," Eduardo said, holding Massú's arm. "Police are determining if more bombs are in there which could detonate."

"But those people taking photographs. They are desecrating the dead," Massú pulled away from Eduardo as he pointed to three people outfitted with masks and gloves taking video and still photographs of the scene. Eduardo figured they were plainclothes crime scene investigators. "If they are allowed in, you can't stop me."

"You must wait here," Eduardo said emphatically. "They are gathering evidence. Law enforcement must get it before it's contaminated by outsiders."

Eduardo was relieved that Massú had not noticed the body bags lined up on one side of the altar, where debris from the explosion had been cleared. *Surely the priest performing the ceremony was killed*, he thought.

The investigators continued to photograph the scene. Others, wearing Tyvek suits and gloves, were sifting through debris, collecting evidence, and placing it in plastic bags.

Two police officers walked past Eduardo. One of them held a shepherd-like dog on a short leash. Floyd came back into the church, right behind the canine unit. He walked up to Eduardo.

"Get back outside," Floyd commanded. "It's dangerous in here."

"I came to check on Carmen and Paula."

Floyd did not hear Eduardo. He turned to Fadi's father, who was still belligerent, and reintroduced himself.

The dog stopped and reacted at the first flower pot near the rear of the sanctuary. Within seconds, the second officer accompanying the canine unit ordered Eduardo, Floyd, and Massú to leave the crypt, explaining that the canine had discovered an undetonated bomb.

"I'm not leaving as long as those photographers and those men in space suits are here," Massú said in an agitated voice.

"If you don't leave, I will have to arrest you," the officer said.

"You miserable son of a bitch, I am not leaving," Massú said to the policeman, taking a threatening stance.

Eduardo and Floyd grabbed Massú and escorted him out.

Once outside, Eduardo watched Massú walk toward the edge of the patio near the fence and take out his cell. Seeing Massú about to tap something on the phone, Eduardo resisted the urge to tackle him and knock the phone away. Instead he only winced and held his breath. When nothing happened, Eduardo exhaled.

CHAPTER TWENTY-THREE

BARCELONA—SAGRADA FAMÍLIA

"Hóstia, ¡llegamos tarde!" Selena cried in her husky voice. She sounded as if she were in excruciating pain. "Fuck, we're late!"

Olani nearly collapsed. Her stomach felt a heavy tightness take control. The imposing basilica of Sagrada Família soared in front of her as she exited the underground metro station at Carrer de Provença, half a block from the church. People flowed in the street, like a river with turbulent water. As she scanned the crowd, she wondered if this was the imminent attack Rosa Gebarra suspected her husband to be orchestrating. If so, then Taiwo would have been a part of it.

Pedestrians ran, spilling like rats into the side streets and disappearing into a warren of alleyways. Dozens of police directed screaming tourists away from the basilica. Empty police cars barricaded Avinguda de Gaudí, a street which dead-ended, like the tip of an arrowhead, at the northeast corner of the famous church.

Olani's heartbeat matched the chaos around her. As she surveyed the area, she spotted a group of onlookers huddled against the walls of buildings outside the taped-off crime scene. She touched Selena's arm as she rushed to join the group. Selena followed. A mosso d'esquadra motioned for them to put their hands on their heads. Olani inquired what had happened.

"An attack in the underground church on the west side of the basilica," the officer said. "On this side we are merely evacuating the tourists from the main church." He warned her to stay away from the other side where bombs could still explode.

Four mossos d'esquadra monitored street activity as their colleagues continued to evacuate those people left behind in the pandemonium. An elderly woman hunched over her walker struggled on the handicapped ramp leading away from the Nativity portico to the street. One small girl in a pink and green dress stumbled and fell to the ground. Blood dripped down her face and onto the front of her dress. Seeing the blood, she screamed hysterically. Her father picked her up and carried her to the edge of the park where he set her down, took his handkerchief, wiped her face and held the cloth to her forehead to stop the bleeding.

Olani walked, with Selena following, toward the convergence of Avinguda de Gaudí with the streets of Provença and De la Marina. From that vantage point, Olani noticed the panicked crowd subsiding. The curious among the hundreds of tourists who earlier had flocked the landmark now stopped their exodus and returned to the edge of the park to catch a glimpse of the ongoing crisis. The bravest among them were standing at street corners, their faces reflecting hesitancy. Yet they were intrigued to observe, from the safety of distance, the consequences of the explosion and the ensuing panic. One couple who had been standing with their arms raised, hands resting on their heads, disregarded police instructions. The woman took out a cell phone. The couple turned their backs to the basilica and took several selfies. That started a trend. Others took their mobiles out and snapped photos and recorded videos of the scene.

Medics placed a gurney carrying an injured person into an ambulance. The driver climbed in and slowly pulled away from the curb of this pedestrian street in front of the Nativity entrance.

Both women stood on the east side of the basilica. Except for the lone ambulance which had left moments before, Olani could not see the injured or the medics working frantically on the west side by the parish entrance.

"Let's go to the west side," Olani said in a whisper. Then she ducked behind Selena as if to hide. "That's Taiwo. Over there. The one with the beard."

"Here? Can't be. Are you sure?"

"The one standing at the corner of the park. On this side of the police line," Olani said. Standing behind Selena, her body as tight as a shadow, her fingers ran up her face and pressed her cheekbones as if her head needed to be held in place. Her hands moved down her neck, her arms crisscrossed over her shoulders to her elbows. Her fingers pressed hard against her elbows.

Selena finally spotted a man with a full, black beard.

"Why is he hanging around?" Selena asked, sounding as if she were in a daze. "He must have set off a bomb. I tell you, that rumbling noise I heard underground came from an explosion. It sounded like the roar of an earthquake. It was loud enough to hear on the train."

The police asked groups of curious people returning to have a look to move back again for safety and to raise their arms again to make sure no one was carrying a weapon.

"I'm going to report him," Olani announced. She moved away before Selena could react.

Olani stepped in stride with three people walking toward a young mosso d'esquadra. She was careful not to let Taiwo spot her. Looking over her shoulder, she saw a couple of pedestrians had stopped to talk with Selena.

Olani approached the mosso.

"I want to report the person responsible for this monstrous act."

"You know who is behind this attack?" the policeman asked. He seemed surprised by her assertion.

"I do. He's in the crowd behind me."

First, the mosso observed Olani's obvious Gypsy attire. Next he waved to a higher-ranking officer to join them. He prepared to record her answers on his small police tablet. When the senior officer arrived, he eyed the witness suspiciously.

"Point out the terrorist," the young officer commanded.

"That bearded man," she said, turning, prepared to identify Taiwo.

Olani searched the area where the Nigerian had been standing, but he had disappeared. Her eyes scanned the area. Unable to locate him, she looked toward the side streets, first to one and then the other. Taiwo had vanished.

"He was right there," Olani said, stuttering, and pointing to the spot where she'd seen him. "He's Nigerian with a full, thick, black beard."

"Are you sure you know what you're talking about?" the second officer asked.

"I do," Olani said in a timid voice.

She remembered Selena's advice regarding the police. To avoid getting involved if she could not deliver Taiwo. The police should not learn too much about her. Olani shook her head, looked down, and mumbled a few words.

"What is your name?"

"Olaniyi."

"Full name?"

"Yes."

She saw the mosso write Olani Yee into his app. "Tell me about the suspect."

"African. Nigerian, I believe."

"Do you know this man?"

"Yes. No. Not really."

"Do you know this man or not?"

She stared blankly at the officer trying to avoid further questions. Olani muttered. "Sorry, I made a mistake. His beard made him look like a terrorist."

"Give us your address."

"I don't have one."

"Don't have an address?" the young mosso asked. He was exasperated. "Everyone lives somewhere."

"Yes, on the street. I came looking for work."

The young one shook his head and the older one opened his hands in a helpless gesture as she turned to walk away.

Shaking with anger as she rejoined Selena, Olani continued to scan the areas cordoned off with crime scene tape. "Did you see where that evil man disappeared to?" Olani asked. She was on the verge of tears.

"Sorry, some people stopped to talk. That distracted me. I missed where he went," Selena said. "Come now, not all is lost. We know he was here. We know he was involved."

"I've lost my chance at justice," Olani said as her shoulders slumped.

"Now, now, Morocco, it's not over yet." Selena put her arms around Olani and brought her in for a hug. "Your fighting spirit is only beginning."

Selena told her the police had killed snipers on both the east and west sides of the basilica. One sniper had been killed on this side, in the green space that was now cordoned off. He had wounded two tourists scrambling out from the Nativity portico before the police killed him. Crestfallen, Olani asked Selena what they should do next.

"See what's happening by the parishioner's church, where the bombs went off," Selena said.

Olani looked up. Her eyes were ablaze with fire. "He's here. I can feel his demonic soul. His evil spirit. I must find him. It would be justice for Kenny. For my daughter. I have to locate him before he leaves." Without hesitating, Olani walked off. She felt so angry she did not even care if Taiwo saw her. She had to catch him.

"Hey, Morocco, you need a bodyguard. Wait for me," Selena said as she quickened her stride to catch up with her friend.

———————

Commotion on the street caught Eduardo's attention—a television crew climbing out of a van. Floyd was crouched down, helping one of the medics.

"TV reporters," Eduardo said, tapping Floyd on the shoulder.

"Good time for us to leave," Floyd said as he stood up.

"I've done all I can here," Eduardo said. "Should we meet up with Interpol?"

Floyd dialed Javier to confirm they were ready to meet with him. Then he turned to Eduardo. "Let's catch a taxi a couple of streets over. Is Nikki going with us? We'll swing by the Majestic and drop Milena off," Floyd said.

"She won't leave until she knows what happened to Carmen and Paula," Eduardo said.

Nikki yelled for Eduardo. He turned and saw her follow a gurney. He rushed to her side.

"How is she?" Eduardo asked in as calm a voice as he could muster.

"Critical. We must transport her to the hospital immediately," the paramedic said.

"I'm going to the hospital with Carmen," Nikki said. "She's alive, but she's lost a lot of blood."

Eduardo took Nikki in a tight embrace and whispered that he and Floyd were catching up with the Interpol contact, Javier de la Mata.

"What about Milena?" Nikki asked. The paramedics were loading Carmen into an ambulance. "She can't stay here by herself."

"We're taking her to the Majestic."

"Good," she said.

"Don't forget, Nikki, watch for an African with a heavy beard. He set off the bomb and he might be after you as well."

"You don't think he'd blow a whole church because I was inside, do you?"

"We don't know. Floyd wants to put us in a safehouse until we learn more."

"No way. Carmen needs me." She kissed Eduardo a quick goodbye and jumped into the back of the ambulance. An EMT climbed in and closed the door behind them.

———

Nikki watched the paramedic work intently, inserting an intravenous needle into her aunt's arm. He connected it to a tube attached to a saline bag to rehydrate Carmen. He lifted her head to affix an oxygen mask. A second EMT had already secured the stretcher into the ambulance and ordered Nikki to strap herself into a seat. Opening a drawer from a built-in cupboard, he helped himself to supplies to clean a bleeding wound under Carmen's ribcage. He locked the drawer and strapped himself into a seat. Still holding a roll of gauze, he applied pressure to the ribcage.

The second medic followed suit by strapping himself into a seat near the front, behind the driver. The two men looked at each other and nodded. The one seated at the front tapped on the driver's window and the ambulance took off, sirens blaring.

Nikki reached out to hold her aunt's hand. With that, Carmen opened her eyes. She looked confused. Nikki spoke softly, reassuring her everything would be fine. Thankful her aunt did not attempt to speak, Nikki could only imagine that Paula and Fadi must be dead. Such news would devastate Carmen and might impact her survival.

As the ambulance sped down interminable streets toward the hospital, Nikki wiped tears from her face. The bombing had taken lives and limbs, and she could not stop thinking about the African man who might be following her. Her mind was too muddled to analyze the few facts she had. But her gut said that Cristóbal Arenas, the man who'd hired an assassin to kill her in Mexico, had found an African to finish the job.

But why kill others in the process? she wondered.

CHAPTER TWENTY-FOUR

BARCELONA—INTERPOL MEETING

Eduardo settled into a booth in a quiet corner of the coffee shop with Floyd and the Interpol agent. Eduardo watched the man log in to his tablet. Javier de la Mata had a mousy appearance and a twitch in his eyes. In fact, Eduardo thought Javier hardly looked like an Interpol agent.

Javier cleared his throat and began to speak in accented English. It hadn't taken long to establish that Javier's English was better than Floyd's Spanish and much better than the little Catalan Floyd or Eduardo could speak. After a few pleasantries, the Interpol agent asked Eduardo to describe the attack on Sagrada Família.

Eduardo organized his thoughts and provided all he knew.

A ding on Eduardo's phone, a message from Nikki, to tell him the ambulance had arrived at the Hospital de Barcelona. She would wait in the emergency room lobby for a doctor to inform her how they planned to treat Carmen.

While Eduardo responded to Nikki, Javier sipped his espresso and keyed a few words into his tablet, using his lightning-speed two-finger method. His jittery eyes seemed to relax as he reviewed his notes. When he commenced the interview again, the twitching returned.

"Read my notes," Javier said when the interrogation ended, and handed his tablet to Eduardo. "See if your declaration on African you chased and how you came by his phone is accurate. And how you saw him on train to Burgos. Tell me changes you think necessary."

Eduardo finished reading the description, nodded, and returned the tablet to its owner. "That's about it."

"Now let's talk about your trip to Burgos," Javier said. "How you think African knew where you were going? How he also got on same train?"

"I've wondered that myself," Eduardo said. "Floyd drove us to the station, so perhaps the African followed us in a taxi and purchased his ticket when he saw us stand in line waiting for the platform to Burgos to open. We already had our tickets."

"When platform opens, it usually deals with two trains. Each one will travel in opposite direction," Javier said.

"In fact," Eduardo said, "part of the reason I dismissed the incident on the train was based on the improbability someone could follow us so precisely. Plus the man wore a uniform, like food service personnel."

Floyd asked if the man could have purchased tickets for both directions and followed them to the one they had boarded.

"Unlikely," Javier said, shaking his head. "Too easy for mix ups. How you purchase tickets?"

When Eduardo explained Nikki had asked the concierge to get them, he saw a glint of insight register in Javier's eyes.

"The concierge must be a snitch," Floyd said.

"My thought exactly," Javier said. "You have concierge name?"

"No, but I will find out and let you know," Eduardo said. He took a sip of cappuccino.

Javier continued, asking if Eduardo and Nikki had encountered the African anywhere else in Burgos or in Barcelona.

Eduardo thought before explaining he had not seen him in Burgos, but perhaps they had at Parc Güell. A man with a nylon stocking over his head had burst out of a cubicle in the women's restroom, startling Nikki.

Javier sipped his espresso as he leaned forward awaiting further explanation.

"The man ran," Eduardo said. "And left the park. We followed him, but he jumped in a taxi."

"Did you get license plate?" Javier asked as two fingers tapped the keyboard on his tablet, recording the information.

"He was too far ahead of us," Eduardo said. "We never saw the license plate or the taxi number before it disappeared."

"When did this happen?" Floyd asked.

"Several days before the trip to Burgos," Eduardo responded.

"Could it be same man?" Javier asked.

"Until today, I never considered it. We did not see his face. In fact, I only saw his back. It was Nikki who saw him up close and described a stocking over his head."

"Did she mention beard under stocking?" Javier asked. "I know police began to search for culprit on closed-circuit TV. I make sure they also look at Parc Güell circuits."

"I don't know," Eduardo said. "We can ask her if she noticed one."

A tone buzzed on Eduardo's phone. "From Nikki," he said. He shook his head and slammed his fist into the top of the table. "Her cousin Paula is confirmed dead. So is Fadi Massú. Carmen is in surgery right now."

As Eduardo typed a response to Nikki, Floyd explained the family relationships and mentioned the late bridegroom's name. He turned to Eduardo and inquired if they had encountered any other suspicious incidents since they had arrived in Spain.

"Looking back, yes," Eduardo said. "I would not have connected any of this before today. A man wearing a skullcap may have followed us on Passeig de Gràcia the day we arrived. Again, it was Nikki who saw him. She thought he may have taken photos of us as we sat on a bench."

Floyd turned to face Javier. "Add skullcap on Passeig de Gràcia to your CCTV search. I don't like any of this. Less than a month ago in Mexico, Nikki was working on a kidnapping case. An attempt was made on her life. She narrowly escaped. Cristóbal Arenas, a Colombian national, hired someone to run her down with a car."

"You suspect connection between Arenas and this threat?" Javier asked. "You think Arenas behind Sagrada Família bombing?"

"Thinking of all the angles is all," Floyd said. "Arenas was related to a job Nikki and I both worked in Colombia. He is presumed to live in Mexico, where he placed a contract on her during the kidnapping case."

"Arenas is reason you originally asked me to meet you in Barcelona. At least the official request you established. Correct?" Javier asked.

"That's right. He's the reason I got Nikki and Eduardo out of Mexico and sent them here. For their own protection," Floyd said. "But when I researched the Interpol database for Arenas, I saw he's a much bigger operator than I originally estimated. He's a big-time smuggler of firearms in Europe. I thought you might share intel with me."

Javier looked pensive and his eyes twitched like crazy. "You think Arenas tied to bombing at Sagrada Família?"

"Don't know about that," Eduardo said. "The coincidence would be too great. As a Christian basilica, it's a target for terrorism. Let's consider connections to the wedding. Was someone trying to bomb the wedding party? After all, the bride was marrying a Muslim. If Nikki is the target, why blow up the whole basilica?"

"What about the Massú connection?" Floyd asked.

Javier told them what he knew about the Massú family, who were well-known in Catalonia, especially Mr. Massú. He advocated for tolerance and understanding between Muslims and Christians and provided financial support to schools in the Middle East promoting education for girls.

"In supporting those schools, he may have powerful enemies who feel he is betraying jihad," Floyd said. "We cannot overlook that angle."

"Massú was late for the wedding. Nikki was outside looking for him," Eduardo said. "The reason she wasn't hurt."

"If Nikki was outside, why bearded man inside the church?" Javier asked.

"She had gone to look for Massú, but she also needed a bathroom," Eduardo said. "Nikki was probably in a restroom when he went searching for her inside the church."

"What about a safehouse for my personnel?" Floyd asked.

"Why don't they return to Miami?" Javier asked in return. "Wouldn't they be safer there?"

"I'm not putting them on a plane. Whoever planted the bombs at Sagrada Família could easily bring a plane down," Floyd said.

"Wait, Floyd," Eduardo said, changing the subject. "Going back to the bombing. After the first responders, a canine unit came into the church. Remember? The dog found undetonated explosives in the flower arrangements. At least in one flower pot. A Muslim florist took care of the decorations. That should be investigated. They could have radicalized employees."

"Many florists in Barcelona. More than one could have Muslim employees. Do you know which shop?" Javier asked.

"I'd recommend elevating this bombing to an international incident," Floyd said.

"Already done. Government considers terrorist attacks international incidents. Sagrada Família is very beloved Catalan monument with international prestige," Javier said, his accent evident as he stressed syllables in a very different way.

"What comes next?" Floyd asked.

Javier informed them the police chief had sent the African's phone to a special forensic lab to verify it had been the detonator. Rapid DNA profiling could identify the perpetrator through touch DNA. Tests for fingerprints could also help.

"That's my handkerchief it's wrapped in," Eduardo said, alarmed. "If you're doing touch DNA testing, you're likely to find mine. Will that mess up the test?"

"Not unless you blew your nose on it," Floyd said. "Plus, they'll take your DNA sample and subtract it out. Wait and see what the tests show."

"On florist, you know name of shop?" Javier asked for a second time.

Eduardo texted Nikki to get the name of the florist, the one Nikki had described as quiet and creepy.

Javier typed on his tablet and Floyd, impatient and restless, went to order another round for everyone. He also asked for a large bottle of water and three glasses along with biscotti to munch as they waited.

"Nikki's texted back," Eduardo said once Floyd returned to the table. "The guy's name is Hassan. No last name. Not aware of the shop's name. Carmen is still in surgery."

"I want to return to the possible involvement of Cristóbal Arenas in this plot," Floyd said. "Interpol should work with the national police to determine his connection to the basilica bombing. Could he be the mastermind? Or was he simply the supplier of explosives and automatic weapons?"

"I could see him as mastermind. Maybe," Javier said. "Bad as attack was, first police report showed minor explosives used."

"It could be ideological," Floyd said. "So he'd have no need to make a ton of money from explosives."

"Unless Nikki was his target and he was trying to make it appear as if she were an innocent bystander," Eduardo said. "Besides, not all the explosives detonated."

"I will escalate idea Arenas is involved," Javier said. "Means police might interview Nikki. She could spend months in Spain."

"If she's needed, that's fine," Floyd said.

"But let me warn you," Javier said, "Spanish authorities see incident as terrorist attack on important Barcelona monument, not attack on Nikki, a foreigner. Interpol role only coordinator for information on international terror incident, not decision-maker."

CHAPTER TWENTY-FIVE

BARCELONA—SMALL MOSQUE

Taiwo, feeling dejected, walked the narrow side street leading to the mosque where he was staying. So much planning and preparation, yet not nearly the damage they had planned. Only the first detonation went off. The idea to detonate multiple explosions to create more confusion and chaos while causing more structural damage had seemed like a good one. More infidels would have died. More infidels would have been injured. Taiwo stopped to remove his shoes. He picked them up as he opened the door to enter the hall maintained for worship. The cleric stepped into the prayer room through a doorway from his adjoining private living quarters.

"As-salamu alaikum," the imam said, his right hand over his heart.

"Wa alaikumu as-salaam," Taiwo responded, also placing his hand over his heart.

"Have you heard the news, brother?" the cleric asked. His lips parted into a half smile as he approached Taiwo to cheek-kiss him on both sides.

"What news?" Taiwo asked, unable to cover the disappointment in his voice.

"An attack on a Christian target, Sagrada Família. Come into my quarters and listen to the television."

Threadbare Persian carpets covered the floor of the musty, dark room that served as the cleric's living room. The pungent aroma of chaat masala combined with fennel, cumin, chiles, and oregano infused the space. Taiwo's salivary glands reacted and he swallowed hard. The imam's wife could be seen through a doorway to the kitchen.

The cleric led the way to a dark bedroom, its two windows hidden by heavy velvet curtains. A small television placed on a long, low table offered the only source of light. He turned the sound up. Despite the dim room, the television's flickering illuminated a jubilant smile on the cleric's face.

A woman's somber voice updated listeners on the events still unfolding at Sagrada Família as the camera panned the landmark. Patrol cars, ambulances, and fire trucks lined the pedestrian street. Then it broke away to a makeshift podium set up on the street, near the small gate to the parishioners' patio.

Flanked by the mayor on one side of the podium and law enforcement personnel on the other, the chief of the mossos d'esquadra stood erect in his impeccable uniform. As he spoke into the microphone with a measured monotone voice, he appeared as stiff as the medals adorning his jacket.

"Barcelona has suffered a terrorist attack at Sagrada Família. Fifteen people are confirmed dead, including a police officer run over by an automobile and three suspects killed by gunfire. In addition, fifty-three injured have been taken to area hospitals."

The chief's statement ended with a plea for citizens to come forward with information, no matter how trivial, and videos taken at the scene of the crime that might show suspicious activity or potential suspects. He also added the description of a person of interest to the police—a man of African ancestry, with a full black beard, reported to have been seen at the site. The police want to interrogate him.

The mayor stepped to the microphone. She urged citizens to remain calm yet vigilant.

"We have evacuated people in the surrounding shops and restaurants. Report any suspicious activity to the police. Especially if you see a man fitting the description of the person of interest. The citizens of our historic city stand united in the face of this attack. We will not be intimidated or defeated," she said. Then she moved away from the podium, returning the microphone to the police chief.

The cleric, looking triumphant, slapped Taiwo on the back. He turned the sound down on the television and they both returned to the hall.

"With that beard, you could be the person of interest," the cleric said, laughing, as they reentered the prayer room.

Taiwo nodded and excused himself, saying he needed to clean up before his prayers.

In the cramped room with the single bed that served as his sleeping quarters, the Nigerian got on his knees and dragged his duffle bag from under the bed. He withdrew a pair of scissors and a disposable razor and headed for the bathroom down the hall.

After turning the light switch on, Taiwo placed the scissors and razor on a stained and dirty porcelain sink. He cut a flimsy paper towel from the roll set on the basin and lined the sink with it before scissoring his beard as close to his skin as possible. Once he'd finished, he gathered the paper towel around the beard trimmings. He threw the crumpled wad into an already overflowing wastebasket. Soaping up his face, he shaved the remaining whiskers. Reviewing the day's events in his mind, he felt his rage surge again.

Taiwo nicked his cheek. Indignant, he threw the razor into the basin with force. Blood trickled down his chin. He tore a piece of paper towel and used it to apply pressure to the gash. When it stopped bleeding, he finished shaving. He ran the tap water over his razor to rid it of the beard residue and to flush down any remaining whiskers in the basin.

Taiwo looked into the tarnished mirror hanging over the sink. His anger rose again as he thought about that man who had chased him at the church, forcing him to drop his phone. Without it, he'd been unable to detonate the remaining explosives. But when the police responded, it became a matter of choosing his freedom or his phone. He had elected to deal later with the man and woman his client wanted killed. Did his client know they would be in the church when the attack took place? He thought about the man with the falcon that he had seen twice on Ibiza and wondered if that was the man who had hired him. If so, had the falconer set out to make it easier to take care of both jobs at the same time? The client, whether he was the falconer or not, would soon know that Taiwo had failed to execute either job correctly. That angered him.

Taiwo spat into the basin.

At least the imam seemed happy with the bombing. He looked again into the mirror.

He smiled.

"Without a beard, I cannot be a person of interest," he said aloud.

CHAPTER TWENTY-SIX

HOSPITAL DE BARCELONA

The antiseptic aroma of the hospital barely disguised the less appealing body odors of sick people: vomit, feces, urine, infection. Nikki grew accustomed to the peculiar corrosive scent of the intensive care unit where Carmen was recovering. Nikki held her aunt's hand. Carmen spoke a few sentences, but did not ask the obvious question. When the nurse informed her that visitation time had concluded, Nikki returned to the gray and white waiting room, where Eduardo and Floyd sat in brown imitation leather chairs. Windows provided a view of rooftops. A large television on the opposite wall offered the only color. Tuned to a music channel running a symphonic program, the low volume had no effect on the melancholic mood.

Eduardo and Floyd stood as Nikki approached, and Floyd embraced her. "How is Carmen doing?" Floyd asked.

"Better than expected," Nikki responded. "Yet she has not inquired about Paula. I think she knows her daughter is gone but is afraid to have it confirmed."

"I know this is a terrible time to talk about the implications," Floyd said. "But we need to consider them. I've asked Javier to join us."

Nikki knew Floyd wanted to move the investigation forward and intended to use Javier's influence with the police to probe those suspects who might intend to harm her.

"Understood," Nikki said. "I'm ready anytime."

The three of them walked down the corridor and entered a small consultation room.

Javier emerged from behind a metal desk to greet Nikki. He expressed his condolences and indicated for everyone to take a chair. He returned to the opposite side of the desk, facing Nikki, and opened his tablet. "First, I ask Nikki questions," Javier said in his heavily accented English. His facial tics and small physique contributed to the impression he was not assertive. "Then we make strategy."

Javier placed the photo of a man on the desk. "Recognize him?"

"He's a concierge at the hotel," Nikki said.

"Concierge who made train arrangements to Burgos?" Javier asked.

Nikki nodded as she tried to identify Javier's accent. It was definitely not Spanish.

"Is name El Saraway familiar to you?"

"El Saraway?" Nikki repeated. She shook her head.

"Eduardo mentioned man wearing takiyah, had beard, and maybe took pictures day you arrived," Javier said.

"Takiyah?" Nikki asked.

"Also called a kufi," Javier answered. "A round cap for the head."

"Ah, a skullcap. A man wearing one did follow us, yes. But as far as his name, I don't have a clue," Nikki said.

"Any chance he could have been man who followed you on train to Burgos?" Javier asked in his heavy accent.

Nikki started. "I never saw—"

Eduardo interrupted. "The man on the train was African and had a black beard, but he was slender. Muscular but slender. The man with the skullcap is Middle Eastern and heavyset."

"Did Nikki ever see African with beard?" Javier asked, his eyelids twitching and brows rising and falling. He glanced at Eduardo.

"I don't think so," Eduardo said.

"Not on the train," Nikki explained. "And I never saw him at Sagrada Família either. I left the church to find Mr. Massú, so I never saw the African. Unless he was the one at Parc Güell. His face was covered with a nylon stocking. That guy could have been African, though I can't be sure. It all happened so fast."

Javier explained that although the police suspected the African in the

Sagrada Família explosion, the detectives had no reason to tie the Middle Easterner to the terrorist attack. At least, not yet.

An image suddenly flashed in Nikki's mind. It flashed through as quickly as the actual incident had happened. At the Paleolithic cave exhibit, she had seen an African with a beard peering at them from the elevator. "Wait," Nikki said. "In Burgos, I did see a guy in the elevator in the museum, but he never got off. He wore a cap and had a beard. I think he had a beard."

"Why didn't you tell me?" Eduardo asked.

"He was just a guy at a museum. I didn't think anything of it, but now I wonder if that's the bomber and he was stalking us. We must find out what's going on," Nikki said. "Or I will never be safe."

"Could the African and El Saraway be separate players?" Floyd asked. "Maybe we should only worry about the African."

"Unlikely. I know from talking to concierge, El Saraway asked questions from concierge to get information on you both," Javier said. "He knew Nikki and Eduardo names."

"You can do an actual investigation?" Nikki asked. "Even though you are Interpol?"

"Before Interpol, I was in police force. Have friends there. If I determine connection between El Saraway and African, I hand information to agent with GEO, National Police Corps. I have good friendship with him," Javier said.

"Can't we speak in Spanish?" Nikki asked.

"Floyd's Spanish not very good," Javier said. "My English better."

Nikki looked at Eduardo and rolled her eyes.

"You don't think the concierge will inform El Saraway that you're making inquiries about their connection?" Eduardo asked.

"Perhaps, but he thinks I'm police officer. He know he go to jail for obstruction," Javier said. "I ask police to check out El Saraway suite. They say no."

"Why?" Nikki asked.

"No reason for judge to issue warrant."

Nikki considered an idea before presenting it to the group. She knew El Saraway was staying at the Majestic. If she and Eduardo could break into his suite, they might find evidence linking him to the African. Or to Arenas. She had to find out who was after her. Living in mortal danger when she wasn't even on assignment was no way to live.

Nikki sighed and glanced at Eduardo. "You can say no if my idea is too farfetched."

"Go on," Floyd said.

"El Saraway is at our hotel," she said. "Maybe we can enter his room and find something."

Eduardo looked confused. "Why us? Why not agents from the Spanish secret police? Or regular detectives from the national police force?"

"Nikki make good point," Javier said. "Our detectives need search warrants. No evidence tying El Saraway to wrongdoing. No wrongdoing, no judge issue warrant. No evidence of El Saraway anywhere. Like guy does not exist."

"I see a pattern," Nikki said. "You already know El Saraway has asked the concierge about us. If the concierge has given out information about our train tickets to the African, then El Saraway and the African must know each other."

"I need surveillance cameras from hotel. If African visit hotel, I ask Eduardo to identify," Javier said.

Nikki knew the African would not appear on the hotel videos. The subjects would have met elsewhere. Unless they were stupid.

"We know El Saraway pay cash for invoices at hotel. He never use credit cards. Even deposit on suite, he give cash. Worse yet, hotel has no address for him. Hotel not know country of origin."

"El Saraway is an Egyptian name," Floyd said.

"Doesn't the hotel require a passport for check in?" Nikki asked.

"Yes, yes. Supposed to," Javier said, his eyebrows rising and plunging like a gymnast on a pommel horse. "But if El Saraway pay cash, and give money to right people, he get a room. No questions asked."

Eduardo was still thinking about Nikki's suggestion. "Getting back to Nikki's idea. If caught, we could end up in jail."

"True," Floyd said. "But if you find information on El Saraway, we might know more about the African. Or even Arenas."

"Basically, you want us to find out who the hell this man is," Eduardo said.

"Yes, yes," Javier said, his eyebrows jumping with excitement. "I like idea. But Interpol cannot get involved. I help you at hotel. I protect you in danger. I call police."

"We need this man's schedule," Nikki said. Her mind raced through several scenarios. Was he a terrorist? If so, what was his interest in her?

Where did he get his money? Why was there no information on him? Why did the hotel admit a guest who did not provide basic identification?

"Does he have security detail?" Eduardo asked.

"None detected," Javier said. "First need to follow him to find out El Saraway's schedule. So you get in his suite, no problem."

"You're asking us to follow him?" Eduardo asked. "No thank you." He looked around the room. Then he made a gesture for Nikki to join him in the hall. "We need to talk this over. We'll be back shortly."

Eduardo and Nikki left the room.

Javier's brows moved up in surprise. He glanced at Floyd. "Did I say something wrong?"

CHAPTER TWENTY-SEVEN

BARCELONA—SANT ANDREU DISTRICT

SUNDAY MIDAFTERNOON

Rafael knocked softly at the door to Selena's apartment, not wanting to alert the neighbors. He hardly recognized the woman who opened the door for him.

"Olani! You look so different," Rafael said. "Your hair. Your face. You look just like Lola."

Olani touched her smooth hair. "Selena calls it a makeover." She moved toward Rafael and gave him the usual cheek kisses.

Rafael followed Olani into the small kitchen and leaned against the sink. He placed an envelope on the countertop. Olani moved a few feet away and glanced out a window. She swallowed, her eyes brimming with tears.

"I did not come here to make you cry," Rafael said.

Selena, who had been rehearsing on her flamenco guitar in the next room, joined them. She carried the small acoustic instrument with her as she gave Rafael a peck on each cheek and asked about Lola and the twins. Rafael took the guitar from her and strummed a few chords.

"Lovely bright sound," Rafael said.

"So it can be heard over the sound of the dancers' shoes."

"Coffee?" Selena asked. Not waiting for an answer, she moved toward a cabinet and pulled the ingredients to prepare espresso.

"I came as soon as I could," Rafael said as he gazed straight into Olani's eyes, now dry. She'd regained control of her emotions. He placed the guitar on the kitchen table. "If you call me again, remember not to give details over the phone. You don't know who might be listening. Understood?"

Olani cast her eyes down. "I'm sorry."

"It's for your own protection." His tone softened. "Tell me about seeing Taiwo at the basilica."

"Selena and I arrived right after the explosion. We walked up the stairs from the metro station. That's when we saw the chaos. Police everywhere. Hundreds of people. They were running. Evacuating from Sagrada Família."

"Where was Taiwo?" he asked.

"Standing by himself. Near the edge of the park. Yellow tape cordoned off that part of the grounds. I went up to a policeman to report him. I want qiṣāṣ, my right to revenge," she said.

"How far away?" he asked.

"Fifteen, maybe seventeen meters. When I turned to point him out, he was gone."

"Any chance he saw you?" Rafael asked.

Olani shook her head, remembering that she'd turned her back to Taiwo when she spoke to the policeman.

"I hate to tell you, Olani," Rafael said, "but he probably saw you."

"He'd never recognize this beautiful woman," Selena said, interjecting to defend her friend. "Just look! A little makeup, no hijab, her hair straightened out, she looks like Beyoncé. No way would he know her."

Olani touched her hair again and looked at Selena.

"Let's hope not," Rafael said. "The police have videos coming in from people who were at Sagrada Família. They are sorting through them to identify possible suspects. Taiwo might be in the crowd."

"Rafa, why would he be there?" Olani asked. "Wouldn't he be afraid of getting caught?"

"It's not unusual for a criminal to return to the scene of his crime," Rafael said.

"Return to the crime scene?" Olani asked. "You scare me, Rafa. What's the chance he will return to Beni Ensar? That's his crime scene too."

"We don't know with certainty Taiwo's involvement in the basilica incident," he said, "but that's a good question."

"I must return home," Olani said, as tears filled her eyes again. "My little girl—"

"In the case of Sagrada Família, he probably wanted to evaluate the extent of the damage he'd inflicted, and he'd feel protected by the crowd and the chaos. But when it comes to you, you must not go back."

"Bring your daughter," Selena said. "Come here to live."

"Selena is right," Rafael said. "You don't want to go back and have him arrive. You'd have no one to help you. Ask your mother to bring the baby to L'Hospitalet. You know Lola wants to keep Dayo with us until you figure out your future."

"I don't want to be a burden to you and Lola."

"That's what family is for," Rafael said, looking at Olani. "We'd love for you to consider moving to L'Hospitalet."

Olani stared at Rafael. "Let me think about it."

"What's to think? It's an excellent choice," Selena said. She handed a demitasse filled with espresso to Rafael. She passed another to Olani. "Yes, Morocco, you must move to L'Hospitalet."

Rafael savored the espresso. He put the cup down next to the envelope he had placed on the countertop. Picking up the envelope, he looked at Selena and then at Olani. He opened it, removed three photographs, and arranged them on the counter.

"Do either of you recognize these men?"

"This one," Selena said, pointing to a young man.

"How do you know him?" he asked.

"Met him. Hassan. He's the husband of one of my friends," Selena said. "Why do you need to know?"

"Does Hassan have a surname?"

"Farooqi."

"Do you know any of the others?" he asked.

Selena picked up the other two photos and shook her head.

"How about you, Olani, have you seen these men?" he asked.

Olani shook her head. "Who are they?"

"The attackers," he said. "Can you tell me about your friend, the one married to this guy?"

"Rosa Gebarra. Roma like me. In fact, she's also a dancer at the supper club."

"Married to a Muslim and she dances at a supper club?" Rafael asked. "Are you sure?"

"Yes, she works with me. He's beaten her up many times in three years. She's very much afraid of him. But they have a daughter. He's threatened to take the child away. Said he'd kill her if she leaves him."

"When did you last see her?" he asked.

"At the club, the last time we performed together."

"Can you be more specific?"

"Three nights ago. We're not always scheduled on the same nights."

"Has she said anything to you?" he asked.

"About what?" Selena asked as her face turned a shade of gray. She bit the nail of her index finger.

"Has your friend ever mentioned her husband's involvement in terrorist activities?"

Selena moved her head. It was not a nod, but it was not a negative response either.

"Did you know Hassan is dead?" Rafael asked.

"Dead?" Selena's eyebrows arched. "¡Hòstia! How the fuck did that happen?"

"Killed by police yesterday. After he opened fire at bystanders at Sagrada Família."

Rafael noticed Olani's blank stare and thought it portrayed the shock and fear she must feel.

"You two need to stop looking for Taiwo. Leave it to the police. Understood?"

Nikki and Eduardo followed Floyd into his suite at the Majestic. Milena had gone to the hospital to keep Carmen company.

A potted calla lily plant from Nikki and Eduardo's wedding was placed on the floor against the wall, across from the coffee table, in the tiny living room. Carmen had delivered it the day after Nikki's wedding. The flowers reminded Nikki of both her fairytale wedding and of the hideous terrorist attack at Sagrada Família. Her knees felt weak, so she sat on a small sofa and put her purse on the floor. Eduardo squeezed in next to her and took her hand.

"Flowers from our wedding," she said. Her chest tightened. "Who would have known? Poor Carmen."

"Have you thought more about your offer to get into El Saraway's suite?" Floyd asked.

"Eduardo thinks I overstepped and will put us in danger if we carry it out," Nikki said. She glanced at her husband and added, "He told me the Spanish police have their own damn investigators and does not understand why Interpol is even meddling in this investigation. What happens if we get caught?"

"Those are all good points," Floyd said. "Javier is meddling because I asked him for help. And you should know that, Eduardo. Now the point is, if we can get some dirt on El Saraway, Javier said the police can investigate. If we establish a link to the African or to the bombing."

"You have not answered what happens if we get caught." Eduardo said.

"Interpol will bring in local police if something goes wrong. And I'm here to help if you need to get out of the country," Floyd said. "Have you both decided to help or not?"

"Eduardo made me reflect on the fact that I don't trust Javier," Nikki said.

"Don't let his squeaky voice and facial tics put you off. He gets things done. And he's good," Floyd said.

"Interpol cannot mobilize police quickly enough if we need them," Eduardo said. "It's only using us to gather information."

"You're right," Floyd said. "But we are using Interpol as a way to get intelligence we can't get otherwise."

Eduardo finally relented and agreed to enter the suite. Floyd high-fived him.

"My life has been endangered twice. I'm thinking it's Arenas, the Colombian. And I want to get him," Nikki said.

They discussed the possibility of Arenas having hired El Saraway, despite both men having very different modus operandi. They could not reach agreement on the African's role, though Nikki figured he might be a *sicario*, or hitman, for Arenas.

"I'm glad we're going to coordinate with Interpol," Floyd said. "We must find answers."

"You have a company to run," Nikki said. "In Miami, remember? You can't stay over here forever."

Floyd laughed. "Whatever it takes. I want to keep my two best people alive."

"Whoa. When did I become part of your staff?" Eduardo asked. "I'm a medical doctor, not a private eye, remember."

"You're part of the team and you know it," Floyd said.

After a moment of silence, Nikki reminded Eduardo of the Barri Gòtic when she saw the dagger and skull.

"We can still apply the antidote," Eduardo said. "Can't hurt."

"I have my tree of life necklace," Nikki said, touching the sculpted jadeite emblem dangling from a gold chain around her neck.

"Antidote? Dagger and skull? What are you guys talking about?" Floyd asked.

Eduardo explained Bishop's Bridge, which spanned a narrow street uniting buildings on opposite sides. The architect, disgruntled at not receiving better commissions, added a skull and dagger on the underside of the bridge, creating a superstition in Barcelona.

"The tradition," Nikki said, "is to close your eyes, twirl around, open your eyes, and if you see the skull and dagger, an evil curse will befall you. It's only a superstition, but I saw the skull and dagger."

"I'm almost afraid to ask about the antidote," Floyd said.

"It's simple," Eduardo said. "Visit a certain stone mailbox sculpted with birds, scales, vines, a crown, and a turtle. The scales represent the balance of justice. The turtle means the slow pace of the legal system. And so on. But it's touching the turtle that cures the curse of the Bishop's Bridge."

"I never thought my work would be influenced by superstitions," Floyd said, rolling his eyes. "But I might tell Milena about the Bishop's Bridge and take her to see it. She loves superstitions like that."

Getting back to the topic they needed to discuss, Nikki asked Floyd if he trusted Javier.

Without hesitation, Floyd indicated that based on his dealings with the man, he did trust him. "Remember Javier can get fired for using his Interpol position to run a clandestine investigation."

They devised a plan to disguise themselves as hotel staff. Floyd would request the necessary passkeys from Javier.

"Before I forget," Nikki said, "I have photos of the florist for Paula's wedding."

"Photos?" Floyd asked.

"Fadi took pictures at our wedding. When he downloaded them to my tablet, he included three shots of his dad and Paula standing near his dad's Ferrari. Hassan the florist was with them," Nikki said. "I don't think Fadi intended to include them."

Floyd handed Javier's card to Nikki. "Javier's email. Send him the photos."

"One more thing," Nikki said, taking the card. "Paula secretly converted to Islam."

"Converted?" Floyd asked. "Secretly?"

"She told you?" Eduardo asked.

"She was in the middle of her prayers when I went to her room to help her dress. Only Fadi knew. She didn't tell Carmen."

"Interesting," Floyd said. He walked to the window.

Nikki sensed Floyd was calculating various implications from that bit of news.

"Why did she want the Catholic ceremony?" Eduardo asked.

"In memory of her father and to avoid upsetting her mother," Nikki said.

"Do you think she was coerced into converting?" Floyd asked as he continued looking out the window.

"She seemed at ease with her decision. Her prayer routine seemed pretty authentic," Nikki said.

"Makes sense," Eduardo said. "She seemed more inspired by Islam than Fadi did."

"I'll ask Javier if he can get a copy of Massú's statement to the police," Floyd said. "Maybe Massú knew the reason behind Paula's conversion."

Nikki and Eduardo talked over the details of getting into El Saraway's suite. Floyd returned with a mobile phone in one hand and a small black box in the other.

"Open it up," Floyd said passing the box to Eduardo. "You'll need to find the right place to hide it in El Saraway's suite, and we're not going to tell Javier about planting it."

"A miniature camera? It's so tiny I could drop it and never find it."

Floyd handed the phone to Nikki. "If you can get access to El Saraway's phone for about thirty seconds, you can download his information to this one. It will also set his phone up so we can follow his every move."

"That's pretty unlikely. Who leaves their cell phone behind?"

"Use it on a tablet if you find one," Floyd said.

"How do I operate it?" she asked.

"Simple," Floyd said, reaching out to get the phone back from Nikki. He angled it to show her the thin side. "Press this button. It needs to turn red. Then set this phone directly on top of El Saraway's phone or tablet for at least thirty seconds. Check the button again to make sure it's turned green. Lift this phone off and bring it to me. That way, Charlotte can follow him from our Miami office."

"Like she tracked me in Mexico?" Nikki asked.

"Similar process," Floyd said.

CHAPTER TWENTY-EIGHT

BARCELONA—SANT ANDREU DISTRICT

After leaving Selena's apartment, Rafael drove to a nearby park. He spent twenty minutes writing up his interview with the two women. Then he dialed Alberto, a detective on his team from the GEO terrorism squad. He'd interviewed Selena and Olani on his own to protect Olani. For the next interview, he'd need a witness. When Alberto answered, he asked his colleague to meet him at an address he'd text as soon as he hung up.

Waiting for Alberto outside Rosa Gebarra's apartment building, Rafael scoped out the neighborhood, a run-down area that looked to be home for immigrants from various countries. He noticed teenagers playing soccer on a side street. He saw Alberto parking his car and walked over to meet him.

The two men proceeded into the building. Musty odors greeted their nostrils. The elevator did not work. Instead they walked up three dark and dingy flights of stairs. Alberto, who had been holding a couple of folded plastic bags, crammed them into a back pocket of his pants leaving part of the plastic hanging out.

On the second floor, the aroma of fried seafood permeated the stairwell. Rafael's physique showed his love of food despite the substantial amount of exercise he got both on and off the job, but the lingering, reeking odor of rancid oil and unsavory seafood accosted his sinuses. He coughed. And then held his breath.

Finally on the third floor, Rafael inhaled. He knocked at Gebarra's apartment. When Hassan's widow opened the door, her face shockingly bruised and swollen, the men flashed their badges, stated their names, and showed her the search warrant.

"Mrs. Gebarra," Alberto said, "was Hassan Farooqi your husband?"

"Yes."

"We're here to have a look around your apartment and to take your late husband's computer and phone," Alberto said.

"And to ask you a few questions," Rafael added, trying not to stare at her bruised face and black eye.

Rosa let the men in. She looked at them with the hollow expression of a woman whose life has been beaten into submission.

"We are sorry for your loss," Rafael started to say.

She interrupted. "I'm the one who's sorry I ever met the bastard."

"We have a few questions about Hassan," Rafael said, noticing how clean the apartment looked. And smelled, compared to the rest of the complex. "I understand you have a daughter."

"At day care."

"Can you give us the names of your husband's friends and associates?" Rafael asked.

"It's a short list," she said. "The most important one is the cleric of the Tarragona mosque."

"Mosques anywhere else?" Rafael asked.

"Whenever he left town, he always told me he was going to Tarragona. He may have gone other places. I don't know."

"What about mosques in Barcelona? Did the two of you attend one here?" Rafael asked.

"I'm Rom. I never went to a mosque with him. We led very separate lives."

"Did you meet any of his friends?" Alberto asked.

"Two. One of them died in the Paris attack in 2015."

"Is the other one still around?" Alberto asked.

"In the morgue," she said, glancing down. "He was in the same car as Hassan yesterday."

"Morgue? How do you know that?"

"His wife. I should say his widow. She called me today."

"Did your husband have a regular job?" Rafael asked. He scanned the room for clues.

"A florist."

"Can you say where?"

"Flores de Primavera."

"We'd like to take a look around the apartment," Rafael said.

"Go ahead," she said, waving a hand. "This is about all there is."

Rafael and Alberto put on gloves and went to work scrutinizing closets and drawers. Alberto checked three plastic containers stored under the bed. Rafael stepped into the bathroom, called Rosa, and asked her to point out her husband's toothbrush. He placed it in a small paper bag he retrieved from his jacket pocket. Before she left the room, he asked her about the three baskets with soiled clothes.

"This one contains my clothes for the laundry," she said, pointing to the one closest to the shower. It was stacked on top a smaller hamper. "That small one is my daughter's and the third basket contains my husband's dirty clothes. Once I wash them, I'll give all his stuff away."

"I'd recommend not washing it or giving anything away for three months. In case the police need to return for an item or two." Rafael searched all three containers, marveling at the Roma preoccupation with cleanliness.

Both men returned to the kitchen where the lone computer in the house, a laptop, sat on a high but narrow table placed tight against the wall. Alberto disconnected and bagged it.

"Did your husband use more than one mobile phone?" Alberto asked.

"The only one I know of he always carried with him. The police must have it," she said.

As the men prepared to leave, they thanked the young widow.

"Who did that to your face?" Rafael asked.

"My husband. Friday after he returned from prayers at the mosque."

"Did he beat you other times?" Rafael asked.

She nodded. "Usually he hit my stomach, legs, or chest. I could continue working as long as my face did not show it."

Rafael took his wallet out and retrieved two business cards. He handed one to her. "This place offers counseling for women. It's free."

Rosa glanced at the card. Her eyes welled up.

He waited a few seconds and handed her the second card, which was his own. "If you think of something, anything at all that can help our investigation, call me at this number."

She started to open the door for them, but pushed it closed and looked at Rafael in a hesitant manner.

"I almost forgot. Hassan told me he'd flown through the Tarragona airport. A few days before the attack. It may have been in preparation for the bombing."

"Reus? How many days before?"

"Yes. Let me check." She pulled up a calendar on her phone. "Two weeks ago tomorrow."

"Twelve days before the bombing. Did he mention which airline?" Rafael asked.

Rosa shook her head. "He mentioned a small plane."

"Ryanair maybe?"

She shook her head again.

"Do you know the names of people he flew with?" Rafael asked.

"Hardly ever did he mention anyone by name. Unless it was someone in the neighborhood."

"Is there anything else you should tell us?" Alberto asked.

"I'll call if I think of something," she said as she reopened the door for them.

Descending the dank stairwell, Rafael detected once again the rancid odor of fried fish emanating from one of the apartments. His body tensed as if that would keep the offensive scent from saturating his clothes.

"He may have had a regular job, but he could take time off work, apparently," Alberto said.

"Interview the owner of the flower shop," Rafael said. "And Hassan's colleagues. See what you can find out. Call me with your findings. Also get a search warrant for both Paula's home and Fadi's place. The initial police report I read had the bride living with her mother."

"Search warrants for the victims' homes? Is that all?" Alberto asked.

"I want to see who they were in contact with on social media, email, telephone."

At street level, Rafael's phone vibrated. When he reached the car, he saw it was an email from his former boss Javier de la Mata, now an Interpol agent. Javier had already provided him with information on the Sagrada Família case and in this email, he forwarded photos taken of one of the alleged terrorists, Hassan Farooqi, the husband of the woman Rafael had just interviewed. In the picture, Hassan was standing next to a Ferrari and two other people. The involvement of a florist had already been mentioned in the news though names were still being withheld from the public.

Rafael studied the photograph. The detective immediately recognized Fernando Massú, father of the bridegroom. The young woman was the bride who had also died in the attack. Rafael typed a quick thanks to his old boss. The Interpol man could not resist trying to get to the heart of a crime. Rafael smiled at the thought.

CHAPTER TWENTY-NINE

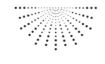

TARRAGONA

Monday Early Morning

As he drove toward the Costa Dorada airport of Reus, Rafael enjoyed the sun-bathed Prades Mountains in the distance. He mentally organized his schedule for the day. First on his agenda would be the visit to Reus Airport, where he would screen security videos. Instead of screening them in his office, he wanted to do it onsite in case he needed to check details at the premises.

Later he would drive into the center of Tarragona, about ten kilometers east of the airport, to make an unannounced call at the mosque. After that, he would walk to El Serrallo, the fisherman's district, and treat himself to cassola de romesco, not exactly a breakfast dish, but he knew a restaurant that served it in the morning. His mouth watered for the vermouth that traditionally accompanied the rich nut sauce and clam casserole. He could not imagine a more perfect brunch before he hit the road back to Barcelona.

Rafael's mind filtered through the bits of evidence already gathered on the bombing of the basilica. The day of the incident, he had tried to interrogate Fernando Massú in the crypt church after the man had identified the bodies of his wife and son. He was visibly outraged when Rafael had started the interrogation. As the counterterror agent continued to question him, Massú's anger had changed to grief. Once the grief set in, the man seemed unable to comprehend the events that had taken place. Consequently, he became somewhat incoherent.

Rafael had seen heartache before and Massú's grief had seemed genuine. But it made it impossible to get a meaningful statement from him. So Rafael had ended his questioning. He would follow up later, he'd informed the man.

The father of the bridegroom had been conveniently away from the church at the time of the bombing, and that bothered Rafael.

His phone rang. It was Teresa, a young agent from his antiterrorist team in Barcelona.

"Regarding the suspect Hassan Farooqi, whom you believe may have flown through the Reus Airport," Teresa's voice said over the speaker in Rafael's car, "I have not found tickets in his name during the window of time you told me to check. Could he have used a different name?"

"He may have flown by private aircraft," Rafael said. "I'll check on it at the airport. Widen your search to include five previous days and call me if you find him."

With his limited information, Rafael hated to draw conclusions. Yet he could not stop thinking about Massú arriving late to his son's wedding. Late as a result of picking up a friend at the airport. The thought kept bouncing around his mind.

Rafael called security to notify them of his pending arrival. A few minutes later, he maneuvered his car into a parking spot and walked to the front door, pulling the folded search warrant from his jacket pocket as he entered the building.

The director of airport security met Rafael by the entrance and ushered him to the second-floor office where they could run the security videos for him. Rafael handed the warrant to the director, who instructed a young female technician sitting at a wall of monitors to start the videos showing arriving passengers.

"Start thirteen, no, let's make that fifteen days ago."

As the young woman worked with Rafael, she moved the digital film forward until he asked her to slow it down whenever he spotted people to scrutinize. After half an hour, she switched to departing passengers and then to the general hallways. Every time Rafael thought he had seen Hassan in the airport, arriving, departing, or in the corridors, it turned out on closer examination not to be the alleged terrorist.

"Would you run videos from the front of the terminal?" Rafael asked.

"Starting fifteen days back?" the technician asked.

"That'd be perfect."

The technician switched to another screen and scrolled the video back by the days Rafael requested.

After forwarding through several days of footage, Rafael became impatient, thinking Rosa may have given him the wrong airport or erroneous information. He continued to watch the monitor.

"Wait. Stop," Rafael said. "Back it up a bit. Right there. Get a look at that car partially in the frame."

"Nice Ferrari," the director said.

"Not what I was expecting, but this can help," Rafael said. "Can you pick up where it parked? Maybe to see who gets either in or out."

As the technician searched three other monitors and ran portions of video to locate the Ferrari, the director picked up a phone and asked a clerk from his office to bring espresso for them.

"The Ferrari has parked where we can't see it," the technician said as she continued searching. After fifteen minutes of reexamining the videos, she picked up a partial roof, rear window, and a door opening as a man wearing a skullcap appeared to get out.

"Stop it right there," Rafael ordered. The three people in the room were staring at a man carrying a hooded hawk on his shoulder. "Please make a still photograph of that screen."

"Any other stills?" the technician asked.

"Yes, the one from the other camera where we can see the Ferrari arriving. Enlarge the license plate if you can," Rafael said, thinking the forensic lab could enhance the video to identify the passengers. "I'll also need a copy of the video covering the entire time the car and the man carrying the falcon can be seen."

A knock on the door alerted them to coffee being delivered. The clerk came in and set a round platter with three cups of espresso, small spoons, and packets of sugar on a desk. Rafael immediately helped himself, adding three packets of sugar to the tiny cup.

Once she printed the still photos, the technician walked to the printer to retrieve them. She handed them to Rafael for his review. She opened a drawer and removed a thumb drive where she proceeded to download the video. After completing the task and handing the external drive to Rafael, she lifted her cup and took a sip. Placing it on her desk, she began running more film.

"Check the footage for this past Saturday," Rafael requested.

Within minutes, she had found the Ferrari again.

This time, the cameras had picked up Massú and the man with the falcon on his shoulder leaving the airport. Rafael had assumed that Massú had meant the Barcelona airport when he said he'd been picking up a friend. Apparently it was Reus. The Ferrari had left the parking lot testing the car's ability to speed.

"I'll take that video and stills of the Ferrari and the men getting in."

"Is that all you need?" the technician asked.

"No, I came looking for someone else. Maybe that person traveled by private aircraft," Rafael said.

"That's a different section of the airport," the technician said. She changed to another camera feed and loaded the footage.

The monitor was gray with fuzzy lines until the video started running. Before joining the technician at the monitor, Rafael sipped his espresso and placed the cup back on the platter.

After a few minutes, Rafael asked the technician to stop.

"That's what I want. Start running it again," Rafael said as they watched about three minutes of video. He instructed her to make stills from the point these individuals come into view all the way to where their backs turn the corner toward the parking lot.

The technician prepared copies of the additional videos and stills. She compiled a nice packet for the detective, which she placed in a box.

———

At the mosque in Tarragona, Rafael felt he was getting the runaround. The imam was gone, god knows where. And no one knew when he might return.

"Who runs the services while the imam is away?" he asked.

"Several men take turns leading the congregation," a young man at the mosque informed him.

Rafael thought about speaking to a couple of those men, if he could find them. He reconsidered as he knew it would be a futile exercise. They would all plead ignorance beyond leading the congregation in prayer. Besides, he had more important interviews to carry out.

Rafael's stomach growled and his palate could almost taste the clam casserole and romesco sauce he had promised himself. His mouth watered at the thought of a shot glass of vermouth to complete a satisfying gastronomic outing before driving to Barcelona to interrogate Fernando Massú again.

CHAPTER THIRTY

BARCELONA—MAJESTIC HOTEL

Attired in a housekeeper's uniform and long black wig, Nikki looked in the mirror to make certain she had not left telltale streaks in the makeup that darkened her face and arms. Slipping on a set of glasses with heavy dark frames and lightly shaded lenses Floyd had provided as part of her disguise, she found they sat heavy on the bridge of her nose. Yet they further transformed her appearance, so she kept them on. Her last step included tucking the special mobile phone Floyd had provided into her apron pocket.

Eduardo, in his maintenance coverall, had been watching Nikki. He called Floyd. "We're ready."

"All clear." Nikki could just make out Floyd's voice over the phone. "I'll meet you at the service elevator."

"Roger, roger," Eduardo responded.

"Roger?" Nikki repeated, chuckling as they walked toward the service elevator in the hallway where the emergency stairwell was also located. "Where did you learn that?"

"Floyd. He said pilots and short-wave radio operators use it."

"Your accent makes it sound sexy," Nikki said.

Floyd held the service elevator open for them and pushed a

housekeeping cart toward Nikki. Then he scanned the housekeeper passkey and punched floor seventeen.

"Javier's had the security cameras turned off on the penthouse floor."

"You're sure?" Eduardo asked.

"As sure as we can be. He's also watching the guest elevators downstairs. He'll call if you need to bail."

As the elevator ascended, Floyd handed Nikki two key cards.

"Door key. Passkey to the safe in the master closet," he said.

Floyd gave a spare door key to Eduardo. "In an emergency, exit to the balcony. From there, you can get to the roof. Then you can use the fire stairs at the back of the building."

Nikki put on plastic gloves she found on the top shelf of the cart. Eduardo followed suit.

"Tell Milena how much I appreciate her staying with Carmen," Nikki said.

Floyd nodded.

They stepped out of the elevator into the plain service hallway, Nikki pushing the housekeeping cart. Floyd opened the door to the richly carpeted hall that guests used and checked for people. When he saw no one, he motioned them through. He would serve as lookout in the hallway near the door to the emergency stairs.

Nikki used the passkey to open the door. With trepidation, she stepped into a dim foyer and pulled the cart in behind her. Without turning a light on, she continued into a living room. She stopped cold when she heard shrieking.

An angry cat?

As her eyes adjusted to the unlit living room, the noise increased. Then she saw it. A cage. A huge cage with a bird inside. Its talons hanging onto the metal bars. Not a parakeet or a parrot, but larger. And it was not happy. It clawed at the bars with its hooked beak as it repositioned its talons. Emitting loud, harsh sounds, its dark brown plumage with copper overtones ruffled up in anger like a rabid fox.

Eduardo rushed around the cart, ready to protect Nikki.

"Must be a hawk," he said. "Looks safe behind those bars. Let's get busy."

Eduardo proceeded, as planned, to the master bedroom and bathroom to make sure all was clear. Nikki covered the small kitchen and the second bedroom as well as a guest bathroom. The bird did not stop its shrieking. They reconvened in the living room. Heavy curtains drawn completely closed gave the expensive suite a stodgy and uninviting atmosphere. Shortly, the raptor settled down and simply cocked its head to one side, keeping an eye on them.

They went to work. Eduardo inspected the contents of the living room and would continue with the rooms on the left side of the penthouse. Nikki took the rooms to the right and entered the master bedroom. First, she checked the bathroom. Finding nothing out of the ordinary, she returned to the bedroom. She opened drawers and examined the contents for clues to this man's identity or what, if anything, he was hiding.

After kneeling to search beneath the mattress and under the bed, she glanced at the floor and noticed a small rug, about two and half feet in width to four feet in length spread out on top of the plush carpeting. She figured it was a prayer mat. As she stood, she moved to the nightstand. The drawer contained a copy of the Koran and Subḥah prayer beads.

A charging station occupied space on the nightstand, next to a lamp with a red base and colorful hand-painted flowers. Of interest to her was the tablet currently plugged into the unit. She took the special cell phone from her pocket. Feeling nervous, she pushed the button on the phone and placed it on top of the tablet. Immediately lighting up, it appeared to be downloading information. After a minute that felt like an eternity to Nikki, it seemed to have completed the job.

Eduardo came in. The cell phone on the tablet showed a green light. She tucked it back into her apron pocket.

"Mission accomplished," she said, looking at Eduardo and feeling exhilarated.

Eduardo took a photo of the setup, where El Saraway probably recharged his phone, camera, and whatever other electronic gadgets he carried in addition to his tablet. Then he returned to the living room. Nikki opened the door to the walk-in closet.

A rectangular safe was bolted to the wall. She took out the key cards Floyd had provided. The second one opened the safe. Inside she found two large bundles of one-hundred-euro bills held together with rubber bands. Next to the money lay an unsealed envelope. As she opened it, her eyes grew bigger. She slid her thick-framed glasses to the top of her head to get a better look at the contents. Her heart beat rapidly as she studied photos of herself and Eduardo.

In the living area, Eduardo stood on a chair he had brought from the kitchen. From that height, he was taking photos of a large screen connected with thick cables to a nearby computer.

"I have something to show you," she said.

Eduardo stepped off the chair and returned it to the dining table. The falcon squawked.

"I placed the spy camera on the chandelier," he whispered. "Does it look okay?"

Nikki looked up and scrutinized the chandelier. She shook her head. "I don't even see it."

"Good," he said.

Nikki showed him the photos—taken not only the day they arrived as they sat on the circular bench on Passeig de Gràcia, but also the next day when they were leaving the hotel. She'd already visited the stylist, and her hair was the more becoming light brown. Nikki held the photographs up, and he snapped the clandestine photographs El Saraway had taken of them. Nikki tucked the photographs back in the envelope. She led him to the walk-in closet and placed the envelope where she had found it.

Eduardo asked her to remove the wads of money for a picture. A receipt fell out. She picked it up and immediately realized it was a 64-character string.

"Bitcoin," she said. "He moves money anonymously. Quick, take a couple of photos."

As a final step, she placed the bitcoin receipt back into the wad it had fallen from. Then she put the money back in the safe and locked it.

"Let's see the kitchen," she said, turning to look at Eduardo.

"I've already covered it. Plus the small bedroom and the guest bathroom," he said. "Nothing there."

"It's time to get out," Nikki said.

Eduardo pressed a button on his mobile phone to alert Floyd they were on their way out.

Nikki pointed toward the falcon. "Reminds me of Sebastian."

"Wait, I should take pictures of him," Eduardo said.

"Hurry," Nikki whispered. "Let's leave before El Saraway surprises us."

"Might need to prove there's a hawk here."

The bird cocked his brown-feathered head and looked at them with his pitch-black, beady eye. His yellow beak cracked open and let out a screech as Eduardo snapped like a real paparazzo.

"Man, I liked that crazy crow in Mexico better," Eduardo said. "Sebastian was a lot friendlier."

Back in the suite, Nikki dialed Charlotte. At this early hour in Miami, she would be at home. She needed Charlotte to look into something.

"Bitcoin transactions," Nikki said. "The best way to research it might be to follow the cookie trail attached to the receipt I'm providing. I think you might find cookies for purchases related to falcons and falconry. Such things as specialty food or radio tracking devices."

She listened as Charlotte explained she would also look at leaks of information from online shopping carts associated with the account Nikki wanted investigated.

"If I can find the blockchains related to this individual's account, we can see his whole spending history, including money transfers," Charlotte said. "Leave it in my hands."

Eduardo had been watching the TV news while Nikki was on the phone. "Won't Charlotte get in trouble for looking into something like that without a search warrant?"

"Have you forgotten I'm a fraud investigator?" Nikki asked with a glint of delight in her eyes. "Blockchain is public. The beauty of that is we don't need a search warrant."

CHAPTER THIRTY-ONE

BARCELONA—SARRIÀ-SANT GERVASI DISTRICT

MONDAY EARLY AFTERNOON OF THIRD WEEK

As Rafael contemplated his next steps, the GEO antiterrorist agent sat on a bench enjoying the tranquility of water lilies floating on the surface of the pond. A figure sculpted in white marble reclined at the far end. Rafael had chosen Jardines Muñoz Ramonet for its sense of peace. Always on the lookout for anything out of the ordinary, Rafael found it easier in a place lacking the clatter of children, the watchful supervision of mothers, or people walking their dogs. He kept an eye on the minimal movement in the bushes, caused by birds hopping from one shrub to another.

He pulled his phone out and dialed a number.

"Following the trail of the now dead suspect in the photo you sent me of the Ferrari," Rafael said, "led me to Reus Airport outside Tarragona. Did you get the photos I sent you?"

"I did," Javier said at the other end of the phone line.

"Who is this man with the falcon?"

"Who?" Javier asked. He sounded annoyed.

"The man wearing the skullcap. Carrying a live falcon on his shoulder. What can you tell me about him?"

"I don't know who you're talking about," Javier said over the phone.

"Thirteen days before the wedding, he got out of Massú's car at Reus

Airport," Rafael explained. "Then on the morning of his son's wedding, Massú picked him up at the same airport."

Javier abruptly told Rafael he would contact him later.

Thanking his former boss, Rafael hung up. He knew Javier was a nervous type who could not multitask easily. Or maybe he was in the company of people and could not speak openly. Still eying the park's plantings, Rafael stood to leave. Wondering why Javier had sounded so abrupt, he took the concrete walkway to his vehicle, climbed in, and methodically started the engine. Turning his thoughts to Lola and their twins, he decided to call his wife before he pulled away from the curb. Once he completed the short conversation with Lola, he drove two blocks to Massú's stately home in the Sarrià-Sant Gervasi district.

Rafael rang the doorbell. As he waited, Rafael stepped back to observe details of the upscale house. Movement through the opaque glass set in the ornate iron grille design of the door and the sound of a key turning focused his attention back to the doorway, where a slender woman now stood dressed in a starched, light blue dress partially covered with a white apron.

The housekeeper gave Rafael an inquisitive stare.

"I'd like to speak to Mr. Massú."

"He is indisposed."

Rafael flashed his GEO badge with the stylized silver snake and gold eagle on a black background. He could see she was not impressed with the badge.

"I've told you he is indisposed. Surely you've heard the TV coverage about the tragedy at Sagrada Família."

"That's why I'm here. To ask a few questions. And find those responsible."

Before the housekeeper could deny him again, Rafael saw the man coming down the staircase a few feet beyond the front door.

"I'll take it from here, Berta," Massú said.

In a well-lit living room with large windows and a high ceiling, Massú waved his hand to prompt Rafael to sit on a sofa. A red, yellow, and orange abstract painting with streaks of black splashed vertically across the canvas hung on the wall behind the seat the investigator took. Its bright colors belied the solemn atmosphere prevailing in the room.

"I'd like to start out again with my condolences for your terrible loss."

Massú pursed his lips and closed his eyes in an attempt to hold back his tears.

"I know this is a bad time to question you, but there will never be a good time to talk about this."

Massú opened his eyes and with his right hand made a rolling gesture, saying go ahead. Rafael noticed Massú's hand trembled.

"Who do you think caused the attack on Saturday?"

"If I knew, I would have told you the first time we spoke. I've stayed awake at night wondering if this was an international terrorist group, or if it was orchestrated right here in this city."

"Are you aware Hassan Farooqi, the florist who arranged the flowers for the ceremony, also drove one of the vehicles who tried to kill people on the streets immediately after the bombing?"

"I've heard it on the news. Not Farooqi's name, but the flower shop. I know he worked there."

"You also know he probably set up the plastic bonded explosives, known as either PBX or C-4 bombs, which were planted in the flower containers?"

"Yes." Massú wiped his eyes.

"And you knew this young man?"

Massú nodded.

"Who recommended him to do the flower arrangements?"

"Paula," Massú said, his voice choking on the words.

"The bride?"

Massú nodded again.

"How did she know him?"

"Through her work. She knew a lot of young Muslim men. Fadi worried about that."

"Your son was concerned about Muslim men she associated with at work?"

Massú picked up a small bell on the coffee table. He rang it vigorously before answering. "Many of them were angry and felt disenfranchised in Spanish society. Fadi was fearful she might be swept up into harm."

"Harm? In what way?"

"Fadi said more than once that desperate people do desperate things. He worried they could influence his fiancée in negative ways. Paula was very idealistic, you know. But my son obviously never considered an event like what happened."

Berta came into the room. Massú asked her to bring coffee.

"Are you saying Paula was easily influenced by people with a cause?"

"She was a good woman. Always trying to make the world a better place. She had converted to Islam, you know."

"When?"

"Recently. A wedding in the Muslim tradition would have taken place later this month," Massú said. He seemed about to break down, but instead, he continued speaking. "They have taken them all from me. My wife, my son, even Paula."

"Who killed them?"

"I don't know. I've said before, I'd kill those bastards if I knew who they were."

Berta returned with a platter holding demitasse cups half full of espresso. In addition, the platter contained a small plate of ma'amoul pastries, green napkins with a gold line around the edge, a sugar bowl, and three small spoons. She set the tray on the coffee table and placed a cup, napkin, and spoon in front of each of the men. She placed the third spoon in the sugar bowl and passed it to Rafael. The plate of pastries she handed to Massú and left the room.

Massú took a pastry, placed it on his napkin, and handed the plate to Rafael, who helped himself.

Rafael nibbled at the shortbread pastry, enjoying the sweet date and walnut filling. He resumed the interview.

"If Hassan was a florist, how did Paula know him?"

"I do not know the answer."

Rafael took his mobile phone and opened a file. He slid the phone on the coffee table toward Massú.

"This is your Ferrari, isn't it?"

Massú moved to the edge of his easy chair to take a closer look without picking the phone up.

"Yes."

"Yet, the florist is pictured here."

"Fadi took those pictures a couple of weeks before the wedding."

"The newscasts have asked for information on an African with a full beard. Do you know anyone of that description?"

"No one I can think of."

"What about a man who is a falconer?"

"Falconer? You mean El Saraway?"

"Who is he?" Rafael asked.

"A close family friend. He has donated significant amounts of money to support schools in Egypt and Lebanon."

"Schools?"

"Yes, coeducational schools to promote understanding between East and West. I've been involved since the attack in New York. Both El Saraway and I have benefited from living in the West. We share a goal to start dialogue between our peoples."

"Did El Saraway attend the wedding at Sagrada Família?"

"By the time he arrived, the attack had already happened."

"You also arrived late. Where were you?"

"I went to the airport to pick him up. Unfortunately, his plane was late that morning."

"What airline did he use?" Rafael asked.

"He chartered a private plane."

"Do you realize you probably would have been killed if you'd been there on time?"

Massú looked through the windows to the garden. "I do. With my wife and son gone, that would have been best. My loved ones are still undergoing forensic work and I don't know when they will be released for burial. Under our religious laws, we bury our dead within twenty-four hours. I'd rather be dead than here suffering."

"Did El Saraway arrive at the basilica with you?"

"No. I dropped him off at his hotel. He arrived after I did. But he brought me home. I stayed at Sagrada Família until the bodies had been recovered. The police asked me to identify them—Jamila, my wife, Fadi, my son, and Paula."

"Was El Saraway with you when you identified the remains of your family members?"

"No. I talked to you. Don't you remember that's when you interrogated me the first time? Right after I confirmed the bodies to the police."

"So when do you think El Saraway arrived?"

"He was late."

"Later than you?"

"Let me think. The television reporters must have arrived while I was with the police down in the crypt. A small room at the back of the church. They had—" Massú's torso slumped. He took his hands to his face and sobbed.

"I'm sorry. Shall we stop and pick up another day?"

"Let's finish," Massú said as he took a monogrammed handkerchief out of his pocket to wipe his face. "I want to find the bastards responsible for this atrocity. Ask whatever you need."

"Can you remember when El Saraway arrived?"

"After talking to you, a mosso escorted me back up to street level. Let me think a minute. From the news coverage, I figure the mayor and the police had been interviewed by the news channels while I was inside the crypt church after identifying the bodies."

"If El Saraway arrived so late, wouldn't he have already heard about the attack?"

"All I know is when I got back to the street, most of the people who had evacuated the basilica had either been taken to hospitals or gone home. Only the police, television crews, and a handful of victims remained. I felt inconsolable, all by myself. That's when I called him. He was in the park and I walked across the street to where he stood."

"You called El Saraway?"

"Yes."

"So he had just arrived?"

"I don't know how long he had been there. My brain was a tangled mess. He brought me home. He must have known I was still there and been looking for me. He stayed with me the rest of the afternoon. Spent the night here too. Neither one of us got any sleep."

"Where is he now?"

"I assume at his hotel."

"He doesn't live in Barcelona?"

"No, he flew in for the wedding."

"And where does he stay?"

"The Majestic on Passeig de Gràcia. He keeps a penthouse year-round."

"Is he a Spanish citizen?"

"Yes, though born in Egypt."

"Are you also Egyptian?"

"Lebanese. My family originated in Jordan, but my parents were born in Lebanon."

"Where does El Saraway normally live?"

"Ibiza, his favorite place. He owns a home in Alexandria and another one in Latin America. He has worldwide business interests."

"What is his business?"

"Chemicals. He exports various ones from Egypt to other countries, including Spain."

"What kind?"

"Solvents and liquid fertilizers mainly."

"How long have you known him?"

"A long time."

"Mr. Massú, do you suspect anyone of masterminding the attack? Do you know who killed your family?"

"I've already told you, if I knew, I would tell you."

"Do you have any information I should know?"

"You've asked a lot of questions about El Saraway. I can assure you he is not responsible for this atrocity. He loved Fadi. Like a son. Yes, Fadi was a son to him." Massú's voice trailed off to a whisper and his eyes looked lost in melancholic memories.

"But Fadi was going to marry a Christian woman. Could that have made El Saraway angry enough to carry out an attack?"

"Bomb the church? Kill people? No, he might be eccentric by Western standards, but he is a very good person. He lost his loved ones in a fire."

"Lost his loved ones? When?"

"A number of years ago. When he lived in South America. He came to Barcelona to start a new life. My wife and I helped him assimilate here."

"What year was that?"

"Early nineties, 1990 or 1991."

"What kind of help did you provide? Give me specific examples."

"My wife helped him find accommodations when he first arrived. That's when he got the penthouse at the Majestic. At that time there were not as many Muslim people here as we have today. So we introduced him to our friends. And he, in turn, introduced us to people he knew."

"I thought he did not know anyone here?"

"That's correct," Massú said. "He introduced us to people from Latin America. Industrialists who would buy my products."

"What products do you sell?"

"Plastics and polymers."

"That will be all. Thank you for answering my questions," Rafael said as he stood to leave.

Back in his car, Rafael buckled himself into his seat. The ma'amoul cookies and espresso had ignited his appetite and he felt hungry again. Having just eaten dessert, he considered where to eat a late lunch. He salivated at the thought of another cassola, but as he patted his belly under the seatbelt, he realized a sandwich was all he should allow himself. Plus a quiet café where he could make a few phone calls.

CHAPTER THIRTY-TWO

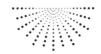

BARCELONA—EIXAMPLE DISTRICT

MONDAY EARLY AFTERNOON

Nikki handed the special cell phone to Floyd.

"Great job, guys," Floyd said. "I'll call Charlotte after she's had time to get her day organized in Miami. Hopefully she can access good intel you've extracted from El Saraway's tablet."

Nikki's phone rang. She cringed. It was Milena calling from the hospital. "What's wrong?"

Milena updated Nikki. Carmen had inquired about Paula and the doctor had talked with her about her daughter's death. Carmen had cried a lot and was now asking for Nikki.

"Tell her I'll be right over."

Eduardo walked Nikki to the lobby, escorting her outside to one of the hotel taxis. When she arrived at the hospital, she rushed to the private room where Carmen had been moved after intensive care. Milena was standing next to Carmen's bed and moved aside for Nikki to approach her aunt.

Carmen embraced Nikki and clung to her with trembling arms. Both women started weeping.

"I hoped against all odds, Paula would be okay," Carmen said as she tried to control her convulsive sobs. She used a hand to wipe away the tears.

"I'm sorry, Tía. I know how hard this is for you."

"She tried to do good. At least what Paula considered to be the right thing. I did not always agree with her. But I loved my daughter so much." Carmen said, her voice quivering. "And I know you understand how difficult it is to lose a child."

Nikki tried not to think about her suffering when she lost her son. Instead she focused on comforting Carmen in her loss. She found herself wondering if Carmen had any idea about her daughter's conversion to Islam. Looking up, she noticed Milena fidgeting awkwardly as if not knowing what to do. Nikki suggested Milena return to the hotel. She hugged her and thanked her for helping.

"I'm afraid," Carmen said, starting to cry again as soon as Milena had left.

"Afraid of what?" Nikki asked.

"My daughter . . . my daughter may have been a pawn in a larger scheme." Carmen wiped her tears as she detailed the news story one of the nurses had told her involving a florist in the attack, a florist who was supposed to be Paula's friend. She wondered why he set her up.

"Evil people do terrible things, Tía." Nikki took Carmen's hand to try to comfort her aunt.

"Nikki, I don't know how much you know about events in Barcelona in September of 2017. A terrorist incident took place on the Ramblas. Sixteen people were killed."

"It was all over the news that year," Nikki said. "Are you suggesting a connection between that incident and the one on Saturday?"

"The Ramblas attack originally included a plan to bomb Sagrada Família. The mastermind was an imam from a town near Barcelona. He accidentally set off explosives at the house where they were manufacturing bombs. Bombs intended for the basilica."

"I remember reading about that incident. Didn't the cleric die when the building blew up?"

"That's right," Carmen said. "After the imam's death, the other terrorists settled for vehicular attacks on the Ramblas here in the city and a second assault in Cambrils, a seaside resort in southern Catalonia."

"So are you saying Sagrada Família was saved by the accidental explosion?"

"Yes, you could say that. After the Ramblas incident, the news all over Europe reported a conspiracy between a secret faction of the Catalan police force and Muslim extremists."

"Are you sure, Tía Carmen? A secret faction of the Catalan police conspiring with radicals? I don't remember reading about a conspiracy."

But then Nikki remembered Eduardo telling her about the short-term goal of both groups being the same, to form an independent nation. The Catalonian people are fiercely independent and almost half of them still want to separate from Spain. Although the long-term ambition of the radicals was to form an Islamic state within Spain, Nikki knew politics made for strange alliances.

"More than conspiring, the Catalan police may have ignored warnings, which then allowed the attack to happen. As a lesson to wake people up," Carmen said. "That event is still being investigated."

"And how does this relate to Paula?" Nikki asked.

Carmen grimaced and started crying again.

Nikki took Carmen's hand and gently squeezed it to provide a little solace.

"We can talk about it later," Nikki said, patting her aunt's shoulder with her free hand. "No need to get upset."

"I need to talk about it now. I'm concerned my daughter was used."

Carmen started sobbing. Tears flowed down her face. Nikki handed her a couple of tissues to wipe the tears.

"Paula would never have participated in an abominable act like terrorism. They set her up, gained access to the church to set their explosives, killed people, and made a statement. All done by the florist she trusted."

Nikki stared at her aunt. "Did Paula have a computer?"

When Carmen indicated that Paula's computer was on the desk in the little office, she suggested Nikki take the keys to the condo and let herself in to retrieve it.

"In fact, why don't you and Eduardo stay at my condo?"

"Thank you, but that's not necessary."

A nurse came in and handed Carmen a pill and a glass of water with a straw. She changed the bottle of saline in the drip. When she completed the task, she turned to Nikki.

"La senyora needs to sleep now. You can visit again tomorrow."

Nikki gave her aunt a kiss on her forehead and asked if she needed anything. Before leaving, she sent Eduardo a text.

Nikki opened the door of their suite for Floyd. After serving herself a glass of orange juice, she poured scotch for Floyd and Eduardo. The three of them sat in the small living room. Nikki had called the meeting to discuss Carmen's thoughts on Paula's innocence.

"Or maybe not so innocent," Floyd said, placing a large brown envelope on the coffee table. "Sorry, Nikki, but we have to consider everyone who might be involved."

"Eduardo and I will go to Carmen's condo after we finish here. She gave me the keys and I'm going to retrieve Paula's computer. Charlotte can check it."

"Good," Floyd said. "If the police have not already confiscated it."

"Carmen's take," Nikki said, "is that the Catalan police may have resorted to this attack to retaliate against the central government in Madrid for interfering with the referendum in October 2017 when Catalonia wanted to secede from Spain."

Eduardo's brow furrowed. "A repeat of Catalan police ignoring radicals intending to blow up the basilica. Could there be any truth to that?" He took a sip of scotch and his brow relaxed.

"The Catalan police came under fire in 2017," Floyd said, "for not stopping an act of terrorism. There were accusations of conspiracy at that time."

"Rumors are easily recycled," Eduardo said. "I've heard it mentioned in news reports since we've been here."

"Prominent Catalonian citizens and politicians were arrested and jailed after the central government in Madrid squelched the referendum. Some are still in exile," Floyd said. "So there is a lot of sensitivity."

"And a few news reports claim the large Muslim population living here would benefit from an independent Catalonia. They dream of returning to the glory days of Al Andalus—the Muslim Spain," Eduardo said.

"Even if there is a separatist conspiracy," Nikki said, "it doesn't explain why the man who may have detonated the bombs is also after me."

Floyd opened the envelope he had placed on the coffee table and removed the contents. He spread nine photos over the glass surface of the table.

Nikki studied the photos and looked at Floyd. "Is there one for El Saraway?"

"No. That's our mystery man."

"So who do we have?" she asked.

"Top row, as you can see, are Paula, Mr. Massú, and Hassan. The middle row shows Fadi, plus the two suspects who died in the attack with Hassan. One is the guy who was riding with him, and the other was the sniper from the east park. These additional two guys were from the first car, the car that ran over the policeman," Floyd said, pointing to the images in the third row. "Then the last one is Cristóbal Arenas, the Colombian."

"What about Jamila, Fadi's mother?" Eduardo asked. "And wasn't there a suspect they took to the hospital?"

"Jamila is not a suspect at this point. The two who drove the first car were taken alive, but Javier said both died on Sunday from their wounds."

"Let's talk motive," Nikki said. "Like who wants to harm me and blow up the basilica?"

Eduardo picked up the photo of Cristóbal Arenas. "He could want you dead for what you did to disrupt his and Manuel del Campo's illegal drug exports out of Colombia. He could have provided the explosives."

"But the coincidence for both jobs is too great," Floyd said.

Nikki thought back to the day they arrived in Barcelona. Neither she nor Eduardo knew Paula was getting married, nor that they would attend Paula's wedding. No one could have connected Nikki to Paula's wedding.

Floyd looked pensive. He studied the sheets he'd printed off with the likeness of each suspect. "Paula is the link between you and the bombing," Floyd said.

Nikki felt her stomach sink.

"Even if I accept Paula as a willing martyr in the terrorist plot, does she have a connection to Arenas?" she asked.

"The other connection is El Saraway," Eduardo said. "El Saraway knows the Massú family and Paula too."

"Could El Saraway be the connection to Arenas?" Nikki asked.

Eduardo shook his head and inquired if Floyd knew anything about Massú's background, and Floyd provided the information Javier had given him—Massú had been a nobody.

"How did Massú make his money?" Eduardo asked.

"Plastics and polymers," Floyd said.

"Plastics? Like in a C-4 bomb?"

"It's possible, but for now let's assume not," Floyd said. "Massú's venture started in the mid-1990s, after he met El Saraway. It became a money maker by 2000. He'd been a clerk in a hardware store. Not a job likely to finance a new business. My question is whether El Saraway provided the money. Does Massú owe El Saraway?"

"At the expense of killing his wife and son?" Eduardo asked.

"Lots of questions," Nikki said. "And no answers."

CHAPTER THIRTY-THREE

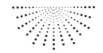

BARCELONA—MAJESTIC HOTEL

"Can you tell me when Mr. El Saraway will return?" Rafael asked the young man behind the concierge desk.

"I am not his secretary. He's a guest at the hotel and does not inform us of his comings and goings."

"I'd like to leave him a message," Rafael said. He ignored the mobile phone vibrating in his pocket.

"He is no longer staying with us," the older concierge said as he approached the desk.

"When did he check out?" Rafael asked, showing his badge to the two men.

"He never checks out, merely leaves on business trips. Keeps his suite year-round."

Rafael thanked them and walked outside. He continued down the gently sloping street until he found a coffee shop offering baked goods. Finding a seat and settling down with coffee and a chocolate-filled croissant, he pulled his phone out to listen to Alberto's short message asking him to call.

"What's up?"

Alberto had interviewed the owner of the flower shop, just as Rafael had requested. "Turns out," he said, "a young woman whose name is Ussam owns it."

Rafael interrupted him. "Do you notice anything unusual about the name?"

"Ussam?" Alberto asked over the phone. "It's a boy's name. This woman's name is Sonia. She told me Ussam is her surname." He continued explaining the woman had been very cooperative and had only good things to say about Hassan. She had expressed shock and disbelief he was capable of such a horrific act.

"That's not what I'm pointing out about the name."

"Ussam?" Alberto asked, sounding confused.

"It's Massú spelled backward." Rafael took a bite of the croissant. Not as good as his wife made, but he took another bite anyway.

Alberto mumbled he had not noticed it.

"Did you ask if any of the other suspects had worked for her?"

Alberto described Sonia's response as a vigorous shake of her head.

"What about Hassan's colleagues? Did they shed any light on his motivation or involvement?"

Alberto confirmed what Rafael was expecting—his coworkers were appalled by Hassan's behavior. Nothing more.

Rafael hung up. He decided to pay Sonia Ussam a visit.

———

Sonia Ussam was closing her flower shop when Rafael arrived. He glanced at his watch and saw it was seven o'clock. He walked up to her and introduced himself.

"I've already spoken to one of your investigators." She pulled the door shut and locked it.

"I have a few more questions."

"Can't you see I'm leaving for the day? I have an appointment."

"This will only take a few minutes," Rafael said. "Unless you prefer to go to the police station."

Sonia opened the door. Rafael followed her inside. He admired the displays in the floral coolers, and then glanced at her.

"How long have you owned this shop?"

"Not quite two years."

"It's in a nice shopping area."

"Thanks, I tried to pick a trendy part of town, to attract moneyed customers."

"Cater to weddings?"

"Every florist does."

Rafael asked her to talk about the shop, specifically what type of businesses purchased flowers. Sonia explained a bit about the usual customers—weddings, funerals, corporate events, and holidays. These included La Diada de Sant Jordi, or feast of Saint George, a celebration of romance and literature. Everyone in Catalonia buys books and roses for their loved ones. He remembered the red roses, wrapped in red and yellow ribbons, the colors of the Catalonian flag, he'd purchased for Lola last April. His mind snapped back to the interrogation.

"You provided the arrangements for Saturday's wedding at Sagrada Família."

"The other detective asked that. I answered him."

"Now you need to respond to me. Did you provide those flowers?"

"Yes."

"Who did you work with—the bride or the groom?"

"On the overall arrangement, with the bride, Paula Azar. We had a meeting to discuss what she wanted. And she paid me."

"Who set up and arranged the flowers?"

"Hassan. He's dead," Sonia said. "He also delivered the flowers. Paula purchased her arrangements here because she knew Hassan."

"What about an African with a heavy black beard? Did he ever come to your shop?"

Sonia looked confused. She stammered that she did not understand his question.

"Do you know a man of African descent with a beard?"

"No. The news media said there's a person of interest fitting that description," she said.

"What about Paula? How did you meet her?"

Sonia hesitated before answering she had met Paula and Fadi for the first time at a function at the Islamic Center. Beyond that, she informed the detective, she had seen her again when she arranged and paid for the flowers.

"Speaking of Fadi Massú, why is it your name is Ussam?"

"It's my surname."

"Are you aware that it's Massú spelled backward?"

Sonia stared at Rafael. He couldn't tell if she was surprised or angry.

She held the keys to the shop in her hand and rattled them in a manner that seemed to Rafael an unconscious nervous response.

"You're a Massú, aren't you?" Rafael asked.

"This is all so unpleasant. Three weddings called to cancel their orders. All since the florist connection to Saturday's attack hit the news. Not that my shop's name has been mentioned, but customers could figure it out for themselves. I'm going to be bankrupted."

Rafael wouldn't let her change the subject. "Your name."

"My family history is something I'd prefer to keep private."

"Did you know Hassan was planning the attack at the basilica?"

"Of course not. He was a soft-spoken man who never expressed anger."

"Did you know he frequently beat his wife?"

Sonia looked at Rafael in stunned silence. When she spoke, she did so with a hint of sarcasm. "Wasn't she a Gypsy or something weird like that?"

"She's a Spanish citizen and a hardworking woman," Rafael answered.

Sonia's eyes narrowed. She bit her lip and attempted to nod, rattling the keys again.

A woman opened the door. Sonia turned and told them she was closed for the day, but the woman didn't budge as she appeared to check out the shop. When asked a second time to leave, she indicated she was there as a newspaper reporter. Rafael moved toward the door and suggested she leave the premises. Sonia locked the door after the woman left.

"Now, tell me what it is about your family history you don't want made public?"

"Fine. You've guessed it. I'm a Massú too. When I was born, Fadi was a year old. My mother registered me under Ussam. To keep my identity secret. My father insisted on it."

"Born to a different mother?"

Sonia nodded. "Fadi was the lucky one to be born to the legitimate wife."

Rafael allowed a pause in hopes she would continue to talk.

"My mother was sent back to Lebanon after my ninth birthday. Fernando Massú paid her off. He had started a business and was making money. With money came social status, and Jamila wanted exclusivity on her husband."

"When did you return to Barcelona?"

"After my mother died five years ago. She knew she was terminally ill. So she contacted my father and demanded he pay for my college education. She threatened to make it difficult with Jamila if he did not cooperate."

"So the threat worked?"

Sonia looked around her shop. Rafael could see the frustration his interrogation caused her. He figured the reporter had unnerved her too.

"It was the way my mother got me back to Spain where it would make it easier for me, a Muslim woman, to attend the university and work after my graduation. Plus I'm a Spanish citizen by birth."

"When did you start your business?"

"After my graduation. It was a gift from that bastard father of mine. Not really a gift, a pay-off to keep me quiet. Gave me cash. A lot of cash and told me to get lost. He did not want either Jamila or Fadi to find out about me. Jamila knew about my mother, but I don't think she ever knew I had been born."

"You used the cash gift to open the shop?"

"Some of it. I bought an existing business. I'm still paying it off." Sonia sighed.

"Could you have paid cash for the business?" he asked.

"I could have. But I did not think that was a good idea. A business should pay for itself."

"So you banked the rest?" he asked. He mentally calculated principal and interest charges a small business like this might make to repay the loan financing the purchase.

"Banks are hardly trustworthy," she responded.

Rafael took a minute to digest Sonia's words. Why not pay the business off when she was apparently sitting on mounds of cash? He figured it had to do with explaining to the tax authorities or other government agencies where the money came from.

"Sounds as if you did not like Fadi or his mother."

"Hated them. Because of them, my father wanted to get rid of me."

"Hated them enough to kill them?"

Sonia looked incensed.

"I'd never kill anyone. No matter how much I hated them. Do you think I would have put stickers with my shop's name on the bottom of the flowerpots if I intended to use them to kill people?"

CHAPTER THIRTY-FOUR

BARCELONA—CARRER DE PROVENÇA

MONDAY EVENING OF THIRD WEEK

Nikki opened the door to Carmen's condo, and her heart raced uncontrollably. She turned to Eduardo and he wrapped his arms around her. Her initial shock expressed itself in sobs muffled by his chest.

"My god," Eduardo said. He blinked at the sight in front of them. "What a mess."

"Why?" she whispered between sobs.

"Someone's trying to get rid of evidence."

"Paula," Nikki said, "Was she implicated?"

"We don't know. But I doubt it would be anything to do with Carmen."

"Carmen will be devastated if Paula was radicalized. All those people killed."

"Don't judge yet. It's hard for me to believe Paula was involved in the attack."

"She loved everything related to the Middle East," Nikki said. "She converted without telling her mother."

"Unless and until proven otherwise, let's assume her conversion was the result of soul-searching, not terrorism," Eduardo said. "Let's not forget that most Muslims are good people."

Nikki wiped her eyes. She slipped out of Eduardo's arms and picked up a broken piece of ceramic flowerpot. The wilted and dried contents lay strewn over the floor and on overturned drawers pulled from a cabinet and a credenza. Plates and glasses had been dumped on the floor, broken testaments of the anger or desperation of the intruder searching for incriminating evidence. She headed to the office, where papers and books had been dumped on the desk and all over the floor. A three-drawer file cabinet had been overturned.

"No computer in sight," she said. "I'll sort through papers while you check the rest of the house."

"I'll find the point of entry," Eduardo said.

Nikki looked at the exit from the office, a door that opened into the common hall a few steps from the building's emergency staircase. It could have been picked without leaving any sign. Eduardo left the room and Nikki picked up books, magazines, and documents from the floor, placing them on the desk. A small, unsealed envelope with Carmen's name handwritten on it caught her attention. The flap was tucked inside. She walked to the living room and joined Eduardo on the balcony.

"The sliding doors were unlocked," he said. They came in through the balcony, bypassing the lobby guard."

"It's not a burglary," Nikki said. "They came for the computer." She held the envelope for Eduardo to see it was unsealed. "Should I open it?"

"Of course," he said.

Nikki glanced at the signature on the handwritten letter and read through it quickly. "It's from Paula, written on the morning of the wedding. In summary, she's sorry for being such a bitch to live with and that Fadi encouraged her to write the note apologizing for her bad moods." Then she read the final part verbatim: *I promise it will be better in the future.*

"You should take it to Carmen. Might console her a little," he said.

Handing the envelope to Eduardo, she walked down the hall to check the bedrooms.

Clothes from the closets had been piled on the beds in both rooms. Contents of every drawer had been tossed on the floor. In Carmen's room, jewelry was scattered on the dresser. Beside the dresser, a jewelry box had been dropped. She examined a couple of pieces without picking them up. To her untrained eyes, the gemstones seemed genuine and the yellow settings appeared to be high-end, fourteen-karat gold.

Eduardo joined her. "I'll take pictures of each room. Why don't you look for specific items you want photographed."

"Start right here with all the jewelry on top of the dresser. Proves it was not a burglary."

Nikki was checking the laundry room when she heard voices, Eduardo's among them. She returned to the living room.

"I'm GEO agent Rafael González," Rafael said, extending his hand to Nikki. He was a stocky man in his early forties. No uniform, but he must have shown Eduardo his badge. "This is special investigator Alberto Mariscal, also with the GEO. We're here to investigate the Sagrada Família bombing. We understand this is where the bride lived."

"It's my aunt's condo. The bride moved in with her mother for a week before the wedding. I think some of her things are already in Fadi's, the groom's, condo."

"When did this happen?" Agent González asked, taking in the mess.

"We found it this way about an hour ago. Carmen, my aunt, asked me today to check on her condo."

"What about the bride's computer, mobile phones, other electronic equipment? Would those items be here or at the groom's?"

"Carmen told me Paula's computer was left on the desk in the office next to the kitchen the day of the wedding. As far as a mobile phone, I have no clue. She may have had it with her at the basilica."

"If any of it was here, it's gone now," Eduardo added.

The detective informed them that Special Investigator Mariscal would take their fingerprints to eliminate them from those they might find. And he'd take their contact data and photos of the condo.

"Not a problem," Eduardo said. "He can set up his fingerprint kit on the dining room table. Then we'll leave so you can get your work done."

Detective González interviewed them, asking about Paula's work with immigrants from various Middle Eastern and African countries.

Nikki gave him the information she knew about her cousin's responsibilities at the Institute for Globalization, Culture, and Mobility at the United Nations."

"And she converted to Islam," Special Investigator Mariscal said.

Nikki nodded.

The interview continued and their fingerprints were taken. Before the detective dismissed them, he suggested that Nikki, now Carmen's closest living relative, stop by the hospital the next day to support her aunt after he interviewed her.

Nikki felt her stomach tighten. It would be so difficult for Carmen not only to face the horrific situation that had taken her daughter's life, but also to be questioned about it. If nothing else, the fact Paula had renounced the religion of her birth and had kept it secret would hurt her mother. Carmen was committed to her Catholicism.

Nikki felt tears forming again.

CHAPTER THIRTY-FIVE

BARCELONA—EIXAMPLE DISTRICT

MONDAY LATE EVENING OF THIRD WEEK

Floyd met Nikki and Eduardo in the lobby bar of the hotel. A musician sat at a grand piano. Yet it was softer than the upstairs bar with its loud beat, a sound to entice a younger crowd, a sound that inevitably became louder as the evening wore on. Floyd had purposely chosen the softer music even if the openness of the lobby bar offered less privacy. He had called the meeting to inform his colleagues about El Saraway leaving the hotel.

When a server approached them, the two men ordered scotch while Nikki asked for a very chilled glass of cava and fresh orange juice on the side. Floyd ordered three plates of tapas to share.

"Left the hotel?" Nikki's voice sounded surprised. "He probably took his falcon out for a hunt."

"Javier's contact from the hotel informed him the man is gone," Floyd said. Javier had investigated where he might have gone, but so far there was no evidence of him leaving through any airport or boarding a train. Nor did it appear he had crossed into an adjacent country.

"Unless he left under an alias or took a boat from an obscure beach," Eduardo offered.

"Could be. Javier indicated that El Saraway owns a house in Ibiza,"

Floyd said. He had more to communicate, but Nikki interrupted him by saying Carmen's condo had been ransacked.

"Looking for something, were they?" Floyd asked.

Eduardo opened the photo app on his phone and showed him the disorder. Floyd whistled. Their server returned with their order of drinks and appetizers.

"We did not find Paula's computer, the main reason we went to the condo," Nikki said, taking a sip of cava. "Even though Carmen said it was on the desk the morning of the wedding."

"Obviously one of the items they were looking for," Floyd said. "But what else could they have been looking for to make such a mess?"

Eduardo helped himself to a bit of grilled swordfish on rustic Barcelona style bread moistened with a mild sauce. He put the tapa down and pulled out the note Paula had written to her mother on the morning of her wedding and handed it to Floyd.

"Not exactly a suicide note, but I don't like the tone of it," Floyd said, handing it back.

Eduardo took a bite of the tapa, his face lighting up. "Nikki, we have to find out how to make this. It's so good."

"While we were at the condo, a detective from the GEO came by. He asked me to join Carmen at the hospital tomorrow after he interviews her," Nikki said. "After he leaves, I'll show the note to Carmen." Then she served herself a swordfish tapa and savored it. "You're right, Eduardo. We must get this recipe."

Eduardo turned to Floyd and mentioned the detective had taken their fingerprints, mostly for elimination purposes, though he knew family members were often considered suspects.

"Except for your prints, the place was probably wiped clean," Floyd said. "On the note, I think it should be given to the detective. Quite honestly, you should have left it in the condo. Changing the subject, Charlotte has found a bit of interesting information I have not passed to Javier yet."

"What is it?"

"In searching through El Saraway's downloaded tablet information, she found emails from Massú to El Saraway." Floyd tasted an appetizer.

"And?" Nikki asked, impatient to hear what had been uncovered.

"The emails urge El Saraway to believe in a US-led conspiracy to weaken and ultimately divide Middle Eastern countries," Floyd said.

Not impressed with the email discovery, Nikki inquired if Charlotte had any news on El Saraway's bitcoin.

Floyd indicated she had not mentioned cryptocurrency.

"Why don't you want to tell Javier about the email finding?" Nikki asked.

"I didn't tell him we downloaded El Saraway's tablet. He'll suspect we've done more without telling him."

"Isn't that the same as withholding Paula's note from the GEO?" she asked.

Floyd gave her a sheepish glance. He noticed a hint of pleasure in Nikki's eyes.

Eduardo wanted to know why the emails were important.

"Massú may not be the benevolent man he tries to portray, that's all," Floyd said. He then informed them Charlotte had been tracking Cristóbal Arenas and found evidence that he may have moved his gun-smuggling operations to one of the Spanish islands.

"Ibiza?" Eduardo asked.

"Spot on," Floyd said.

"Both Arenas and El Saraway in Ibiza? Sounds like Armageddon," Nikki said, shaking her head. "The Egyptian conspiracy and the Barcelona separatists' movement. It's all lies and propaganda. Add in a crazy drug lord from Colombia and I could write a crime thriller."

Floyd steered the conversation back to serious business, sharing his discussion with Javier about Arenas operating out of Ibiza. His Interpol friend had theorized that Arenas and El Saraway could be business partners, or have some other connection, a situation not to be ignored.

Eduardo moved nervously in his chair. "Do you suppose Arenas and El Saraway could be the same person? Especially since the Interpol database contains info on Arenas but not on El Saraway."

"Unless El Saraway is a suspected criminal, part of an ongoing investigation, a fugitive, or a person of interest in international criminal activity, there's no reason for El Saraway to be flagged on Interpol," Nikki said.

"Dual identities are possible," Floyd said. "But in this case, I think one is an Egyptian and the other one is Colombian. Not the same man."

"What's next?" Nikki asked.

They discussed giving Javier the information they had downloaded from El Saraway's tablet in case Interpol considered it worth disseminating. But first they needed to confirm whether El Saraway had left the hotel. The hidden camera had shown the man leaving with the falcon on his shoulder, but that alone did not confirm he had left. Only going in again would verify if the man was gone.

"Do you still have the passkeys to the penthouse?" Eduardo asked.

Floyd responded affirmatively. And he dialed his colleague's phone to make sure Javier could deactivate the security cameras on the seventeenth floor. "Let's get ready. He said give him fifteen minutes to contact his guy in the hotel. He'll call back to confirm." Floyd removed the keycards from his pocket.

CHAPTER THIRTY-SIX

BARCELONA—EIXAMPLE DISTRICT

Tuesday Morning

Olani glanced at Selena as they stepped off the metro at the Carrer de Provença station. She admired her Roma friend. *Not only has she taken me into her fold, she has also walked every step with me to find justice. When I set out, I had no idea what to do other than depend on Rafa. Instead Selena has shown me a world where I can depend on myself*, Olani thought.

Olani was still thinking about Selena's friendship when a musty odor caught her attention. The stench grew overpowering. Olani suppressed the urge to throw up. Both women quickened their pace toward the stairs.

"It gives me chills to come here again. It was so scary last Saturday. The explosion, the people, seeing Taiwo in the crowd. Worst of all was letting him get away."

"It's not your fault, Morocco."

But Olani did blame herself. If she'd acted sooner, the police would have arrested Taiwo. They were here to find that monster by posing as beggars. She mentally reviewed Selena's instructions about covering her face with the shawl and using the fan to signal her if she saw him.

"Let's make ourselves somewhat invisible as we beg. Can't attract too much attention. Police are sure to be in the area."

"Invisible?" Olani asked. "With that guitar?"

"I need to add music so I can earn money for you, Morocco."

"Begging is giving me a pretty good living." Olani smiled. "I may want to make a career of it."

"I thought you were going to look for a job teaching school?" Selena asked.

"That's what I'm trained for, but begging is easy money."

"You're joking, right?"

Olani took a second to respond. "Maybe."

Selena knew the perils of panhandling, besides the fact that begging only works in good weather and during the tourist season. "Look," she said as they stepped onto the street level, "tourists have abandoned Sagrada Família. The minute they smell trouble, they run away like scared cats."

"So why should we be here?" Olani asked.

"Remember, Rafa said murderers always return to the scene of their crimes."

Other than a few mossos d'esquadra policing the area cordoned off with police tape, the basilica was deserted. Gone were the swarms of tourists. Absent were the aggressive vendors who vied for space on the sidewalk of Gaudí Park. They, like the tourists they depended on, had decided on better places to spend time. Gone too were the guides holding up signs or umbrellas.

"We'll catch Taiwo if he comes back," Olani said, "but he'd better hurry. Nothing is stopping me from meeting my mother at the airport next week."

Selena smiled. "I can hardly wait to see your baby. I'll sing lullabies to your little gadji. If you stay in Spain, I'll teach her how to sing."

Olani missed her daughter terribly. And she feared Dayo would not remember her. But she reminded herself she had to get justice.

Selena handed Olani a bag containing her lunch and a bottle of water, and told her where to stand while she set up across the street.

Olani watched her friend cross the pavement to the opposite corner. Strands of curly hair had fallen over Selena's forehead. When Selena flipped them back with a sensuous toss of her head, Olani wondered why such a woman had taken her in. *There are good people everywhere*, Olani thought, *and Selena is one of them.*

After a quiet morning, Selena put the guitar on her back and rejoined Olani.

"How much did you make?" Selena asked.

"Eight euros," Olani said. "I take back what I said about easy money."

The women walked to a bench in the park and sat down to eat lunch.

"We're not having much luck finding Taiwo here," Selena said as she unwrapped her sandwich. "Can you think of a more promising place?"

"What about a mosque?" Olani asked.

"Good idea. But which one? There are about three hundred places to choose from."

Olani's eyes widened. "I haven't seen a single mosque since I've been here."

"Right. I'm talking about locations for worship, called model oratories or something like that. Places where people meet to pray, but they are not formal mosques. At least not buildings with minarets."

"What about calling your friend Rosa. Maybe she knows where her husband went to pray while he was alive. It could be a place to start looking for that bastard murderer."

"That's a great idea, Morocco. Instead of begging for a living or teaching school, you should ask Rafa about becoming a detective."

"If you think I'm so good, then why don't you call Rosa?"

CHAPTER THIRTY-SEVEN

BARCELONA HOSPITAL

TUESDAY MORNING

Rafael was surprised to find Fernando Massú next to Carmen's hospital bed, speaking in an aggressive tone. Sensing the tension between them, he paused in the hall just outside the doorway without announcing his presence. He overheard Massú say that Paula was the guilty one.

Carmen was crying and though she responded, Rafael could not make out her words.

"Paula converted to Islam, you know," Massú continued. "And she had radical friends, like the florist. Don't tell me she was not part of this attack. She associated with the wrong people."

Rafael continued listening as Carmen defended her daughter.

"I saw Jamila standing by herself near the altar," Carmen said with anguished words. "So, tell me, where were you? Absent for your own son's wedding? One might think you set off the explosion. Don't come here accusing my daughter when you well could be the guilty one."

A nurse walked past Rafael into the room.

"You rang for me, Senyora. What can I do for you?"

Massú greeted the nurse. "We are having a little family discussion." His tone of voice was considerably warmer.

"The senyora seems upset."

"Of course she is. Her daughter passed away recently," Massú said.

Seeing movement in the hallway, Rafael caught sight of Nikki darting around an aide pushing a medicine cart. She weaved between visitors and hospital personnel until she reached Carmen's room.

Rafael stopped her, gesturing silence with a finger to his lips.

"Senyora, you need to remain calm," the nurse said, studying the monitoring equipment. Turning to look at Massú, she resumed. "Her doctors do not want her agitated. I'll be back with medication for her, but you should leave right now."

Massú left the room, looking surprised to see Rafael and Nikki.

The detective followed Massú a short distance down the corridor. Nikki remained in the hall outside Carmen's room.

"Mr. Massú," Rafael said, "any information or evidence you have on the bombing, you need to turn it over to the police, not lash out at an injured woman in the hospital. So tell me right now what you know."

Massú shook his head. "I don't know anything. Only trying to find out if Paula had anything to do with the attack."

"What makes you suspicious?"

"That she converted. That she was friendly with the florist. I've wondered if she was radicalized by the people she worked with."

"What about your son? Could he have radicalized her?"

"Fadi? No, he was too much a businessman. And too Spanish to become a jihadist. Plus he was a secular Muslim. He did not care if she converted. It was Paula's decision."

"Are you aware that withholding evidence is obstruction of justice?"

Massú again denied having knowledge of anything. He turned to leave, but Rafael told him he was not through with him.

"What about your daughter?" Rafael asked.

"Daughter? I don't have a daughter."

"Sonia Ussam is not your daughter?" the detective asked.

"Where did you get that information?"

"Does not matter where. Do not deny it. She's your daughter, isn't she?"

Massú moved his head as if to nod but seemed to reconsider. Instead he spoke. "Her mother claimed I was her father. But one never knows for certain until DNA tests are run, right?"

"The flowers with the imbedded explosives came from her flower shop." Rafael said.

Fernando Massú's jaw tightened. He stared at the detective and nodded curtly.

"So who planted the C-4 in the vases?" Rafael asked.

Massú's eyes hardened. "I don't know."

"The money you gave her. That was a large sum. Why so much?"

Massú seemed to consider thoughtfully before responding that he had given her cash for her graduation.

"Was it advance payment for blowing the parishioner church up?"

"What do you think I am?" Massú's jaw tightened to the point it caused a spasm in his left eyelid. "Killing my own son? My wife?"

Rafael knew Massú was a liar. After all, he had claimed El Saraway had driven him home from Sagrada Família. When the investigators checked the CCTV around the basilica, it showed Massú drove himself home. When the detective asked for an explanation, Massú blinked.

"That was a terrible day for me. I lost my family. I don't remember what happened. Everything was so confusing. I thought he'd taken me home. Maybe he just showed up at my house to check on me."

"But guess who does appear in the CCTV footage?"

Massú stared blankly at his interrogator.

"Sonia. Sonia Ussam is standing at the edge of the park," Rafael said. "She was there before the bombs went off. Then she left. Explain that to me."

Massú stared at the floor.

Rafael demanded an answer.

"I can't say. I don't know why she would be there. Ask her."

"You were not at your son's wedding, but Sonia was outside. Rafael reminded Massú one more time that willful interference in the process of justice is a criminal offense that he could be arrested for.

"Yes, yes, I am aware of this. I assure you, I don't know anything regarding the bombing. Or why Sonia was there. But if I learn something, I'll call you," Massú said. "I'm traumatized. That's all. Traumatized."

Rafael noticed Massú was visibly upset and his hands were trembling. He tried to assess whether Massú was deliberately stalling, hiding incriminating evidence, or shell-shocked and unable to act rationally.

"I will give you twenty-four hours to come clean," the detective said. "On what you know or what you think you know."

"I cannot confess to crimes I did not commit," Massú said.

"Then stay away from Senyora Azar," Rafael warned.

By the time Rafael returned to Carmen's room, Nikki was at her aunt's bedside holding Carmen's hand. He figured she had eavesdropped, but that did not matter to the detective.

CHAPTER THIRTY-EIGHT

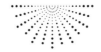

BARCELONA—EL RAVAL DISTRICT

Taiwo had gone for breakfast at one of the halal restaurants in the neighborhood. He returned to the mosque to perform the noon salah. If he were out on the street, he would have dismissed the prayer. Instead he walked to the prayer room and took a rug out and spread it in front of the mihrab.

Taiwo felt good. He completed the second prostration and adjusted his left leg to sit on it. Facing the mihrab, he positioned his legs and feet. A gentle rustle from behind him forced him to turn slightly. It was the imam entering from his living quarters. The cleric waited quietly as Taiwo completed his prayers. When he finished, Taiwo rolled up the prayer mat and turned to look at the imam.

"I see you nicked yourself again as you shaved this morning," the imam said, laughing. "Without a beard, no one can identify you as the man of interest. Though the Prophet would not approve of your hairless face, it might keep you from getting arrested."

The religious man laughed with a zeal that amused Taiwo. Nodding and laughing along with him released a bit of the stress Taiwo himself was feeling.

"The beard is part of the fitrah, the natural order," the imam said as he stroked his own beard. "Allah would want you to grow it back. You should honor the Prophet. Will you grow your beard back when the police catch the bearded one?"

The imam's wife rushed into the room. "You must come see this. The news just showed a picture of a man wearing a baseball cap. Fuzzy picture. But it looked like you. Maybe you should not wear your cap out on the street."

The woman's comment burned through Taiwo's gut like a red-hot iron rod. Even though he realized it was a warning, it also confirmed that the imam and his wife knew Taiwo was involved in the bombing. The Nigerian had learned never to trust anyone. He felt the same burning gut when he thought about his mother and his twin brother. If he hadn't been able to rely on them, why should he confide in people he hardly knew? Even a religious man and his wife.

Taiwo did not want to stay to watch television. Instead, he would check his phone for the latest news. He waved his hand in a carefree gesture at the invitation to watch the newscast. "Caucasians think all Africans look alike," he remarked, showing no emotion.

Needing a place to stay until he completed the job, which would bring in a respectable amount of money, he politely took leave of the cleric and his wife and returned to his small room, closing the door. Lifting the bedcovers, he reached under the mattress to retrieve the Nagant revolver he had hidden there the night he had arrived. First, he checked the barrel and chamber. He snapped the suppressor into position. Next, he held it as if to shoot and placed his finger on the trigger. He opened the box of bullets and inserted four. Satisfied with its working condition, he tucked the gun into his pants at the waistline on his back. He retrieved his duffle bag from under the bed and took out a windbreaker. Before putting it on, he pulled his shirt out of his pants to provide another layer covering the gun.

The imam and his wife had been helpful, so he engaged in small talk before he left the mosque to hit the streets again. He had changed his appearance, so he could buy a bit of time. The police were not yet closing in on him, but he knew he was on borrowed time in Spain. He could return to Nigeria, but not before completing one more job in Barcelona. Once he returned to his own country, he would be safe. Extradition requests made to Nigeria from other countries were often ignored or took years to process. Afraid to use Kenny's passport for fear Olani may have reported it, he would use the forged passport.

As Taiwo approached the corner where the alley leading from the mosque dead-ended into Carrer de San Gil, he noticed a Gypsy woman strumming a guitar. And she was singing. A mournful piece. Taiwo tuned in the noise of the traffic to drown out her raspy voice. He crossed the street and headed for the Sant Antoni metro station. On this route, he had noticed a convenience store and now walked toward it. A second Gypsy woman, her head and face covered by a shawl, stood near the shop. Even her eyes were hidden behind sunglasses. She was vigorously fanning herself. He paid no attention when the woman turned and slipped away in the opposite direction.

This street is full of gypsies today, Taiwo thought as he entered the shop. *Spain is full of gypsies.*

An assortment of hats and caps were displayed on several shelves against the far wall. He went straight over, noticing most were touristy. He tried on a couple of straw hats with narrow brims, cocking his head from one side to the other to catch his reflection in the glass doors of the commercial refrigerator. Deciding they made him stand out too much, he returned them to the shelf.

Instead he selected a black aero-bill golf cap. It contrasted with the light tan one he had worn the day of the attack, now being broadcast in the news media. The attendant, who was watching a movie or video on his smart phone, barely looked up, took Taiwo's money, and handed him a plastic bag containing his purchase. Taiwo went to the bathroom, removed the sales tag, and put the cap on. Dropping his old one in the bag, he knotted it closed.

Once outside, he turned right and walked toward the metro, dropping the bag with his old cap in a trash can. When he entered the station, he thought how easy his task would be if only the targets would use the metro. He could push them into the path of an oncoming train. He had sought that opportunity when he was traveling on the same train to Burgos, but it never presented itself. And his attempts by the museum and the cliff overlooking Burgos had also failed. But today would be different.

Taking a seat on the train, he brought up the internet on his phone to search for the latest news on the basilica bombing.

The cleric's wife is right. It's not a very clear photo, he thought with a flicker of relief. *Today I must finish my work in this city.* He pursed his lips, suppressing a smile at the thought of the money this job would bring him.

The train slowed as it approached the Avinguda Diagonal station.

Taiwo scrambled onto the platform with a feeling of exhilaration. Today was his day. His heart palpitated in anticipation of the challenge he faced. He trotted up the steps to street level, his rapid footsteps echoing his pulse. A rush of adrenaline brought on the feeling a transcendent moment was about to happen. He passed other pedestrians in the stairwell, almost knocking two old ladies over, too excited to notice.

At the street level, he continued to walk for two blocks on Passeig de Gràcia. When he arrived at the cross street of Carrer de València, he found a bench on the median where he could look straight across the median to the hotel on the corner.

Today must be the day, he thought. *If only they come out, I will find an opportunity.*

CHAPTER THIRTY-NINE

BARCELONA—EIXAMPLE DISTRICT

TUESDAY AFTERNOON

Olani and Selena covered their heads with shawls and followed Taiwo onto the train, boarding the car behind his, Selena's guitar strapped across her back. They watched each stop through the window. When Taiwo got off at Avinguda Diagonal station, they mirrored his steps, keeping a safe distance.

Three days after the attack on Sagrada Família, people were out in swarms on Passeig de Gràcia. The streets had been devoid of pedestrians the first two days following the bombing, but the city was proving life goes on. Even after atrocities. Men in suits and women in business attire scurried toward meetings or returned to their offices after lunch. Mothers with toddlers meandered on the sidewalks admiring displays in the shop windows or followed as their children chased birds, oblivious to the tragedy. One mother showed her kids how to feed the pigeons.

When Olani and Selena saw Taiwo take a seat at a bench in the median, they ducked behind a building on the corner. From the edge of the building, Olani peered out to make sure Taiwo still sat on the bench in the median of Passeig de Gràcia.

"We should call the police," Olani whispered to Selena despite the distance between the two women and the object of their surveillance.

"They are still seeking an African with a beard, but he shaved it off. We need to tell them."

"Here, take this, Morocco." Selena handed the guitar to Olani. "Let's follow him a bit longer. That way we can see what he's planning next."

Olani looked surprised. "Sorry, I can't play," she said, holding the instrument away from her body.

"Just hold it for me. I want to take advantage of all these people to get a few euros. Be prepared to follow me, or if he comes this way, I'll signal for you to walk away." Selena reached into a deep pocket in her skirt and removed a tarot deck and a small bowl. "And stay out of sight." She kept the bowl in her hand but returned the cards to one of the many pockets of her skirt.

As Olani leaned against the wall of the building, she felt the warmth the stone wall had collected from the early afternoon sun. The comfort of the pleasant weather as she observed mothers playing with their children lulled her into daydreaming about her own daughter. She imagined holding Dayo, caressing her chubby face.

Selena approached a group of mothers. The women monitored their children, mindful of activity on the street, as the toddlers scrambled around the birds, tossing breadcrumbs and seeds. Pigeons and sparrows took flight as the children jockeyed for position. Turning their attention to the beggar, a couple of mothers scrutinized the immediate surroundings. All but one pulled money from their purses, handing the change or one-euro bills to their preschoolers, who lined up to drop the money in Selena's begging bowl. One boy about five tried to keep the money for himself and started crying when his mother made him cast it into the bowl. For another half an hour, Selena collected money.

When Olani witnessed a mosso d'esquadra park his motorcycle half a block away, she saw her friend immediately put the bowl, money and all, into a large pocket in her long skirt. Holding her breath to see if the officer was going to accost Selena for panhandling, Olani exhaled when the man entered a café. She knew Selena could handle the mosso, but it might cost part of her earnings.

Shortly after the mosso entered the coffee shop, Olani saw Taiwo stand up. A chill ran down her spine until she reasoned Taiwo had been oblivious to the police officer and his attention had focused on a different matter. She picked up the guitar she had leaned against the wall and waited to see what he would do. Selena moved closer to Olani.

Taiwo crossed the avenue. Olani observed all the strangers on that side of the street to determine if the Nigerian was about to approach one of them. He did not. She noticed two men who had exited a tall building across the street shortly before Taiwo had moved. They took a few steps toward the intersection and stopped at the corner. As the men paused, Taiwo dawdled. A cab drove into a narrow area between the street and the sidewalk meant for taxis either dropping off or picking up passengers.

"He may be following those two guys."

"Which ones?" Selena asked.

"At the street corner. One is opening a taxi door. Where a woman is getting out. They obviously know her. See them? The second one is looking around but has not spotted Taiwo."

As the three people stood near the intersection, one of the men pointed in the direction of the old port down Passeig de Gràcia.

"Why would Taiwo be interested in them?" Almost as soon as Selena said it, the three crossed the street and started strolling along the wide avenue. Taiwo followed them.

"You said he was up to no good," Olani said. "I'm not sure we should follow him. It could be dangerous. Maybe I should call Rafa?"

"And say what?"

"That we've located the man who set off the bomb."

"Rafa will be angry with us for ignoring his advice. Let's make it worth our while. Keep an eye on our exact location in case we need to call him," Selena said.

Olani and Selena followed Taiwo until the foreigners stopped to read a menu at the door of a restaurant. After a few seconds, the three proceeded to enter the eating establishment. Taiwo walked to the median and placed an order at a food kiosk. After being handed a can of Coca Cola and food wrapped in foil, he sat on a bench under a tree. He kept an eye on the restaurant.

"There's no doubt he's following those people," Selena said. "But why?"

"Who are they?" Olani asked. "They look like tourists."

"Let me get a photo of Taiwo for the police." Selena reached into her skirt to retrieve her mobile phone. "May I borrow your sunglasses?"

"Be careful."

"Don't worry," Selena said as she covered her head with her shawl and put the cheap sunglasses on. "I'll be back with lunch." She crossed to the median and continued walking toward the food kiosk, where she approached from the rear where Taiwo could not see her.

While Selena waited for the order, Olani watched her friend snap clandestine photos of Taiwo's profile.

CHAPTER FORTY

BARCELONA—EIXAMPLE DISTRICT

The dimly lit interior of the restaurant featured an extra-long bar with a marble counter over an elaborately carved wooden base. Panels of mirrors covered the wall behind the bar, and inset lighting projected soft illumination on dry-cured hams dangling from a metal bar embedded in the ceiling for that purpose. Behind the bar, two tall and slender yet muscular men—the younger could have been a matador—prepared drinks for the whole restaurant and took food orders from customers at the bar. Nikki noticed their main role seemed to involve carving thin slices of the cured hams. The younger of the two performed the cutting with almost reverential ceremony.

Chaos with periodic equilibrium seem to reign within the establishment. Soft classical guitar music in the background was drowned out as the noise level rose when patrons sitting at a long table against the side wall reacted with peals of laughter to humorous remarks made by one rather jovial man in their group. After their bursts of hearty laughter, individual chatter would increase until that guy caught the attention of the group once again, and all his friends turned toward him to listen and laugh again.

"I've never seen so many hams in one place," Nikki said during one of the less boisterous moments. She looked overhead at the hanging hams.

"You're seeing double because of the reflection in the mirrors," Eduardo said.

Nikki laughed. "That's true!"

Floyd ordered red wine and a large portion of food to be shared.

The younger bartender set wine glasses and white cloth napkins in front of them. He served Floyd a taste of wine for approval. Floyd held a napkin up against the glass to see the color, swirled the wine, stuck his nose over the rim to smell it. Then he took a sip, taking time to appreciate the finish. Floyd nodded his approval to the young bartender. Matador-man poured for Nikki and Eduardo.

The noisy group behind them erupted in jubilation and applause to an obviously hilarious comment. Nikki swiveled on her tall bar stool to take a look at the commotion.

"That high-spirited man at the table behind you," the bartender said, "the one who makes everyone laugh, he's a famous adventure guide. He loves to tell funny stories of people he takes on his crazy escapades."

The guitar music that had been drowned out periodically by the jovial table behind them suddenly became louder as "Concierto de Aranjuez" reached a fever pitch. Eduardo tapped his foot on the barstool. "One of my favorite tunes," he said.

Nikki smiled. Then she reflected on recent events and her expression changed. "I feel guilty enjoying myself."

"Don't," Eduardo said. "You need to relax."

The young barman moved to the other side of the bar as his middle-aged colleague placed small plates and utensils on the counter. Soon the young man returned with a large platter of ham he had cut. He had filled out the platter with cured cheese, olives, and crackers in an artistic arrangement.

"El mejor jamón ibérico," he said underscoring the quality of the ham as he placed the platter in front of Floyd. "Es jamón cien por ciento de bellota."

"One hundred percent acorn fed. I'm sure it will be outstanding," Eduardo said, pushing the platter toward Nikki.

The younger bartender returned carrying a bowl of sausage and a platter with Spanish tortilla, fresh pimento slices, shrimp, and a breadbasket with a whole baguette.

The tantalizing aroma reminded Nikki of the dinner Carmen had prepared for them, complete with appetizing tapas.

"If this tastes as good as it smells, I'm going to gain a ton," she said.

She served herself a sampling of each item and waited until the men had served themselves before tasting. Her mouth watered in anticipation of the first bite of jamón ibérico.

"It's too early for tapas," Floyd said, "but then we can act like tourists. For lunch, paella is the dish of choice, but you need to try this ibérico de bellota. It's the best anywhere."

"It should be for what they're charging," Nikki said. "It's like a mortgage payment."

Floyd took a bite of the ibérico. His entire countenance changed. "It's so rich and savory," he said with a satisfied smile.

"You look like a happy man. I wish Milena could have joined us," Nikki said, knowing Milena had scheduled a tour of Gaudí's architecture around the city. Besides, she didn't want to interfere with her husband's work.

"Does Milena's tour include Sagrada Família?" Eduardo asked. He savored a bit of shrimp, his expression reflecting pleasure.

"It's off limits since the attack. For obvious reasons." Floyd took a bite of Spanish tortilla and smacked his lips in appreciation. Then he dabbed his mouth with a napkin.

"Figures," Eduardo said after taking a sip of wine. He dipped a slice of baguette in olive oil, piled on a couple of slices of jamón, and topped it off with olives and pimento.

"I need to tell you about my visit to the hospital," Nikki said. She took a sip of wine and continued. "Rafael González, the detective we met last night at Carmen's condo, was already there. More surprising was to find Fernando Massú talking to Carmen. He was implying Paula was involved in the attack."

"If he has evidence, he should present it to the police, not upset Carmen," Floyd said.

"Absolutely," Nikki said. "Rafael told him the same thing. In fact, the detective told Massú he could arrest him for obstruction of justice if he knows something and does not inform the police."

Expressing concern that Massú would upset Carmen that way, Eduardo suggested the man had an ulterior motive. He helped himself to another piece of jamón and placed a slice of tortilla and a couple of olives on his plate.

"The man arrived late for his son's wedding," Nikki said. "It seems more and more suspicious."

"Consequently, he kept himself alive," Eduardo added.

"The detective questioned Massú about his daughter," she said.

"A daughter?" Eduardo asked. "I thought Fadi was an only child. He never spoke of a sister."

Nikki explained she was Fadi's half-sister, but he did not know she was his sister. Massú had kept it a secret.

"Well, well, well. Where does she live?" Floyd asked.

"Right here in Barcelona. Her name is Sonia. She owns a flower shop. The one that provided the flowers in Saturday's bombing."

Floyd stopped eating.

Eduardo put his wine glass down.

"Was she at the wedding?" Floyd asked.

"Not as a guest," Nikki said.

"This could be a game changer," Floyd said, interrupting.

"Get this. Massú gave her cash for her graduation," Nikki said. "She used it to buy the shop."

Eduardo pushed his plate away. It still contained a couple of thin slices of tortilla, pimento, and olives. He used his napkin to dab his mouth.

"What's more, I overheard the detective tell Massú his daughter was caught on CCTV at Sagrada Família the day of the wedding. Apparently at the park across from the entrance to the parish church."

"This is ominous." Floyd said. "How much longer is Carmen going to be in the hospital?"

"She's recovering so well, they might release her as early as tomorrow afternoon, but the doctor will decide in the morning. Most likely, the day after tomorrow."

Eduardo suggested going to the condo to clean it up. Otherwise, it would depress her to find the mess. Plus she was in no shape to do it herself.

"One of her friends arrived at the hospital before I left to join you," Nikki said. "They've organized a whole group who will be cooking for her and checking on her. Even staying with her overnight."

"That's wonderful," Eduardo said. "Otherwise, Nikki, you and I would be pulling double duty taking care of her for a couple of weeks. Or at least I would if you returned to work."

Floyd reminded them they could stay in Spain as long as necessary. They decided to return to the hotel and continue to discuss the salient points of the investigation there. Perhaps figure out what to do next and call Javier to see what news he could report.

Nikki turned to signal matador-man to bring the check.

"My treat," Floyd said as he tried to catch the attention of a bartender. Both barmen were busy serving food and spirits to other customers sitting at the bar. Finally, the young matador look-alike noticed Floyd signaling for the check.

"Let's walk," Nikki suggested, when Floyd started to flag a taxi. "Both Carmen's condo and the hotel are close. Walking always clears my brain."

"Never mind my brain, it's my digestive tract that could benefit from a short walk," Eduardo said as he glanced at his watch. "It's almost seven p.m. With this very late lunch, we won't need dinner."

The three of them walked for a couple hundred feet without talking. As they continued toward their hotel, Floyd broke the silence.

"Nikki, before meeting you for lunch, Charlotte called. She's accessed the blockchain sequence for El Saraway, but has not had time to analyze the transactions. Said she'd email it to you. More importantly, she reported El Saraway has gone silent. His tablet must be in a steel safe or deep cave."

"Or he changed passwords," Nikki said. "That would do it."

"True," Floyd reasoned. "Last night you confirmed he's abandoned fort."

"Certainly the falcon was gone," Eduardo said, "and the safe was empty."

Nikki concluded they must have spooked him. El Saraway must have discovered his suite had been invaded and bugged. She wondered aloud if they had left evidence when she and Eduardo had entered the first time.

Eduardo had removed the hidden camera on their second visit to prevent it from falling into the wrong hands.

"He might know someone was able to remotely access his tablet," Nikki said. "While it's not impossible, it would take very sophisticated equipment and knowledgeable IT guys to discover our hacking in."

"Maybe the falcon tattled on us." Eduardo chuckled at his own joke.

Nikki laughed but Floyd rolled his eyes.

"The other thing Javier told me is that none of the CCTVs show El Saraway at Sagrada Família on the day of the bombing," Floyd said. "Yet Massú told the investigator that El Saraway took him home from the basilica and stayed the night at Massú's house. There's no CCTV in

Massú's neighborhood, so we can neither confirm nor disprove the last portion of Massú's statement."

The three of them stopped at an intersection and crossed as soon as the light turned green.

"Massú is a complicated, contradictory fellow," Nikki said. "Why would he lie about El Saraway?"

"You can also wonder why he verbally abused Carmen at the hospital," Eduardo added.

"Has Massú's house been searched?" Nikki asked.

"Only Fadi's condo. And Carmen's," Floyd said. "They found nothing suspicious at Fadi's. They took his computers and so far, Javier tells me, they have not found any ties to terrorist groups or to the bombing itself. Paula did not leave any electronic equipment at Fadi's place."

The doormen at the Majestic opened the heavy doors. Floyd stepped through and turned to Nikki and Eduardo.

Nikki thanked Floyd for a great dinner.

"We'll clean Carmen's condo and call you if there's anything you should know," Eduardo said.

"When you get back from Carmen's, no matter the time, come straight to my suite," Floyd said, heading toward the elevators.

Nikki and Eduardo continued their walk to Carmen's condo in the waning warmth of the late afternoon sun.

"This has been a superb evening," Nikki said. "If we did not have the tragedy to deal with, life would be perfect."

CHAPTER FORTY-ONE

BARCELONA—EIXAMPLE DISTRICT

Olani nudged Selena when she saw the three people Taiwo had been tailing leave the restaurant. The two women hid behind an old newspaper kiosk. They watched the three foreigners cross the intersection and continue walking on the crowded Passeig de Gràcia. When Olani saw Taiwo start to follow them, she quickly stepped closer to the kiosk and covered her head, making sure the shawl covered the lower part of her face too.

"It's time to send Rafa the pictures," Olani said, whispering to her friend through the fabric of the shawl.

"Good idea."

Selena opened the photo app on her phone, selected three photos, picked the text message icon, and keyed in Rafa's phone. She quickly wrote a message and pressed the send button. Seconds later her muted phone lit up with an incoming call. Though she answered, she did so in a whisper.

Olani watched her friend. Selena listened for a few seconds and responded, giving their location at Passeig de Gràcia at the corner with Carrer d'Aragó, and confirming the pictures she had sent. "It's Taiwo," she said. "He's shaven his beard."

Olani's stomach gnawed at her. Fear made her heart rhythm speed up.

She did not want to lose Taiwo this time, so she took a few steps away from the kiosk and focused on him as he walked up the boulevard following the foreigners. She was still close enough to hear Selena's phone conversation.

"He's following three people. All four of them are heading toward Diagonal," Selena said, pausing to listen to Rafa and then describing the three individuals Taiwo was tailing. She hesitated a few minutes, then responded. "That's fine, Rafa. Yes, yes, Olani is fine. She's with me. I'll take care of her."

As Selena completed her conversation, she turned to Olani.

"Rafa wants us to stop what we're doing immediately."

"Of course. We knew he would say that. But I'm not losing Taiwo this time. Let's go."

The two women turned the corner onto Passeig de Gràcia and tailed Taiwo. They held back as the three people reached the Majestic Hotel. The couple returned to the street and Taiwo started following them again.

Olani and Selena watched as the two subjects of Taiwo's interest turned right onto Carrer de Provença. Olani noticed Taiwo reach behind him and grab something from his waistband before following them around the corner.

"A gun! He's pulled a gun, Selena."

"You stay here. Understand? Don't let him see you," Selena said. The last words were uttered in haste as she hustled away.

Zipping after her friend despite the warning, Olani felt the guitar on her back swing around and bounce over her arm. With one hand she pulled the cord to keep the musical instrument from swinging too much. She saw her friend reach into her pocket to retrieve an object. *Does Selena carry a gun of her own? Or could it be a knife?* Olani thought, her stomach sinking. When Selena turned the corner after Taiwo, Olani ran to the intersection to make sure she could watch her friend and protect her if necessary.

Olani dialed Rafa. Out of breath, more from fear than exertion, she told him Selena was on Carrer de Provença and needed help.

When Olani stepped onto Provença, she muffled a scream. Her friend appeared to be accosting Taiwo. Selena brandished her hands in Taiwo's face. The artifact she had withdrawn from her pocket was still in her hands. Tarot cards. Olani suddenly recognized the cards used in fortune telling.

Selena was flashing them in the man's face, taunting him. He turned and grabbed her by an arm. That's when Olani saw him point the gun at Selena's head. Taiwo pushed her up against the wall of the building and used the weapon to hit Selena over the head. She crumpled to the ground.

Olani did not suppress her scream this time. Anguish tore at her and she covered her mouth with her hand. Overcome by fear, she thrust herself against the wall, the guitar hitting first. She held her breath. She tried to think how to run to Selena to find out if she was seriously hurt or not. But her body would not move. Her thoughts were in a tailspin.

Nor did she hear or notice a patrol car as it turned its siren on and flashed its lights.

But she watched Taiwo retreating from the fortune-telling woman. He was running away from the patrol car Olani now noticed. He was running straight toward her. She felt faint. She prepared for his attack. With her hand over her mouth, she held her breath as she pressed against the building. Fear overtook her and she slid into a sitting position, the guitar bumping down the wall. Taiwo sprinted by swiftly. After he had passed, she realized he would not have seen her if he had knocked her into the gutter. Sirens and flashing lights filled the street.

A second patrol car stopped. Two policemen exited with guns drawn. Both of them raced after the man. As the officers sped on foot after Taiwo, Olani hustled to her friend's side. Selena lay flat on the sidewalk. Pedestrians had moved toward safety except for two people Olani saw walk up when she knelt next to her friend stretched out on the concrete.

"I'm a medical doctor. I can help," the man said as he crouched next to Olani. To check for a pulse, he felt the side of Selena's neck. He glanced at Olani. "She's unconscious, but she's alive."

The doctor tapped the victim's shoulder vigorously and asked his companion to lift the victim's legs to get blood to her head.

This time the doctor tapped her shoulder a little harder, and Selena opened her eyes. Once she regained consciousness, he took his handkerchief and used it to wipe the side of the victim's forehead, where her wound was bleeding.

"What happened?" Selena asked Olani as she focused on the man whose face was looking down at her.

Another patrol car arrived with lights flashing and parked behind the two already on the street. An officer and a man in plainclothes stepped out.

Olani squirmed in close to her friend to hold her hand. "Taiwo hit you with the grip of his gun."

"Where is he? Are you in danger?" Selena asked.

"Last I saw, the police were running after him." Olani suddenly saw two pairs of shoes plant themselves near Selena's feet. She followed the pant legs up to the waistlines and torsos and on up to the faces peering down at her. She saw a policeman and another man. Olani's facial expression changed from the concern and fear to total surprise.

"Rafa? Where did you come from?" Olani asked.

"Is Selena okay?" Rafael asked.

"I'm fine," Selena responded from her supine position on the concrete. "Glad you found us."

"You're supposed to be taking care of Olani. How can you take care of her if you are passed out on the street?" Olani noticed Rafael looking around, taking in the total scene.

Cards scattered on the sidewalk around Selena made the setting appear part of a ritual. Rafael leaned over and picked one up.

"Tarot cards?" he asked, slipping the card into his pocket. "I asked you to take care of Olani."

"Olani's taking care of me instead," Selena said. She managed to laugh.

Rafael looked at the other two people. His face gave away the fact that he recognized the couple. "What are you doing here?"

"We heard a scream and turned around to help," the woman said. "We were on our way to my aunt's condo."

"Running into you is quite a coincidence," the doctor said. "You're like Batman, you're everywhere, man."

"I'm afraid this is not a coincidence," Rafael said in a somber tone. He told them he needed to talk to them as soon as he had made sure the two women had been taken care of. "Get to the condo and stay inside until I come by or call you."

"The woman was unconscious," the doctor said. "She's probably suffered a concussion and needs to be checked at an emergency room."

The detective nodded.

CHAPTER FORTY-TWO

BARCELONA—EIXAMPLE DISTRICT

TUESDAY NIGHT

"Why did he say it's not a coincidence?" Nikki whispered once she and Eduardo were beyond the officers' hearing.

"Probably connected to the break-in at Carmen's or to the bombing," he responded.

"Oh my god," Nikki said. "The man who attacked the woman—could he be the African? Did you notice if he was African?"

"I only caught a glimpse of his back when the woman screamed. He ran off too quickly."

"The woman said he used a gun to hit her friend over the head. What's scarier, if he's the African, he may have been stalking you again."

"Why did he hit her?" Nikki asked. "Why not come after me?"

Eduardo suggested asking the detective when he called them.

"I'd also like to know the connection between the two women and the detective."

"I wondered that myself," Eduardo said. "They're probably undercover agents working with him."

"Dressed as fortune-telling Rom? Really, Eduardo? It doesn't make sense to me."

"Why not?" Eduardo asked. "We wear disguises in our undercover work. Or have you forgotten, my lovely chambermaid?"

"Umm, makes sense," she conceded. "But tarot cards were strewn around on the sidewalk? I think they were real Rom."

"Maybe so," Eduardo said. "If you were undercover as a Rom, I'm sure you'd include tarot cards as part of your disguise."

"She looked vaguely familiar to me."

"Which one?" Eduardo asked.

"The one who was knocked out," Nikki said. She keyed the code into the security panel while Eduardo unlocked the door into the lobby in Carmen's building.

The guard wished them *bona nit*, good night, as they walked to the elevator.

"Something happened on our way to Carmen's condo." Nikki spoke in a feverish pitch as she and Eduardo entered Floyd's suite. "Rafael González, the detective, arrived on the scene and he later came to talk to us."

"The African suspected in the bombing followed us on our way to Carmen's," Eduardo said. "Rafael told us the guy is from Nigeria and he's dangerous."

Nikki saw Milena and apologized for her ranting. In a calmer voice she explained about the incident, including the Rom women who saved them from the Nigerian attacker.

Floyd invited them to take a seat.

Milena excused herself, saying she was glad Nikki and Eduardo were safe, but they needed to talk investigations with Floyd and she would watch TV in the bedroom.

"Get this," Eduardo said, looking at Floyd without slowing down. "Rafael told us the guy killed his own twin brother in Morocco to steal his passport and use it to get into Spain. The man was arrested tonight right after our incident."

"Did Rafael have assets tailing the Nigerian? Is that how he knew the guy was following you?"

"That's what Eduardo thinks," Nikki said in a calmer voice. "The two Rom women must have been disguised GEO agents. Otherwise why would they put themselves in danger?"

"That makes sense," Floyd said. "Wait here. I have something to discuss with you."

Floyd stepped into the hallway connecting the living area to his bedroom and returned with a corkboard. He set it upright on an easy chair across from Nikki and Eduardo. Then he placed a pen and a stack of index cards on the coffee table before taking a seat in the other easy chair.

"You've been busy." Eduardo whistled as he looked at handwritten notes on cardstock and photos thumbtacked onto the corkboard.

"Trying to make sense of what little we know. In no particular order, I've written down additional questions we should consider. I'll communicate any worthwhile ideas to Javier. Let's go through these," Floyd said, pointing to a card in the upper left side. He read aloud:

Home invasion at Carmen's house–who stole Paula's computer?

After reading the first card, Floyd glanced at Nikki and asked if she had given Paula's letter to Rafael.

"I didn't even think about it," she said. "We can give it to Javier."

Prefacing discussion of the next two cards by stating they would know a lot more if they only knew the answer to one of these questions, Floyd read the cards aloud.

Why is Massú lying? Why is he accusing Paula?
Does Sonia Ussam have a motive to kill Jadi? Or is she a jihadist?

After talking it over, they concluded they did not have answers, except for Massú trying to frame Paula. Floyd touched a fourth card:

Who hired the African? Arenas? Massú? El Saraway?

Floyd remained quiet for a few seconds.

"Floyd, please continue," Nikki said.

Arenas and El Saraway both have businesses in Ibiza–Partners?
What about Massú and Arenas? Are they partners?

"Speaking of photographs, I'd like to speculate on a couple of thoughts," Floyd said as he made a sweeping motion over all the photos he had tacked onto the board, including the snapshots Eduardo had taken of the photos they discovered in El Saraway's safe. Then Floyd touched two cards, which he also read aloud:

What use did El Saraway have for Nikki's and Eduardo's photo. El Saraway is our mystery man. No data and no photo for him.

"Charlotte sent me the blockchain history on El Saraway," Nikki said. "I've analyzed it and the only suspicious part is possible money laundering, but I've given Charlotte instructions on further work."

"With biometric data on passports and driver licenses," Eduardo said, "how does a man live without driving or traveling?"

"Plastic surgery and avoiding biometric data banks," Nikki said. The she pointed to a card and read it.

Is a terrorist group responsible for bombing? Or stand-alone cell?

"That's a good question," Eduardo said. "As things are shaping up, I'd say this is a stand-alone cell. TV carried a story of two terrorist groups lauding the incident, but not one has claimed responsibility."

Floyd read the last card tacked to the board:

Did police with separatist sympathy allow attack to happen?

"I'm thankful for the pattern I see emerging here," Nikki said.

"What's that?" Eduardo asked.

"Paula is innocent."

Floyd blinked several times as he tended to do when he was thinking. "Sorry, Nikki, but I cannot rule Paula out. Remember her computer was stolen. It must have had incriminating evidence on it. It's too early in the game to rule anyone out."

"What about Fadi?" Eduardo asked.

"What about him?" Nikki asked.

"He seems too squeaky clean. That's never good, in my mind," Floyd said.

CHAPTER FORTY-THREE

BARCELONA—CARRER DE BALMES

Rafael and Alberto entered an interrogation room in the building of the General Directorate of Police on Carrer de Balmes, which also housed the national police offices in Barcelona. Taiwo was handcuffed. He looked up as the two men sat down across from him. His movement was further restricted by his handcuffs being tied to a hook on the side of the steel table, which was embedded in the floor. A very old public defender sat next to him.

Rafael checked the camera for the red indicator light. Recording was on.

"Taiwo Adebayo, we are here to ask you a few questions," Rafael said in a stern voice.

Taiwo stared at the top of the table.

"Who hired you?"

The stare continued.

"Who wanted to blow up Sagrada Família?" Rafael asked.

No answer.

"Did you intend to blow up a Christian church?"

No answer.

"Or were you hired to kill specific people?"

After more than an hour of unanswered questions, Alberto spoke for the first time during the interrogation to inform the suspect the sooner he answered, the sooner he would be out.

"You're going to lock me up no matter what I do." Taiwo's response was worded in good Spanish suffused with his Nigerian accent.

"That might be true, but you're not going to eat a morsel until you talk to us. You had no breakfast. You will have no lunch, no dinner. We get to eat, so we can hold out for days, weeks even, if needed. So who did you work for?" Alberto asked.

The public defender cautioned Alberto not to make threats and he told the suspect not to let the threat intimidate him.

Rafael sensed Taiwo's indignation. "Who did you work for? It will help if you cooperate with us."

"I don't have a name for him," Taiwo said. He looked at his handcuffs with an expression of contempt.

"How did he contact you?" Rafael asked.

"An intermediary met me out on an island."

"Which island?" Rafael asked.

"Ibiza."

"Give us the guy's name." Rafael made the request knowing the suspect was stalling.

"He never told me." Taiwo's brow showed tiny beads of perspiration and repeated the man was merely an intermediary.

"So how did he hire you?" Rafael asked.

The room was silent for a minute before the suspect began.

"I was given a phone number to call. The person said they needed a job done. When I agreed to do it, they gave me another number to call. A week later, the same man approached again. He told me they had a second job for me and gave me an international number to call. Some numbers were local, some were international. Every time I made a call, the person I spoke with gave me a new number to use for the next part of the assignment."

"So where were you when you got the first number to call?" Rafael asked.

"In Nigeria."

"Where in Nigeria?

"A mosque."

"Where is the mosque located?"

"In Èkó."

"Èkó. Do you mean Lagos?" Rafael asked, allowing his annoyance to color his voice. "For the record, I need a confirmation or denial."

"Yes, Lagos."

"And you knew this person?" Rafael asked. "The one who gave you the initial phone number?"

The suspect wiped beads of sweat on his forehead with the back of his hand. He stated Lagos is a big city and he'd never met the person before. The man had approached him inside the mosque the first time and outside a week later."

"You were following a foreign couple last night. Why did you intend to kill them?"

"I did not kill anyone. A Gypsy woman confronted me. Distracted me with those fortune-telling cards. She tried to pick my pocket. That's what that was all about."

"There was no Gypsy at Sagrada Família. Yet you detonated a bomb. You killed people." Rafael's jaw was tight as he spoke. "You would have killed more if you'd had the opportunity to set off the other bombs."

Taiwo glared at Rafael.

"You placed flowerpots where you could maximize damage on the foundations of the church by detonating the bombs in a rolling fashion," Rafael said. "Why were you not able to set the other bombs off?"

"I did not make any pot placements," Taiwo said.

"You need to tell me what the target was at Sagrada Família. The basilica itself or the woman you were following last night?" Rafael asked.

"I did not have a target," Taiwo said. He stretched his head to one side as if he felt pain and needed to relieve it. His shoulders slumped.

"Don't deny you had a target. We have matched your DNA to the DNA found on the phone you used as the detonator. All you need to tell me now is what or who your objective was." Rafael's voice was harsh and commanding.

"It was a job."

"Did you help to place the flower containers inside the church?"

"That was Hassan. And the woman who owns the flower shop. He died on Saturday, but the woman is still alive."

"Did the woman help?" Rafael asked.

"It was her flower shop."

"Hassan's job was to get the flower containers inside the church with the explosives," Rafael said. His voice was unforgiving as he continued the interrogation. "And your job was to set the explosives off and blow up the church?"

"Yes."

"So you admit to setting off the explosion at Sagrada Família this past Saturday?" Rafael asked.

Taiwo cast his eyes down. His shoulders slumped more until he looked as if he had aged a decade during the interrogation.

"My phone was programmed to set off the bombs. Yes."

"Who hired you for that job?"

"I've told you. I don't know who hired me."

"It's best for you if you tell us."

"I think it's a man who owns a falcon."

"A falconer? You met with him?"

"No."

When asked why he would identify a person he'd never met with, Taiwo indicated he'd seen the man twice. First on a cliff overlooking an isolated beach when he was hunting with the falcon and the second time in Ibiza Village as he passed by with the bird on his shoulder.

"Is that why you followed the woman and her husband yesterday? You were carrying out orders to kill them?"

"I was the one being followed. That Gypsy woman tailed me. I saw her in the morning and later that night."

"Answer my question. Why did you follow that couple last night?"

"That man went after me at the church. I wanted to get back at him for not letting me complete my job."

"So why did you follow them on the train to Burgos? That was a week before the bombing."

Taiwo stared and said nothing.

Rafael called for a meeting with the four agents who reported to him. Normally he and Alberto handled the most critical aspects of the terrorist investigation his group was assigned to, but the other three detectives performed specialized research, questioned witnesses, examined CCTV footage, and followed up on loose ends. All members of the team were commandos with cross training in explosives, combat driving, special environments, and more mundane tasks such as lock picking and gathering evidence with search warrants. All five were expert marksmen.

One person on the team was a computer expert. Rafael had hand-selected his team and was very proud of them.

Rafael convened two formal meetings a week—usually on Mondays and Fridays. Additional meetings were held when necessary. This gathering was in a small conference room with TV monitors and access to CCTV files. After the initial greetings and small talk, Rafael asked Teresa, the newest agent assigned to his group, the one who performed most of the online research, to share her findings with her fellow detectives.

"Regarding yesterday's CCTV footage from the Passeig de Gràcia incident," Teresa began, turning on a video. "Of interest here is the suspect we apprehended after yesterday's incident on Carrer de Provença, half a block off Passeig de Gràcia. You can see him walking away from the camera on the main boulevard. He is following the three foreigners. These three people also attended the wedding on Saturday."

"The bride's cousin, Nikki Garcia," one of the agents said.

Rafael nodded.

Teresa used a laser pointer to highlight two men and a woman, also heading away from the camera. Then she moved the laser beam to the suspect and enlarged the part of the video she was emphasizing. "See here, he pulls a gun hidden on his back, tucked into his belt." Teresa brought the video back to normal size. "A bit further away, we also see two Rom women. One of them bolts into action when our suspect turns the corner. She leaves her companion behind."

"That's good work," Alberto said.

"Yes, it is," Rafael said, nodding in approval.

The young agent instructed her audience to turn their attention to the second screen as she ran a video showing a different angle on the boulevard. "Wait. Of more interest to me is a man who also appears to be following them." Teresa directed the laser light on a small black GLC 300 Mercedes coupe.

The investigators in the room watched the car stop. A man stepped out of the Mercedes from the rear seat shortly after the suspect turned the corner onto Carrer de Provença. The man adjusted a felt fedora and passed in front of Casa Milà at the intersection of Passeig de Gràcia and Carrer de Provença.

"Notice how our subject waits for his driver to move back into the stream of traffic before he moves around the corner and leans against the wall to watch our suspect," Teresa said.

"Looks like the tracker following the foreigners was also being tracked, not only by the two women but also by the man in the fedora," Alberto said.

"We never see the man's face," another agent said. "He has checked out the CCTV placement."

"For that matter we have not seen the African's face either," Alberto added. "He wears that golf cap low over his face and he never looks up. He's also verified the camera angles."

"Or he is simply good at keeping his head down and hidden under the cap," Teresa said.

"Do we know for certain that this Nigerian we have in custody is the one who set off the bomb at Sagrada Família?" one of the other agents asked.

"Our Rapid DNA testing team matched the suspect's DNA to that found on the phone dropped on the street right after the bombing. He's also admitted to detonating the bomb," Rafael said.

"Although we never see his face at Sagrada Família or on Passeig de Gràcia, I've compared body images from both locations and they match perfectly," Teresa said. Then she used the laser again. "Now as we return to the video on Passeig de Gràcia, you will see the two Rom women following the suspect. The question is whether the Rom women are ever aware of the man in the fedora."

"When you informed me early this morning of the man following them in the car, I questioned the women," Rafael said. "They were oblivious."

"By the way, do we have those women in protective custody?" an agent asked.

"No, they are in a safe house," Rafael said. "I thought they would be more comfortable. You know how the Rom are."

"Averse to anything to do with law enforcement," Alberto said, nodding in agreement.

Rafael had informed his boss of the connection between himself and Olani and Selena, but the team didn't need to know.

"Let's listen to Teresa," Alberto said to focus the agents on the reason for the meeting.

"Here's another look at the Rom women. We've already seen the one on the right side run after the suspect when he pulls the gun right before he turns the corner," Teresa said as the men watched the suspect disappear around the edge of the building. "She removes something from her pocket, which we will see shortly turn out to be tarot cards."

Teresa stopped momentarily and switched to a third monitor. The agents watched a long view of the street on the video showing the woman waving her hands in the face of the suspect. "When she uses the cards to distract the suspect, he retaliates by knocking her unconscious. Now let's refocus on the man in the fedora. When he sees the suspect knock the Rom down, he takes a couple of steps as if he's going to interfere in the squabble between our suspect and the woman. At least until he sees a patrol car arriving at the incident."

The agents in the room saw the man in the fedora return to the sidewalk and walk away from the patrol car.

"As you can see, the man in the hat removes a phone from his pocket and makes a call as he moves tranquilly toward the boulevard," Teresa said. "I'm not going to take your time, but I can tell you we have traced the car on Avinguda Diagonal, past the University of Barcelona to the Parc de Pedralbes. That's where we lost him for lack of CCTV. We should be able to close in on him in a few days."

"We don't have a few days," Rafael said. "What about the tags on the car?"

"Registered to a foreign woman. We have not found any information on her. Absolutely nothing. The address on the registration is a guest house in Poble Nou. My search found a driver's license in her name showing that same address. We know the guest house is a remodeled factory and caters to businesspeople. Been open for about four years."

"Alberto, you need to check out the guest house, the owners, the guest register. You know the ropes," Rafael said.

"Going back to our CCTV, look what happens here," Teresa said as she stopped the video and froze the frame of a man's face fully visible under his hat.

"Did you run it through the facial recognition app?" Rafael asked.

"Yes, I did. Do you want to venture a guess?" the young agent asked.

The room was silent.

"Not a single hit on that face. I asked myself how that could happen in today's world of infinite digital information. So I printed the photo and hit the streets asking people if they had seen the face. It was fun." Teresa paused. "Actually I only went one place. The Majestic Hotel. In the meeting on Monday morning, Rafael mentioned an aloof character, someone of interest, staying there. The concierge identified him as El Saraway, a hotel guest."

"Good job, Teresa," Rafael said. "Now let's all get back to work."

CHAPTER FORTY-FOUR

BARCELONA—GENERAL
DIRECTORATE OF POLICE

Wednesday Midmorning

With the meeting adjourned by eleven, Rafael asked Alberto to walk with him to his office. Rafael opened the top drawer of his desk and took out a folder.

"Here are two search warrants I got signed this morning. We need to pay a visit to Sonia Ussam's flower shop. After that we'll go to her apartment to see what she might have stashed away there."

Both men walked down the corridor to the elevator, getting out at the basement level and moving through the underground parking garage to Rafael's car.

"Do you think Sonia might be implicated?" Alberto asked as Rafael drove.

"At first I didn't. She was tough, yet a real cool cookie when I interviewed her. I decided it was not necessary to formally question her at the station. But I've changed my mind after interrogating Adebayo."

As Rafael approached the flower shop, he started looking for parking on the street. Unable to locate a spot, he had no choice but to drive into an underground garage used by patrons of the shopping district where the shop was located.

The two men climbed the stairs to the street and walked to the shop.

"Coño," Rafael said. "Damn my ass. It's closed. Let's get to her house."

Not wanting to drive to her apartment, Rafael hailed a cab and both men got in the rear seat. He opened the file to check the address before instructing the driver where to take them. Twenty minutes later Alberto paid the fare as Rafael hurried out of the taxi before it came to a full stop. Alberto followed his boss into the apartment building, flashed his badge at the concierge on duty, and got into the elevator with Rafael.

"You're in a rush."

"I'm concerned she may have fled."

Rafael knocked on the door to Sonia's apartment. After three attempts, Alberto pulled a Bogotá-style rake from his pocket and started picking the lock. He manipulated the rake by employing a scrubbing motion first and then jiggling it to cause the pins within the chambers to rotate to an open position.

"You are the master of break-in operations," Rafael noted as Alberto opened the door.

The men walked into the apartment. When Sonia did not respond to Alberto calling her name loudly three times, they pulled disposable latex gloves from the back pockets of their pants and went to work looking for evidence.

Rafael entered the bedroom. The bed was unmade with the sheets and bedspread on the floor. Several pairs of panties and socks plus two bras were scattered on top of the sheet covering the mattress. When Rafael lifted a pillow near the headboard, he found a clear plastic bag crammed full of lipsticks, two small jars of makeup, eye creams, and a tube of hand lotion. Rafael deduced Sonia had intended to pack it but forgot it in her haste. Rafael walked to the doorway and raised his voice enabling Alberto to hear him.

"Someone was in a hurry to get out of here."

"The kitchen corroborates that fact. Scrambled eggs are in a skillet, cooked but left untouched," Alberto yelled back. He started down the narrow hall toward the bedroom. "Have you found anything of interest to take with us?"

"The closet has clothes on the floor. I kicked them aside and there's a laptop computer there we need to bag and bring with us."

Rafael headed to the chest of drawers. He opened each drawer and searched through it. Remembering Sonia's distaste for banking institutions, he returned to the mattress and removed the fitted sheet. He inspected the three sides that were easily accessible. With his hand, he felt between the mattress and the box springs. Finding nothing, he asked Alberto to help him move the mattress away from the headboard. And there it was—an obvious hole on the fourth side.

Rafael stuck his hand through the slit into the cavity. His fingers touched an item and he nudged it out. It was an envelope. He opened it, removed three sheets of paper, and unfolded them. The first was a letter from Massú. The other two sheets were test results from a genetics laboratory associated with the University of Barcelona.

Rafael saw Massú's and Sonia's names at the top of one of the sheets. Massú's name was also at the top of the last page but instead of Sonia's, it was Fadi's name. When Rafael read the results, he saw they were genetic tests to determine the markers for Parkinson's disease.

"Offhand, I'd say Massú has a paternity issue." Rafael's eyes scanned the letter from Massú to his daughter. "Massú knows Sonia is his daughter, but he also knows Fadi was not his son. Obviously Sonia knows it, too."

"How did you know where to search?" Alberto asked as he waved his hand toward the mattress while Rafael was still reading the test results.

"When I interviewed her at her shop, she made a remark about not trusting banks. She also mentioned stickers she places with the name of her shop on the bottom of the pots."

"If all the bombs had detonated, there would be no evidence of those stickers," Alberto said.

"That's right. Sloppy work. I think we have a new suspect to apprehend," Rafael said, "with a motive—inheriting her father's money." He folded the sheets of paper, placed them in one of the evidence bags, and removed his gloves.

"From the appearance of the apartment, I think our new suspect is running from the consequences of the bombing," Alberto said. "Shall I ask Teresa to put out a national alert to stop and arrest her?"

"You close up here and take the evidence bags," Rafael said. "I'll call Teresa from the street. To issue an order to keep her from leaving the country. And her father, too."

CHAPTER FORTY-FIVE

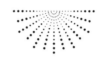

BARCELONA

Nikki and Eduardo arrived at the hospital. Carmen would be discharged by early afternoon and they planned to take her home and spend part of the day with her. Nikki explained to the doctor that one of Carmen's close friends, Ramona, would arrive midafternoon, have dinner with Carmen, and stay the night. Nikki and Eduardo would return the next morning to check on Carmen's recovery. Another one of Carmen's friends would arrive and remain through the day and cook meals.

The doctor informed Nikki he had arranged for a nurse to visit Carmen every day for two weeks to clean and dress her wounds, but overall, he was certain the patient would continue to recover.

"The symptom to watch for is depression," the doctor said. "After all she's been through, she is certain to be on an emotional roller coaster."

"In addition to everything else," Nikki said, "her condo was broken into after the bombing. Last night my husband and I straightened as much up as we could. We need to tell her about the break-in before we take her home."

"Why don't you both go to her room now and tell her. If she becomes upset, I can always keep her another night for observation."

Nikki walked in and saw Carmen sitting up in bed. She leaned over to give her aunt a kiss on the forehead and Carmen held her hand out to grab Nikki's.

"I'm so glad to see you. Thank you for doing so much for me."

"Oh, Tía Carmen, I wish we could help. With everything that's happened, I hate to add more bad news."

Carmen looked at Nikki with apprehension.

Eduardo handed Paula's letter to Carmen.

Carmen sat up straighter in bed. "Paula gave me the letter at breakfast the morning of the wedding. We discussed it. She couldn't express herself so she had to write, but she also mentioned our relationship would improve because she'd promised Fadi she would work on it." She handed the letter back to Eduardo.

"We should give it to the detective," Nikki said.

"I told him about it," Carmen said, "the morning he came to interrogate me. I told him he could have you get it for him."

"When you asked me to pick up Paula's computer at your condo," Nikki said, "we discovered someone had broken in and gone through the entire apartment. I'm so sorry to have to tell you. They made a mess of things."

"Material things can be replaced easily enough. It's Paula and Fadi and his mother, and Carlos, my late husband's only brother. And all those other people who lost their lives. That's what causes me anguish."

Nikki felt tears forming in her eyes. Carmen was right. Material items are the least of one's concerns when faced with tragedies. But above all, Nikki sensed the courage Carmen was marshaling to overcome the sad events of the past week. She also realized for the first time that Carmen would be able to confront the sorrow and move on with her life. Not immediately, but with time. Nikki knew from experience it would never be easy, but the pain would subside into the background.

"And there is another matter I need to bring up to you and Eduardo," Carmen said. "You have started a new life together. Try to retain the good memories of your wedding, of Paula and Fadi, and of Spain. Don't let the terrorists who carried out this atrocious act claim victory. We must win, not them. We must carry forth and live productive lives."

Nikki was crying. She threw her arms around Carmen. Eduardo, also with tears in his eyes, came over and embraced them.

Two hours later, Eduardo pushed the wheelchair off the elevator. Nikki rushed to unlock the door and hold it open as Eduardo rolled the wheelchair into Carmen's condo. The sweet, rich fragrance of jasmine greeted them. The dining and living rooms were covered with containers of fresh flowers, including white jasmine. Every tabletop, every shelf on every cabinet had vases overflowing with blossoms and greenery. And three of Carmen's closest friends rushed over to greet her.

Nikki and Eduardo went into the kitchen to give the women time to shed a tear, hug, and support one another. Soon Carmen was calling her niece and nephew to rejoin the group. Ramona showed Nikki a schedule they had worked out to assist Carmen through her convalescence.

"We'll leave for now, but we're only a phone call away. I'll return for dinner this evening. And we will have a pajama party after that," Ramona said. She patted Carmen's shoulder gently. "Just you and me."

Carmen smiled, yet her eyes showed sadness.

The women left the condo and Eduardo closed the door behind them.

"Can I get you anything?" Nikki asked.

"Yes," Carmen responded. "I need to know about Paula's computer. Did you find it?"

"I'm afraid not. That's probably why the break-in happened," Nikki said.

Carmen covered her eyes with her hands. She started crying.

"I'm sorry, Tía. I wish we had thought of it and come here sooner."

"I'm so concerned Paula was part of this conspiracy," Carmen said. She sobbed as she tried to get the words out.

"What makes you think that?" Eduardo asked.

"Many things. She converted to Islam. Never told me, but I know my daughter. She was attending a mosque every evening. Why she gave up flamenco. I'm sure that's why she arrived late the night I prepared paella."

"Did Fadi attend the mosque with her?" Eduardo asked.

"Fadi was not a practicing Muslim. He may have gone once or twice with her, but not on a regular basis. And something else worries me. Fernando Massú came by the hospital. He practically told me Paula was involved."

"That man has some nerve," Eduardo said. He fought to keep his anger against Massú from showing. "He's the one who arrived at the basilica after the bombing had occurred."

"If Eduardo had not seen the man who detonated the bombs, I would suspect Massú himself had done it," Nikki said.

"Don't believe Massú," Eduardo added. "He might be casting blame on Paula to cover up for himself."

CHAPTER FORTY-SIX

BARCELONA—MAJESTIC HOTEL

Wednesday Early Evening

Nikki and Eduardo were settled on the sofa in Floyd's suite, waiting for Javier to arrive. Nikki disliked the Interpol agent, but she sat there thinking she had to be fair. After all, he had been as forthcoming with information as he could be. In fact, he should not have shared any information with them. But then he had gained intel from their breaking into El Saraway's suite.

Floyd opened the door for Javier. He greeted everyone and turned to Floyd to ask about Milena. Floyd explained Milena was with him, but since she'd never visited Barcelona before, she was taking advantage by going on every city tour she could.

Javier's accent and eye tics intensified Nikki's dislike of his demeanor. His accent sounded artificial to her, part of the reason he seemed so fake.

"I was looking forward to meeting her, but we work now." Javier sat on the easy chair closest to him.

Floyd plopped down heavily on the other chair.

"This meeting is update on bombing. My friend Rafael," Javier paused. "GEO Agent González, apprehended Sonia Ussam and Fernando Massú at airport. We believe they hired African. He's Nigerian. Bad guy. Very bad."

Nikki reached out to touch Eduardo.

"Rafael not sure how many others involved, but he thinks Nigerian, Sonia, and Massú collaborated," Javier said. He added that Rafael got Massú to talk by fabricating a story that Sonia had planned to get rid of her father in a year or so after the Sagrada Família bombing was no longer a top headline. She intended to inherit all the Massú holdings.

"Give us more details," Floyd said.

"Data too preliminary. Cannot disclose," Javier responded.

Nikki asked about Paula in a very hesitant manner. She wanted to know if her cousin and Fadi had participated in the plot. She turned to Eduardo and asked him to give Javier the letter Paula had written to her mother.

Javier read the letter and told them Rafael already knew this information. "But on Paula's innocence, very hard to tell if Paula and Fadi involved. My guess no. Could be paternity issue. Parkinson's tests show Sonia is Massú daughter, but Fadi not his. Sonia has financial motivation to kill Fadi. She one smart woman with Machiavellian spirit."

Javier's words silenced everyone in the room.

Nikki shivered thinking of the lives lost in the bombing. Could it all have been the consequence of one woman's greed?

"What about Nikki's safety?" Eduardo asked. "Someone is trying to hurt her too."

"Maybe both of you," Floyd said, adding to Eduardo's remark. He turned toward Javier. "You know the Nigerian was tailing them yesterday. And could have killed them if it had not been for that Rom fortune teller."

"Were the Rom women undercover agents?" Eduardo asked.

"Cannot say. That woman also responsible for apprehension of bad guy," Javier said. "I think Nikki safe from harm now all of them under arrest." He informed them he had ordered a review of CCTV footage from the front side of the Burgos museum. It showed a bearded man with a baseball cap standing behind Nikki and some children. "He pushed Nikki into bad fall, and walked away."

Nikki turned white. "I thought that was an accident. Even the teacher who kept me from falling into oncoming traffic had the boys apologize to me." She had not been vigilant enough and determined she'd return to her usual watchful self.

Everyone in the room spoke at the same time, each saying how lucky Nikki had been. Javier's eyebrows kept jumping up and down his forehead as he repeated he thought Nikki was safe now that the African had been apprehended.

"I'm so thankful!" Nikki said, standing up. "That means Eduardo and I can visit another Gaudí monument before we leave."

"Not so fast," Eduardo said. "What about El Saraway?"

"Not sure where Egyptian is hiding, but police looking for him," Javier said. "Don't know his involvement. Agents know area of city where he might be hiding. He cannot pull nonsense. He hears news, so he knows others already jailed."

"He will probably run, but until we know for sure, Nikki, we're going to stay right here," Eduardo said with authority. "We need to know who's been trying to kill you."

"I've felt confined to mostly the hotel. A bit in the hospital or Carmen's condo. With things getting settled, I'd like to visit a place called Bellesguard," she said. "We'll be leaving Barcelona soon, so I want to visit this Gaudí site. It's not so grand but comes with plenty of history, like all his buildings."

"Confined to a hotel?" Javier asked. His eyebrows darted upward. He glanced at Floyd. "Isn't that what newlyweds want?"

Floyd grinned. As he turned serious again, he asked Javier if El Saraway's background had been uncovered or if a connection had been established between the Egyptian and Cristóbal Arenas.

"Cannot say," Javier said.

"Bellesguard Tower," Nikki repeated as if no one had heard her, "is waiting for us. We can see nearby Palau Reial de Pedralbes where Gaudí left his style when he remodeled the place. Both are near Tibidabo."

Javier suggested taking a bus or taxi to the top of Tibidabo, adding that it was the prettiest view of Barcelona, where the entire city could be seen, including Passeig de Gràcia.

"Or you can take the funicular to the top," Floyd said.

"Funicular?" Eduardo's voice became animated. "Nikki, let's do it."

"I don't know," she said, remembering her dislike of heights.

"Funicular built on ground, all way up mountain," Javier said. "Takes you to Sagrat Cor de Jesús. In English, Sacred Heart of Jesus. Better known as Temple of Tibidabo."

Nikki turned to glance at Eduardo and then Floyd. Her solemn expression gave way to a faint smile. "I'll decide about the funicular tomorrow. Bellesguard Tower may take all our time."

"Bellesguard good idea to visit," Javier said. "For beauty of location.

For history. Last monarch of House of Barcelona, Martín I the Humane, built palace there in fifteenth century. Palace now in ruins, near house Gaudí built. Plus contains history of bandolero Serrallonga."

"Javier, you're as bad as Nikki on this Gaudí stuff," Floyd said.

"Who is Serrallonga?" Nikki asked.

"Bandit who stole from royal caravans passing through Barcelona and gave goods to peasants and farmers. Joan de Serrallonga very popular with poor people. Was executed in 1634."

"Sounds like Robin Hood," Floyd said.

"Robin Hood at least a century before Serrallonga," Javier said.

"Be careful," Floyd admonished. "I don't like the fact El Saraway is still on the loose."

Eduardo suggested another option for the following morning. After checking on Carmen, they could take Floyd and Milena to visit the Gothic Quarter to show them the Bishop's Bridge. Floyd could find a place for luncheon tapas. He invited Javier to join them.

"Tapas are for eating at night. Paella is tradition for lunch in Barcelona," Javier said as he shook his head and appeared confused by the banter.

"I forgot about the skull and dagger," Nikki said. "If they see it, we need to take Floyd and Milena to the antidote too." She reached for her world tree necklace and held it up for Floyd to see. "This is my cure. It protects me from all evil."

Floyd laughed. "You really are superstitious, Nikki." Then turning serious, he looked at Javier. "What do you think? Will they be safe doing the touristy thing tomorrow?"

"El Saraway probably running scared," Javier said. "I think Nikki okay playing tourist. But always be cautious. I know Rafael ordered police to follow Egyptian in area where he is hiding out."

"That does it. I have Javier's permission, so Bellesguard and Tibidabo, watch out. Here we come!" Nikki said.

"Eduardo, be sure you call me if emergency happen," Javier said. "Also, I invite all of you to good tapa bar tomorrow night after Tibidabo. Floyd, please bring Milena."

CHAPTER FORTY-SEVEN

BARCELONA—SARRIÀ-TIBIDABO DISTRICT

THURSDAY EARLY AFTERNOON OF THIRD WEEK

"I really loved Bellesguard. I'm so glad we went there," Nikki said to Eduardo as she stopped for a look at the rail tracks heading straight up the hill to Tibidabo. "I think I can do the funicular just fine."

She and Eduardo stepped in the line to purchase tickets from a young woman sitting behind a thick bulletproof transaction window, like the ones banks use to protect their tellers from armed robberies.

After purchasing their tickets, they walked up the stairs and boarded the blue and yellow car. Once the car closed its doors, Nikki realized how many children and teenagers had also boarded. Each of them was either laughing or talking loud enough to be heard over the din of voices and the clangor of wheels against the train tracks. The earsplitting noise became more deafening than a rock concert. She hung her purse strap over her neck and shoulder and moved toward the front of the cabin to look out the windows. Eduardo followed her. On each side of the tracks she noticed the vegetation and was surprised to see a diverse assortment of cacti—prickly pear, century plants, and dragon trees.

"Look at the prickly pear out there. And the century plants," Nikki said. She leaned toward Eduardo's ear and spoke loudly so he could hear her over the cacophony.

The funicular slowed down as it approached the small station at the top and then came to a complete stop. When Nikki and Eduardo stepped off and climbed a few steps, they halted to observe their surroundings. They watched as teens ran toward an old-fashioned amusement park, yelling their preferences for the ride they wanted. Parents trying to become oriented to the immediate area held the hands of younger children before they headed for the park. One little boy dressed in a blue outfit fell as he ran. His mother scolded him for getting his clothes dirty as she yanked him up from the ground.

"Poor kid," Eduardo said. "His mother is more interested in keeping him clean than letting him have fun."

Nikki gazed through the arches of a salmon colored building to the left side of the park that offered places to eat, public restrooms, and gift shops. Still taking the landscape in, her eyes settled on the imposing façade of Sagrat Cor de Jesús rising from the top of the mountain like a lion protecting its territory. As she admired the details of the church, Eduardo seemed engaged in catching a last glimpse of the kids heading toward the park entrance.

"Nikki, I know I'm overly cautious, but turn slowly and take a look at the two men leaving the funicular station. What do they look like?"

"A couple of grandfathers trailing behind," she responded as she noticed two stragglers who appeared to be dawdling at the view of the city below.

"Grandfathers? They're not that old. They're about our age. I thought they might be Middle Eastern."

"They seem Latin to me," she said. "Do you think we should be concerned?"

"Not really, but as Javier said, we need to be cautious. That's all."

Nikki reached into the secret compartment of her purse to make certain she had her Taser. Her fingers wrapped around it. "We're safe. And while we're here, I'd like to see the interior of Sagrat Cor. Shall we see if it's open?"

"I doubt you'll like it," Eduardo said as he put his hand on Nikki's shoulder to guide her toward the church.

Nikki shot Eduardo an inquisitive glance.

"You love Gaudí's architecture so much, this won't be as interesting," he said.

"Agreed. Gaudí is extraordinary. Plus the history. But we should still see the church here. People always compare it to Montmartre's Sacré Coeur in Paris."

"When we leave, would you mind walking down to Avinguda Tibidabo?" Eduardo asked. "It's steep but there are beautiful old homes. Carlos Ruiz Zafón mentions the Aldaya mansion in my favorite book by him. It's at 32 Tibidabo."

"That's at the bottom of the hill," Nikki said. "But it'd be a nice walk."

CHAPTER FORTY-EIGHT

BARCELONA—TIBIDABO DISTRICT

<small>THURSDAY EARLY AFTERNOON</small>

"We're following the black Mercedes coupe. It's heading to the top of Tibidabo." Rafael spoke to Alberto over his phone as Pepe, one of the other GEO agents, drove the unmarked car they were riding in. "We're on Avinguda de Vallvidrera, a safe distance from the subject. He's obviously after Ms. Garcia and her husband. You met the couple at Carmen Cardoso Azar's condo. They are supposed to be visiting Tibidabo today."

Rafael looked out the windshield and saw a pink roller-coaster track on the side of the mountain. He continued talking, giving details to Alberto about the guy they were tailing. "The Mercedes has a driver and one passenger. I presume it's El Saraway. But a gray Nissan sedan with two more people is following the Mercedes."

Rafael asked for Alberto's location. He then instructed his subordinate to drive up Carretera de Sant Cugat, the shorter route to the top, and park at the lot near the funicular station. "From your position, you should get there before we do. Walk toward the parking lot behind the church. Try to get there to identify the subject's two vehicle convoy. Follow them if they leave their vehicles."

When his subordinate asked if the Nissan was stalking the Mercedes, Rafael replied that he thought the cars were together, not antagonistic toward each other. He gave Alberto the license plate number of the second car.

Pepe slowed down as they approached the curve near Gran Hotel la Florida so that neither driver would suspect they had a tail.

Rafael made another call, to the police supervisor whose officers were assigned to provide backup. "Be ready to surround the perimeter of Tibidabo Temple and the amusement park. Spread your men out, but don't come in too close yet. I don't want to scare our subject away. Let me remind you we can't let him harm a foreign couple, a man late thirties and a woman, midthirties, he seems to be following."

Rafael asked Pepe to allow El Saraway's motorcade time to park and the passengers to step out. "I want to see what they're planning. My guess is they will go into the church or the museum."

"Or even a restaurant at this time of day," the driver said.

"The hard part for us is to look like tourists," Rafael said.

"We could be hikers. I have my gym clothes in the luggage compartment. You can even wear the clean set. I'll wear yesterday's." Pepe chuckled as he spoke.

"Good idea. Stop and let's change."

"Collserola is a big park. Isn't that why you requested police backup?" Pepe asked as he steered the car into the parking area of the nursing home facility, Llar d'Avis Nostra Senyora de Fátima. Trees delineating the facility's property kept their vehicle hidden from the lot which faced the rear of the Tibidabo Temple complex, the lot where El Saraway and his men had parked.

Pepe got out, popped the luggage compartment, and removed his gym bag.

After changing into shorts and a sweatshirt, Rafael got out of the car. He adjusted the sweatshirt over the gun and the bullet proof vest. He weaved between bushes of sweet-smelling honeysuckle to hide behind the trunk of an Aleppo pine, surrounded by smaller evergreens and a deciduous oak. The air smelled pure. Yet he knew it would not take long before his allergies would awaken, and his sinuses would activate. Preferring to remain hidden, he peered through the branches to monitor the group's activities. Both cars had parked, and he observed the occupants ease out of their vehicles. El Saraway and his driver took the easy route by crossing Avinguda Vallvidrera and headed toward the church while the two in the second car disappeared into the wooded area.

Rafael called the police supervisor again to describe the subject's position.

Pepe left the gym bag on the back seat but pulled his handgun and tucked it into the small of his back. Like Rafael, he let the sweatshirt hang over his shorts to cover the gun and vest. He locked the car and positioned himself a few feet behind his boss.

CHAPTER FORTY-NINE

BARCELONA—TIBIDABO TEMPLE

THURSDAY EARLY AFTERNOON OF THIRD WEEK

Nikki and Eduardo admired the view of the entire complex, first taking in the lower structure called the crypt church even though it was a stand-alone construction. Built from rough-hewn Montjuïc stone to resemble a Romanesque fortress, it had been the initial construction and formed the smaller section of the Sagrat Cor de Jesús complex. They saw the stairs on both sides of the lower church soaring upward, climbing the hill to the upper church whose dome was capped with a Christ figure extending its arms as if to embrace the entire city of Barcelona, stretching out in the valley below.

"Christ's open arms seem to hug everything all the way to the port. Including the Mediterranean," Nikki said.

"Could have been the sculptor's intention," Eduardo said. "He may have also wanted to echo the embrace of the Christ figure on Corcovado Mountain in Rio across the Atlantic."

"They do look pretty similar," Nikki admitted. She turned back toward the city to enjoy the view. "Javier told us yesterday we could see Passeig de Gràcia if we looked closely at the city streets."

First they located the familiar Sagrada Família towers in the distance and spent several minutes trying to find Passeig de Gràcia without success. Nikki's memories of Sagrada Família would always be bittersweet. A breathtaking monument designed by the architect she loved so much, yet it's where Paula had died.

"It's a unique structure," Eduardo said. "Remember what Tía Carmen told us about keeping the good memories."

"Passeig de Gràcia is also where we encountered El Saraway. Not a pleasant memory." She looked both nostalgic and sad as she turned toward the crypt church again. "But I still love Barcelona."

"Doesn't Casa Milà bring you good memories?" Eduardo asked.

Nikki glanced at him. "For sure. I will never forget the feeling of wonder and love when we said our vows on our favorite rooftop in the world."

Filled with emotion, Nikki turned toward the crypt church again to avoid becoming sentimental. She grabbed Eduardo's hand and they walked to the crypt's main doors. From where they stood now, the walls of the lower church obstructed the view of the upper church. Still feeling melancholy, Nikki stopped to study the crypt's ornate entrance with its three semicircular arches. Above the arches, a richly decorated semicircle with inlaid mosaic brought the entire façade into a unified design.

As they entered the crypt, brightly painted frescoes decorated the walls of the apses at the far end of the church. The main nave spread out in front of them with two more on each side. The central nave was the widest and its altar was set apart from the front pews by a gold-plated railing on low supports of white marble. Each nave was separated from its neighbor by large columns made of the same Montjuïc stone of the exterior, only this stone had a smoother finish.

"Nobody's in here," Nikki whispered. "The calm is nice after all those noisy kids."

Nikki walked toward the main altar and leaned against a tall column on the right side of the central nave near the railing. Her head rested against the rock pillar. She studied the fresco painted on the hemispherical vault high above the altar.

Then Nikki heard footsteps. She turned and saw Eduardo moving across the marble floor to join her. In her peripheral vision, a figure flashed across the opposite side of the church to the pillar at the edge of a secondary nave. Her hand went into the secret compartment of her purse. She pulled out her lipstick-case Taser.

"Eduardo, when you moved, I saw someone dash for cover behind that column," she said, pointing. "It reminded me of the nightmare I had a couple of weeks ago. A figure hiding behind pillars. It's creepy. Let's get out of here."

"I don't see anything, but I'll check." He watched for movement as he inched closer to the pillars supporting the secondary nave Nikki had pointed out.

Nikki held her breath and gripped the Taser. Eduardo circled the pillar where she thought she had seen a figure take cover. Yet he found no evidence of anyone hiding. Eduardo searched the nearby altar and several other thick columns. She saw him wave that all was clear, and she walked over to join him. From the altar, she surveyed the entire chapel and walked around the stone pillars Eduardo had already checked.

As she came around the last pillar, Eduardo stopped her and moved close to embrace her. "Your nerves," he said, "are a bit frazzled after the week we've had. Would you prefer to leave?"

"It's okay. We've never been to Tibidabo before and it's legendary. Let's take a look around." She put the Taser away.

For the next twenty minutes, they enjoyed the frescoes and stained-glass windows and eventually stumbled upon the access to the Perpetual Adoration chapel that had been carved directly into the mountain. The obvious reason it was called a crypt church, Nikki reasoned. She saw Eduardo's expression change to joy when he glanced at the chapel floor. When she looked down, the light from the church filtered through the doorway behind them onto brilliantly colored mosaic. She realized they were walking on images assembled from tiny pieces of colored stone.

"Tesserae," Eduardo said.

"Can you imagine cutting and assembling these miniature stones and gems for people to walk on?" she asked.

Eduardo faced her and smiled. "Barcelona is full of surprises, like you."

As they stepped farther into the chapel, the lighting quickly became much dimmer and they lost the details of the mosaic. Nikki looked up and saw the central nave with a narrower one on each side culminating in sparsely illuminated apses at the far end of the chapel. Each nave, as in the church, was divided from its neighbor by heavy columns. Paintings in the vaulted ceiling reflected subdued electric lighting placed along the ribs of the vaulting. Without the artificial light, the architectural space of the windowless chapel would have been as dark as the far side of the moon. From where they stood in the central aisle, an outline of pews could be seen on either side. They walked a few more steps down the aisle.

Eduardo took out his mobile phone and turned on the flashlight. He knelt as he beamed the light to the floor. Nikki took a seat on the edge of a wooden pew. She shifted her torso sideways and placed a hand on the pew in front of her to angle herself into the aisle. She leaned over even more to observe the patterns Eduardo pointed out. She loved listening to his enthusiastic description of the intricate labor involved in creating a tapestry in stone.

"Such beautiful work," she said. "Reminds me of Pompeii. Just different subject matter."

A low rustling sound interrupted them. Eduardo stood up. He turned the flashlight off. Nikki tensed with fear. She felt a choking sensation in her throat. Her hand trembled as she reached inside her purse, searching for the secret compartment.

The shadowy figure of a man appeared from behind a column on the opposite side of the chapel. He slipped back into hiding.

Reaching for Nikki's arm, Eduardo pulled her up next to him to shield her from danger. He guided her into the darker area of the chapel, the wall opposite the pillar sheltering the lurker, an area where they were less likely to be seen. Finally able to grab her Taser, she positioned it to be used if necessary.

Wanting to flee, Nikki realized she needed to stay with Eduardo as they inched their way along the wall toward the doorway they had entered minutes earlier. But before they had made much progress, two more figures slipped through the doorway. She saw them split, one to each side, into the darkness against the chapel walls.

Terrified, Nikki pulled on Eduardo's hand. Together they slithered as best they could toward their only choice for cover, the stone pillars on their side of the chapel.

"We're trapped," Nikki whispered as they huddled together, their backs against the cold stone of a pillar near the altar.

"I'll get Javier." Eduardo let go of Nikki's hand and turned to face the column.

When she saw him hunch his head over his chest to create a cavity between his body and the pillar to conceal the light emanating from his phone, she angled in next to him to help mask the light. *Maybe not the best time to send Javier a message for help*, she thought.

Nikki heard steps approaching them. Her heart was thumping more loudly than the oncoming footsteps. She placed her hand over her chest to settle the palpitations. *Be quiet,* she reprimanded her heart. *Don't alert our stalker of our hiding place.*

Eduardo took Nikki's hand again and slowly they crept around the pillar, pressing against it as if trying to become part of the stone. He stopped abruptly, and she felt his arms spread out to protect her.

"Go this way. Follow me," A man's voice whispered, thick with a foreign accent.

It was dark. She could not see, but she felt Eduardo move. More shuffling noise brought a panicked realization that Eduardo was confronted by more than one stalker. Almost instantly she heard a struggle.

"Get out now," Eduardo's anguished voice told her.

The thud of a crushing blow came next. She reached in front of her to feel for Eduardo, but his body went limp and she knew he had lost consciousness as he crumpled to the floor. A mobile phone slammed onto the floor lighting up the area sufficiently for her to see a huge figure standing before her.

"Leave now," the same accented voice said.

Nikki reacted. She zapped her Taser wildly at the bulk of a man, unsure if her shaking hand had aimed precisely until he fell to the floor near her feet. He made garbled sounds as if trying to scream or articulate words. Nikki had fired the Taser's darts and had continued to use the stun gun backup capability, giving her from five to thirty seconds to get herself and Eduardo to safety, depending on the accuracy of the hits.

The sound of running feet echoed in the chapel. She dropped to the floor next to Eduardo. Searching for a pulse, she detected it at the side of his neck. On the floor, the phone still lit up a small section of the tesserae giving away their exact location. She reached to turn it off, but before she could grab it, strong arms seized her shoulders and dragged her toward the altar. His hold on her was so painful, she let go of the Taser. As the powerful arms continued pulling her, she realized this was not the man she had tased, but another perpetrator.

When her assailant stopped yanking her, he clenched her body against his. She cried out in pain.

"Shut up," a hoarse whisper of a man's voice said.

He shifted her into an awkward sitting position with her head held tightly in place against his torso. She detected dim lights and did not know at first if it was an illusion in her brain caused by the pressure he put on her head, or if the illumination came from within the chapel. She pushed into his chest and twisted her head into a contorted position. Two or three figures with flashlights stood at the entrance to the chapel.

"Don't move," the man's voice said near her ear.

She felt him let go of her head. Almost instantly, the cold steel barrel of a pistol pushed into her temple.

"Police," a voice shouted from the entrance. The words echoed in the chamber. "Drop your weapons."

Total silence reigned.

Nikki's assailant rose, pulling her up with him. She could feel the gun steady at the side of her head. He pressed her body tightly against his own as he moved into a standing position with her in front of him functioning as his shield.

"Drop your weapons and surrender," the voice from the entrance said again.

A shaky but accented voice spoke from the floor. "I have no weapon. Two men are armed. Be careful. They have the woman and could hurt her."

Shots rang out, ricocheting off the stone column where the shaky voice had been heard. Nikki thought she heard shuffling on the floor. Her captor held her tight against him with one arm, and with his free hand, he kept the gun digging painfully into her temple. She focused on breathing.

So who was firing at Eduardo? she wondered. For a split second, her captor moved the gun away from her head and shot at the floor where the shuffling sound had come from. Before she could react, the barrel was jabbing her again.

"Surrender. Drop your weapons. Police are surrounding the entire mountain. You will not escape," a police officer said. His voice, despite echoing, still came from the area near the entrance to the chapel.

Suddenly the whole chamber was brightly lit. Nikki squinted and closed her eyes. When she reopened them, she saw El Saraway on the floor. Her heart beat faster than ever. Eduardo was next to him. The two were partially hidden behind a pillar. Had she tased El Saraway? Eduardo tried to move. She saw El Saraway stretch his arm over Eduardo's torso to hold him down. Eduardo mumbled incoherently.

Nikki trembled. She hoped the police would see she was held at gunpoint. She prayed silently none of them would shoot at the man holding her and hit her instead. She also prayed Eduardo had not been shot.

"It's my turn to give orders," her assailant said. He spoke with a heavy

South American accent. "If any of you move, I will put a bullet through this woman's skull."

A Colombian accent, Nikki thought. But then she was not sure. Her brain was scrambled. Confused. Panicked. Her training had taught her to think under stress, and she willed herself to calm down, to focus on staying alive instead of panicking. Eduardo was semiconscious at best. And that's what scared her the most. The police were not yet in control. It could be up to her to get them out of this mess. She needed a cool head.

"If you want this woman alive, you must leave the church," her assailant said in a very self-assured voice.

This time, Nikki identified the Colombian accent for sure. Automatically her thoughts went back to that country. She had never heard Cristóbal Arenas speak. Her thoughts tumbled forth, spilling over like a hiker falling off a mountain. She tried to grab onto insights, anything to make sense of the situation. If this was Arenas, why did he want her dead? Was it revenge? She knew he had hired a hitman to kill her when she worked the kidnapping case in Mexico. Or maybe his business partner in the illicit drug business, Manuel del Campo, wanted revenge. Nikki considered del Campo; the man was serving a life sentence in a Colombian prison as a result of her investigation in Medellín. Maybe del Campo was the person ordering her assassination. Maybe del Campo was orchestrating her demise from his jail cell.

Groans filtered up from a few feet away, bringing Nikki back to the present moment. She glanced at Eduardo, still lying on the floor next to El Saraway, and realized he was regaining consciousness. *Thank you, God*, she prayed silently.

"All you pigs leave now before I start shooting people," the assailant said.

Nikki felt him move the gun away from her temple. She thrust her head forward very quickly and then back into his. The gun fired. She lunged forward, turned and kicked her assailant in the groin. He wobbled. She saw the gun drop from his hand, but before she could reach for it, El Saraway, from his position on the floor, picked it up. She heard police rushing in. Thoughts whirled in her head, fear cast its net on her, and she lost the focus she had experienced seconds before.

Nikki's and El Saraway's eyes locked. He moved in closer. She saw a determined look in his face. At the same time, she sensed movement on the floor. Her assailant had recovered and was coming toward her. She screamed. Before she could react, El Saraway had landed a couple of blows to the man's head. The Egyptian towered over the South American. For the third blow, El Saraway used the grip of the gun to send the man tumbling to the wooden planks of the altar. At that moment the police were upon the man on the floor, one officer placing handcuffs on as another informed him of his rights.

Nikki rushed to Eduardo's side. She hardly took notice of a man in gym shorts approaching her.

"An ambulance has arrived," the man said. "Paramedics are coming in to take your husband to the hospital."

Nikki recognized that voice. She looked up and nodded at Rafael. As she started to speak to him, the medics arrived. Eduardo reached for her hand.

"Go with him to the hospital. I'll try to drop by later," Rafael said. He turned to address one of the medics. "Take care of this woman's injuries after you take care of her husband."

"Is this place secure now?" Nikki asked. She looked across the chapel and saw two men in handcuffs, her assailant and another one she had not seen before, being escorted out. El Saraway walked with another officer.

"Absolutely, or we would not allow the ambulance crew in."

Rafael watched as the paramedics triaged Eduardo. Although he was able to stand, the medics insisted on putting Eduardo on the gurney so they could wheel him out to the waiting ambulance. Rafael picked up the phone and Taser still lying on the floor and handed them to Nikki. He came in very close to whisper in her ear.

"You won't be surprised when I tell you that Tasers of this caliber are not legal for civilians to use in Spain."

"It may have saved my life," Nikki said as she put both articles into the purse still hanging around her neck.

"I think you hit the wrong guy," Rafael whispered. "El Saraway helped you. The other two were the dangerous ones."

Nikki did not respond. Instead she took Eduardo's hand as the medics started rolling the gurney over the uneven floor of miniature tile.

CHAPTER FIFTY

BARCELONA—TIBIDABO CRYPT CHURCH

Thursday Afternoon

Rafael saw Alberto crossing the chapel to join him.

"The man who held Ms. Garcia hostage claims to be El Aremi, Palestinian," Alberto said. "Speaks perfect Spanish with a Latin American accent. His accomplice seems to be a Saudi. Does not speak much Spanish and has not talked except to say he's called 'the captain.' Handed me a card in Arabic with his name. We don't have anyone with us that reads Arabic."

"Our guy Omar reads Arabic," Rafael said. "He'll get the captain to sing after we get him to the station. You said both suspects are ready to be transported?"

"We're ready."

"What about El Saraway?" Rafael asked.

"Said his driver would take him to the station to answer questions," Alberto said.

"Let's go outside. Ride in the same vehicle with Aremi. I'll see you at the station. I'm stopping at the hospital to ask Ms. Garcia and her husband a few questions."

Rafael headed toward the vehicle Pepe had parked at the nursing home. As he got closer he spotted Pepe opening the passenger door for him.

"That was easy," Pepe said as Rafael slipped into the front seat.

Rafael scoffed. "Why don't you ask Ms. Garcia how easy it was."

"Didn't think about it from her angle. Guess a gun at my head might change my perspective," Pepe said, his voice sounding apologetic.

Rafael noticed Pepe had already changed back into regular clothes. He asked his driver to take him to the Barcelona Hospital. He would change there.

Rafael and Alberto entered the interrogation room where El Saraway and his attorney were already sitting at the table. Rafael sat down, looked at the monitor, and requested the video begin recording. After everyone stated their names, the GEO agent asked the Egyptian to state what he knew about the suspects in custody, starting with El Aremi.

"That was his birth name, but he migrated to Colombia and changed it to Cristóbal Arenas to fit in. Yet he never integrated into life there. Not even with other Middle Easterners, like Lebanese, who live in Medellín. Arenas is Massú's cousin. That's how I met him. I lived in Medellín for seven years and we became friends. At least that's what I thought."

"Explain yourself," Rafael said.

"I needed someone to handle my chemical import business in South America and I turned to him since he was Massú's relative. I offered him a job managing the business. He was well compensated but never happy with his earnings, so he decided to enter the most lucrative business in Colombia."

"Illegal drugs?" Rafael asked.

"He wanted me to join him. I flat out refused. It was drugs and guns. We parted ways." El Saraway shook his head. His eyes turned very somber.

"Can you go on?" Rafael asked.

"Things turned ugly. He tried to provoke me. I ignored him, but he would not let it go," El Saraway said. His eyes displayed a hollow sadness. "I never understood why he was furious with me. It became an obsession for him."

"Carry on," Rafael said.

El Saraway started to speak but his voice broke. He looked away and pursed his lips and then looked back at Rafael. "One thing led to another. My business demanded a lot of travel. I was still opening markets in Latin

America, calling on customers in various countries. My wife and three children lived in Medellín."

El Saraway's eyes went moist.

"I never thought he'd hurt them. He burned the house down. Killed my family. All of them. My mother also lived with us. We had household help and they died, too."

"Arenas burned your house down to kill people inside? Where were you?" Rafael asked.

"In Brazil. São Paulo. For years I did not know who set the fire. The police told me it was arson, but never gave me a name."

"When did this happen?"

"In 2010. Arenas had been jailed a few months for his illegal activities and had just been released. His business partner, a guy by the name of Manuel del Campo, got him out. Paid bribes to high level officials. Then Arenas moved to Mexico. He and his partner continued their illegal businesses."

"How do you know he killed your family?"

"I hired a private detective to look into the arson. I had moved from Colombia to Spain. I could not live in Medellín after I lost my family. The pain was unbearable. So I worked even harder than ever to keep my mind busy."

"You have a place in Ibiza?" Rafael asked.

El Saraway explained that Spain fit his growing European business, and Ibiza's climate suited him. As a widower, he no longer needed a social life, having almost become a hermit, except for his business contacts, which he administered through his worldwide network of managers.

"Do you fly overseas?" Rafael asked.

"Haven't for several years. I charter a small plane for my personal use and I fly back and forth between the Reus Airport and Ibiza. No passport is required for domestic travel."

"Do you have a passport?"

"No. I could always get one if I needed it. My business is big, but very simple. If I need to speak to my managers or even customers in person, I fly them here."

Rafael found it difficult to believe an entrepreneur with a worldwide business didn't travel, but saw no reason to contest the issue at this point. "You also keep an apartment here?"

"A hotel room. The Majestic. Though I'm staying at the Sofia Hotel right now."

Rafael questioned him about paying cash for everything at the Majestic.

"Nothing illegal about paying in cash. I do it to protect my identity. Fell into that habit when I was keeping my whereabouts secret to prevent Arenas from finding me."

"Why did you move to the Sofia?"

"I've been following the trail to Arenas. I had to get out of the Majestic to avoid having him find me first."

"Explain yourself."

"My detective got his hands on the arson investigation five years ago. Arenas himself committed that crime. Killed my family. He could have no idea of the pain he caused me. You see, he has no children. His wife could not conceive."

"So how did you locate Arenas?"

"Four years it took me to find him. My detective informed me over a year ago that a female investigator from the States had put an end to a lot of his easy money. Del Campo, his business partner, is serving a prison sentence since the Colombian government closed down their little drug scheme."

"Who is the woman?"

"Nikki Garcia."

"The Nigerian you followed that led to his arrest said he worked for you. He called you the 'man with the falcon.' Why would he say that?" Rafael coughed. The allergies caused by the vegetation on Tibidabo were still bothering him.

"No way did he work for me," El Saraway said emphatically. He squirmed in his seat. "My investigator discovered Arenas moved part of his operations to Ibiza last year. Even before that, Arenas had a presence smuggling weapons through there to European and Middle East markets, including Syria. My detective thinks his customer in Syria was ISIS."

"Why Ibiza? Because you were there?"

El Saraway replied that he did not think Arenas knew of his hideaway in Ibiza. Most of his excursions on the island, he explained, were to exercise his falcon. Arenas, he surmised, used Ibiza as a place to bring in boats carrying weapons and explosives, warehouse and sort the goods, and reship them. But El Saraway did not think Arenas spent time on the island.

"When was the last time you saw Arenas?" Rafael asked.

"It's been years. Until he showed up at Tibidabo today."

"You never answered why the Nigerian called you the 'man with the falcon.'"

"From information my detective gave me, I kept an eye on the coming and going of Arenas's boats from the isolated coves he uses. They are small ocean-going vessels. I saw the Nigerian with Arenas's people twice. He must have seen me with Shaheen, my falcon, and assumed the man he met worked for me."

"So you knew about the Nigerian?"

"My detective and I followed him. In Ibiza and here in Barcelona. We knew he was a hired killer. And dangerous."

Impressed with the detective's work, Rafael made a mental note to arrange a meeting with El Saraway's detective. Interpol had issued a red notice for Arenas, yet he'd escaped arrest. The man even arrived in Spain without detection, a fact Rafael would investigate.

"My detective followed Ms. Garcia from Mexico to Spain. It was a strange coincidence, bizarre in fact, that she was related to the young bride who was killed at Sagrada Família."

Rafael thought of inquiring about Sagrada Família but decided to pose that question later. Instead he asked about El Saraway's friendship with Fernando Massú.

"He was my business partner starting about 1993 when my business expanded into Spain. We were both young and he worked for me, became my partner, and then left to start his own company. Back then, he and Jamila, that was his wife, took me into their circle of friends. Jamila helped me find a place to stay in Barcelona. I've kept the hotel room at the Majestic for three decades. Basically since Fadi was born in 1990."

"So you knew them since before Fadi was born?"

"That's right. Over the years we were friends, yes. Jamila was a good woman. She introduced me in 1995 to the beautiful woman I later married."

"We have you on CCTV with Massú at the Tarragona airport the day of the wedding. What did you know about the planned bombing of Sagrada Família?"

"Nothing at all. And I regret knowing nothing about it. If I had, I would have told the police. Fadi and Jamila would be alive." El Saraway's voice was choking up.

"Did you suspect anything?"

"About the bombing, no. Fernando Massú acted strangely the morning of the wedding when he picked me up at the airport in

Tarragona. At first, I thought his son's wedding had him nervous. He's a conflicted individual."

"Conflicted? Explain yourself."

El Saraway described a temperamental man who could be a generous donor to an organization founded to create better understanding between the Middle East and the West one day, and the next preach about conspiracies of Western governments to obliterate the Middle East. He had the capacity to behave erratically with people, being naturally suspicious and paranoid that everyone was out to get him.

"Give me an example."

"Paula, his future daughter-in-law. Some days he extolled her virtues. Other times, he criticized her greed and ambition, saying she converted to Islam to ingratiate herself with him to get his money."

"Was there any truth to his accusations of Paula?"

"I've known her for a couple of years. She seemed like a gentle soul, a bit too idealistic. On the other hand, Fadi was like a son to me. I knew him from infancy. When he was a child, he wrote poetry and I spent time reading with him. He was like Jamila, a steady heart and fun loving."

"Like a son, you said. Is there any chance he could be your biological child?"

"No, none at all. But in Tarragona, the morning of the wedding, Fernando Massú accused me of double-crossing him. Said he had proof Fadi was mine."

"What proof?"

"I don't know. I never knew what he was talking about."

"Will you voluntarily submit to a paternity test to see if Fadi is your son?"

"Yes, of course. But I can assure you he is not my son."

"So what happened when he accused you?" Rafael asked.

"He got so furious about twenty kilometers outside of Tarragona, he stopped the car and ordered me to get out."

"And did you?"

"Of course. He was rabid. I thought he'd kill me. In fact, as I stepped out, I was not fully out as he took off. It knocked me to the ground. I was lucky I did not get dragged by the car. Even now, I have bruises on my face and body," he said, pointing to a laceration on his right cheekbone.

"He drove off and left you there?"

El Saraway nodded.

"For the record, can you answer out loud?" Rafael asked.

"Yes, on the side of the road. I walked back to Tarragona to take the train into Barcelona. I missed the wedding. When I arrived at the train station, I heard the news of the bombing."

"What time was that?"

"Around four p.m. Well after the bombing."

"Did you spend the night of the attack at Massú's house?"

El Saraway looked perplexed. "Massú did not even answer when I called his mobile phone. I called his house. Berta, his housekeeper, told me Massú wanted me to stay away. She also informed me about Jamila and Fadi. Though I'd heard on TV that the couple, no names, getting married at Sagrada Família had been killed. I was sick about it all. Too reminiscent of my own family tragedy."

"Let's go back to your detective. Why did he follow Nikki Garcia to Spain?"

"The old adage 'the enemy of my enemy is my friend.' I told him to follow Nikki thinking it would bring Arenas out of hiding," El Saraway said. "I knew Arenas well enough to know he would eventually feel he had to show up to handle Nikki himself. Just as he burned my house down and let my family die inside. He's obsessive."

"How did you find Arenas in Barcelona?"

"Again, my detective. We knew Arenas was closing in on Ms. Garcia. He would have killed her husband, too. In fact, I personally followed Ms. Garcia a few times, but I think she became aware of it, so I hired two more people to help my detective. In addition to locating Arenas through her, I did not want more bloodshed."

"Not a clandestine operation you should have done on your own," Rafael said.

"Maybe not, but Arenas has eluded law enforcement for years. My idea was to turn him over alive to the police whenever I found him."

"Still you should not have taken the law into your own hands." Rafael said.

"My mission is now accomplished," El Saraway said.

Rafael noted the man's expression of satisfaction.

CHAPTER FIFTY-ONE

BARCELONA—BARCELONA HOSPITAL

Floyd came through the main entrance to the Barcelona Hospital. The smell assaulted his nostrils. He coughed, pulling out his phone to send Nikki a text. When he glanced up from his phone, he saw her checking her messages.

"The nightmare is over." Floyd said as he caught up with them. He embraced Nikki and patted Eduardo on the shoulder. "How are you, Eduardo?"

"Ready to take my board exams so I can practice medicine in Miami," Eduardo said. "Safer job."

"He suffered a concussion, but they found nothing to suggest serious problems," Nikki added.

"If you both feel up to it, Javier wants to take us to dinner tonight and update us on the interrogations of Massú and Sonia arrested yesterday. Wants to explain how Sonia masterminded the bombing with help from her father. Apparently, Massú wanted revenge on his wife for having been unfaithful to him."

"But how could Massú kill innocent people?" Nikki asked. "Including Fadi. He may not have been the biological father, but he *raised* Fadi."

"Evil people do evil things," Floyd said.

"How about dinner tomorrow instead?" Eduardo asked. "We'd prefer to see Carmen this evening and see how she's getting along."

"Good idea," Nikki said. "Javier may also have more information to share by tomorrow."

"Turns out El Saraway was a modern-day vigilante," Floyd said. "Those photos he took of you were used by the two people he hired to help his detective protect both of you. And he did protect you."

"Protect us?" Nikki asked. She was wide-eyed. "You must be kidding. He could have contacted us and saved us a lot of stress." She made a mental note to contact Charlotte about the cryptocurrency as soon as she returned to the hotel.

First to step through the hospital's revolving door, Nikki turned back to look at the men. The late afternoon sun pleasantly cast long rays through the glass in the turnstile. The sunlight hitting the glass prompted rainbow-colored patterns to fall on Eduardo and then Floyd as they came through the turnstile. *That's a much better image than my nightmare coming to life this afternoon at the chapel. Thank God we're safe now. The rainbow,* she thought, *must be a good omen.* She touched her tree of life necklace. It must have helped her overcome the dangers at Tibidabo.

Nikki heard Floyd say he had a limo waiting. "The driver can drop you off at Carmen's and take me to the hotel. And I'll call Javier about scheduling dinner for tomorrow."

CHAPTER FIFTY-TWO

BARCELONA—GENERAL DIRECTORATE OF POLICE

Friday Morning—Week Four

O nce again, Rafael walked into the interrogation room. This time instead of having Alberto present, he brought Omar.

Rafael looked at the muscular, middle-aged man waiting to be interrogated and glanced up at the monitor, signaling the recording to start.

After names were stated, Rafael asked the man his citizenship, his address, and his passport number, though Rafael knew the police had taken the document.

"I'm Emil El Aremi from Lebanon," he said in perfect South American Spanish. Then he stated his six-digit Lebanese passport number and his address as 176 Dekwaneh, Apartment 36 in Beirut.

"That's unusual," Rafael said. "I have facial recognition information that you are a wanted drug trafficker and gun smuggler, a Colombian national, living in Mexico."

Arenas's eyes scorched Rafael's face.

After more than two hours of questioning, Rafael informed Arenas that if he would cooperate by turning over the names of his Russian gun suppliers and delivering names, sources, and everything else he knew about the Sagrada Família plot, a judge might grant him some mercy. But

Rafael would have to verify the information before a judge would consider any leniency.

"Let's start again," Rafael said. "What is your name in Colombia, South America?"

Arenas turned to look at his attorney, who nodded.

"Cristóbal Arenas."

"Are you aware the paternity test we took yesterday came back a positive match between you and Fadi Massú?"

"I did not kill him," Arenas responded.

"That's not what I asked. Did you know Fadi was your biological son?"

Arenas looked aghast. "My son?" he asked. His voice trembled. "But I don't have any children."

"When you provided the bomb-making material to Sonia Ussam and her group of makeshift terrorists, did you know Fadi was your son? That they planned to kill him?"

Arenas's head slumped ever so slightly.

"Did you know Sonia Ussam used a radicalized young man who worked for her and convinced him and his friends to bomb Sagrada Família on the day of Fadi's wedding?"

"I supply customers what they pay for. No questions asked."

"When you provided the bomb-making materials, did you know she planned to eliminate Fadi so she could inherit the Massú wealth?"

"Of course not. I had no idea she was going to kill Fadi. Or Jamila." Arenas raised his voice and glared at his interrogator with hatred. "I did not know what she was planning."

"So you knew he was your son?" Rafael asked in a very calm voice to counteract Arenas's outburst.

"Many years ago I wondered if he was my son, but Jamila denied it," Arenas said. His manner was much more subdued.

"But you sold Sonia the explosives, and you also put her in contact with the Nigerian who detonated the bomb that killed Fadi and his mother."

Arenas continued to glare.

"Answer me. Did you provide Sonia the explosives for the attack at Sagrada Família? And did you put her in contact with the Nigerian who set off the explosion?"

"Yes. No. Not directly. She needed a computer expert with knowledge of explosives."

"Did you receive an invitation to the wedding?"

"No, they did not invite me," Arenas spat out the words with venom.

Rafael calculated that Arenas's line of business made him unworthy to have at the wedding.

"How did Sonia get your name for the explosives?"

"Though they excluded me from their social life, for business reasons, I was contacted. Massú gave her my phone number. She called."

"What did you know about the plans of the attack?"

"I knew nothing." Arenas stared back at Rafael with an empty look instead of hatred.

"How did you get the explosives to her?"

"By boat. My captain, the fellow you have also detained, brought them to Barcelona. Sonia sent one of her flower shop terrorists to pick up the delivery."

"What about the Nigerian?"

"What about him?" Arenas asked.

"Why was he following Ms. Garcia and her husband with intent to kill them?"

"I had unfinished business with Ms. Garcia," Arenas said. His voice sounded hostile again and his eyes were blazing with hatred. "She destroyed one of my operations. I had reason to exact revenge."

Rafael ran the pros and cons in his mind about bringing up revenge against El Saraway and his family, but decided to keep his questions strictly about the issues at hand.

"So it's not a coincidence the Nigerian was involved in the attack at the basilica and also sent to eliminate Ms. Garcia?"

Arenas glanced at his attorney and sighed. "The Nigerian missed his chance to kill her on the train to Burgos."

"Train to Burgos? How did he know she would be going to Burgos?"

"The concierge at that woman's hotel gave me the information. My people passed it on to the Nigerian. He messed up. His second chance would have been at the church. I did not know she'd be there. I never knew what target was being blown up."

"Now tell me about the Nigerian," Rafael said.

"The man's worked for me before. I told you, Sonia needed an electronics expert for the explosives. My involvement was giving her a number to call. With my people, she arranged for the expert to arrive at her flower shop to set up the explosives and detonator right before the bombs were taken to the target location. The expert was the same man."

"The Nigerian?" Rafael asked. "Electronics expert and a hired gun?"

"You could say that." A half smile slipped across Arenas's lips.

"He mentioned meeting with a man on Ibiza. He thought that man represented someone else."

"That's good. Most people who work for me never know who they are working for. Like the Nigerian, they never meet me. Keeps me safe."

"Not this time," Rafael said.

"We have not gone to trial yet," Arenas said with a sadistic smile.

CHAPTER FIFTY-THREE

BARCELONA—BARRI GÒTIC

The two couples—Nikki and Eduardo, Floyd and Milena—visited the Bishop's Bridge and walked on to the site of the turtle antidote before arriving at the Azul restaurant in the Gothic Quarter of the city. They were seated at a large, well-worn table constructed of wide wooden planks.

Feeling relaxed for the first time in days, Nikki looked around. The restaurant's low ceiling over massive medieval walls gave the place a centuries old atmosphere, especially as the dim lighting accented the rough-hewn rocks of the walls. *These stones must have stood by as a lot of history passed on the cobblestone street*, she thought.

Eduardo broke her musings by mentioning Carmen "She's a remarkable woman. Devastated by the death of her loved ones yet she's meeting this heartbreaking challenge with fierce pragmatism."

"She's even insisted we take our honeymoon through the caves of northern Spain and southern France," Nikki said, "but we will spend three days with Carmen before we leave. We want to be with her for the memorial services for Paula and Carlos, Carmen's brother-in-law. Also to inter their ashes." She turned toward Milena and explained Carmen had chosen to take the ashes to Cementiri de Montjuïc, a place not usually selected by families in Barcelona since it's on the tourist trail. But Paula and her uncle shared a love for Joan Miró, the painter and sculptor, who was a native son of Barcelona. With Miró buried there, she felt they would both appreciate having their ashes near the painter's burial site.

"That will bring some closure," Eduardo said. He took the opportunity to thank Floyd and Milena for their support throughout the ordeal. And he mentioned their appreciation for Nikki's extra time off from work so they could take their honeymoon.

"Not a problem. When you get back, there will be plenty of work. In fact, we may have a case in Hong Kong."

"I'd hate to be in Carmen's shoes," Milena said, still thinking about Carmen. "I don't know how I'd deal with such sorrow."

"You'd survive," Floyd said. "Somehow we find the fortitude to deal with life's hardships."

"Tía Carmen was so relieved to know her daughter was not involved in the plot," Nikki said. "She was concerned about that during the days she was in the hospital. It's made a huge difference in how she feels."

Floyd brought the conversation back to the investigation, mentioning how glad he was El Saraway turned out to be a good guy. Nikki agreed. She hesitated, feeling disloyal to the person who helped save their lives, but added she'd discovered El Saraway had moved millions in digital currency through a Panamanian-based crypto exchange company where withdrawals were made in US dollars.

"Does not sound good," Floyd said.

"I know. I debated about telling you. We don't know that he's laundering money, but it sounds suspicious."

"I'll mention it to Javier tomorrow when I have a closing meeting with him. Now to complete the story about the Rom women," Floyd said. "Javier's told me only one is Rom. That was the one who was attacked by the Nigerian. It turns out the other one is the Nigerian's sister-in-law."

Nikki grimaced. "His sister-in-law? That does not make sense."

"Yes, it does, when you consider the Nigerian killed her husband to steal his passport so he could get into Spain. That woman also happens to be a cousin of Rafael's wife."

"What a small world. Now it makes sense that he seemed to know them," Eduardo said.

"Javier may want to add more details tonight," Floyd said, "but what we know is Sonia Ussam masterminded the attack. Once she discovered Fadi was not Fernando's biological son, she took advantage of her father's anger and set out to eliminate Fadi and his mother so she could inherit the Massú money. Of course, Fernando Massú is fully implicated since he colluded and brought Arenas into the scheme."

"Who was Fadi's biological father?" Nikki asked.

"Don't fall over when I tell you," Floyd said. "The guy who hired hit men to get you. Cristóbal Arenas. Massú and Arenas are cousins. Arenas confessed to a love affair with Jamila but did not know Fadi was his son. DNA tests confirmed his paternity."

Chills ran down her back. Nikki's expression of surprise remained on her face as she shook her head, thinking how lucky she and Eduardo had been to escape Arenas's attempt on their lives.

"Massú set it all in motion when he tested his offspring for Parkinson's," Floyd said. "That's when he found out Fadi could not possibly be his son. He shared that information with Sonia. Together they decided to bomb the basilica to make it appear as if it had been a terrorist plot."

"How could they do something so cruel?" Milena asked. "He raised that boy. That makes him his son."

"Exactly what I said," Nikki offered. "Fadi was such a great guy. It's all so sad."

"Sonia knew one of her employees was at least partially radicalized," Floyd said. He continued telling them Sonia had known of Hassan's connection to the imam with extremist views in Tarragona, the one who deals in false documents, gun trafficking, and illegal drugs to get money for his causes. Then Massú put Sonia in contact with Arenas, knowing his cousin sold weapons and explosives.

"If Sonia executed the plans," Eduardo said, "she was an amateur at it. They did a lot of damage, but it could have been far worse. That explains why her employee used a Honda Beat instead of a sturdy vehicle to mow people down."

"Sonia confessed she'd purposely left her shop stickers on the vases to make it appear she was innocent since a guilty flower shop owner would never have left such incriminating evidence," Floyd said.

"Bad reasoning on her part," Eduardo said.

"The Tarragona imam had a connection not only with Hassan, but also with Arenas's organization on Ibiza," Floyd said. "The Nigerian had a gun on him the night he intended to assault you. Arenas's intermediary arranged for the imam to provide it. It was an old Russian pistol. The Nigerian flew to Tarragona on a small aircraft provided by Arenas and they could not risk the Nigerian getting caught with it at the airport."

"It's the same the world over. Criminals from one type of illegal activity deal with criminals involved in other things," Nikki said.

"Drug lords in Latin America deal with the human traffickers all the time," Milena added.

"Oh, absolutely," Nikki said. "Let's also remember there are a lot of good people in this world. Look at the two women who risked their lives when Eduardo and I were walking down Carrer de Provença. They could have walked away but did not. Eduardo and I might not be here tonight if it were not for them."

"Would you believe they want to meet you? Javier might bring them with him tonight," Floyd said.

"Speak of the devil. Here's Javier now," Eduardo said as he looked toward the entrance.

Three tall, striking women, one carrying a baby, walked in with Javier and Rafael. A fourth woman, petite with a dark complexion, was Asian.

Chinese, perhaps, Nikki thought.

As the group approached the table, Javier greeted everyone and proceeded to introduce the women, starting with Lola, Rafael's wife. Next he presented Olani and elaborated on her brave quest to seek justice.

"The twin brothers were similar to the story of Cain and Abel. Like Abel, Olani's husband was the younger one, the good one, who was murdered by his jealous and greedy older brother."

Javier introduced them to Selena, mentioning she's a flamenco dancer and teacher in Barcelona.

"Oh, we saw you at Tablao Flamenco," Nikki said as she stood. She felt emotional at being introduced to the women who'd saved them. "We saw you dancing at the Tablao Flamenco. Your dancing is incredible."

Selena took a mock bow.

"But saving our lives was even more incredible," Nikki said. "My husband and I thank you."

Selena reached for Olani's hand, and they both took another bow. Dayo giggled when her mother swung into the bow.

Nikki stepped toward the women and gave them warm embraces. "And now I know why you looked familiar when you were sprawled out on the sidewalk." Nikki embraced Lola and continued to stand until Javier finished talking.

"And this is my wife, Jia Li," Javier said. "We met in Hong Kong when we were growing up. My father was stationed there. I'll bet you did not know I speak fluent Mandarin, one of the reasons I have the job I do."

No wonder he speaks English with an odd accent, Nikki thought as she approached Jia Li and embraced her too.

"El Saraway sends his best wishes and message. He wanted to join us tonight but was afraid of Nikki's Taser," Javier said, waiting a couple of seconds as everyone laughed.

"I thought I was tasing a bad guy," Nikki said with an apologetic shrug of her shoulders.

"He said to tell you he is glad guilty ones arrested. Soon they be brought to justice." Javier smiled and asked everyone to find a seat at the table. "Oh, this is baby Dayo. Not quite one year old."

"The United Nations at one table," Nikki said. "I count eleven of us with Dayo. And if I'm correct, we have five nationalities represented— Spain, the US, Colombia, China, and Nigeria."

"Dayo gives us six nationalities. She's Moroccan. Though I'm happy to say we will be legal residents in Spain very soon. Thanks to Rafael." Olani beamed as she looked at Rafael and Lola.

"We have all been hit by Sagrada Família tragic events," Javier said. "But tonight we enjoy one another's company before we go back to our separate corners of the world."

"And he wants you to enjoy the tapas he loves so much," Jia Li said as she glanced at her husband. "His favorite is the roasted pepper and goat cheese. He preordered by phone so we don't have to wait."

As soon as Jia Li had spoken those words, wait staff appeared with plate after plate of tapas. Wine bottles flowed to the table as a few final points on the investigation were clarified.

"One thing I did not understand was Paula's missing computer," Eduardo said.

"Sonia confessed she tried to take advantage of Paula's conversion to Islam," Javier said. "Sonia stole computer after bombing to plant software and information on it to frame Paula as mastermind. Make it appear Paula had martyred herself with home-grown terrorists. But Nigerian not expert on electronics that Arenas's contacts claimed, so it didn't get done."

"No, but he was adept enough," Nikki said. "Look at the innocent people he killed."

"True," Rafael said. Up to now he hadn't spoken. "But I think we need to celebrate the good things about life, good company, good food, good drink."

"Salud," Floyd and Rafael said simultaneously, holding up their wine glasses.

Even Olani jumped into the toast. Her glass contained carbonated water, but she held it high as she toasted and thanked Selena for helping her. Then she added a thank you to Lola and Rafael for welcoming her and Dayo into their home.

The evening progressed past midnight with laughter, tears, joy, and sorrow depending on the topic of the moment. At one point when Dayo starting crying, Nikki took her in her arms and walked in the narrow aisles between tables until Dayo fell asleep.

By the time they had all finished eating, talking, and drinking, they were all hugging and cheek kissing each other as if they had known one another for a lifetime. Nikki even gave Javier a warm hug.

CHAPTER FIFTY-FOUR

BARCELONA—MAJESTIC HOTEL

EARLY HOURS OF SUNDAY MORNING

Eduardo opened the door to their hotel room. As soon as he closed it behind them, Nikki slipped her arms around his neck and squeezed against him as if she could not bear to let go. He bent down slightly, his lips searching for hers, and they kissed with such passion, Nikki was not sure if Eduardo carried her to the bed or if they flew. The dream state continued as they unclothed. Time magically stopped ticking. They were alone in the universe, the two of them, in a dimension Nikki had never known before. She felt the thrust of her breasts against his chest, her legs wrapped around his body, her hands on his buttocks rocking with the motion of their desire. Their bodies responded to each other's rhythm in perfect harmony. She had never felt happier.

In the moment of ecstasy, they surrendered to each other completely.

As they lay together, their legs entwined, Eduardo touched Nikki's face with the back of his hand and brushed a wisp of her hair from her cheek. He propped himself up on his elbow with the pillow bunched under his armpit. Looking at Nikki, he said "You look happy and relaxed."

"What a great way to resume our honeymoon," she said looking at him through dreamy eyes. "After our honeymoon, where shall we go next?"

"How about staying right here making love night and day for a full month?" Eduardo's lips parted into a whimsical smile.

Nikki playfully smacked his arm with her hand. "Get serious. I have to get back to work and you have your board exams."

"I was also thinking," Eduardo said, "how fortunate we've been. In Mexico Juana la Marihuana took care of you, and here you've had Selena and Olani."

"I never thought I'd find people like Juana again. We owe them so much."

"So what's next for us?" Eduardo asked.

"Hong Kong as Floyd suggested? He'll fly you over for a week or two. Or should I stay in the States, where I can be home for weekends?"

"Any place where no one's waiting to kill us is fine with me," Eduardo said. He leaned in and kissed her again.

A NOTE FROM KATHRYN

Thank you for reading *Revenge in Barcelona*. If you enjoyed it, I would very much appreciate a review on Amazon, BookBub, and Goodreads so others may also find Nikki Garcia.

If you'd like to learn about my new releases, please sign up for my newsletter at kathryn-lane.com.

— Kathryn Lane

MISSING IN MIAMI SAMPLE

CHAPTER ONE

C arefully moored yachts glistened in the late afternoon sunlight. Nikki Garcia sighed. "It's spectacular! I could stay here forever." She snapped some pictures of the marina with her smartphone, then looked up at Eduardo. His sunglasses reflected miniature versions of the graceful white vessels.

Her husband smiled. "Think what you'll miss when you leave for Hong Kong."

"I'll miss *you* much more."

Nikki opened her phone's browser and read a description she'd brought up on the drive to Miami Beach Marina. "Victoria Harbor is a natural landmark, where the sky kisses the mountains and skyscrapers accent the greenery over the blue waters of the Hong Kong harbor."

"I'm jealous," he said playfully. "Your boss always makes offers you can't refuse."

They were here to meet Floyd Webber, Nikki's boss, and the founder of Security Source. He was also a former CIA operations officer.

"You know I'm more effective in foreign countries. And I'm going to ask Floyd if you can join me after your exams." She saw a speedboat approaching and recognized the man at the helm. "Speak of the devil."

Floyd slowed the speedboat to a crawl, angling into the dock. Then he reversed the engine, halting the boat and making little waves. A black-backed gull that had been walking along the pier stopped to watch.

An attendant ran to secure the boat and the bird retreated. With a burp from the outboard, the stern settled against the slip. Floyd and his wife, Milena, took off their lifejackets. The attendant helped them onto the floating walkway.

"That was great docking," Nikki said. "I hope you enjoyed the trip over."

Milena hugged Nikki. "I haven't seen either of you since Barcelona."

Eduardo and Floyd bumped elbows, then they all followed Eduardo to the car. It was just three miles from the marina to their borrowed condominium with its gate and camera-secured subterranean parking.

Once in their living quarters, Milena exhaled. "This is lovely."

"Eduardo will show you around and serve drinks while I get hors d'oeuvres ready." Nikki headed for the kitchen. She nestled sea scallops on twelve clam shells she'd cleaned earlier in the day. She dribbled lime juice, butter, and Peruvian Pisco over them before generously sprinkling Parmesan cheese on each half shell. Using an oven glove, she pushed the platter under the broiler.

After a brief tour of the condo, Floyd took a seat by the marble countertop that separated the kitchen from the great room.

"Nice place," he said.

Nikki faced Floyd. "I have a favor to ask. I'd like Eduardo to join me in Hong Kong after his medical board exams." She glanced toward the beige sectional sofa, where Eduardo was talking quietly with Milena.

Before Floyd could respond, his phone buzzed. He glanced at the number. "Gotta take this." He slipped outside to the balcony.

Nikki cut two limes in half, wrapping each half in cheesecloth and tying it with a green ribbon. She sprinkled salt and a spice blend over a bowl of habas saladas. The crunchy Peruvian snack's texture would complement the soft sea scallops.

Floyd returned to the marble countertop and leaned against it. "We need to rethink Hong Kong." He studied her face.

"Why?" she asked, hoping her blank expression didn't change. Floyd had been coaching her on keeping a poker face. "Showing emotion can be deadly for a private investigator," he'd advised her.

"I need you for a case here in Miami," Floyd said now.

"Miami?" she repeated, disappointed.

"A teenage girl has vanished."

"Kidnapped?" Nikki felt her stomach churn. Cases involving kids reminded her of her twelve-year-old son's tragic death several years before.

"All I know is that she's disappeared. That was the mother who called —Delfina Morales. The father is Yoani Rodríguez. She said they haven't yet reported her missing."

"That's strange. It's the first thing they should have done."

"If you take the case, you can follow up with the parents tomorrow and ask them."

"If a child's missing, I should go right now," Nikki said.

"I offered. I told the mother how important the first few hours are. But she insisted on tomorrow morning at nine. Said her daughter might return home tonight."

"Let me call her from your phone." After several rings, it went to voicemail. Nikki left her number and asked the mother to call her.

Her chest tightened at the thought of working on a missing teenager's case. "I'd rather take the Hong Kong job. Can't Hamilton do this? Or one of the junior investigators?"

"Your work on missing children is exceptional. Think about it and give me your answer at the marina when we—"

Nikki grabbed the glove and yanked the oven door open, coughing as she pulled out the platter.

"Burnt Parmesan!"

Floyd covered his nose.

"That smells awful," Eduardo muttered, approaching the kitchen. "Scorched scallops?"

"Like rubber," Nikki said, flipping on the exhaust fan. "Change in plans. Take the wine, cheese, and crackers to the balcony while I bag this for the garbage."

"Good thing the fire alarm didn't go off," Eduardo said.

"I just hope security doesn't tell the owners I'm stinking up their beautiful condo." Nikki ran cold water over the burnt scallops and dumped them into a plastic bag, then put the sealed bag in the freezer.

Eduardo showed their guests to the balcony. The condo, in the Faena District of Miami Beach, boasted a wraparound terrace from the primary bedroom all the way to the great room. Glass walls extended the indoor-outdoor feel of the living space.

Nikki could see Milena outside on the balcony, holding onto the railing. With her own fear of heights, Nikki could never get that close to the edge, not twelve stories up, not even if she grabbed the railing for support. She picked up the bowl of habas saladas and joined them, taking a seat on a chaise longue. A fresh, warm breeze blew a wisp of dark hair across her face.

Milena peered down at the white sand beach. "What an incredible view."

"It's gorgeous all right," Nikki said. "But it's not us. I feel like an intruder."

Eduardo refilled Floyd's wine glass. "I keep telling Nikki we should enjoy it while we can."

"How much are you paying in rent?" Floyd asked.

"Nothing. We're house sitting," Eduardo said. "They wanted to pay us. Can you imagine? They insisted so much that in the end, we let them pick up our utility bills. Even that makes us uncomfortable."

"And the owners—"

"Off on a world tour for one full year," Nikki said.

"Milena and I can take care of it if you don't want to." Floyd chuckled.

"Then we'll move out tonight," Nikki said, getting up from the chaise longue in an exaggerated manner.

Taking a seat, Milena suggested Nikki relax and pretend to be on vacation for a year.

"A vacation in Hong Kong sounds more exciting," Nikki said, hoping she sounded calm. She took a seat again. Just because she'd been eaten up by anxiety from the moment Floyd told her about the missing teenager was no reason to ruin everyone else's evening. "I was supposed to fly out next week."

Eduardo dabbed Stilton on a cracker. "When my surgeon friend offered us the condo, we thought it'd be a great idea. Let us get to know the city before we buy our own home. We didn't realize the stress of living in a picture-perfect place. We're afraid of chipping the paint or spilling coffee and staining that Italian marble countertop." Eduardo gave his wife a devilish glance. "Or god forbid, Nikki burning the place down with Parmesan scallops."

Nikki laughed. "From now on, we'll order pizza every night."

"That'll work while I'm studying for my exams." Raising his glass, Eduardo toasted his wife's upcoming trip to Hong Kong.

"I may not be going to Hong Kong after all," Nikki said.

"In that case, we can invite Floyd and Milena for Peruvian conchitas next week. With luck, they won't be charred." Eduardo lifted his glass again.

Milena took a sip of wine and glanced toward the beach, in the direction of candy-cane-striped umbrellas at the beach club. "You'll soon love it here. You won't want to leave when the owners return."

"That's the next issue," Eduardo said, nibbling on habas saladas. "We'll fall in love with it and we'll have to leave. We can't afford a property like this. I haven't worked for over a year and I still have to take my exams to get my medical license."

"Yeah, I'm supporting him." Nikki laughed and winked at her husband.

As the others helped themselves to habas or cheese and crackers, Floyd told them he'd asked Nikki to take the case of a missing Miami teenager instead of working in Hong Kong. He apologized for disappointing her.

"I wouldn't burn this place down if I were in Hong Kong," Nikki said, laughing.

Nikki wondered how she could hide her unease about working on the missing teen case in Miami. She would have loved the Hong Kong job. Anything would be better than a kid in danger. Her gut twisted at the thought.

"Tomorrow is a workday," Floyd said. "It's time we leave."

Eduardo and Nikki drove their guests back to the marina.

It bustled with people. Couples pushed baby strollers, children darted here and there, and singles walked their dogs along the brightly lit street near the waterfront. Eduardo parked and the four of them headed toward the dock.

"We must plan an outing in the boat," Milena suggested.

Eduardo responded with enthusiasm.

Floyd asked Nikki what she'd decided on the Miami assignment.

"If a girl is missing, I'll give it everything I've got to find her."

He nodded. "Are you sure?"

"I'm committed," she said. "There's no turning back now."

"That's great." Floyd was not one to waste words. Motioning to a dock attendant for assistance, he handed him a tip. He took his wife by the elbow, and they boarded the boat, then put on their life jackets.

Floyd started the engine and the attendant untied the boat.

Before he cast away from the dock, Floyd joined Milena at the gunwale and waved to Nikki and Eduardo.

"Must be nice to own your own boat," Nikki said.

"Let's walk that way." Eduardo pointed toward three anchored yachts. "And dream about owning one of those." He took her hand.

"When I met you in Colombia, you told me you were not wealthy. They're beautiful, but it'd take real money to own one."

Ignoring her comment, Eduardo stopped and turned her to face him. "What happened to Hong Kong? You'd told me you're more effective in foreign countries."

Nikki looked into her husband's eyes.

"A teenager is missing. How could I possibly not try to find her?"

CHAPTER TWO

E arly the next morning, Nikki stopped by Charlotte's office to chat about the change in assignment.

Tall and thin, Charlotte never had to diet. Her outdoorsy lifestyle and organic, vegan cooking kept her in shape, she claimed. A computer expert, she handled online research to support cases for Security Source. She also supported the team of investigators. Her work frequently provided breakthroughs in tough cases. The firm depended on Charlotte to dig up information that they would not have even known how to access online.

Besides the huge computer monitors dominating the walls in her office, the geeky young woman displayed a collection of elephants. One was an elephant alebrije, whimsical folk art from Mexico that Nikki had given her. Charlotte claimed it warded off evil spirits.

"Andrea Rodríguez is the missing girl," Nikki said, giving her the few details Floyd had mentioned the night before. "Her father dropped her off at school but she never made it to class. She simply vanished. Apparently, the mother was so distraught when she called Security Source that Floyd's not certain when she actually disappeared."

Charlotte keyed the name into her computer. "That's weird. No missing person report."

"Not good. I'll tell them they must file one. Look up the parents, Yoani Rodríguez and Delfina Morales."

"Here's the parents' residence," Charlotte said, tapping on the keyboard.

Nikki looked over Charlotte's shoulder to check the map on the screen while her assistant texted her the address on Paradise Point Drive in Palmetto Bay.

"It's a couple miles south of Coral Gables, in a frou-frou neighborhood." Charlotte's typing speed was impressive despite the green and yellow acrylic nails on her fingertips. "Interesting, there's nothing on Yoani Rodríguez," she said. "That's the wife's house. The county records list Delfina Morales as the sole owner."

"Please get all the information you can on the parents. Where they were born, educated, and their employment records—both past and present. Are they separated? Divorced? Any issues? Arrests, criminal records, financial difficulties, bankruptcies, DWIs, whatever. You know the drill," Nikki said.

Twenty minutes later, Charlotte sent Nikki an electronic file containing her research. And she followed up on the intercom. "I can't find much on the father. He must pay to erase his digital footprint. No social media on either parent. Andrea did have postings. Nothing unusual, typical teenage stuff. Though she doesn't seem to have a lot of friends. Her last post was six days ago."

Nikki studied the information before calling Delfina for an appointment. On her way out, she let Charlotte know she was meeting with Andrea's mother at the home address. She always felt more secure if someone knew where she was.

———

Nikki took US Route 1, the longer but more scenic drive. Her GPS chirped instructions to take SW 152nd Street east until it narrowed and became Paradise Point. Stopping at a guard shack, she provided her driver's license and signed the roster of visitors.

She glanced at the map on the navigation system. It showed a single street, Paradise Point Drive, meandering on a narrow stretch of land resembling a finger pointing to Cutler Channel in Biscayne Bay. Studying the map, she realized she'd passed over a small bridge right before the guard shack. Paradise Point was actually an island.

Getting clearance from the guard, Nikki left the window down as she drove toward the bay to get a feel for the neighborhood. The first section had expensive-looking condos to her left. Beyond the condos, boats were anchored at a marina along the canal. On her right, a wild and densely wooded area appeared to have been untouched since the days of Ponce de León. She deduced that developers had left the mangrove forest on the south side of the finger-shaped island to keep storm surges from damaging the community.

Despite the mangrove forest, the air smelled like citrus and ginger. Driving on, she encountered a huge cul-de-sac with magnificent homes. Each mansion overlooked the channel. She slowed to a crawl. Big and impressive, the showy places sprawled across manicured lawns. She wondered how they fared in hurricanes. Storms didn't care whether a community was gated, a home simple or lavish.

Spotting Delfina's address, she pulled into the driveway. A white-crowned pigeon was perched on a weathervane on the roof. It flew off when Nikki closed the car door.

A petite woman, casually dressed, invited her into the two-story great room. Nikki sat on an extra-long white sofa with decorative throw pillows in navy blue and bright orange. Delfina sat in a black leather and steel Barcelona chair angled toward the sofa.

Nikki detected a faint aroma of vinegar. Maybe coming from the rug under the sofa and chairs. An attempt to get rid of pet odor? Or perhaps it was a scent diffuser. In any case the architecture was far more interesting. It seemed like a hybrid of two distinct styles. An Acapulco geometric design, accented by a curved staircase, contrasted elegantly with the simplicity of open interior spaces in cantilevered construction, creating the illusion of modern architecture reminiscent of Mies van der Rohe.

A gigantic rug in orange and black hung from a vertical white marble partition, the only solid wall in the great room, added color to the sparse décor. Natural light filtering through wall-length windows fell on the monochromatic furnishings, casting sharp-edged shadows that generated a tapestry of angles.

"You spoke to Floyd about your daughter. Is that right?"

Delfina nodded. "Only by phone."

Other than a rhythmic Cuban intonation further emphasized by a nasally accent, Nikki noticed her client spoke excellent English. To a casual bystander, the woman's swollen eyes might have appeared to be defined with red liner, but Nikki knew tears had caused that illusion. "Tell me about your daughter's disappearance."

"My husband dropped her off at school."

"Which school?"

"Everglade Academy. It's excellent. My daughter always calls me from the cafeteria to tell me she's there. As usual, she called that morning. She's a responsible student, so I was shocked when the principal's office called me around ten to ask why Andrea was not there."

"Your daughter called you every morning. Why?"

"It became a ritual for us. I wanted to make sure she was okay."

"Okay?" Nikki asked, surprised. Then she remembered Floyd's advice not to show her emotions. "Okay from what?"

"A mother's reassurance is all."

Nikki took another angle. "What day did she disappear?"

"Friday."

"Five days ago?" Nikki inhaled. Today was Wednesday. Most abducted children and teenagers are killed within the first twenty-four hours after they're taken. "Have kidnappers contacted you to request ransom?"

Delfina shook her head, pursing her lips together.

"Why haven't you reported it to the police?"

Delfina looked away, glancing out the windows to an enclosed patio with several flowering Buddleia bushes against a stone-veneer wall.

"We thought she'd return by now, but it's a long story."

"I have time," Nikki said.

She turned and looked straight at Nikki. "We're Cuban. We have green cards now, and Yoani does not like to rock the boat."

"When did you arrive?"

"In 2012. We'd tried to come here for many years. We decided it was then or never. We had a six-year-old. Coming by raft was too risky. We flew to Nicaragua on business, knowing they had a friendly policy toward Cubans trying to get into the US. Once there, we thought it'd be easy to fly to Mexico, and then cross the border into the US.

"We miscalculated. At the airport, we learned we needed visas to Mexico and special migratory documents to pass through that country. After we were denied legal entry to Mexico, we traveled overland with a smuggler from Nicaragua. Grueling trip. Our daughter got very sick."

Delfina's knuckles grew white. She choked as she started to speak. Sounding distant, she recounted the toll that the hazardous journey had taken on the six-year-old. "Dizziness, headaches, and exhaustion—they all seemed normal under the circumstances."

"I can imagine," Nikki said in a comforting manner.

"It got worse," the woman said, taking a deep breath. "She developed an infection and ran a fever. Lost weight. It impeded our progress. We had no money. The smuggler had demanded so much cash to take us to the US border, we could not afford to take her to a doctor. Plus I am a physician. I still get angry at myself for not recognizing the symptoms.

"After three horrendous months, we crossed the border at Laredo, Texas. A nightmare, all of it, but the smuggler gave us the name of a clinic that would take care of her. She was diagnosed with leukemia."

"How is she now?"

"The irony is," Delfina said, looking pained, "we'd left a country where medical treatment was free. Here, doctors gave us professional courtesy, so we didn't pay them, but we had to contribute toward the therapy. Both of us started working. I'd found a good job and my husband started managing our friend Urbano's business. That was before Yoani became his partner. We asked Urbano to take Andrea to Cuba for stem cell transplantation. He stayed with my gordita until she could travel again. Andrea was cured."

"That's wonderful," Nikki said.

"Yes, but there was another issue. Stem cell transplant is only as good as the cells that are used. There can be side effects."

Glancing at Delfina, Nikki was unsure what to say.

"At fourteen, she developed lupus. Now she's on medication all the time. Even heavier doses during flareups." Delfina looked away. "And eighteen months ago, she had chest pains. It took several months to diagnose. It turned out to be primary spontaneous pneumothorax, PSP for short. It's also called blebs. I'm convinced she also developed these from the stem cell therapy."

"I'm sorry to hear that," Nikki said. "I know about lupus, but I've never heard of PSP or blebs."

"It's genetic. Neither Yoani nor I have ever had it. It's the abnormal accumulation of air in the chest cavity between the lungs and the pleural sac. Air pockets form in the lungs. When the blisters, called blebs, burst, the air builds up in the chest cavity and can cause partial or complete collapse of a lung. One of Andrea's collapsed."

"I can't imagine what you're going through. We'll do our best to bring her back."

Delfina nodded mutely, looking miserable.

Nikki paused a moment before asking questions she hoped would elicit useful information. She took notes on her mobile. Inquiring about doctors who treated Andrea, she keyed in their names, marking the primary care doctor, Corrado López, with an asterisk.

"Is there any reason Andrea may have run away?"

"None that I can think of."

"Have you checked with her friends?"

"All of them. More than once."

Surprised the school had not involved the police, Nikki wondered if the principal had informed the parents of their obligation to report Andrea's disappearance. "Why didn't the school call the police?"

"My husband handled it. I'm not sure how he convinced them not to call law enforcement. You'll have to ask him."

Nikki had been surprised not to see Yoani Rodríguez at this meeting, but she'd follow up with him later. "Does your daughter have a boyfriend?"

"Once boys find out about her medical condition, they dump her," Delfina said. "In fact, she doesn't even have many friends. She's very studious."

"Do you have her cell phone?"

"No. She had it with her when she disappeared from school."

"Have you tried calling her?" Nikki asked.

"It's either turned off or the battery is dead. It goes directly into messages. Do you have an expert who can examine her computer? I'm not savvy enough to make the type of search required in this situation."

"As her mother, you can access her computer. Surely you know how to access email, social media sites, check her search history. It's basic stuff."

"We don't have her passwords."

"Federal law prohibits us from doing it," Nikki said, not mentioning that Charlotte had already accessed Andrea's social media sites. She could not disclose that. "The police can search her computer once you file a report. Plus they can add Andrea's case to national crime databases."

"As I said earlier, Yoani is reluctant to get the police involved."

"If you don't, you can get into trouble for failing to report it. What specific reason does Yoani have for not reporting it?"

"We came here as undocumented foreigners. Only recently we received our green cards."

"Did Andrea have any disagreements with her father? Or you?"

Delfina shook her head and looked down at the floor. "Well, three weeks ago, my husband and I had a terrible fight. She may have overheard, but things had calmed down. So there was no reason for her to run away."

Seizing on Delfina's openness, Nikki asked her what the fight had been about.

"All marriages have issues."

"Did this fight involve Andrea?"

"Indirectly." Delfina stared at the floor and ran her hands through her hair.

"Can you share it with me?"

Delfina paused, as if searching for an answer. "It concerned her medical treatment, about having stem cells for the lupus. I did not want to expose her to PSP again. I'm always involved in decisions on her health issues."

"What about Andrea's father? Is he involved?"

"He has to take care of the business. He handles the travel agency."

"Is that why he's not at this meeting?" Nikki asked.

"I'm on a leave of absence until we find our daughter. But Yoani has a partnership to manage."

"Who is your husband's partner?"

"Our friend Urbano, who came from Cuba years before we did. The one who arranged our flight to Nicaragua. He was instrumental in our decision to come here."

"What's the company called?"

"SunNSand Getaways."

"And his partner's full name?"

"Urbano Barriga."

"You said Barriga? Like in belly?" Nikki asked.

Delfina glanced down and half smiled for the first time. "We Cubans are known for our unusual names, but it's normally our given names. In Urbano's case, Barriga is his family's surname." She glanced at Nikki. "You may be aware that our country controls everything. The one liberty every family has is to give their children distinctive or one of a kind names. That's the reason Cubans have memorable names."

Nikki thought about the name Delfina, the feminine form of dolphin. An actual name, but definitely unique.

The questions continued, with Nikki asking about the travel agency's business address. When she requested Andrea's photo, Delfina invited her to a study down a hallway past the curvilinear staircase.

"Your home is beautiful," Nikki said.

"And it comes with a monstrous mortgage. To my husband, this represents our success in America."

The study was cozy. The lower ceiling and the glass wall looking out to the enclosed patio gave it a charming feel. Nikki noticed a table with three chairs on the patio near a built-in grill. A half-hipped roof provided cover over part of the patio, sheltering a large-screen TV hanging on the opposite side of the stone-veneer wall from the grill. Butterflies flitted from one Buddleia shrub to the next.

Nikki turned toward three silver-framed family photos on the desk.

Delfina opened the desk drawer and pulled loose photos out. Smiling, she handed Nikki an eight-by-ten glossy of a pretty teenager with brownish shoulder-length hair falling on a lavender blouse.

"This is my gordita."

"Tell me what she was wearing the day she disappeared."

"A tan outfit, pants, and a matching sleeveless blouse. Sandals, beige."

"Any jewelry?"

"Yes, the necklace she's wearing there," Delfina said, pointing to the picture in Nikki's hand. "For her sixteenth birthday a month ago, I took her shopping and that's what she selected, including the lavender blouse. She loved the ruffles around the collar and down the front where it buttons up. It had matching pants you cannot see there."

Glancing down, Nikki noticed a "Be Happy, Be Me" pendant with two medallions on a gold chain. Andrea's name was engraved on the outer edge of the larger one.

Nikki took a picture with her phone. "May I also keep this copy?"

Delfina nodded and Nikki slipped the photo into her purse.

Looking on the desk, she saw Andrea's photo in the same lavender outfit, holding a Chihuahua puppy. "Does your daughter have a dog?"

"Oh, that little munchkin. Another one of her birthday gifts, from Urbano. It's at the kennel right now. I can't deal with him. Reminds me too much of Andrea. Plus Pepito is not house trained."

"Is there anything else that might be important to our investigation?"

"Nothing I can think of," Delfina said. Her voice broke and it trailed into a whisper. "Please find Andrea."

"We'll work hard to find your daughter. But the best advice I can give you is to report her to the police. She's been gone five days. The longer she's unaccounted for, the more serious her situation."

"You mean she could be dead?" Delfina lost her composure. She wiped away tears, took a deep breath, and looked into Nikki's eyes.

"Because of our green cards, Yoani does not want to involve the police. Besides, he's positive Andrea will return on her own."

"Let's hope he's right," Nikki said, trying to be reassuring. "But now that I'm involved and aware of her disappearance, the law requires me to file a missing person's report."

"My husband will be upset." Delfina uttered an anxious, almost tormented sigh.

"If he'd taken time to be here, I would've explained it to him. I recommend you file the report. If it's not done within four hours, I'll have to do it." Nikki pulled a card from her purse and handed it to Delfina. "Call me anytime, day or night."

CHAPTER THREE

Aﬀer driving back over the Paradise Point bridge, Nikki looked for a place to stop and text Charlotte. A sign directed visitors to the Deering Estate, so she pulled into the museum grounds and parked. An oversized welcome sign advertised environmental lectures, kayak rentals, and a nighttime ghost tour. She made a mental note to schedule a moonlight kayak outing. According to the sign, Charles Deering had been an art collector, philanthropist, and one of the first environmentalists of the early twentieth century.

Unfastening her seatbelt, she sent Charlotte a text asking her to find the address for SunNSand Getaways. Then Nikki took a few minutes to review her interview notes on her mobile. As she went over them, the gnawing sense that Delfina was hiding something grew. *Why was Delfina's husband so distrustful of the police? Could he have a criminal record in Cuba? Or in the US? Did his mistrust of authority come from his years in Cuba?* Yet Charlotte had not found his name connected to any crimes.

Charlotte smiled as she dialed Nikki. "I've sent you the address you wanted. And I had time to do some quick research on the firm. It's a travel agency owned by Yoani Rodríguez and his business partner, Urbano Barriga."

Nikki thanked her for the address.

Charlotte continued. Something about the firm was odd. "The travel company moved recently to its current location. It seems to move at least once a year."

"Maybe they keep upgrading their offices. Delfina's house is damned expensive. Someone is making a lot of money," Nikki said.

There was another thing Charlotte had to tell Nikki. "Just so you know, I set up an alert for missing people in Miami."

"Delfina said they haven't filed a report."

"Right, but I thought they might," Charlotte said. "A notice came through that didn't mean anything until now, but it can't be a coincidence. Looks like Barriga's wife was reported missing. Her parents filed earlier today."

"How long has she been gone?"

"Unknown. Her parents estimated several days, maybe a week. Her name is Raquel Álvarez. Married to Urbano Barriga."

"Look up Barriga's home address," Nikki said. "I'll swing by later and try to find out why he didn't report his wife's disappearance."

Charlotte texted the address and looked back at her monitor. "But wait, there's something else. Raquel rented another house a few weeks ago. Maybe she and Barriga split up."

Nikki was silent.

"Are you thinking Andrea's abduction is connected to Raquel going missing?"

"I think I have to act quickly on Raquel's disappearance now that the police are alerted. Once they start investigating, I won't have as much access. And yes, I think the two cases are somehow related. Send me Raquel's new address."

"Texting it now," Charlotte said.

"I'm off to Raquel's first. Call me if anything important comes up. Oh, and please dig up whatever you can on Dr. Corrado López. He's Andrea's primary physician. I'll visit him tomorrow."

Charlotte grinned. She was on the hunt.

Nikki headed south on Old Cutler Road and arrived twenty minutes later at the address on Blistering Street. She pulled into the driveway, facing a medium-sized house with shrubs and trees lining both sides of the drive.

She knocked on the front door and rang the doorbell three times. No answer. She tried the front door. It was locked, so she walked to the street. A canal bordered the property. There was no fence between the yard and the canal. Through the bushes, Nikki could see a path along the waterway and a small dock. She took the path around to take a closer look at the backyard. But a large bundle, trapped under the wooden dock, caught her attention.

Walking on, a rotten odor assaulted her senses. A corpse. She jumped back. Pulling the phone from her purse, she speed-dialed Floyd.

"Oh my god, I've found a body. Under a dock."

"Where are you?" he asked.

"Charlotte found a missing person's report on the wife of Rodríguez's business partner. I came to check it out. I'm in the Cutler Bay area, near Southland Mall on Route 1. It's a house on a corner lot with a canal running along two outside boundaries. Charlotte can give you the exact address and details."

"I'll call the medical examiner. His office will coordinate with the investigations bureau and get the police out there. Take pictures. Document anything unusual."

"I'm already on the pathway and I'll wait for the first responders. I advised our client to file her daughter's disappearance with the police. Told her to do it within four hours or I'd be forced to do it myself."

"Good," Floyd said. "Call me after you leave."

Nikki documented the scene in the canal. She snapped pictures from where she stood to avoid disturbing any evidence. She didn't want to risk falling in, either. Alligators could be lurking under the surface. Stories of them in the canals often appeared on the news. After taking a few photos, she felt as if someone was watching her. Looking around, she saw nothing.

Nikki walked the pathway back to the street. Two vehicles drove up.

As the first car parked, Nikki noticed its license plate—4N6—phonetically spelling forensics. *Cute*, she thought.

The medical examiner introduced himself. "Call me Smithy," he said. "So you work with Floyd. Good man. We've worked a few cases together over the years."

He gestured at the house and surrounding foliage. "The house is a bit isolated. It could be a crime scene." He didn't usually come out to the scene of an accidental death. He was here because Floyd had asked him.

A middle-aged woman with a huge camera dangling from her neck walked around the car. "I'm Lila, Smithy's evidence technician." She and Smithy were fully suited up in forensic clothes. "We always come prepared."

Nikki assumed Lila was referring to their forensic outfits.

Two men in their thirties got out of the second car. Over their suits, they wore vests that said they were crime scene workers.

"Show us where you found the body," Smithy said.

With a slight jerk of her head, Nikki indicated the rear of the house. "In the canal under the dock."

The medical examiner asked everyone to follow him. He talked to Nikki while he led the team around the bushes and shrubs on the side of the house toward the waterway. "I suppose you took care not to trample any evidence."

"If anything's tampered with, it happened before I got here," she said.

Everyone stopped to take in the overall scene.

"The smell indicates this body's been here a few days," Smithy said, walking closer to the dock. "I'm surprised it wasn't found sooner."

The guys in the vests taped off the area. Lila took photos while Smithy put on his gloves and approached the dock. He pointed to an object wedged between a couple of boards at the edge of the dock. Lila put her own gloves on and nudged it free. Holding a woman's shoe up for everyone to see, she placed it in an evidence bag.

Nikki wondered if the victim could have fallen in accidentally, perhaps after drinking too much. Someone unable to scream or whose screams were not heard.

One of the vests, the one who appeared to be the crime scene manager, headed for the street and Smithy suggested Nikki go with him.

She introduced herself to three police investigators, two men and a woman, who had just arrived.

"I'm Sergeant Maldonado," a stocky man said. "You found the corpse?"

Nikki nodded.

The crime scene manager and the other male police detective told Maldonado they would check the perimeter of the house.

Maldonado waved at the female investigator. "Please record our witness's statement and get her contact data before she leaves." Turning to face Nikki, he asked why she had been on the pathway.

Nikki hesitated, wanting to protect her clients. "I'd come here to talk to the woman who rented this house. When she didn't answer, I walked around to the path. Her parents had reported her missing. I wondered if she was simply avoiding them."

"Did they hire you?"

Nikki shook her head.

"So you're an ambulance chaser?"

"Private investigator." Nikki pulled out her wallet and showed him her license.

As he turned at the edge of the house, the sergeant stopped and glanced around the small backyard and the canal. The young female officer continued scribbling Nikki's responses on a paper pad.

Smithy's guy in charge of the crime scene and the other male police detective returned to report they'd found two dead alligators on the patio.

"Left near the back door," the male detective said.

Maldonado told them he'd get to it when he completed his interview with Nikki.

"Did you notice anything unusual?" Maldonado asked Nikki.

"Other than the body, no," Nikki said. "You can see for yourself. It's an isolated street, new construction, three empty lots to the closest neighbor. Could be an accident, but probably not. It's an easy place to access without being noticed."

"Did you walk the perimeter of the house?" he asked.

"No. Only the path by the canal."

She glanced toward the canal and saw the body had been retrieved from the water. Lila, taking photos, obscured most of the corpse. She bent down to bag a couple of small items. Nikki couldn't tell what they were.

The technician moved in for more photos, partially obscuring her view. Nikki stepped toward the corpse. The sergeant stopped her, informing her he'd finish taking her full statement and then she'd have to leave.

Still taking pictures, Lila moved to the opposite side to photograph the human remains from that angle.

With the body in full view, Nikki gasped.

Alligators or other predators had severely damaged the corpse. The skin was blotchy. An arm was missing, the face was mauled, and the pants were shredded where the legs were mangled. Yet it was not the mutilated remains that had made Nikki gasp. It was the blouse, which looked lavender under all the filth. A torn ruffle ran down the front. The resemblance to the one Andrea wore in her birthday picture had stopped her cold.

CHAPTER FOUR

After leaving Raquel's place, Nikki called Floyd and told him about Smithy, his forensic team, and the police. Once she'd seen the blouse on the corpse, she'd had no choice but to inform the police about the missing girl.

Floyd suggested she call Delfina. She could explain to their client why she had to report Andrea's disappearance to the police.

"I was planning on that, but I really hate to tell her about that blouse. When the police took my statement, I had to tell them why I'd been there."

"We have to tell Delfina the truth too."

Nikki cringed. "Right. Of course. I'll do it."

Looking in the rearview mirror, Nikki saw a white Honda Accord with tinted windows behind her that she'd first noticed a street past Raquel's house. She shuddered, thinking how killers often revisit the scenes of their crimes.

To make sure he wasn't following her, she took a right turn. At the next intersection, she took another right. Checking the mirror, she didn't see the car. She'd been so preoccupied rehearsing, in her mind, the conversation to have with Delfina that she forgot to take the license plate number. She chastised herself for such a foolish mistake. Probably being paranoid, but she still couldn't shake the sensation someone had been watching her at the canal before the coroner arrived.

Pulling into a Walmart parking lot, she turned the engine off. Delfina answered immediately. Nikki explained about the missing person report that had prompted her to check out Raquel's house. Then she dropped the bomb: she'd had to explain about her job to the police investigator.

Silence.

"Delfina?"

"You should have left us out of this."

"I understand," Nikki said, "but I was a witness and once we called the medical examiner, there was nothing for me to do but tell the truth. And there's something more you need to know. You might be called to identify the body."

"Why me? Urbano should do it. Didn't he file the report?"

"Her parents filed it."

"Then they should be the ones to identify her."

"I'm so sorry, Delfina, but there's more. I'd prefer to tell you in person, but I don't want the medical examiner's office or the police to be the ones to inform you. And keep in mind until an autopsy is performed, we won't know the identity, but the body had a lavender blouse with a ruffle—"

"Oh my god, it's Andrea—"

Nikki heard a scream. And something hitting the floor. After a few seconds, she realized the phone had gone dead. She decided to drive to Delfina's. On the way, she called Charlotte to let her know where she was going.

"Do you have protection?" Charlotte asked.

"My Glock. It's in my purse, like always."

Nikki reversed the route she'd used earlier to get to Raquel's house. All she could think about was her own son. Her chest tightened as she recalled the worst moment of her life, at Abbott Northwestern Hospital in Minneapolis, when the doctors informed her of Robbie's death. He'd been twelve. His death still felt as if it'd happened yesterday. Whenever she dwelled on it, she'd get nightmares and couldn't sleep.

She reminded herself to think about the present, about the case she was working. Two women were missing, a teenager and a woman in her forties, and there was a chance this body was not Andrea's. Maybe Raquel had a blouse similar to Andrea's birthday outfit. And if that were the case, the teenager's mother was being put through unnecessary hell. *But what was the chance of two similar blouses?*

A flashy new gold Mercedes coupe filled the driveway. Before getting out of her own car, Nikki snapped a photo of the license plate. She'd ask Charlotte to check it out.

A man answered the front door. Wearing a stern expression and expensive-looking athleisure, he asked if she was the private investigator his wife had hired.

"I'm sorry to bother you, but I've given Delfina bad news. I came by to make sure she's okay." Nikki noticed that Yoani's accent was much thicker and harsher than his wife's.

"As okay as anyone in these circumstances. Come in. I'm Yoani."

Delfina stood in the entry, a few steps behind her husband, leaning on a console table.

Nikki apologized to Delfina for the way she'd delivered the news. "And it's important for you to understand that until an autopsy is performed, you won't know for sure."

Those words set Delfina into another bout of grief. She bent over, holding her stomach, and cried out in heartbreaking anguish.

"If an autopsy is needed, then the body must be in bad condition." Rodríguez moved back a few steps to get near his wife.

"Unfortunately, that's correct. It's been in the canal a few days."

Delfina stood straight again and wiped her nose with a tissue, making a visible effort to regain a bit of her composure. "I haven't heard from the medical examiner yet. Of course, I've met him, though he wouldn't remember me."

"One bit of information gives me hope," Nikki said. "I thought you told me she was wearing a beige outfit the day she disappeared."

"That's what I thought, but she could have changed. The lavender blouse was her favorite," Delfina said, turning to face her husband. "You drove her to school. Do you remember?"

"I have no idea what she wore," he said.

"Since you're both here, let me remind you to report this to the police."

"You're forcing us to." Rodríguez sounded angry.

"State law requires it, not me," Nikki said.

Rodríguez's lips tightened before he spoke. "Well, as soon as we report it, she *will* show up. Trust me. That won't be her body."

"Why are you so certain she'll return?" Nikki asked.

"I can feel it in my bones," he replied.

"Listen, Yoani, when I tell you that the longer she's gone, the less likely she is to return, I mean it. Those are the statistics on minors," Nikki said. She could feel Delfina's anguish as she pronounced those words, words that caused the bereaved mother to turn away.

Rodríguez opened the door, suggesting it was time for Nikki to leave.

Nikki had one more point to discuss with the mother. "Now that the police are investigating, Security Source will refund the retainer you paid. If you have any questions, please call me."

Delfina looked at Nikki. "I don't want a refund. There's still work I need. The police are not trustworthy. In fact, you *must* continue investigating. I need to know what happened." Her voice faded to a whisper.

"I don't think this private investigation is necessary any longer," Yoani said to his wife.

"Yes, it is," she responded resolutely.

Order on Amazon and Continue Reading Missing in Miami

ALSO BY KATHRYN LANE

Waking Up in Medellin

Danger in the Coyote Zone

Missing in Miami

The Nikki Garcia Mystery Series: Box Set

Backyard Volcano and Other Mysteries of the Heart

AWARDS AND PRAISE FOR KATHRYN'S BOOKS

WAKING UP IN MEDELLIN (A NIKKI GARCIA THRILLER)

Waking Up in Medellin was named "Best Fiction Book of the Year—2017" by the Killer Nashville International Mystery Writers' Conference and also won Killer Nashville's "Best Fiction—Adult Suspense—2017." It was also a finalist for the Roné Award—2016.

DANGER IN THE COYOTE ZONE (A NIKKI GARCIA MYSTERY)

Danger in the Coyote Zone won first place in the 2018 Action/Adventure Category of Latino Books into Movies Award, named a finalist in the Thriller Category at the 2018 Killer Nashville International Mystery Writers' Conference, and a finalist in the 2018 Book Excellence Awards.

REVENGE IN BARCELONA (A NIKKI GARCIA MYSTERY)

Revenge in Barcelona won first place in Latino Books into Movies-Latino Themed TV Series Category 2020; won the Silver Medal in the Mystery Category 2020 by Reader Views Literary Awards; Finalist in the Eric Hoffer 2020 Book Awards; Finalist for Silver Falchion in the Best Suspense by Killer Nashville; Finalist in the Suspense Category by Next Generation Book Awards; Finalist in the 2020 International Latino Book Awards; Awarded Five Stars by Readers' Favorite

BACKYARD VOLCANO AND OTHER MYSTERIES OF THE
HEART (SHORT STORY COLLECTION)

***Backyard Volcano and Other Mysteries of the
Heart*** was named "Best Short Story Collection
—2018" by the Killer Nashville International
Mystery Writers' Conference.

ACKNOWLEDGEMENTS

I am indebted to countless individuals, many of them from book clubs I have visited, who express the desire to read more Nikki Garcia adventures and offer suggestions of future locations for Nikki's investigations. Their recommendations provide an impetus to continue writing Nikki's adventures.

It is impossible to name the many friends, family, and fans who deserve specific mention. People who contributed directly to *Revenge in Barcelona* are listed here.

My husband, Bob Hurt, who supports my writing endeavors and also happens to be my most enthusiastic fan.

Mercè Iglesias, Josep Redento, and Mercè Puig, friends residing in Barcelona, who arranged for me to meet with a Spanish counterterrorism agent to discuss the various police and counterterrorism forces working in Catalonia.

Ryan Gable, Constable of Montgomery County, Texas, who offered expert advice.

My incredible beta readers – Maureen Donelan, Brenda Gottlieb, Patricia Hogan, Jorge Lane, Nancy Miller, and Josep Redento.

Dean Herr, Dan Rich, Ralph Bivins, Andre Edwin, and Roger Stacy—my writing group in Houston—whose suggestions and comments improve my stories.

The many friends and fans who keep asking for Nikki's next adventure—thanks for the wait!

Special thanks to my editor Sandra A. Spicher, Heidi Dorey for the beautiful cover design, Danielle Hartman Acee for the book interior and, more importantly, for her valuable technical expertise, and Maureen Donelan for the Tortuga Publishing, LLC logo.

ABOUT THE AUTHOR

Kathryn Lane is the award-winning author of the Nikki Garcia Mystery Series.

She draws deeply from her experiences growing up in a small town in Mexico as well as her work and travel in over ninety countries around the globe during her career in international finance with Johnson & Johnson.

Kathryn loves the Arts and is a board member of the Montgomery County Literary Arts Council. Kathryn and her husband, Bob Hurt, split their time between Texas and the mountains of northern New Mexico where she finds it inspiring to write.

Kathryn's Website
Kathryn-lane.com

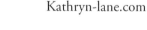 amazon.com/~/e/B01D0J1YES

bookbub.com/authors/kathryn-lane

facebook.com/kathrynlanewriter

twitter.com/kathrynlanebook